CHANGED FOREVER

Slowly but firmly, Dev eased back from the kiss, pulling away, even when she would have deepened their embrace. His hands gentled her, stroking down her back from her shoulders to her waist. When only their lips touched, he lifted his head and pulled Bess to him. She could feel the thunderous beating of his heart matching the cadence of her own. Wonder mixed with giddiness and a sense of unbridled elation. If he let her go now, she would float away.

Dreamily she opened her eyes. Though they stood in the dark shadows, light from a nearby lamp glinted in Dev's eyes, making them glow like coals in a midnight fire. She read passion in them, and a depth of hunger she couldn't begin to meet. Half frightened, she took a step back.

Dev moved his hands to her shoulders, cradling her gently. "It's all right," he said soothingly. "Nothing more will happen."

She could see, even in the half light, that he was as surprised as she by their kiss. She felt the fine trembling in his arms and realized just how much strength of will it had taken for him to bring their embrace to an end. She felt a surge of feminine power, an inkling of what it could be like to love and be loved, to let passion rule her life. Elation and trepidation filled her — the need to know battling with an instinct that told her now was not the time, and this

PASSION BLAZES IN A ZEBRA HEARTFIRE!

COLORADO MOONFIRE (3730, $4.25/$5.50)
by Charlotte Hubbard

Lila O'Riley left Ireland, determined to make her own way in America. Finding work and saving pennies presented no problem for the independent lass; locating love was another story. Then one hot night, Lila meets Marshal Barry Thompson. Sparks fly between the fiery beauty and the lawman. Lila learns that America is the promised land, indeed!

MIDNIGHT LOVESTORM (3705, $4.25/$5.50)
by Linda Windsor

Dr. Catalina McCulloch was eager to begin her practice in Los Reyes, California. On her trip from East Texas, the train is robbed by the notorious, masked bandit known as Archangel. Before making his escape, the thief grabs Cat, kisses her fervently, and steals her heart. Even at the risk of losing her standing in the community, Cat must find her mysterious lover once again. No matter what the future might bring . . .

MOUNTAIN ECSTASY (3729, $4.25/$5.50)
by Linda Sandifer

As a divorced woman, Hattie Longmore knew that she faced prejudice. Hoping to escape wagging tongues, she traveled to her brother's Idaho ranch, only to learn of his murder from long, lean Jim Rider. Hattie seeks comfort in Rider's powerful arms, but she soon discovers that this strong cowboy has one weakness . . . marriage. Trying to lasso this wandering man's heart is a challenge that Hattie enthusiastically undertakes.

RENEGADE BRIDE (3813, $4.25/$5.50)
by Barbara Ankrum

In her heart, Mariah Parsons always believed that she would marry the man who had given her her first kiss at age sixteen. Four years later, she is actually on her way West to begin her life with him . . . and she meets Creed Deveraux. Creed is a rough-and-tumble bounty hunter with a masculine swagger and a powerful magnetism. Mariah finds herself drawn to this bold wilderness man, and their passion is as unbridled as the Montana landscape.

ROYAL ECSTASY (3861, $4.25/$5.50)
by Robin Gideon

The name Princess Jade Crosse has become hated throughout the kingdom. After her husband's death, her "advisors" have punished and taxed the commoners with relentless glee. Sir Lyon Beauchane has sworn to stop this evil tyrant and her cruel ways. Scaling the castle wall, he meets this "wicked" woman face to face . . . and is overpowered by love. Beauchane learns the truth behind Jade's imprisonment. Together they struggle to free Jade from her jailors and from her inhibitions.

PHYLLIS HERRMANN
DESIRE'S DREAM

ZEBRA BOOKS
KENSINGTON PUBLISHING CORP.

To our wonderful agent, Joyce Flaherty
whose faith and drive
have been an inspiration

And to our editor, Beth Lieberman
who was there for the first book
and now the fifth and sixth

ZEBRA BOOKS are published by

Kensington Publishing Corp.
475 Park Avenue South
New York, NY 10016

First Printing: July, 1993

Printed in the United States of America

Prologue

Kansas City, 1870

Elizabeth Richmond gazed up at the steep gables and mansard roof. Like it or not, this was to be her home for the next few years.

"Come on, darlin'. Don't be shy," her father said, tugging on her arm until she stepped up onto the well-swept path leading to the front steps.

"I don't want to stay here, Papa," she whispered, forlorn.

"You haven't given it a chance yet, Bessie." He let go of her arm and put his hands on her shoulders, turning her to face him as he bent forward to peer into her face. His eyes were green, unlike her own blue; his hair ash brown, though like her, he'd been blond as a child. Only her hair had never darkened. A strand of it tore loose in the wind and whipped across her nose and mouth. With loving care, her father reached up and tucked it back behind her ear.

"This is the best school in these parts," he said with a touch of defiance. "Miz Fine is a genteel lady. She'll teach you all you have to know to be a lady, too."

"I don't want to be no lady, Papa. I want to be with you."

Her father sighed and looked away. Bessie could feel tears gathering in her eyes and blinked rapidly. She would not have him see her cry; she had too much pride for that.

"I want to be with you, too," he said at last, his voice strangely husky. "But this is more important. I won't have these city folks look down on you 'cause you don't know their ways. You'll thank me for this when you're grown, I promise you."

She flung her arms around his waist, hugging him tight. "I don't care about no city folks. I just want to be with you. Please, Papa. I'm sorry I took Black Devil out for a ride. I'll never do it again—I promise."

The tears she'd been fighting all day won out, soaking her father's best shirtfront, the one he saved to wear to the city. Bessie was past caring. All she wanted was to convince him of the truth of what she said, to make him take her back to Carlinsville with him.

Though his voice was hoarse with emotion, Bert Richmond would not be swayed. "This has nothing to do with Black Devil, little girl. You and I both know you can handle that crazy horse a damn sight better'n anyone else."

He sighed and held her away from him so he could look her in the eye. "And that's exactly the problem, Bessie. Your mama made me promise I'd do right by you afore she died. I aim to keep that promise the best way I know how."

She tried to turn her face away from him, but he wouldn't let her. He grasped her chin gently, but firmly. "Listen to me, girl. There's more to life than living over the jail house with your pappy and running in the streets of a small town like Carlinsville. I want you to grow up proud of yourself. I want you to be a lady, like your mama—refined . . . special. I don't like hearing the snide remarks about Sheriff Richmond's brat."

The quiet appeal in his eyes got through to her more

6

than his words. For reasons she could not begin to understand, this was important to him — more important than her love and devotion, more important than her presence in his life.

She tugged more forcefully this time, and he let her go. Staring down at the ground, she said, "I understand, Papa. I'll do my best."

She started up the path to the towering mansion again, keeping her eyes averted so that she missed the look of pain and loss that crossed her father's face before he put on a bland mask and followed her up the steps to the front door.

One

Bess stood before the cheval mirror and inspected her handiwork. The dress was perfect and in the latest style. The low, square neckline, softened round the edges with a whisper of lace, set off her cameo pendant—her only legacy from a distantly remembered mother. The blue and white princess basque fit snugly, flattering her every curve. The splash of red poppies on the skirt added the perfect touch, making the outfit ideal for the Kansas City Board of Trade Spring Ball: patriotic red, white and blue.

The dress was her armor. In it, she could face them all—even Anna and her new husband, Wylie Moore.

Wylie. Just the sound of his name caused a wave of pain and loss to crest inside her. So many dreams abandoned, so many hopes destroyed. She closed her eyes and took a deep breath. It was over now, she told herself, and no one need ever know what a fool she'd been. No one.

Having made that promise to herself, Bess turned back to the mirror to check her coiffure. No sooner had she pinned the white heron's feather aigrette to the top of her head than a knock sounded at her door.

"Are you ready yet?" Alice Covington asked, poking

her head into the room. "Oh! You do look lovely. Where ever did you get that dress?"

Bess smiled at her friend's enthusiasm. "I ordered it from New York." She twirled around in a circle. "What do you think?"

"I think I hate you," Alice answered, her brown eyes twinkling merrily as she grinned back. "There won't be a single eligible man looking my way once you walk into the room."

"Now, Alice, you know that isn't true," Bess retorted, and they both laughed. Alice was a terrible flirt and always had at least three beaux hanging on her every word. But for once Bess hoped her friend was right. Tonight she wanted to make an impression, to show the world she was not cowed by Wylie's desertion.

"We'll find out soon enough, if you're ready to leave," Alice said. "Father has already sent for the carriage."

Bess took a last look at the mirror. "Yes, I'm ready," she agreed. *Ready as I'll ever be*. That last thought she kept to herself.

The ballroom of the Harkness Hotel had never looked lovelier, Bess decided as she gazed around at the artfully placed bouquets of flowers, the beautiful china place settings, the gleaming silver and glassware. Yards and yards of tricolored bunting were hanging high on the walls of the cavernous room and shrouded the tops of all its supporting columns.

"Oooh, I can't believe it! They've really outdone themselves this year," Alice exclaimed. "This is the best party ever, even better than last year's. Don't you think so, Papa?"

"Last year we were still reeling from the Panic of '73 and the grasshoppers of '74," Edward Covington intoned, his mind on business, as usual.

"Grasshoppers?" Alice mouthed from behind her

hand and rolled her eyes at Bess. Her father continued, "This year, everything's turning around. More and more people are moving out West, not just to Missouri, but to Kansas, as well. This area's got possibilities, you mark my words."

"Now, Edward, you promised you wouldn't spend the entire evening talking business," Harrietta Covington said to her husband, slipping her hand into the crook of his elbow. "We must introduce the girls around."

Her pointed remark was not lost on either Bess or Alice. Harrietta Covington had decided "her girls" must get married — and the sooner the better. Alice made a face at Bess, who shrugged philosophically. There was no tactful way of stopping Mrs. Covington once she had this particular bee in her bonnet.

"Why, yes, of course, dear," Edward said and patted his wife's hand absently as he scanned the room. "Ah, there's Walter Moore over there. Let's join him. I see he has that Philadelphia fellow with him — Devlin O'Connor. I've been meaning to catch up with him for a few days now."

Mrs. Covington pinched her husband's arm. "Edward, you haven't heard a word I've said," she complained.

"That's not true, dear. Didn't I mention Mr. O'Connor is single? And most eligible, I might add. His father is a major financier, and I understand the boy is handling all of his business affairs now."

Mrs. Covington smiled her approval and allowed Mr. Covington to lead her away. "Come along, girls," she said over her shoulder.

Bess took a deep breath as she and Alice walked behind the Covingtons. The time had come to start playing her part. She only hoped she was a good enough actress to carry off the role. She wished she were a little taller so she could see over the couple in front of her and know exactly whom she had to face, but fate was

11

not so kind. When the Covingtons moved to the side to greet Walter Moore, Bess got her first good view of the small group surrounding him. Too late, she recognized the young man at Moore's side — his son, Wylie, standing proud as could be, his new bride hanging proprietarily onto his arm.

Bess gasped involuntarily, her indrawn breath making the softest of sounds, but not so soft that Alice didn't hear it.

"Are you all right?" Alice whispered solicitously, looking anxiously at Bess's face.

"Yes, I'm fine," Bess insisted, squaring her shoulders. She hadn't anticipated running into Wylie quite so soon, nor having to face him with Anna Hobart — no, it was Anna Moore now — on his arm.

The introductions went by in a blur as Bess concentrated on maintaining her poise.

"Why, Bess, how nice to see you," Walter Moore said, his false solicitude grating on Bess's nerves. Mr. Moore had been less than gracious when he thought his son might wed her instead of the well-connected Anna.

"It's nice to see you, too, Mr. Moore," she lied out of politeness. "And may I wish you well on your birthday."

"You are most gracious," Walter Moore acknowledged, then immediately dismissed her when Edward Covington spoke.

"I understand we are celebrating tonight. May I extend my best wishes."

"Oh, yes," put in Mrs. Covington. "This is quite the occasion."

Walter beamed at the attention he was receiving, then turned to explain to the newcomer what all the fuss was about. "I am fifty-five today, and my wife has arranged a portion of tonight's events in my honor."

"Then may I add my felicitations," the tall man replied. "I am indeed fortunate to be in Kansas City this week."

12

His accent and his dress indicated he was newly arrived from the East. His dark sable hair was impeccably groomed; his frock coat buttoned high, revealing only the edge and points of his stiffly starched collar. A fine gold chain glinted at his waist, and he leaned with negligent grace against a gold-headed ebony cane, the epitome of the fashionable businessman. His name escaped her, as she had barely had her wits about her during the introductions.

"I'm the one who's lucky," Anna cooed, tightening her grip on Wylie's arm as she batted her eyelashes at the stranger. "If Wylie hadn't decided to come back early from our wedding trip, we would have missed you entirely."

She rubbed her cheek against Wylie's shoulder and sent Bess a smoldering look.

Bess took up the challenge, pasting a brilliant smile on her face. "I must say, marriage seems to agree with you. You're both looking well."

Wylie glanced at her in surprise, meeting her gaze for the first time. He visibly relaxed.

"It more than agrees with us, doesn't it, Wylie?" Anna replied, reaching up to pat Wylie's cheek. Though the display was unseemly in public, it made her point: Wylie was hers now. "I'm so sorry you missed our wedding, Dev. That was just about the time your father broke his leg. Papa was most devastated to hear of it."

"I'm sorry, too, little one," the man called Dev replied, smiling down at Anna with genuine affection. Bess realized this must be the eligible Devlin O'Connor she'd just heard about. His next words confirmed that. "My father was just as upset that he couldn't make this trip. He was looking forward to spending time with his old friend and anxious to see you married, as well. But that fall down the steps put an end to it, I'm afraid."

"I'm so glad you took over his business and came out

13

in his place," Anna replied, flashing her dimple at him. "And so is Wylie, aren't you, dear?"

"Yes, love," Wylie said, smiling at his new wife while his eyes sought out his father's approval. "We've had some very profitable discussions which I'm sure will lead to beneficial results for us all."

The men in the group sprang upon this opening to turn the conversation over to their abiding interest, the local business scene, leaving the women to talk amongst themselves.

"We had a wonderful wedding trip," Anna announced, still clinging to Wylie's arm. "We went to Boston and New York and even spent a couple of nights at a secluded country inn. It was most romantic."

She spoke to the group at large, but her gaze kept returning to Bess to see how she was reacting.

Firm in her resolve to let no one know of her humiliation and loss, Bess smiled and bantered with the others, looking away only when Wylie tried to catch her eye.

"Did I hear you say you visited New York on your wedding trip?" Devlin O'Connor asked Anna as the gentlemen rejoined the ladies, leaving further business conversation to another time. "You could have popped down to Philadelphia for a day or two. I know my father would have loved to see you."

Bess watched him gaze fondly at the couple. There was something about him she didn't like. Maybe it was his rather foppish air, or his accent, or . . . she wasn't sure what it was. Most likely it was his obvious approval of Anna Hobart Moore—that would be reason enough in Bess's present state of mind.

Anna nodded with regret. "We would have loved to, but we did have to get back for this party. You will give him our best wishes, I hope?"

"I will be most happy to," the Easterner replied.

"At least Wylie and I did manage to visit Delmonico's in New York, and I must say, it was grand," Anna said,

14

once again addressing herself to the group. "You really can't appreciate how provincial Kansas City is until you've traveled. Don't you agree, Bess?"

Bess lifted her chin. Anna knew far well that she'd never been east, but the other girl did so love to press her advantage. She must have sensed Bess's vulnerability "I really wouldn't know, Anna. I haven't your experience, you know."

"But, Bess, everyone at Miss Fine's always said you were so clever. I can't believe you don't have an opinion. Aren't you surprised, Wylie?"

Wylie colored and mumbled something noncommittal under his breath.

"Now, Anna, just because Bess—" Alice started to say, her voice angry.

"Not now," Bess murmured under her breath and put a restraining hand on Alice's arm. Then, smiling brightly, she turned to one of the young men who'd just joined them and said, "Frank, you've traveled all over. What do you think? Is Kansas City terribly provincial?"

Frank turned red as a beet as all eyes focused on him. He glanced at her with helpless adoration. "I don't know, Bess. I guess I kind of like it here, myself."

Bess smiled approvingly at him. "Well said, Frank," she applauded. "I like your loyalty to home and hearth."

Frank brightened, basking in her approval while Anna frowned.

"And what do you think, Mr. O'Connor?" Bess asked. She lowered her lashes and looked coyly up at him. She could play games as well as Anna, and if that was what it took to get her through this night, then that was what it would be. "You're new in town. Do you find us unbearably provincial?"

"I've not been in town long enough to make any judgments," he said, his dark brown eyes gazing down into hers. Bess's heart did a strange flip-flop as their eyes made contact.

15

"In that case, we'll have to wait until you've enjoyed what our fair city has to offer before we can come to any conclusion," she said, smiling up at him.

He smiled back. Again her heart skipped a beat. Before she could react, a shrill laugh broke from Anna.

"Why, Bess, it's a sign of how provincial you are that you would even think Kansas City might have anything exciting to offer Dev," Anna said. "He's from Philadelphia, you know, and used to life on a much grander scale than here."

"Now, Anna, dear, Bess was just making conversation," Wylie put in placatingly. "You're looking very nice tonight, Bess. Is your dress new?"

"Yes, I ordered it specially for tonight," she said, her gaze darting to Wylie and then quickly away. She didn't need another sample of Anna's sniping. Besides, looking at him was too painful.

"You see, Wylie, that's exactly what I mean," Anna said, recapturing her husband's attention. "In New York and Philadelphia there's no need to order a dress from out of town. Then again, not all of us would feel the need to be dressed to the nines on every occasion." She looked pointedly at Bess. "Bess doesn't actually live in Kansas City, you know," she continued, ostensibly addressing herself to Dev. "She comes from a small town miles away, barely a dot on the map. Isn't that so, Wylie?"

"Bess is from Carlinsville," Wylie put in. "But she went to school here in the city with Anna and Alice. They're all good friends." He smiled uncomfortably.

Just then the orchestra began tuning up, and Mrs. Covington descended on the group. Bess felt a wave of relief rush through her. Even Alice's mother's matchmaking would be better than what she had just been through.

"The dancing is about to begin, children," the older woman said, encompassing the entire group with her

16

glance. "Now, Alice, dear, why don't you show our out-of-town guest to the dance floor. Frank, you take Bess for the first dance, and Wylie, we all know with whom you want to dance."

She tittered happily, beaming at the newly married couple as she herded her daughter in Devlin O'Connor's direction. Bess watched as he handed his gold-tipped cane to a nearby hotel steward and put out his arm for Alice.

Frank, once again fiery red in the face, stumbled over his feet in his eagerness to escort her to the dance floor. If she hadn't been so relieved to be away from Wylie and Anna, not to mention the disturbing stranger from the East, she might have felt uncomfortable with Frank's all-consuming infatuation. As it was, she was happy to have a few moments away from the others to rebuild her defenses. How she wished this evening were over.

But the evening dragged on. She managed to keep away from Wylie and Anna once the dancing began, but was glad of a respite some thirty minutes later. She and Alice found two empty seats by one of the tables lining the walls of the ballroom beneath the overhanging balcony. They had barely caught their breath when Harrietta Covington found them.

"Girls, girls, why are you hiding out here?" she asked, clearly displeased.

"We're just taking a rest, Mama," Alice answered for them both.

Bess stayed hidden in the shadows, in no mood to parry Mrs. Covington's none-too-subtle matchmaking.

"You're too young to need a rest, both of you. You should be out on the floor, dancing and mingling with all the other guests."

"We'll be along in a second, Mama," Alice placated. "We just want to freshen up first."

"Well, don't take too long. This ball is special. Every-

17

one here is quality, and you don't want to miss a minute," Harrietta Covington said and swept off in search of her husband.

As soon as she was out of earshot, Alice turned to Bess. "I'm afraid if we stay here, Mama will just come back to get us. Do you want to go upstairs or would you prefer a breath of air?"

One of the upstairs rooms had been set aside for the ladies so they could primp or gossip and take care of other personal needs. Bess knew it would be crowded and hot, the air filled with the scents of hundreds of perfumes and powders. She didn't think she could face the noise and closeness of the place.

"I think I'd prefer stepping outside for a few minutes, but don't let me take you away from the festivities. I can go alone."

"Not on your life, Bess Richmond. Right now you need company more than anything. I'd rather stay with you."

"You're a wonderful friend, Alice. I've missed seeing you more than I ever thought possible."

"And whose fault is that?" Alice demanded. "I told you to visit me more times than I can remember. You know Mama and Papa love to have you. You're such a 'good influence', Mama always says."

Bess saw the gleam in Alice's eyes and laughed as she was supposed to. Both girls knew full well that most of their mischief in school had been directed by Bess. Somehow, though, Alice had always been the one to catch the blame.

"Besides," Alice added, "if you think I'm going to venture within ten feet of Mama by myself, you're sorely mistaken. Especially when she's on one of her campaigns. Why do you think I invited you here in the first place?"

Bess knew her friend was only teasing, hiding her concern under the wave of banter. Though she really would have preferred some time alone, she wasn't about to hurt Alice's feelings by saying so.

"Let's go out to the terrace, then, before we attract your mother's attention again."

The two walked arm in arm out of the ballroom and down the hall leading to the flagstone terrace. Outside, Chinese lanterns were strung between the trees and lampposts, giving a festive air to the enclosure.

"It's nice out here," Bess commented as she strolled to the low, white-columned wall surrounding the terrace. "Quiet and cool."

Alice sat on a wrought iron bench near the low wall and gave Bess a few moments to enjoy the solitude and peace before asking, "How are you holding up?"

"Fine, I hope. Why? Are people looking at me strangely?"

"No . . . only Anna. She's being a real cow, but I don't think anyone's really noticed. Anna's always throwing her weight around about one thing or another."

"I can't say I really blame her, under the circumstances." Bess sighed.

"You're the one who should feel bad, not her. I remember last year at school how Wylie was the only thing you talked about. All the girls thought it was kind of sweet, the way you carried on—except Anna, of course. To be frank, I was sure you would marry him as soon as you left Miss Fine's."

"So was I," Bess confessed, "especially when he visited me so often at home. Right up until three months ago, that is. Papa was so pleased. All he ever wanted was for me to be a lady and marry a fine gentleman—you know, the kind of man he thinks my mother should have married." Bess shook her head as painful memories swept through her—her father's guilt over her mother's untimely death, her own futile attempts to make it up to him. "I don't know what was worse, disappointing Papa or finding out I'd made such a fool of myself."

"You're no fool, Bess. If anyone's a fool, it's Wylie — the dumb jackass."

"Alice!"

"Well, it's true, and you know it. That Anna isn't all she appears, as Wylie will find out soon enough. Just because her daddy's the richest man in town, she thinks she's entitled to anything she wants. Do you think she really loves Wylie?" Alice asked, but before Bess could even attempt a response, she answered herself. "Not a chance! She just wanted to get back at you 'cause you're prettier than she is and everyone liked you better at Miss Fine's. And that Wylie — he looks at her and all he sees is a gold mine. As my papa likes to say, you mark my words. Those two deserve each other. You came out ahead on this one, Bess."

"I'm afraid you're right," Bess agreed sadly. In the last few months, she'd come to see the truth about Wylie. How could she have made such a terrible mistake? Even Alice, who was sometimes as flighty as her mother, could see through Wylie. Why had it taken Bess so long? Her heart had outwitted her for the last time, she resolved; in the future, she'd be much more careful about trusting it.

"Some things are not meant to be, Bess," Alice went on. "It's not anything you did. I hope you realize that."

"I know," Bess responded, forcing a smile. Wylie's defection had done a lot to undermine her sense of confidence. Once again she'd felt like a second-class citizen — Bess Richmond, the sheriff's daughter who lived above the jail, not quite good enough for the best society — but she wasn't about to let anyone see that side of her. Not even Alice.

"Wylie's the one to be blamed. No doubt about it," Alice affirmed. "You're a wonderful girl, Bess. Just look at how much my brother Barrett likes you. He talked of no one else before he left for Philadelphia."

"I liked him, too," Bess admitted, though she didn't reveal that Barrett's affection could hardly make up for the loss of her dreams.

Wylie Moore had been a young girl's fantasy come true, especially when the girl in question had been brought up with only one goal: to be a lady who would marry well and respectably, to a man her father could be proud of. Never mind that the goal had been Bert Richmond's rather than her own. Over the years, Bess had fought her own nature trying to please her father, and with Wylie she thought she had finally succeeded. Her shock at seeing his wedding announcement in the *Kansas City Ledger* had been profound and shattering. She still had not recovered. Nor had her papa.

Alice's invitation to visit Kansas City had been a welcome reprieve from his puzzled glances and sighs of disappointment. Bess had hoped to escape the entire situation, little realizing that Wylie and Anna would cut their honeymoon trip short to be in town for Walter Moore's birthday.

"I guess it's just difficult facing up to the mistake I made," she finally confided. "Especially the way Anna's behaving. She's having a great time rubbing it in."

Alice patted her shoulder soothingly. "What you need to do is get away from here. A change of scene will brighten you up and get your mind off your troubles."

"I don't know . . . Where would I go? I can't drop in unannounced and uninvited on just anybody."

Alice laughed and clapped her hands. "Not on just anybody," she said, her voice filled with excitement. "How about on me? As I said, Barrett was quite taken with you. My family and I are going to Philadelphia to see his new offices. He's going to be the greatest architect there ever was. Why don't you come along?"

"To Philadelphia?" It sounded so far away. Overwhelmingly so. "But, I couldn't—"

"Why not? I'm sure Mama and Papa won't mind. It would be so exciting. We could see all the sights and go to the Centennial Exhibition. Imagine spending the Fourth of July in Philadelphia! It's going to be the most spectacular event in the world. And even if it doesn't work out with Barrett, much as I would like it to, there are bound to be scads of young men visiting the Exhibition. We'll have an absolutely wonderful time. Say you'll come, please."

"I don't know. Let me think about it."

Though Bess was filled with doubts, Alice had no reservations. "I'll check with Mama as soon as we get back to the ballroom. I just know she'll agree."

Wrapped in her excitement, Alice rattled on about Philadelphia and her brother's architecture firm.

Bess heard her out while she tried to sort through her choices. She had graduated from Miss Fine's Academy last year, but finishing school had not provided her with the kinds of skills she needed to get on in life — except as the wife of a well-to-do man, a possibility she would not countenance again. Her dreams of love and marriage had been shattered by Wylie's unfeeling rejection.

Her father wouldn't hear of her teaching school, one of the few professions open to genteel young women, though he had allowed her to tutor. But she had found her temperament quite unsuited to the teaching profession and that left her with few possibilities other than keeping her father's house, a prospect that would daunt the staunchest of women. Once she was ensconced in there, she would never be able to leave. Was her only option to live the rest of her life above the jail?

Maybe Alice was right. Maybe she should go away. This might be her only chance to take control of her life and find a new direction — for herself this time, not just to please others. She would certainly give the idea some serious thought.

Devlin O'Connor watched Anna Moore flit from group to group around the edge of the dance floor, her manner brittle and edgy. Every few minutes, she'd stop and avidly scan the crowd until she located Wylie. If he was with a group of men or standing alone, she would continue on her way. If she saw him with another woman, she seemed compelled to join him and flaunt their relationship shamelessly.

Why would a newly married bride carry on so, he wondered. What made her so insecure? The child he remembered from long-ago visits had been cheerful and happy, even if a trifle spoiled. What had happened to give her such a desperate edge?

At that moment, Anna saw him and made her way through the crowd to his side.

"Dev, what are you doing here all by yourself? I expected to see you on the dance floor or, at the very least, consumed with business affairs like all the other men."

Her gaze slid past him to fasten on Wylie again. He stood deep in conversation with several other young men, all of whom Dev recognized as part of Kansas City's up and coming business establishment. There was a wistfulness to Anna's expression.

"I much prefer being right here talking to you," he said gallantly.

"Do you?" she asked, her face lighting up. "I'm so glad you came. Papa needs something to distract him from his loneliness now that I'm gone, and there's nothing better than an old family friend."

Dev winced. At twenty-nine, he wasn't so old that her disingenuous remark didn't prick his vanity. Had he become so staid in her eyes?

"He seems very happy about your marriage," Dev said.

She smiled, showing her dimple. "Yes, he is. Wylie is quite a catch, if I do say so myself." She laughed. "All the girls are envious of me, and Papa couldn't be prouder."

Something in her response bothered him, but he couldn't put his finger on what it was. Maybe it was the fact that she hadn't mentioned her own feelings.

"Are *you* happy?" he asked.

"Oh, yes. I've got the most wonderful husband in Kansas City. None of the other eligible bachelors can hold a candle to him. His family was one of the first to settle out here. They're considered the finest in Missouri, and they know everyone worth knowing."

"So I've been told." Too many times to count, Dev thought, as if the listing of personal assets was all that mattered in life.

"By whom?" she inquired, her expression inquisitive and proud, all at the same time.

"Oh, quite a few people — businessmen mostly."

She nodded, clearly pleased. "That's Wylie's doing, you know. His family has a fine, historical name, but absolutely no mind for money. His papa can turn gold to dross without even trying." She sounded uncannily like her father, and Dev assumed she was repeating Gunther Hobart's lines word for word.

"A reverse Midas touch, eh?"

She regarded him uncomprehendingly. "Who's Midas?"

He sighed. Maybe Kansas City *was* as provincial as she had claimed earlier. "He was an ancient king who turned everything he touched into gold."

"Oh, I see." She gave him a puzzled look, clearly not understanding what he'd meant. "Anyway, Papa is setting Wylie up in business and teaching him everything he knows. Before long he'll be running the factory by himself. Won't that be grand? He's exactly what Papa's been looking for, someone to handle the business when he gets too old."

Suddenly the full range of Anna's insecurities became clear. She worried that Wylie had married her for the factory as she had married him for his name. For all Dev knew, he had. Gunther was an astute businessman who would stop at little if he thought it would benefit his factory or his family. From the older man's point of view, this marriage did both: provided a prominent place in society for his daughter and guaranteed that the business would be in safe hands when he retired. No wonder Anna was so high-strung.

"Speaking of your father," he said to distract her, "do you know where he is? I haven't seen him for the last half hour."

"If you promise not to tell, I'll show you where he's hiding out." She smiled conspiratorially, and he nodded his agreement, seeing in her expression vestiges of the impish child she had been long ago. "He always heads to the back parlor." She lowered her voice. "We ladies are not supposed to know they meet there, but I can point you in the right direction."

She pulled him toward the side exit of the ballroom and showed him a studded, burgundy leather door set unobtrusively in the wall.

"I'd best leave you here," she whispered.

Just as Dev was about to suggest he spend the time with her instead of her father, Alice Covington walked by, heading for the ballroom. Anna's smile vanished, and she gave a nervous glance over her shoulder. "I need to get back to the dancing."

Before he could offer to escort her, she disappeared around the corner after Alice.

Poor Anna, Dev thought. She'd seemed particularly upset at seeing Alice, and he couldn't help but remember her reaction to Alice's friend Bess. If anything, Anna seemed more anxious about Bess than any of the others—perhaps because Wylie seemed so much more aware of the blonde, at least from what Dev had seen. And the blonde seemed aware of Wylie, too, though she was plainly trying to hide her feelings. Dev wondered if Gunther knew of all the subterranean intrigue.

Gunther Hobart, Anna's father, was an old family friend, and one of the reasons Devlin had acceded to his father's request that he take over this business trip. Ordinarily he stayed out of his father's affairs, but this time he hadn't had a choice. On the eve of this trip Patrick O'Connor had slipped on the outside stairs of his house, breaking his right leg in two places which effectively immobilized him. Though he could have sent one of his senior employees, Patrick pleaded with his son to go in his stead, arguing that only Devlin would be accepted as his substitute. Devlin knew Patrick still harbored the hope that he would join him in his business and intended this trip to entice Devlin into the fold.

While Devlin had very little interest in the business of making money, he could not refuse the request — his father asked little enough of him and he owed the man more than his life. So here he was, stuck among the monied crowd of Kansas City, feeling bored and trapped by circumstances and ready for a diversion.

"Devlin O'Connor! Just the man we were talking about!" boomed the familiar voice of Anna's father as Dev entered the smoke-filled masculine sanctum. "Come over here and meet my friend, Edward Covington. He's more than eager to do business with your firm. *Nicht wahr*, Edward?"

Gunther Hobart jovially pounded Edward Covington on the back before shaking Devlin's hand and completing the formal introductions. He then added, "Edward is heading for Philadelphia in a couple of weeks to look for investors. I've told him your father is the man to see."

"That was very kind of you, Gunther. My father will be most appreciative." Devlin smiled down at the short, rotund German, a self-made businessman proud of his accomplishments.

Edward Covington nodded his head. "Mr. O'Connor has already given me his card and an invitation to meet with his father. I was hoping he'd consider making the trip back east with us. My family would be most honored."

He smiled benignly at Devlin, but Devlin detected a crafty gleam lurking in Covington's eyes. What was he up to?

"I'll do my best, but it's hard to predict how long things will take. I trust you and your family will not take it amiss if our plans don't fall into place," Devlin responded, leaving himself an out.

"I can hardly ask for more than your best intentions, Mr. O'Connor. My wife would be delighted if you could find a way to fit your schedule in with ours."

The crafty gleam deepened at the mention of Mrs. Covington, and Devlin suddenly understood. He was unmarried, and so was the Covington daughter. He'd already had her pushed into his arms once this evening. Not that she wasn't a lovely girl, but he preferred to do his own asking. He was relieved when Gunther Hobart changed the subject back to more immediate business concerns.

The two other men discussed business prospects for a while longer, carefully including Devlin in their conversation, until the wall clock chimed the hour.

"I'd better get back to the ballroom," Edward Covington declared. "Harrietta will have me tarred and feathered if I hide in here all evening."

Gunther laughed. "You let your wife boss you around too much."

"No more than you do your daughter."

"*Ja, ja,* that is true. A beautiful woman can always get what she wants. Come, we will go now before they both come after us with a switch, *nein?* You, too,

27

Devlin. If we have to suffer, we might as well have company."

Dev laughed but begged off. He'd had enough of the frenetic celebration and longed for some fresh air to clear his head of the alcohol and tobacco fumes. He also wanted a few moments alone to escape the constant pressures of business dealings that seemed to dog his steps even here at a ball.

Gunther went off with Edward in search of Anna while Devlin made his way down the hall toward the terrace.

Bess lingered outside for a few minutes after Alice left. She wished she didn't have to go back inside, but knew she had no choice; her hostess would consider it rude if she spent the entire evening out of doors.

As she passed through the rear hall on her way back to the ballroom, she heard steps coming from behind her.

"Bess. At last," a familiar male voice called out breathlessly. "I've been waiting all evening for a chance to catch you alone."

Wylie! She stopped and looked over her shoulder. He was advancing on her, a determined expression on his face. She didn't want to face him, especially not alone. She quickened her pace, eager to make her escape, but he caught up with her, his hand closing around her upper arm to hold her in place.

"Wylie, you know that this is highly improper," she protested, "and most certainly unwanted."

Wylie ignored her words and pulled her back down the hall, away from the ballroom.

"Let me go," she snapped in a hushed undertone, her satin dance shoes slipping on the slick marble floor as she tried to dig in her heels.

"Just talk to me for a minute, please, Bess. Surely you owe me that."

How did he dare? She owed him nothing! If anything, it was the other way around. "Let go of me. Now," she demanded furiously, still keeping her voice low. She took a deep breath to let him know she was more than ready to create a scene if he did not obey.

"All right, all right. Just hear me out, please." He let her go and backed away, turning the corner of an adjacent hall. "Come closer," he whispered and looked worriedly down the hall they had just left.

Bess did not care for his furtive actions. If he wanted to talk to her, why hadn't he spoken in the ballroom with others around, as befitted a married man who wished to converse with a single woman of twenty years. Now she wished she had gone back with Alice. "I'm as close as I intend to get. What do you want?"

"I made a mistake, Bess," he said, and reached for her hand.

"What?" she asked too startled to pull away from him.

"Marrying Anna. I didn't realize . . . you know what she's like. You're the one I love. Surely you realize that?"

He eased her down the hallway as he spoke, turning her so he stood between her and the main hall. "I could tell that you'd forgiven me when I saw you earlier. You're the only woman I could ever love."

This couldn't be happening, she thought. These were the exact words she'd waited so long to hear — too long.

"Wylie, we both know better. It's too late." She tried to shake off his hand, but he wouldn't let her go.

"Listen, Bess, just for a minute," he urged. "It doesn't have to be over. Hobart's given me the job of second-in-command at his meatpacking factory. I'll be making quite a fair wage." His tone had turned boastful. "We can be together, as long as we're discreet. I'll get you your own place, and . . ."

He continued speaking, his words fast and intent,

29

blurring as her mind sought to comprehend the total depths of nightmare to which her dreams had decayed. Her heart's betrayal was second only to his. And now he thought he could have it all — a rich wife *and* a mistress on the side.

Bile rose in her throat. "Stop it. Stop this minute!" she cried out, but Wylie put his mouth over hers to silence her. Revulsion lent her strength, and she tore her lips from his, then shoved with all her might.

Freed from his embrace, she angrily wiped his taste from her lips and glared at him as he stood blocking her way with his aggressively masculine stance. "Get out of my way and don't come near me again. Ever!" she got out through bruised lips, anger blazing through her.

"Bess . . ." Wylie looked genuinely confused, as if he couldn't believe her rejection of his plans.

How could she have ever thought well of him, this selfish, scheming, dishonorable man? She started to push past him, but he grabbed her elbow, halting her progress.

"Be reasonable, Bess. Take some time to think over my offer. Don't think you'll get anyone better — not with your prospects."

His arrogant, self-confident sneer had her hand moving to strike him. He caught her by the wrist and pulled her close.

"Think about what I said. I'll be in touch," he murmured, then drew back and headed toward the ballroom. The look he cast in her direction was filled with smug satisfaction and self-confidence. She could see he had no doubt that she would come around to his way of thinking.

At that moment, she made up her mind. If Alice's parents agreed to take her along, she would go to Philadelphia. And she'd tell them right now.

Determined to waste no time informing Alice of her decision, Bess hurried back to the main corridor. Just as she turned the corner, she collided with something tall and hard. For a moment, she wasn't sure what had happened. Then a voice asked solicitously, "Are you all right?"

Devlin O'Connor. Why of all people did she have to run into him? "I'm fine," she murmured, her cheeks flaming. "Please excuse me. I'm afraid I didn't see you."

"My fault, entirely," he replied, taking the blame as befitted a proper gentleman.

"Nonsense, I ran into you," she countered, an angry edge in her tone. She didn't need this right now. There was something about this man that set her nerves jangling, as if she needed them any more finely drawn. She straightened to her full height, unimpressive though that was, and sent him a look that dared him to challenge her.

"As you say," he conceded politely.

"Please accept my apology," she said and turned again toward the ballroom.

"Apology accepted," he said evenly, and stepped out of her way.

She nodded her head and then swept by him without a backward glance. At the entrance to the ballroom, she stopped to search the crowd. All she saw was the crunch of people standing by the walls, talking and watching the dancers. How would she ever find Alice in this throng?

Two

Bess worked her way farther into the large ballroom. The room had filled with guests and because of her height, she made little headway in her quest for Alice. She dared not glance behind her. With some sixth sense she could tell that Devlin O'Connor was still staring. She could feel the imprint of his piercing gaze on her back.

Her skin tingled where he had touched her, his hands neither too soft nor too rough. His scent, too, stayed with her. She had run right into his chest and for an instant, her face had been pressed against the front of his white silk shirt. He'd smelled clean, of soap and starch, with a hint of tobacco. And his muscles had been harder than she'd expected, revealing a strength she'd never anticipated in an Eastern tenderfoot.

A shiver ran down her spine. What was she doing thinking of him? Hadn't she just sworn off men with their fickle hearts and conniving minds?

Where was Alice? In her overwrought state, Bess felt desperate to confirm her plans, to ensure that one way or another she'd get away from a situation that held nothing good for her. Unable to spot her friend, Bess stepped into a small alcove built into one corner of the ballroom. The area was dimly lit, a refuge from the noise and color of the main arena.

"Well, Bess Richmond! What are you doing here?"

Bess started, then recognized the voice of her favorite teacher from Miss Fine's. "Miss Christy, I didn't realize you'd be coming to the ball." She moved deeper into the alcove now that her eyes had adjusted to the low light.

"Arthur insisted. He's on the Board of Trade, after all, and like all men, he tends to think he knows what's best for the rest of mankind, and me in particular. Though he didn't have to prod too sharply. The Board of Trade balls are always memorable occasions."

"Then why are you hiding in here?"

"Hiding? Is that why you came in?"

How neatly she'd turned everything around, Bess thought. But then Miss Christy had always been clever, keeping one step ahead of even her brightest students. Bess laughed. "You caught me there. Actually, I was looking for Alice Covington, and when I couldn't find her, I thought I'd try to catch sight of her from here."

"I see," the other woman said though her skeptical gaze told Bess she believed only half the story. "I'm afraid your aigrette is somewhat the worse for wear," she commented as she finished scrutinizing her. "You must have knocked into something."

Bess put a hand to the top of her head. The beautiful white feathers felt limp, and one of them was bent at an unnatural angle, the result of her tussle with Wylie or the subsequent collision with the tall Easterner; she didn't know which. She felt the heat of a blush rise from her neck to her cheeks.

"I must have been careless," she mumbled, knowing just how careless she had been, allowing Wylie to corner her the way he had. She couldn't very well admit that to Miss Christy, however, even if it was the real reason she'd taken refuge in this alcove.

33

"Why don't you sit in this chair, and I'll see if I can't put it to rights," her former teacher offered.

Bess obeyed without question. Few students dared thwart Miss Christy more than once, and though she hadn't been a student in almost a year, Bess's response was ingrained.

"Your dress is lovely," Miss Christy said as she poked and prodded, rearranging Bess's hair and smoothing her feathered ornament. "I imagine you've drawn more than your share of admiring glances this evening."

Bess looked up sharply. This didn't sound in the least like her teacher. "My father bought it for me. He takes great stock in these events, you know."

"Of course, men usually do. And what about you? Are you enjoying yourself? Alice may be flighty, but surely her brother Barrett is taking better care of you."

"How did you know I was seeing Barrett?" Bess asked, surprised. She'd only met with Barrett a couple of times and that had been since Wylie's defection.

"Arthur keeps me abreast of all the social goings-on. Says he doesn't want me to be embarrassed when I'm in polite company. When I hear something that interests me, I remember."

"Well, Barrett couldn't be here. He had to go back to Philadelphia. I came with Alice and her parents."

Miss Christy narrowed her eyes. "No wonder you're not happy. What could Barrett be thinking of, squiring you all over town and then leaving you high and dry before the Board of Trade Ball?"

"Barrett couldn't help it," Bess felt compelled to defend. After all, Alice was her best friend. Surely her brother deserved some consideration. "I'm afraid his firm insisted he go back to Philadelphia right away."

"Well, don't you worry. I'm sure we can find someone to take his place," Miss Christy said, patting Bess on the arm.

"Really, Miss Christy, I'm quite happy—"

"Call me Laura," Miss Christy insisted. "Now that we're no longer in the classroom there's no need for so much formality."

Bess could only nod. Call her Laura? Why, Miss Christy was at least . . . No, now that Bess really thought about it Miss Christy — Laura, that is — wasn't that old at all. In fact, she was several years younger than Bess's father, and Bess had never thought of him as old. It was just that as a teacher she always seemed so knowledgeable, so much in charge of whatever situation she was in, so much more mature than Bess's friends.

"Now, come along," Laura continued, urging Bess to her feet and leading her to the edge of the alcove before she could gather her wits to refuse.

Together they surveyed the crowd. The women were dressed very fashionably, their richly ornamented gowns rivaling any New York or Boston could boast of: satin and silk, muslin and brocade, diamonds and feathers, point lace and flowers — all sparkled in the hundred points of light from the chandeliers. The men wore dark suits and ties, their shirts brilliantly white, their shoes and boots shined to a high polish.

Everywhere Bess looked she saw only couples. Nervously she swept her gaze over the crowd once more, searching, seeking . . . then finding. Wylie and Anna were dancing less than twenty feet away.

Bess's hands grew cold. She did not want to face either of them again tonight.

"Now there's a possibility," Miss Christy said as she moved closer to the dance floor.

"Possibility?" Bess hung back.

"Now don't be shy, Bess. I've found the perfect solution to your escort situation."

To Bess's dismay, Miss Christy was turning out to be just like her brother Arthur, rearranging other people's lives without so much as a by-your-leave. With some trepidation, Bess stepped out of the alcove. Then she saw him. Devlin O'Connor. Tall and slim, leaning nonchalantly on his cane. Brown eyes ensnared hers, trapping them. The noise of the crowd fell away.

"Yes, I think he'll do quite nicely," her teacher was saying. "Come along, and I'll introduce you."

"If you mean Mr. O'Connor, we've already met," Bess answered with some desperation. The expression on his aristocratic features was remote and disapproving; moreover he was Anna's friend. "Besides, Mrs. Covington has her eye on him for Alice."

"Why, that will never do. I'm afraid Harrietta Covington will have to find someone else for Alice. They're not at all suited. He needs someone with more backbone. He's quite the dashing man from what I recall."

Laura Christy was the only daughter of an extremely proper Philadelphia family and had moved out to Kansas City to live with her brother when her parents had died. The girls at school had long since decided she wouldn't know what to do with a man even were she to find one, so the thought of her describing a man as dashing was altogether new.

"Have I shocked you, dear?" she asked and held up one hand. "Don't answer that," she continued, still smiling. "I wasn't born thirty-six years old, though I'm sure you girls at school liked to think so. Now, let's not keep him waiting." Clasping Bess's hand, she began working her way around the dancers.

"Please," Bess entreated. "I'm not sure now is the best time to meet someone new."

Laura gave her a shrewd look. "*Now* most certainly is the best time," she said firmly. "But the most important factor is to meet the right man." She emphasized the last words, and Bess saw her glance disdainfully in Wylie's direction.

"You know about Wylie?" Bess had been so sure her

secret was safe, and now not only Alice knew of her poor judgment, but Miss Christy, too.

"Don't worry, Bess, dear, I know only because I make it a point to find out about the people for whom I care. I think your secret is safe from the others here tonight." She sighed. "I had hoped you would put him behind you once you left school and were out socially."

"Well, he's behind me now," Bess said with resolve, knowing she'd not pine over Wylie Moore ever again.

"So what are you going to do about it?"

"Do?" She wasn't ready to jump feet first into the Kansas City social whirl just yet, but Miss Christy did not seem to believe her.

"Yes, do. You can't spend your life visiting friends and living with your father." Miss Christy narrowed her eyes into her most penetrating, schoolmarm's glare. "Languishing away doesn't become a young woman in today's society. There are things to be done, people to meet. You can't let one bit of bad judgment set you back. Besides, as far as I'm concerned, Fortune smiled on you this time. Worse things could have happened. Wylie might have married *you*."

Her words were an uncanny echo of Alice's.

"You're very different from the way I remember you at Miss Fine's School," Bess said. In those days, teachers never discussed anything this personal with their students.

"No, child, you're different — you're growing up." Miss Christy gently stroked Bess's cheek with her hand. "I wouldn't want you to repeat the mistakes I made as a girl. Believe me, it's not worth throwing your life away over one rotten apple, not when there are so many others in the barrel. Right?"

There was a definite twinkle in the other woman's eyes. Bess was even beginning to think she might get used to calling her Laura when a shadow fell across her face.

37

The teacher looked up, then scowled. "What are you doing here, Wylie?" she demanded in the dry, piercing voice Bess remembered from school. "Shouldn't you be with your wife?"

Wylie tried his most bewitching smile. "I thought perhaps Miss Bess might like a whirl across the dance floor. Anna and I have only just parted, and Miss Bess has been standing by the wall for so long now."

"Thank you, Wylie, but no," Bess got out through gritted teeth. How dare he come near her again? Her insides quivered with indignation.

"We were about to meet a friend, Wylie," Miss Christy put in, not taken in by him at all. "If you would be so kind as to excuse us."

"Surely one dance would be no great imposition?" Wylie insisted, stepping between the two ladies.

"I'm afraid it would, Wylie, old man. This dance has been promised to me."

Devlin closed the gap between himself and the trio. He'd been trying to get Wylie alone ever since he'd witnessed the man tangled in what seemed to be an embrace with the petite blonde now before him. That there was more going on between this couple than met the eye was obvious, especially to a trained observer like himself. The events of the evening could not be denied: the way Wylie had jumped to the blonde's defense when Anna pushed too hard, the way Wylie had stared after her when she went off to dance with someone else. The hungry look in his eye whenever he was near her. Like now. Dev would bet that whatever Wylie was up to, it didn't bode well for his marriage. No wonder Anna was so high-strung.

As one of Pinkerton's best operatives, Devlin knew better than to accept a shallow, surface interpretation of events. Nonetheless, his instincts could not be ignored—they'd served him too well in the past. Deftly he positioned himself next to the blonde, cutting out Wylie.

"I believe we met earlier, Miss Richmond," he said, taking her hand in his and bending over it.

She looked up at him, her eyes wide and blue as the summer sky. For a moment, he felt he was floating, up and up into their cloudless reaches. His reaction startled him, and he let go of her hand.

"Why, Devlin O'Connor, we were just making our way over to see you," Laura Christy said with a friendly smile. "Weren't we, dear?" she added, nudging Elizabeth Richmond none too delicately with her elbow.

The younger woman faced him, looking as if it was the last thing in the world she wanted to do. He was determined to dance with her if that was the only way to thwart Wylie. He was marshalling arguments to deal with her refusal when she surprised him by saying, "Yes, we were."

Laura beamed. "I was just saying to Bess that she should meet some new people, and there you were. Now don't let us—" her nod took in Wylie as well as herself "—keep you. Go along now, while the music is playing. I'm sure Bess is eager to be on the dance floor now that she's had a chance to catch her breath."

Dev took pleasure in the expression of impotent anger on Wylie's face at being outmaneuvered by the sly teacher. The young pup certainly deserved to be put in his place. Turning his attention to his partner, Dev extended his arm and said, "Miss Richmond."

"Thank you, Mr. O'Connor," she replied and placed her hand on his arm, her touch feather-light, as if she wasn't quite ready to go off with him.

Not giving her a chance to change her mind, he swept her onto the dance floor and spun her away from the temptation of Wylie Moore. From the corner of his eye, he saw Anna approach her husband. Dev smiled, satisfied now that he had intervened. Gunther had such high hopes for the newly married couple, though they were very young and seemed extremely immature. Dev could already see they would need a lot of help to make their marriage succeed.

"It was most gracious of you to accede to Miss Christy's request," Bess said to him as they danced, her tone more polite than sincere, completely ignoring the fact he'd asked her to dance even before the older woman had spoken.

"The pleasure is mine, Miss Richmond," he said, ignoring the ambiguity. To his surprise, he did indeed feel a certain pleasure.

Up close her eyes were clear and guileless, their color enhanced by the deeper blue of her peau de soie gown. Her ivory skin glowed beneath the rich light from the ornate gas chandeliers overhead. Though not very tall, her figure was perfectly formed, softly curved in all the right places.

No woman had fit him like this . . . not since Julia. Curiously, thinking her name no longer hurt as much as it used to. He felt a stab of guilt that he was holding another woman in his arms, then he experienced a quiet elation. How long since he had even considered holding, caring, loving? Could it be that he was finally healing?

Lost in his thoughts and the subtle pleasures of dancing with such a responsive partner, Dev didn't watch where he was going. Suddenly an arm jabbed him roughly in his side.

"My mistake," Wylie apologized, though the glint in his eye belied his words. He was partnering Anna whose smile was both apologetic and beseeching. "Please excuse us," she said.

Dev inclined his head, choosing to accept Wylie's graceless apology, before moving away with Bess.

"They make a nice couple, don't you think?" Dev asked deliberately. He hadn't missed the way Wylie stared at Bess.

"Oh, yes, made for each other," Bess replied, a fine edge to her tone.

"Exactly." He gave her a pointed look and felt her stiffen in his arms, putting more space between them though she did not pick up on his conversational gambit. He debated whether to force the issue. Initially, he had hoped to speak to Wylie, but since that plan had not worked out, he had to change his tactics. Though he did not usually involve himself in others' affairs, something impelled him to intervene in this case. Most likely it was the long-standing family friendship between his father and Gunther Hobart that prompted his action. Surely that had to be the reason.

Just then the music came to a rousing finish followed by silence as the musicians conferred on what to play next. Dev was forced to let Bess Richmond out of his embrace.

"Thank you for the dance," she said and turned to leave.

"Wait," he called out, unwilling to let her get away quite yet.

She looked over her shoulder at him expectantly. "Is there a problem?"

Without stopping to think he blurted out, "Wylie seems inordinately fond of you."

"I beg your pardon?" She sent him a frigid look.

"I said, Wylie seems fond of you, unusually so." He kept his voice as bland as he could. "Don't tell me you didn't notice."

She paled, then blushed to the roots of her hair, but did not drop her gaze. "Tell me, Mr. O'Connor, are all Easterners as rude as you?" Without waiting for him to answer, she continued, "As far as I can see, my personal life is none of your business. I'd appreciate your keeping your comments to yourself."

"Then you're not denying what I said?" For a moment Dev was speechless. Whatever he had expected, it was not this calm admission of her relationship with Wylie. His stomach twisted—how could he have found such pleasure in her arms when she was so cold-bloodedly unscrupulous?

"I am neither admitting nor denying anything," she said into the silence. "I am simply refusing to discuss such personal issues with you."

She turned to go again, and Dev knew he couldn't leave matters like this. "It's Anna's life I'm most concerned with at the moment," he said to her back. "Not yours. I think you are a very strong threat to her happiness."

When she didn't stop, he started after her. "Anna and Wylie are newly married," he reminded her. "There are a lot of adjustments they're going to have to make. They don't need any outside interference at this delicate point in their lives."

"Let me assure you, Mr. O'Connor, the furthest thought from my mind is interfering in Anna's life."

"It didn't look that way earlier in the hall with Wylie."

That stopped her. "In the hall?"

He nodded.

"Maybe you didn't really understand what was happening," she said.

He would have believed her to be as cold as her tone if he hadn't noticed her balled fists, half hidden in the voluminous folds of her skirt, the knuckles stark and white. "Would you explain it to me then?" he asked, his voice softening.

"The only person I have anything to explain to is Anna, if she should somehow find out. I owe no one else an explanation, certainly not you."

"Maybe you're right, and it is none of my business, but I've known Anna since she was a child, and I don't want to see her hurt."

"How noble of you, but you are misdirecting your efforts, Mr. O'Connor. I suggest you talk to Wylie. He is her husband and the ultimate source of her happiness."

So saying, she turned on her heel and was about to escape when the musicians resumed playing.

Without missing a beat, he pulled her into his arms. "One more dance, I think," he murmured, and gathered her close.

"Let me go," she protested, but he would not release her. Her refusal to explain her behavior intrigued him.

"Don't make a scene. Wylie and Anna are looking this way." He wasn't sure how she would handle his audacity, but counted on her pride to keep up a semblance of good manners in front of the cream of Kansas City society. "Smile. Pretend you're enjoying yourself."

She looked over her shoulder, and he could see her swallow her protest as she caught sight of Wylie and his new wife. She let him lead her away then demanded he let her go when they were out of earshot of Anna and Wylie.

"Why?" he asked. "We're doing just fine together. See?" He nodded toward the far wall. "There's Laura Christy watching us. Look how pleased she is. You really can't disappoint her. Besides, I'm told I'm quite a good dancer."

Her only response was to deliberately step on his toe. "Ouch," he whispered in her ear. He increased the distance between them but kept his hold firm, biting down a smile. After that, they danced in silence.

"Have you been to Kansas City before, Mr. O'Connor?" she asked, after a while, her resigned tone signaling her readiness to play the polite partner.

He decided to go along with her. "No, this is my first visit. Have you lived here all your life?"

"Almost. I grew up in Carlinsville — a small town east of the city. I went to school here, though, and I consider this my second home."

"It seems very civilized. Perhaps I might return

43

again some time."

"I'm sure Wylie and Anna would be pleased to see you."

Dev detected an underlying bitterness in her words. He narrowed his eyes but did not reply. They danced on, circling the large ballroom with the rest of the crowd.

The light from a wall sconce glinted in Bess's hair as he twirled her, turning it into a golden aureola. He felt a sudden urge to run his fingers over her cheek, to feel her skin satin-soft beneath his fingertips as he breathed in her flowery scent.

Instead, he looked away and pondered his attraction to her. She was definitely not his type, at least not from what he had seen so far. High society was all well and good—for some. For himself, however, the empty chit-chat of the drawing room and parlor had never appealed.

He preferred people who lived life with a purpose and goal, not those who pursued money for its own sake. Unfortunately, the time spent in Kansas City on his father's business had thrown him into the company of Wylie and his ilk more often than he liked. They were exactly the type of shallow-interest people he was most eager to avoid, while Bess Richmond seemed to seek them out.

"So, what do you do with your life other than coming to galas and balls?" he asked, driven by some perverse demon.

"Oh, let me see now. Sometimes I meet the gracious gentlemen who also come to galas and balls. Other times, I'm not so lucky." She gave him a bland look.

"Am I to take it that tonight is not one of the lucky times?"

"Good manners prevent me from answering, I'm afraid."

Dev couldn't prevent the chuckle that rose from his

44

chest. It was his first genuine laugh since meeting her.

"So we are striving for good manners at the moment, are we? At times during this conversation I haven't been sure. Not that I'm pressing for an answer, mind you, unless it's suitably flattering," he added with a smile.

Just as she would have replied, the music stopped again, and the dancers regrouped. Dev led her to the side of the room. He didn't want to lose her yet. "Could I get you something to drink, Miss Richmond?" he asked. "It's rather close in here."

He sensed that a refusal was on the tip of her tongue. She looked around, as if desperately searching for another escort. Fortunately for him, none was handy.

"I—um, yes, thank you. A lemonade would be wonderful."

"I believe there are some seats up on the balcony." He indicated the overhang at the near end of the ballroom. "I'm sure it's less crowded up there."

He escorted her up the stairs behind the ballroom. The balcony covered a section of the dance floor and swept around the edge of the ballroom on two adjacent sides. They walked to a small seating group—a padded bench and two chairs around a low table, with a view of the dancers below—and he waited until she was seated, her skirts arranged neatly, before he went after their drinks.

Bess watched him walk away. She didn't want to notice that he had a litheness about him which his slender build disguised. She didn't want to remember the feel of his muscles bunching and releasing beneath the hand she had rested on his shoulder as they moved across the dance floor. She certainly didn't want to recall his enticing masculine scent.

This man had no liking for her; she'd seen that clearly enough. In fact, he thought so little of her that he'd all but accused her of trying to come between Wylie and Anna. If she had any brains at all, she would disappear while he was gone. But good manners had been ingrained in her, and by the time this errant thought occurred to her, Devlin O'Connor was already coming back bearing a silver tray with two full glasses and a plate of small sandwiches.

"Here, you must be hungry. I know I am."

How like an Easterner, she thought, to worry so about creature comforts. He placed the tray on the low table by her bench and sat on an ornately upholstered chair opposite her. She watched him recline lazily, one arm draped over the back of his chair, one ankle resting on the knee of his opposite leg. In some circles, he would have been considered a prime catch—sophisticated and worldly, at ease with himself and society.

But Bess now knew that was not enough. Wylie, too, was a city boy, exactly the kind of man her father had taught her to seek, and look how he had turned out. If she ever decided to take a chance on a man again, and right now that didn't seem likely, he would be someone completely different, someone more like her father— honest and hardworking, a man of the West, where honor was prized over manners and social position.

From everything she could see, Devlin O'Connor and Wylie Moore were cut from the same cloth: handsome, self-assured businessmen, used to having their own way without regard to others' feelings, pressing their ideas on all and sundry. She'd had more than enough of that.

"What do you usually do, Mr. O'Connor, when you're not traveling to the uncivilized wilds of Kansas City?" she asked as she reached for her glass of lemonade.

"Oh, a bit of this and that, whatever comes to hand," he answered evasively. "Right now, I'm here on business, as you heard."

"And do you enjoy it?"

"Enjoyment is not the issue. I am doing what is necessary, that's all."

"For your father, I understand."

"You're well-informed."

"And must you always do what is 'necessary?' "

"I certainly try to, but then I have different goals than you, I'm sure."

The coldness in his tone sent a chill down Bess's spine. She hadn't meant to question his attitudes, but it was evident he had taken her remarks that way. She'd been lost in her own thoughts, trying to decide how to explain to her father why she no longer wanted to marry and start the requisite family—those things he felt were so necessary, but that she no longer desired.

"Goals have a way of changing when we least expect them to, Mr. O'Connor." She put down her glass and clasped her hands in her lap.

"And what goals have you set for yourself, Miss Richmond?" he asked, narrowing in on her most vulnerable point.

"None, really," she answered honestly. Her goals had all been imposed from the outside, except for one—teaching. "Actually, I did try tutoring, but without too much success, I'm afraid. I don't think I have the patience to handle children, especially if they have special problems."

"Maybe you simply need to gain more experience. Everything improves with practice. You can't expect to do things perfectly the very first time."

"You're probably right, but I don't think teaching is my vocation. I'll have to find something else."

The look he sent her spoke more loudly than words. He thought she was taking the easy way out. Little did he know how hard she had fought for the opportunity to teach, how disappointed she had been at her lack of success. Her father, out of misguided love, had deftly used her failure to push her back into society.

"Do you have anything in mind to try?" he probed.

"I don't know yet, but I'm sure I'll find something. I've been thinking of traveling for a while." She didn't mention that her plans had been made just this evening, providing, of course, that Alice's parents agreed to them.

He did not look impressed. "Have you traveled before?"

"No. I've been to visit my friends from school—like Alice."

"A charming young woman, as are her parents."

Bess felt hot color rise to her cheeks at his lightly mocking tone. She remembered all too clearly how Alice's mother had cornered him, pushing Alice on him as a dance partner. Mrs. Covington had had only one thing on her mind—matchmaking. Had Devlin O'Connor figured out her plans? Flustered, Bess reached again for her drink, nearly knocking it over.

With a quickness of which she wouldn't have believed him capable, Dev reached over and righted her glass, his fingers closing over her hand.

A shock of heat traveled up her arm. At the same time a chill raced down her spine, leaving her unnerved. She quickly retrieved her hand and stood.

"I'm afraid I've been taking up too much of your valuable time, Mr. O'Connor," she said, suddenly realizing she'd opened herself to a complete stranger on first acquaintance. "We really should go back downstairs."

Before he could respond, Alice's voice rang out across the balcony. "Bess! At last!"

"Alice! I was looking all over for you. Where have you been?"

"Looking for you, of course." Alice sashayed over to Bess. "Have you two been up here all this time?" she asked archly, fluttering her lashes at Devlin O'Connor.

Bess had seen Alice's arrival as a reprieve, providing

her with a perfectly natural way to leave Mr. O'Connor's overwhelming presence, but right now it was clear Alice wasn't going anywhere. Not as long as Devlin O'Connor was around, anyway.

"Hello again, Mr. O'Connor. I never expected to find you up here with Bess."

He gave a slight bow in Alice's direction. "Miss Christy was kind enough to re-introduce me, and we've been having a very interesting conversation."

"I didn't realize you knew Miss Christy," Alice said.

"We share mutual friends in Philadelphia."

"Oh, that's right. You're both from Philadelphia. How interesting. Will you be going back there soon?"

"Not right away. I still have some business to take care of here in Kansas City."

"Why that's wonderful. We have such a lovely town here, you'll have time to see some sights. I'm sure my father would be happy to be of help if you need any assistance."

With every word she spoke, Alice edged closer, until she stood right by Mr. O'Connor's side.

"It's very kind of you to offer, Miss Covington," he said graciously.

Too graciously, Bess thought irritably. Couldn't he see through Alice's flirtatious ways?

"I think we should go back downstairs," Bess said, her voice uncharacteristically sharp. Alice and O'Connor both looked questioningly at her. "Everyone will wonder where we are," she explained, ignoring their real question since she had no answer to it.

"Why, yes, you're absolutely right," Alice declared, "especially with the orchestra still playing. Everyone will expect us to dance, you know."

She placed her hand in the crook of O'Connor's elbow and smiled up at him. "Shall we go down?" she cooed.

O'Connor nodded and Bess clenched her teeth, a

knot forming in her chest. She didn't know why she felt so aggravated. Alice's flirting had never set her off before.

She followed the other two back to the ballroom and smiled politely when they excused themselves to dance. She should have been relieved to see them go, but instead she felt abandoned, alone in a world of happy couples. She found an empty table in a shadowed corner and gratefully sank into a chair. More than ever, she realized she needed to give her life a new direction. The only question was what to do.

Women had few choices if they wanted to maintain their respectability, and for her father's sake, that was a primary consideration. Marriage was the most suitable arrangement, but failing that, a woman could move in with a married relative or friend. Bess shuddered at the prospect—what could be more horrific than living life as a perpetual extra?

There were women who pursued careers, she knew, and only a few of them married, the others preferring to devote their lives to their work. She'd read about them here and there and wondered how they survived, ridiculed in the press as peevish spinsters, spurned by a society which regarded single women beyond a certain age as essentially worthless.

What kind of existence was that, she wondered, and what kind of career could she choose for herself at this late date? She had considerable energy and drive, but no focus on which to expend them. Her life in Kansas City had been carefully circumscribed, deliberately so, by her doting father and society's strict dictates.

Before tonight, she'd never questioned her place in the scheme of things, merely accepting the status quo in a safe and predictable world. Suddenly, in the space of an evening, everything she had taken for granted was threatened, as much by her own change in attitude as by any concrete event that had taken place.

Her only hope was that Philadelphia would provide her with a new perspective, a new sense of purpose. She stood, needing to find Alice and make sure the invitation to join her family had been approved. She didn't know what she would do if the Covingtons turned her down.

Just then Alice hurried across the floor and came to a stop in front of Bess. Her cheeks were flushed, and her brown eyes held an unnaturally bright sheen.

"Oh, Bess, I just had the grandest time!" She pirouetted on the smooth, wooden floor. "Mr. O'Connor really does dance like a dream! He's just the most exciting man I've ever met. Don't you agree?"

Something about Alice's attraction to Devlin O'Connor bothered Bess more than she wanted to admit, though she couldn't imagine why. The man had made clear his low opinion of her, and right now she didn't think too highly of him either.

"You say that about every new man you meet," she said teasingly, not wishing to make her true feelings known.

"I know, but it's always true. Do you think I have a character flaw?"

Bess groaned dramatically but said nothing. Alice could be too silly at times.

"Now don't make fun of me. I'm serious." Alice put her hands on her hips, prepared to be indignant, then thought better of it. "Oh, well, who cares? Right now, I'm having the time of my life, and you should, too. I bet all the men back east are like Mr. O'Connor. Real city men are *so* much more sophisticated than these Kansas City boys, don't you think?"

City men, Bess thought. She'd had enough of them for one day, but she forced a smile to her face.

"I guess so," she acknowledged, not wanting to dampen her friend's enthusiasm. After all, Alice still had stars in her eyes and a future secured by her father's wealth.

"I can't wait until we get to Philadelphia," Alice declared. "You are coming, aren't you? Did I tell you? I talked to Mama and she's *so* excited about you coming with us. We'll have such fun; the best time ever!"

Bess breathed a silent sigh of relief. "You're sure it's all right with both your parents?" she asked, needing the reassurance. Philadelphia had become the answer to her dilemmas.

"Oh, yes — Papa was right there, and he gave his usual absent-minded agreement." Alice giggled. "He probably wasn't even listening when we asked, but he won't back out of it. Mama will see to that. All we have to do now is get your father to agree. You don't think that will be a problem, do you?"

"Oh, no, I'm sure my father will think it a wonderful idea," Bess said with more conviction than she felt. Even if he refused, she would find a way to convince him to let her go. She had no choice — Kansas City held a future too dismal to consider; Philadelphia held a hope too bright to ignore.

Three

A late spring rain had dampened the dust near the train station earlier in the day, but by mid-afternoon the sun had worked its way through the clouds. The crowd was small; few people were leaving today. The rest were mostly ne'er-do-wells and young boys hoping the incoming train would bring some excitement into their humdrum lives.

Bess stood by her bags, her father at her side, relieved that the time to leave had finally come. Bert Richmond had vacillated back and forth about letting his only daughter go off to Philadelphia, and for a while Bess had been certain he'd say no.

She peeked at her watch to make sure the train from Kansas City was not past due.

"Don't worry, Bessie," her father said. "The train will be here soon enough."

Her father's use of her childhood name brought forth fond memories, each reminding her how far from home she would be traveling.

"I was only worried my watch might be wrong," she said, afraid he had been hurt by her impatience with the train.

"I'm sure it's just fine. You checked with the jeweler three times this morning to get the correct time."

"Are you going to be all right while I'm gone?"

"Sure, don't worry none. I'll manage, just like always. I'm more worried about you."

Bess smiled. They were so alike. "I'm a bit worried, too," she confessed. "I've never traveled so far away before."

He took her hand between the two of his. He felt warm and solid, a bulwark against all threats, real and imagined. "You'll do fine, sweetheart. You've grown into quite the young lady—everything I ever dreamed of."

She could see the approval in his eyes as he took in her new traveling ensemble. No matter how she'd objected, he'd insisted she get a new wardrobe for the trip, and now she'd become exactly what he'd always wanted her to be—well-dressed, articulate, and educated, the perfect young woman for some eligible young man.

Bert gave her a hug. "You'll have beaux from all the best families lining up in front of your hotel wanting to take you to all the fanciest places. You'll be the belle of the ball."

He smiled down at her, and Bess knew exactly what he was thinking. He had agreed to this trip primarily because Mrs. Covington had promised to introduce her to the best of society. Bert still hoped to see his daughter married to a gentleman. She hadn't had the heart to tell him marriage was the last thing on her mind.

Feeling a twinge of guilt, Bess hugged him back and stood on tiptoes to kiss his leathery cheek. "I love you, Papa," she whispered as her eyes filled. "I'll miss you so."

"I'll miss you, too, Bessie girl, so don't forget to write. I'll be thinking of you every day."

Her arms tightened as she wondered how he'd feel if he knew her secret plans. Would he be disappointed in her? She hoped not. She didn't like keeping things from him, but she'd learned that her will was no match for his. She loved him too much to openly challenge him, and he knew it. She could only imagine his reaction if he found out she wanted to contact her mother's family in Philadelphia. His protective instincts would overwhelm his good sense in less than a second, and she would find herself stuck in Carlinsville for the rest of her days.

She knew little about her Philadelphia relatives — her father was always most circumspect when the subject came up — but over the years, she'd learned to read between the lines. They had disapproved of her parents' marriage and had never forgiven him when their daughter died. Nor had he forgiven himself. The sorrow of Bess's childhood had been her inability to make it up to him. One of the many blessings of her love for Wylie had been her father's satisfaction with the match.

But Wylie had been a terrible mistake, and Bess had learned a hard lesson: the best way to live her life was to please herself. But in order to please herself, she first had to find out who she was. And like it or not, that involved learning about her mother's family. Once she'd contacted them, she could set about reordering her life, setting new goals and finding new directions.

"I think I hear the train coming," her father said, his voice heavy despite the smile on his face.

Bess gave him another quick hug. She blinked rapidly, trying to dispel her tears, and listened carefully. She, too, heard the rumble down the track. The train whistle sounded in the distance, and the crowd came to life, the travelers picking up their parcels and checking their luggage for the last time while the young boys crowded around them, offering to help — for a tip.

Bess's heartbeat quickened. She had never contemplated taking so daring a step. For the first time she was trying to change her destiny, to give direction to her future. She didn't know what she was capable of, but she was determined to find out.

As the train chugged up to the station platform, steam billowing from its engine, she looked around, her eyes soaking up every detail. The station master would see that her trunk was loaded onto the train. All she had to do was say her goodbyes and board. For a second she wished she could change her mind and stay.

Bert gave her a last hug. "Off you go, sweetheart," he whispered in her ear.

She hugged him back in sudden desperation. " 'Bye, Papa," she said, then took one more quick look at her childhood home before boarding the train. There was no turning back now.

Once aboard Bess passed through two cars without seeing a familiar face. She had just decided she was either on the wrong train or the Covingtons hadn't boarded in Kansas City when she heard her name called. She looked up and saw Alice rushing toward her down the long central aisle.

"Isn't this too exciting? I can hardly wait till we get to Philadelphia," Alice proclaimed as she met Bess and gave her a quick peck on the cheek. "Your traveling outfit is lovely — perfect for this time of year."

"Thank you. I'm glad I finally found you. I was beginning to think I was on the wrong train." They both laughed as they started down the aisle in the direction Alice had come from.

"You'll never guess who's on the train with us," Alice said conspiratorially, stopping before they'd gone more than a few feet. She leaned close, her eyes sparkling and mysterious. "I couldn't believe it myself. I know this must be fate. The trip will be ever so much more interesting now."

Bess waited for her to continue, but Alice kept silent, smiling smugly as a well-fed cat. "Well, aren't you going to tell me who you're talking about?" Bess prompted.

"No. I want to keep it a surprise. I can't wait to see your face when you find out." Alice giggled. "I'll tell you this, though, I was just as surprised as I could be when I boarded the train."

Bess listened patiently for a few minutes longer while Alice prattled on. Then the hamper her father had packed for her began to get heavy. She glanced around, but there was no sign they were anywhere near their seats.

"Is this our car?" she asked when Alice paused to catch her breath.

"Oh, no. We're back several cars. My father got us tickets for the day coach and the sleeper."

Bess couldn't imagine Mr. and Mrs. Covington traveling in anything less than the best. It wasn't enough that he was a well-known Kansas City banker, they wanted everyone else to know it, too.

"Why don't you show me the way?" she suggested before Alice could start in again on her "exciting secret." Right now all Bess wanted was to sit down and catch her breath.

They were just about to enter the farthest car, Bess in the lead, when she barged into a man exiting the door. She was so busy trying to steady her packages that she didn't realize who it was until he spoke.

"Why, Miss Richmond, what a pleasant surprise." Strong hands gripped her shoulders as the train began to move. Dev's soft, gravelly tone was somewhere between sincere and mocking. Bess wasn't sure which he intended.

"What are you doing here?" she blurted out, her own tone none too friendly. She wanted to give Alice a shake for having kept this to herself. If there was one person Bess didn't want to see, it was Devlin O'Connor. He was everything she'd hoped to escape in leaving Kansas City. He reminded her all too sharply of her humiliation at Wylie's hands.

Dev raised an eyebrow and looked down at her from his great height. She bit her lip, wishing she would

57

learn to hold her tongue around this infuriating man. She only hoped he had a seat at the opposite end of the train from the Covingtons.

"Thank you. I've been quite well, and yourself?" he responded pleasantly, his hands still supporting her.

Bess purposely stepped back, shrugging out of his hold with what she hoped was a casual disregard. She didn't want him to know how his touch affected her. But her move was too jerky, and she stepped on Alice's toe in the process.

"Careful, Bess," Alice chided. Then in a hushed voice only Bess could hear, she whispered, "So what do you think of my secret? Isn't it just wonderful?"

Bess didn't know what to say. She'd assumed Mr. O'Connor was back in Philadelphia if she considered him at all, though he had come into her thoughts more than once. Her daydreams had painted him quite differently from reality. In her dreams he'd been heroic and rugged—the type of man she'd sensed she could trust. Now, barely two minutes after seeing him again, she knew how foolish her daydreams had been. Why she had made him over in her imagination, she had no idea. He'd made his disdain for her quite obvious, and not only over Wylie and Anna. He seemed to find her trivial and useless, which scared her since lately she felt exactly that way.

"I was just wondering where our seats were," she said, trying to get Alice's mind off Mr. O'Connor. Her ploy didn't work, for it was O'Connor who answered.

"Your seats are back there." He indicated the left side of the car behind him. "Mrs. Covington was afraid you might have gotten lost—or worse, left behind. She was quite frantic when the porter told her the train would soon be pulling out. I offered to find you both."

Though he spoke to the two of them, his gaze remained on Bess. With a sinking heart she realized he wasn't just on the train but traveling with the Coving-

58

tons. Now she would be forced to spend time with him, like it or not.

"It was all my fault, Mr. O'Connor," Alice confessed. "When I spotted Bess, I forgot about everything else and just started talking. Please forgive me?" She smiled up at him.

"I believe it's your mother who needs the apology," he replied, returning her smile. "She only sent me to find you."

Bess watched the exchange between O'Connor and Alice, surprised at how much she resented Alice's coy tone and flirtatious behavior. She'd heard her friend use those exact same words any number of times and it had never bothered her before. Now every syllable grated on her nerves.

"Come on, Alice. We'd better let your mother know we're safe." Bess hated to admit Devlin O'Connor was right about anything, but at least he'd given her an excuse to break up this little tête-à-tête.

"Mother gets into a tizzy about every little thing," Alice complained and pouted charmingly, "but I suppose you're right. She'll probably harp on this for the rest of the trip if we don't soothe her."

Edging past Bess, Alice sent a regretful look in O'Connor's direction and hurried down the aisle. Bess started to follow, but he stepped in front of her.

"Allow me," he said and reached for the hamper she was still holding.

"I can handle it. Thank you, anyway." His nearness flustered her, and she held on to her basket with both hands. Up close she could see the different shades of brown in his hair, some dark as the Missouri soil, others a rich auburn color. His clothes were impeccable as always, his suit a summer-weight wool, his shirt pristine white. He smelled clean, of soap and something else more subtle and elusive. She didn't want to notice anything about him, much less his scent,

59

but she couldn't help herself.

He spoke again, and his breath caressed her cheek. "But why should you, when I'm more than willing to take it for you?"

The fine hairs on the back of her neck stood up as the velvety timbre of his voice curled through her. "Because I'm more than capable of handling it myself, that's why," she snapped, needing to distance herself from him and the strange effect he was having on her. Did he think her so totally incompetent that she couldn't even manage a small hamper?

"As you wish, milady," he said with a nod of his head, his gaze holding hers for a brief moment before he turned toward his seat.

She really shouldn't have acted so uppity, but she'd wanted to show him she could take care of things on her own, that she wasn't completely useless. Now it appeared she'd only aggravated the situation. The tone he'd used when he'd said, 'milady,' told her all she needed to know. His low opinion of her was all too clear. Even if she were interested in him, which she definitely wasn't, her feelings would not be reciprocated.

Carrying the hamper in front of her and balancing her purse, she followed him down the center aisle, the unwieldy basket bumping up against several passengers as she passed. She could hear their muffled complaints and was sure the man ahead of her heard them too, but it was too late to regret her behavior. Instead, she resolved not to let him get to her again, even if it meant ignoring him.

Devlin led the way to the seats without once looking back. Ordinarily his innate good manners would have insisted he cajole her into handing over the hamper, but something about her made him back down. She seemed to have something to prove, either to herself or to him, and he was too much the gentleman to force things.

He stood patiently while Bess greeted Mrs. Covington, stored her hamper under the empty seat, and took her place across from the older lady. Then he purposely sat down next to her. She gave him a startled glance, her blue eyes wide with surprise, but before she could say anything, Mrs. Covington spoke up.

"Bess, we're so glad you're traveling with us. And how lovely you look. Don't you think so, Mr. O'Connor? Such a beautiful girl and growing up so fast. Why, before you know it, she'll be getting married and having a family of her own."

"Mother!" Alice admonished under her breath and sent Harrietta Covington a quelling look. Turning to Devlin, she smiled and said more loudly, "I thought Bess and I would sit near each other. That way we could talk more easily."

Devlin noted the calculating gleam in her eye and wasn't about to move. He was actually quite pleased with the seating arrangement, more so than he wanted to admit. Fortunately Mrs. Covington intervened.

"Why don't you change places with me, dear? I'd prefer sitting away from the window anyway. I would have thought you girls would be out of things to say by now. After all, you were together for two whole weeks." She smiled indulgently and then urged Alice to her feet so they could trade places.

"But, Mother, I thought you and Bess would . . ." Alice started to say, but Mrs. Covington settled down in her seat and immediately began a conversation with Devlin.

"Mr. O'Connor, you must tell me more about your business. I'm sure we would all find it most fascinating." She turned to look at Bess. "Mr. O'Connor was telling us the most interesting stories before you arrived, dear. I know you won't want to miss a word."

Without missing a beat, Mrs. Covington gave her at-

61

tention back to Devlin. "You know Edward is fasci-
nated with business dealings himself. Isn't that so,
Alice? And I must confess he's so happy that you're
traveling with us. Why, just last night he was
saying . . ."

Devlin allowed Mrs. Covington's voice to wash over
him without really listening; his mind was centered on
the woman sitting beside him and his reactions to her
presence.

Bess was even lovelier than he remembered; Mrs.
Covington was certainly right about that. Since their
first meeting, he had carried Bess's image with him as
he went about his work in Kansas City, unable to put
her out of his thoughts.

They had seen each other at several social functions
after the Board of Trade ball, but she had stayed aloof
even to the other young men who attempted to flirt
with her. Her attitude had intrigued him, piquing his
interest where Alice's more blatant approach left him
unmoved. But Alice's attentions had their uses since she
was more than happy to talk about Bess when subtly
primed. At least Dev hoped he'd been subtle; he didn't
want to leave the impression he was interested in any
relationship at the moment, because of course he
wasn't. Still, there was something about the Richmond
girl . . .

Images of her filled his dreams at night — erotic images which would shock her, if she guessed he thought
of her at all. He'd wake up longing for her and feeling
guilty as hell. He'd try to remember Julia, but though
he strained, the only face he saw had blond hair and
blue eyes. Julia had died so long ago, almost in another
lifetime, and the longings Bess aroused made it clear
the time had come to let Julia go.

Memories of the dance at the Board of Trade gala
would float through his mind, and he would once again
smell wildflowers and feel Bess's soft, feminine curves

pressed against him. His uncharacteristic thoughts interfered with his business when he could least afford it. His years of celibacy seemed finally to have caught up with him. One way or another, he knew he had to do something. The only question was, what?

From Bess's responses she obviously hadn't been losing any sleep over him, which was probably all for the best. With his life the way it was, he couldn't afford any entanglements, especially not any permanent ones. Since Julia's death he'd led a double life, often disappearing for weeks to investigate some crime. There was no place for a woman in his scheme of things.

But the feel of Bess's leg pressed up against his in the cramped seat pushed all his logical rationalizations out the window. Closing his eyelids halfway to conceal the direction of his glance, he leaned back in his seat and watched as the afternoon sun glinted in her hair, turning it into spun gold. The trim blue jacket of her traveling suit hugged her figure, accentuating the smallness of her waist, the fullness of her breasts.

Her rounded chin expressed defiance even in repose, and a faint blush colored her cheeks. Was she aware of his scrutiny? Did she feel the same heat he did where their bodies touched?

His mental meanderings were brought sharply back to earth with the arrival of Mr. Covington.

"Hello, everyone. Ah, Bess, I see you've arrived safely. Good, good."

"Hello, Mr. Covington. It's good to see you again."

"The pleasure is mine, I assure you," he said, nodding approvingly before directing his attention to his wife. "And how are you managing, my dear?"

"It's been a wonderful trip, Edward. Mr. O'Connor has been most helpful. It was so nice of his father to allow him to extend his visit so he could ride with us to Philadelphia. Having a man who's so well versed in traveling by rail will be such a help." She looked up at

63

Devlin, who had stood in deference to Mr. Covington's arrival. "Both you and your father have my undying gratitude."

"I am more than happy to be of service," he responded with a slight bow. Though it hadn't been his idea to travel east with the Covingtons, for his father's peace of mind he'd agreed. Stepping into the aisle, he addressed his father's business associate. "Mr. Covington, please, may I offer you my seat."

"No, no, my boy. Stay and talk with the girls. Harrietta, why don't you move over here and give the children some room?"

Devlin was faintly amused at being referred to as a child. It had been a long time since he'd felt the carefree irresponsibility of childhood, though he could see glimpses of those traits in both Bess and Alice.

As soon as he was reseated, Alice leaned forward and gushed, "Mr. O'Connor, you must tell me — us — more about your business."

Devlin felt Bess shift in her seat as she tried to ease closer to the window. He knew he was leaving her less and less room, but he couldn't resist prolonging the surreptitious contact with her. Even through the layers of fabric separating them, the heat of her body burned along his.

"I'm afraid my business is a very boring subject, Miss Covington," he managed with the portion of his mind that was not distracted by the tiny catch in Bess's breathing.

"Please call me Alice. All my friends do." Alice punctuated her offer by laying her hand delicately on his knee.

While Devlin wasn't taken aback by the young woman's action, he could tell Bess was shocked. Her small gasp of surprise reached his ears if not Alice's. "In that case, *Alice,* you must call me Devlin," he said as he moved his leg subtly out of her reach.

Alice pulled back her hand, undisturbed, and pursued the conversation. "The social reports in the newspapers are full of references to grand parties, and as I've found out from Father, a great many business deals are conducted on such occasions. Surely you've met some interesting and important people?"

"Yes, on occasion." Devlin was more than happy to answer Alice's questions just to keep Bess by his side. While he found business dealings boring, it didn't mean others did.

"But don't you find them stimulating?" Alice questioned, opening her eyes wide and clasping her hands together.

"I'm sure Mr. O'Connor spends most of his working life attending such functions and must find them run of the mill," Bess said, her voice tight.

Devlin looked at her, but she wouldn't meet his eye. What had he done now to cause such a reaction, he wondered. Something in her tone pushed him to goad her.

"Please call me Devlin, Bess. And one can never be bored with the likes of a Vanderbilt or a Rockefeller," he said mildly, even though he didn't believe a word he was saying. He watched as she strove for something to say, sensing her indignation at his use of her first name. He hid his smile as Alice broke in.

"Vanderbilt?" Alice squealed, "You've met Cornelius Vanderbilt? What is he like? Is he as impressive as the papers say?"

Dev spared a quick glance for Alice as he satisfied her curiosity about the financial and social circles in which he traveled. But his gaze kept returning to Bess, gauging her responses, trying to read from her expression what she really thought, how she really felt, about herself and about him. Though he was talking to Alice, he knew deep inside that it was really Bess he was trying to please, Bess he was hoping to impress. It was

65

foolish, he knew, but he couldn't help himself. She reached inside him to some deep, essential part he'd thought long gone. In her presence he could dream of possibilities . . . and for just a few moments he could indulge himself without hurting anyone.

A couple of days later he was closing his eyes and settling in for a quick nap when he felt someone sit down beside him. He opened his eyes a mere crack — just in case Alice or her mother had joined him. Between the two of them, they had managed to keep up a nonstop barrage of inane chatter, and he needed a break. He wouldn't want either of them to know he was awake.

To his surprise he saw Bess. She'd done her best to avoid him the past two days, and to have her sit beside him . . . He caught himself up quickly, remembering how crowded the car was. She probably had little choice in where she sat. He gave no sign he was aware of her presence as she arranged her skirt and opened her book, but he continued to watch her through heavy-lidded eyes.

Ordinarily long train trips made him restless. The relentless clicking of the wheels along the track only added to the monotony of the endless rural landscape dotted by the occasional bison or farm animal. But the presence of Bess on the trip had eased his boredom.

It was rather a new experience for him to meet a woman who wasn't impressed with his moderate good looks, exemplary family background, and practiced conversation. The fact that she found him wanting both amused and irritated him. His more honest self admitted that he hadn't been the most pleasant person when they first met, but he'd thought he had good reason. He had since discovered his error. Wylie Moore might be interested in Bess, but she'd gone out of her way to avoid him. Unfortunately, she was giving Dev no chance to apologize. Though he treated her with the utmost regard, she kept him at arm's length, and he found he couldn't resist the occasional barb just to get her attention.

Why her attention and good opinion were of such import he wouldn't speculate. Nonetheless, he'd been looking for an opportunity to get in her good graces. Maybe now was the time.

He was about to speak when a rising wave of angry voices erupted from the front of the car. The voices increased in volume as a man passed down the central aisle, weaving from side to side and muttering to himself.

"Whatcha doing hangin' over the arm? Let a man through," the man complained as he tripped over his own feet. He righted himself by grabbing onto the back of a seat. An uncorked bottle leaned precariously out of the pocket of his dirty overcoat, intermittently sloshing red-eye onto the floor.

Devlin tensed, ready to spring into action, though he continued to feign sleep. Through the mask of his lashes, he watched every move the drunkard made, biding his time. If possible, he preferred to keep his skills to himself. Too many questions would be asked if he played the hero, and he wanted no one to suspect his real occupation. On the other hand, he couldn't allow anyone to get hurt.

When the man got halfway up the aisle, he leaned over and whispered something in a lady's ear, then laughed. The woman gave a startled shriek and recoiled. The drunkard laughed harder, running his fingers through his greasy hair.

The gentleman sitting next to the lady stood and challenged the drunkard. An ominous quiet fell over the railcar as his laughter stopped and the drunken man pulled out a knife.

"I was just havin' a bit of fun," he whined and flicked

the knife unsteadily back in forth in front of the lady's face. It glinted evilly in the afternoon light. "Can't blame a fellow for wantin' to have some fun."

Devlin's hand surreptitiously slipped to his own knife, hidden in the boot he had propped on the seat in front of him. If he had to, he could stop the drunk with one lightning-swift strike, expertly placed. He glanced in Bess's direction and saw the fear in her eyes, but he kept still. Fear in and of itself was no reason to take a man's life. He kept the drunk's knife hand in his sight and waited to see what would happen next.

From the corner of his eye he noted that the porter and another passenger were slowly approaching the drunken man from his blind side. In a few seconds they would be within reach of him.

The gentleman standing in front of the wavering knife also saw the approaching men. Realizing the import of what was happening, he tried to distract the drunk. "Look, we don't want any trouble here. Why don't you just go along now?"

"What do you mean, I should go along? You think I ain't good enough to be here with the likes of you? I got as much right as anyone. I paid for my ticket. Nobody tells me I don't belong."

The train lurched as it went around a curve, and the drunk staggered, then pitched forward.

Devlin's hand tightened on his knife, half drawing it out. Just then the porter grabbed the knife-wielding man from behind and wrestled him to the floor. Devlin relaxed his taut muscles and eased his knife back into its hiding place.

The man was led out of the car, protesting all the while about his rights. The stench of raw alcohol and unwashed body lingered in his wake, feeding the excitement and nervous elation of the well-bred passengers in the car. Rarely did they see the seamier side of life from so close. They'd be talking about this incident until they reached Philadelphia.

Within minutes Alice came rushing from the car behind. "Bess! What in the world has been going on? One of my father's acquaintances said there's been a stabbing in this car."

Bess shook her head, unable to say a word. She'd never been so frightened in her life. Maybe it was knowing her father wasn't nearby to protect her or having had the violence confront her so closely. Whatever it was, she was still feeling the shock of the incident.

"Devlin, maybe you can tell me what happened. Bess seems to have lost her tongue. Won't one of you tell me something? I'm going absolutely crazy with wondering." Alice's face was flushed with impatience.

Bess watched Devlin lazily sit up in his seat, straighten his tie, and brush the wrinkles from his coat. How could he be so blasé? Her anger with him overcame her lingering fear, channeling it in a direction with which she could better cope.

"Mr. O'Connor doesn't know what happened. He slept through the whole affair."

Alice looked absolutely scandalized by the information. Bess might have taken pleasure in bursting the bubble of perfection Alice carried around about O'Connor except there was also a vague sense of disillusionment coursing through her. Had she secretly wanted him to be more heroic? The notion was too ridiculous to pursue.

"Must have been the quietest stabbing in the history of the Union Pacific," was his only comment, but the look he cast in her direction mirrored her own defeated expectations.

Alice looked back to her for an explanation.

"Well, no one was actually stabbed," Bess admitted, looking neither at O'Connor or Alice.

"No one was stabbed?" Alice sounded disappointed.

"No, but this man did have a knife, and he was

69

swinging it around."

"Did he swing it at you?"

"Well, . . . no."

"Was he close to you?"

"Not that close."

Alice's questions made Bess wonder at her own fear. Maybe the situation hadn't been as bad as it had seemed at the time.

"Alice, you must allow Bess her little excitements. After all, this is a long and boring trip." O'Connor turned in his seat and smiled indulgently.

At his words Bess felt so much indignation swell within her she could think of nothing to say. How had she ended up looking the fool? He was the one who'd slept through the whole episode and offered not the least bit of reassurance when it had all been going on.

"Well, it sounds like nothing much happened after all," Alice put in, dismissing the incident as no longer worthy of her attention. "Mother sent me back here to find you both. She's preparing a little snack for us. We've found facing seats, and we can have a lovely little tea. Minus the tea, of course." Alice giggled at her own joke.

"That sounds just the thing," O'Connor said. He stood, momentarily blocking the light from the window. "And if Bess will move along, we won't keep your mother waiting another moment."

His superior attitude added to Bess's pique. As far as she was concerned, his behavior during the frightening episode with the drunk had been inexcusable. A real man would have awakened and intervened. A real man would have been more concerned for her safety. Mr. O'Connor had done nothing, and now he dared to make her feel as if she were the one lacking in insight. Before this trip was over she'd make him look at her with respect if it was the last thing she did.

She swept into the aisle without looking back to see if

he followed. But for all her indignation, she couldn't completely ignore the core of disappointment inside her, the sense of having missed something, of having lost a chance at something more.

Four

Bess sighed and twisted her hands in her lap as she leaned back in the cab and watched the Continental Hotel fade from sight . . . and with it, all that was familiar. Philadelphia was a far cry from Kansas City. She'd been in the city almost a week, and it still felt unfamiliar. Everything was so much bigger, so much busier, so much more impersonal. She wished she could have invited Alice along for moral support, but her errand today demanded secrecy.

As the aged horse and driver slowly ambled west up Chestnut, Bess had more time than she wanted to contemplate her rash actions. Her father would think it a betrayal, this going behind his back to see her mother's family, but she so longed to meet them. Her only consolation was that he didn't have to worry about her loyalty since he knew nothing of her plans.

She took the small scrap of paper out of her reticule and read the name and address written on it. *Olivia Babcock, Rittenhouse Square. Philadelphia.* Her great-aunt. Bess knew little about her, other the address she had copied off an old letter hidden in her father's strongbox. Butterflies fluttered in her stomach. She hoped she was doing the right thing. What if Mrs. Babcock didn't want to see her? *Stop it,* she scolded herself. There was no point in borrowing trouble.

Seeking a distraction, she looked out of the wide opening of the cab. Elegant stores and magnificent buildings lined both sides of the street, each more palatial and imposing than the last. She was admiring the facade on a particularly dramatic store front when she caught sight of a tall, slim man walking briskly in the same direction as her carriage. The man carried an ebony walking cane, and beneath his dark hat his neatly combed hair was a familiar color. Her heart tripped over itself. Could it be Devlin O'Connor? She hadn't seen him since they'd disembarked the train in Philadelphia, and though she didn't like to admit it, she'd missed his company.

The cab reached the corner just as the man did. When he looked up, their eyes met.

"Bess?" Devlin signaled the driver to stop, then doffed his hat and poked his head into her window. "Where are you off to this fine morning?"

She'd forgotten how dark his eyes were, how his smile set her insides quivering. At any other time she would have enjoyed seeing him, but not now. Right now, the last thing she needed was a witness to her activities. Why did he have to have such uncanny timing?

She blushed and hurriedly returned his greeting. "Mr. O'Connor. This is a surprise."

He cocked an eyebrow at her. "I thought we agreed you would call me Devlin."

Her blush deepened. "I don't believe we ever really discussed the matter."

Devlin threw his head back and laughed, a rich, heart-warming sound she was hard-pressed to resist. His brown eyes sparkled with good humor. "I guess you're right about that. Nonetheless, after traveling

73

in each other's company for so long and surviving our many adventures together, I would think it strange if we weren't on a first name basis. What do you say?"

She wanted to give in, to yield to his warmth. He was so different today from that day on the train when the drunken man had scared her so. Though she had yet to show him her competence, he seemed friendlier, more open.

"The traffic is backing up around us, Devlin," she said, conceding the point. She wished she could linger, but she needed to hurry if she were to meet Alice back at the hotel at one. "I really must press on."

"May I ask where you are going at this time of day? Perhaps you'd like an escort?"

"No, no, I'm fine," she put in hurriedly. The last thing she needed was an escort, improper though it might be for her to make this trip alone. "I'm merely sightseeing while the Covingtons go about their business," she prevaricated, desperately hoping he wouldn't defeat her plans.

"Are you sure you're all right?" he asked, pitching his voice so only she could hear it. He gave the driver a thorough going-over, then looked at her hands which were trembling slightly. What a time for him to turn protective!

"Of course I'm fine," she said more abruptly than was strictly necessary. "What could possibly make you think otherwise?"

"Nothing at all, milady," he tossed out, obviously stung by her sharp retort. "Carry on, driver," he ordered, stepping back from the carriage, all signs of his earlier openness gone from his face.

She'd done it again—offended him when all she'd intended was to save herself from hurt or interference. She sighed. He was only doing what any self-respecting gentleman would do, offering his protection to a lady of his acquaintance. No doubt his poor impression of her was only being reinforced by her actions, but what could she do? She could hardly trust him with her secret. He thought little enough of her now. What would he think if he learned she was defying her father? Surely the same gentlemen's code that led him to offer his help would require him to thwart her. She only hoped he wouldn't decide to interfere despite her reassurances that she needed no help.

The cab turned left on Seventeenth, and she leaned forward so she could catch a final glimpse of him. He too had hailed a carriage and soon disappeared from sight. Her cab continued, turning right onto Walnut toward the elegant houses of Rittenhouse Square as she mulled over her meeting with Devlin O'Connor.

In the middle of the next block, the horse stopped in front of a four-story mansion overlooking the open square.

"The Babcock's, miss," the driver announced. When she didn't immediately alight after he'd opened the door for her, he asked, "Isn't this the right place?"

"Oh, I'm sure it is," she answered quickly and looked again at the impressive facade of the house. "I'm just getting my bearings," she explained and stepped down to the sidewalk.

The cabman gave her a strange look, then shrugged his shoulders and climbed back up to his perch. The horse walked slowly away, and Bess found herself out of excuses. Her fears returned with a rush as she turned toward the house. It took all of her willpower to keep from calling back the cab and leaving. Admonishing herself not to be a fool, she walked up to the front door and rang the bell.

The door opened, and the butler looked at her expectantly from his great height, a frown creasing his brow. "Yes, miss, how may I help you?"

Bess had to crane her neck to look him in the eye. Now that the moment of meeting her mother's family was upon her, she didn't know quite how to explain herself.

"How may I help you, miss?" he repeated. "I don't believe you are expected. We normally don't receive callers before tea."

Though the butler's manner was gruff, his expression held a certain friendly interest, enough that Bess found the resolve to stammer, "I—I came to see Mrs. Babcock. Is she in?"

"Mrs. Babcock, is it?" He shook his head. "She doesn't do her business here, miss. You'll have to see her at the League office. Strict orders, you know. If you leave your card, I'll tell her to expect you Tuesday."

Tuesday? That was too far away. She'd never get her courage together again. No, it had to be today. Besides she had no card to leave. "I can't. I must see her today. It's very important."

The butler straightened his shoulders to fully block the doorway. "Mrs. Babcock cannot be disturbed. She will be available Tuesday as usual. At the League."

The League? Things were getting more and more confusing. The butler started to close the door, and Bess felt she was losing control of the whole situation. "This has nothing to do with the League. Please," she implored, seeing her last chance disappearing. "Is she in?"

"What's going on, Evans? Who's at the door?" a voice called from inside. A pair of blue eyes not un-

76

like her own peered over the butler's shoulder. The woman was only a few years older than Bess, but her light red hair was pulled back in a severe coiffure, accenting the sharp angles of her rather thin, aristocratic face. "Do we know you?" the newcomer inquired, squinting at her.

"No. I'm afraid not. That is, not directly, but one might say indirectly. Yes, I'm quite certain you know *of* me though we've certainly never met. That is to say, you'd know of me indirectly if you're related to Mrs. Babcock." Bess knew she was babbling and probably making very little sense, but at least the door hadn't slammed in her face. "Are you? Related to Mrs. Babcock, that is."

"Well, Evans," the other woman said, ignoring her question. "What do you make of this?"

"It sounds rather confused to me, ma'am," the butler admitted. "Perhaps the young lady would care to leave her card as I suggested earlier, and we'll let Mrs. Babcock decide what to do next. How would that be?"

He looked rather sympathetically at Bess, his expression both hopeful and wary. Bess wondered what manner of visitors Mrs. Babcock normally received to give the butler such finesse at turning away unwanted guests.

"I don't think that would do at all," she said apologetically. "I really must see Mrs. Babcock today if at all possible. Is she at home?"

"Neither Evans nor I could possibly give out that information," the redheaded woman said haughtily. "If you don't wish to leave your card, that is entirely your concern." As she spoke, she edged in front of the butler and placed her hand on the side of the door. "I'm afraid there's nothing more to—"

"Who are you talking to, dear?" A diminutive

woman worked her way between the two at the doorway. She gazed at Bess through round, wire glasses. Her eyes, too, were blue, and her hair snow white. "Do I know you?" she asked Bess. "You do look familiar, you know, but I'm terrible about remembering names. Isn't that so, Catherine?" She smiled up at the redheaded woman.

"We've never met," Bess said, "but you may have heard of me."

A sudden panic struck Bess. Suppose they hadn't heard of her! Just because she'd found a letter with Olivia Babcock's name on it in her mother's effects didn't mean her mother had ever mentioned Bess's existence to them.

"Heard of you? How interesting. What's your name?" the old lady asked. "No, wait, don't say another word until you come in. Evans, be a dear and open the front parlor, and then tell Cook we'd like a bit of tea. Is that all right with you, dear?"

She beamed at Bess, her eyes crinkling along well-established laugh lines, as though smiling came naturally and happily to her. The woman at her side frowned — her face also falling into what seemed to be it's usual expression.

"Now, Grandmother," she admonished, "what are you doing? You know Mother would be most upset if she—"

"Don't worry about your mother, Catherine. I've handled her for more years than she'd care to have me mention. You can join us, too. Come along." She led the way into the front foyer, then called out, "Evans, make that three cups. Catherine will be staying after all.

"We should probably introduce ourselves if we're having tea together. I am Olivia Babcock, and this is my granddaughter, Catherine Sinclair. Her mother is

78

my daughter, as you've no doubt gathered. Here, have a seat." Olivia Babcock indicated a fully-uphol-stered rocking chair, its seat covered in a delicate petit-point pattern.

"My name is Bess, Bess Richmond," Bess said as she sat. "My mother was Victoria Hendricks before she married."

"Evie's Victoria?" the older lady exclaimed, examining Bess's face with intense concentration. "Why, of course you are. No wonder you look familiar. You look just like your mother. No doubt about it."

"I do?" Bess couldn't believe the pleasure that surged through her at those words. At last she knew where her upturned nose came from, and her bright blue eyes so different from her father's, not to mention her rounded chin. A profound sense of belonging filled her.

"No doubt about what? Surely you aren't taking her word for this?" Catherine's exclamation grated on Bess's ears, shattering her momentary euphoria. "Grandmother, you have no proof. Who knows what this person—" the word reeked of distaste "—wants from us."

"Don't mind Catherine," Olivia Babcock said. "I can see just by looking that you must be related to Victoria. Now what brings you to Philadelphia?"

"Well, if that isn't obvious, I don't know what would be!" Catherine put in, her tone as disagreeable as before. "Don't forget she's also related to that odious Bert Richmond, and we all know what he wanted."

Bess was unable to stop her gasp at Catherine's words. This was something she'd never anticipated. She could see Olivia Babcock was just as shocked.

"Catherine, I fear you've listened to far too much

family gossip. And since you've never met Mr. Richmond, you can hardly stand in judgment. Now mind your manners or I'll be forced to exclude you from our conversation." She glared at Catherine until she took a seat on the green and yellow striped settee by the opposite wall.

"I'm only concerned about you, Grandmother." Catherine's voice had changed becoming soft and cajoling, but her eyes remained narrowed as she stared at the newcomer. Bess was taken aback by the dislike in her gaze and looked away.

"Catherine, that will do," Olivia warned in a low voice.

Catherine pouted, her lower lip thrust out in exact mimic of the portrait hanging above her. The entire room was filled with portraits, both large and small, of family members. Those that didn't hang on wires from the ceiling molding, stood in frames covering every flat surface in the cluttered room.

"Please excuse Catherine's behavior," Olivia said to Bess, distracting her attention. "She's usually more courteous, and I'm sure she's already found her manners."

Bess had her doubts on that score. Bert had always excused his wife's family's indifference by claiming he didn't get along with them. He'd never given her any details, but Bess had always suspected their differences ran deeper than he let on. Faced with Catherine's animosity, she finally understood why her father had never attempted a reconciliation.

Fortunately Olivia Babcock shared none of her granddaughter's prejudices. She smiled warmly at Bess and said, "Now, as soon as Evans brings the tea, you must tell me all about yourself."

Evans entered the room at that moment, bearing a tray laden with cups, plates, a silver tea service and an assortment of cakes and biscuits. When he left Bess told her great-aunt of her life in Missouri. The older woman listened attentively and peppered Bess with questions.

Before she knew it, Bess heard the grandfather clock strike noon. She had spent the entire morning talking about herself!

"I hope I haven't bored you. I didn't realize how much time had passed," Bess said, standing to take her leave.

"I enjoyed every minute of it. You so remind me of your mother—such a tragic loss." Olivia clucked sadly. "We all miss her, as I am sure you do."

Olivia stood, followed by Catherine, who'd spent the morning looking bored and making it obvious she found the whole conversation tedious and dull.

Bess felt a pang of regret that the visit was over. She had so wanted to hear about her mother, and now, just when Olivia mentioned her again, it was time to go.

"Thank you for spending this time with me. I hope I didn't inconvenience you," she said,

"Nonsense, child. How could meeting a long-lost relative be anything but a pleasure? When will we see you again?"

"Grandmother!" Catherine whispered in protest. "Mother will be furious."

Olivia ignored the outburst. "I will be visiting the Women's Pavilion at the Centennial Exhibition on Tuesday. Would you care to join me? Several of the women meet there regularly to work on charitable causes. We can always use a new recruit."

"I'd love to," Bess readily accepted, relief making her almost giddy. Catherine Sinclair might not want to accept her as family, but clearly Olivia had no such qualms. Bess was quite taken with the older

81

woman. Maybe on Tuesday she would learn more about her mother. She could hardly wait.

Bess had lied to him, Dev thought after discreetly following her cab to the Babcock mansion. She hadn't been sightseeing at all. Was she in some sort of trouble? Was that why she'd lied? All of his protective instincts rose to the fore. And why had she come here, of all places? The Babcock name was well-known in Philadelphia, particularly the name of Mrs. Olivia Babcock whose charitable works kept her in the papers regularly. Less well-known was that Devlin O'Connor was Olivia's friend and confidant, and Olivia had never mentioned Bess Richmond.

Dev couldn't help but wonder what Bess wanted with his friend and why she was so nervous about the visit. She'd looked so fragile and vulnerable standing in front of the large house, as if she was steeling herself to walk up to the door. He'd ached to go to her and help her with whatever was so troubling, but he knew she didn't want his help. She'd made her feelings for him quite clear: he didn't live up to her image of a hero.

Nor did he want to. In his opinion heroes caused more problems than they were worth, taking unnecessary chances and putting other people's lives in jeopardy. Such unseemly displays weren't for him. He preferred caution and a well thought out plan of action. If that made him less of a man, so be it. At least he'd never lost a client.

Right now, though, he had more pressing concerns, such as his meeting with his Pinkerton contact. Reluctantly he turned his steps away from Olivia's house and headed for Thirtieth Street and the train station. Bess and her secrets must be put aside for the moment.

A short while later he pushed through the turnstile nearest the horsecar depot and entered the Centennial Exhibition grounds. Spread over many acres in Fairmount Park, the Exhibition was the United States' major undertaking to mark the centennial of its birth. Not only were the products and inventions of the United States on display, but the world had been invited to participate as well, paying homage to the republic's anniversary with artwork and inventions of every imaginable type.

Dev was to meet his Pinkerton contact in the Machinery Building at twelve noon. Since it was only eleven-thirty, he had a half hour to spare, but he felt itchy. He wanted the meeting over and done with and to be on his way. He'd been uneasy since receiving the urgent message on his arrival in Philadelphia.

After paying the fifty-cent admission, he stood in front of the massive, light brown Main Exhibition Building and marveled at its size. The red ornamental stripes only added to its massive look, while the sound of thousands of flags and streamers from the roof snapping in the breeze assaulted his ears. He entered the building and headed for its western exit, where Machinery Hall, his rendezvous point, was located.

Devlin walked through the huge expanse barely noticing the exhibits, his mind on the information he would be receiving from his contact. They had planned their meeting carefully. If Dev was to be of any use in Pinkerton's investigation of a burglary ring, no one must guess he was involved. Dev had the unpleasant feeling that as a consequence of today's meeting he'd be spending time undercover again, trying to pick up more information.

"This is a mighty big building, isn't it?" The clear voice came from below him, almost obscured by the noise from the surging crowds. Devlin looked down. A small boy of about seven years was standing beside him. From the looks of his clothes the boy must have slipped in unobserved for he didn't look like he had the price of admission.

"You get mighty thirsty walking around in here, you know," the child said. "I was told you could walk ten miles just in this here building."

Devlin smiled at the youngster's obvious ploy, since they were standing by the Tufts Arctic Soda Water concession. "It certainly is warm, but you'd expect that in summer, wouldn't you?"

"Yes, sir. It's been hellatious so far, hasn't it?"

Dev knew he'd buy the young boy the drink he was angling for so obviously. He understood that in the boy's world you took advantage of every opportunity that presented itself. "Want a drink?" he offered and watched the boy's eyes light up.

"I wouldn't mind. It sure is awful warm." He was already licking his lips. "I could give you a tour of the building to pay you back if you like. My name's Danny."

"No need, Danny. I have an appointment in a few minutes."

As the boy thirstily gulped down his drink, Devlin glanced around. He wasn't surprised when he didn't see anyone looking for the child. The problem of abandoned children in the bigger cities had only grown worse in the years since the war. The boy was probably living on the streets, fending for himself, perhaps stealing to get by.

Devlin turned to ask Danny if he wanted something to eat, but the small boy had disappeared, vanishing into the crowd as quickly as he had appeared. There would be no finding him unless he wanted to be found, Devlin realized with true regret. Touched by the boy's plight, he'd wanted to help him, spurred on as much by memories as by the child's predicament.

Devlin shrugged in acceptance of events he couldn't change and hurried to his meeting. The sooner he got his business over with, the sooner he could get back to Bess and her mysterious trip to the Babcock house.

When Devlin entered the Machinery Building, the hum and click of the enormous Corliss Steam Engine filled the air. He stood at the entrance and looked down the vast hall. The huge engine, the largest steam engine in the world, was displayed prominently in the center of the building and marked the assigned meeting place.

Devlin pulled his watch out of his pocket and snapped it open. Casually, as if he had all the time in the world, he walked down the center aisle of the building, his eyes surreptitiously searching each face he passed. He wasn't sure who'd be meeting him, but he bet it would be Quinton. Besides himself, Quinton knew as much about the assignment as Allan Pinkerton himself.

Machinery Hall was an excellent choice for a meeting place, Devlin acknowledged as he walked toward the engine. The vast majority of visitors to this exhibit were men and boys who came to marvel at the machinery on display from around the world. Neither he nor his contact would stand out in this crowd.

At the same moment that Devlin spotted Quinton standing by the massive fly wheel, Quinton made eye contact and motioned him to the left. They met directly in front of the engine.

"O'Connor," Quinton said in brief greeting. "The boss says to tell you he's sorry to pull you away from your father's business, but something's come up."

Quinton was one of the head men at the Philadelphia office and had direct contact with Pinkerton himself.

"I take it this has to do with the trouble we've been investigating," Devlin said.

Quinton nodded and pretended deep absorption in the mechanical marvel before him. To anyone passing they looked like ordinary exhibition visitors, strangers to one another. "The men who contacted Pinkerton's are getting desperate," he whispered. "This crime gang has to be stopped, and soon. The Centennial celebration is heating up, and our clients are none too happy about having this crime spree reflect badly on the city."

"Without more information to go on, there's not much we can do."

"I told that to the boss himself," Quinton said. "But these men are all very influential so he wants some action fast. Besides, I have a couple of leads for you."

Devlin looked away from Quinton for a few moments despite his excitement that there was a break in the case. It wouldn't do for anyone to suspect that the two of them were exchanging more than a few pleasantries about the huge engine. After a suitable interval, Dev looked once again in the direction of his colleague.

"Some of the stolen jewelry has shown up," Quinton said. "One of the jewelers we'd alerted bought back a couple of pieces."

"From whom?"

"That's the problem. He bought them off a bloke who claimed he found them. The next time the chap showed up, we were waiting. Turns out he's a well-known petty crook that wasn't opposed to cutting a deal if he told us what was going on."

"And did he talk?"

Quinton walked a few steps to the side and admired the engine from the new angle. After a while, Dev eased over that way too, so Quinton could finish his tale.

"Apparently he was contacted anonymously to sell the jewels for a cut of the profits. All he knows is that he dealt with a gentleman."

"A gentleman?"

"He didn't recognize him or anything, just knew his clothes were of quality fabric and his shoes of the finest leather."

Devlin was the one to walk away this time. A gentleman crook—could that be possible? The more he thought about it, the more reasonable it seemed. The jewelry that had been stolen was all owned by Philadelphia's high society. Someone had to know when and where it would be worn, when and where it would be accessible for stealing. Moreover, the pickpockets and petty thieves roaming the Centennial Exhibition seemed to know what to look for. What could be more logical than that the person organizing them also provided the extra information?

"Do you have any idea who the gentleman might be?" he asked.

"No. The petty thief I mentioned was killed before we could get him away. In cold blood, I might add. Whoever is behind this is a dangerous man, no question about it."

"What do you want me to do?"

"I came to tell you Paddy's indicated he's ready to deal," Quinton said. Paddy was one of their informants, a denizen of the sleazy underworld of crime and poverty in the city.

"And?"

"He'll only deal with you, or rather, your alter ego."

"Has a meeting been set up?"

87

"For the middle of next week. Down by the docks . . . we think that's where the gang's headquarters is located. Will you be able to do it?" Quinton asked.

"It shouldn't be a problem."

The only good part about his meeting with Quinton, Devlin thought later as he made his way back to the center of the city, was that he'd have time to find out what Bess was up to before he disappeared. His interest in her had grown far more than he wanted yet he couldn't stop himself. Already he was planning what he'd do with her tomorrow — and how he'd get the Covingtons to help arrange it. Whistling under his breath, he entered the Continental Hotel and asked for Mr. and Mrs. Covington.

Getting an invitation to join the Covingtons for dinner that night was even easier than Devlin had anticipated. The only drawback to his plans was the unexpected presence of Barrett Covington. Apparently the young architect had been neglecting his family and chose that night to make it up to them. Dev gritted his teeth as he watched the younger man fawn over Bess.

"Bess, you look exceptionally lovely tonight," Barrett remarked as soon as she disembarked from the elevator. "I must apologize for not seeing more of you, but my work has been very demanding. Had I known what I was missing, I would have found a way to escape into your presence sooner."

Bess smiled at his compliment, her pleasure obvious. "You're looking uncommonly handsome yourself," she replied, giving him an admiring glance, the kind of glance she had yet to bestow on Dev. Dev scowled as he watched her flirt with the young man.

"Come now, children," Harrietta Covington called. "Our table is ready. Barrett, you bring Bess along.

Devlin, if you would be so kind as to escort Alice."

Bess looked around, noticing him for the first time. He was set to smile at her when he saw her daring decolletage and the way Barrett was leering when she wasn't looking. He frowned at the man, hoping to catch his eye. Instead Bess intercepted his look. She stiffened and lifted her chin as she placed her hand on Barrett's arm. "Why don't we join your parents? We shouldn't keep them waiting," she said.

"An excellent idea," Devlin said before Barrett could reply. Dev hoped the young man would be more restrained with his parents in the room. Just to make sure Barrett knew he was being observed, Dev added, "We'll follow in right behind you."

Bess sent Dev a haughty glare, but he paid it no mind. That young upstart needed to be taught some manners, and Bess knew it even if she wouldn't admit it. Before he could explain himself, Alice placed her hand on his sleeve and moved closer to him.

"I'm so glad you were able to come," she cooed. "This is such an unexpected surprise—and so much the better for being unanticipated."

Dev knew he'd been invited specifically for Alice's benefit so he smiled indulgently at her.

"I'm more than happy to be here," he replied and escorted her into the dining room behind the other couple.

Harrietta beamed at them as they approached. "You make such lovely couples, so handsome the four of you. It makes me feel young at heart. Don't you think so, Edward?"

"Whatever you say, dear," Edward responded, his attention elsewhere. "I say, Harrietta, isn't that Roland Atherton over there? I think I'll invite him over. He's someone we definitely need to cultivate. He has lots of contacts in the city, you know."

"Surely you can wait until after dinner," Harrietta admonished. "We've hardly had a chance to see Barrett. He's been so busy." She took her place at the round table set aside for the family and motioned to the rest to take their seats.

Once everyone was seated, Harrietta turned to Bess. "It's a shame you were out this morning. Barrett arranged for us to tour his office. We had so hoped you might join us. Isn't that so, Barrett?"

"Why, yes, Bess, I missed you." Barrett took her hand and raised it almost to his lips. "Perhaps another time," he offered gallantly, his eyes fixed on hers.

Bess looked uncomfortable at his actions so Devlin refrained from saying anything that might increase her discomfiture. He couldn't help feeling relieved when she quickly reclaimed her hand, though he didn't care for the conciliatory smile she sent his rival, for that was how he was beginning to think of Barrett.

"I'd love to see your office," she said and sent Dev a defiant look, as if she guessed at his disapproval of the younger man. "Perhaps tomorrow?"

"Oh, not tomorrow, Bess," Alice said. "Don't you remember? We're going to the Centennial Exhibition. Barrett even got time off to join us. Isn't that right, Barrett?" Without stopping for Barrett to answer, she continued, "Maybe you can join us, too, Devlin. It will be ever so much fun."

"It sounds wonderful. What time shall we meet?" Devlin asked with alacrity. The young woman was unknowingly abetting him, and he didn't want to give anyone else a chance to interfere.

Devlin spent the next few minutes in an expansive mood. Even Alice's obvious flirting didn't bother him, particularly when he caught the look of confusion on Bess's face every time Alice leaned over to whisper something in his ear. Perhaps she wasn't as indifferent as he feared.

When the main course was over, Edward Covington excused himself and crossed the room to talk to Roland Atherton.

"Who's Daddy talking to?" Alice asked.

"That's Mr. Atherton. I understand he's new to the city but quite influential," Barrett informed her.

"Do you know him?" Alice asked Devlin, opening her eyes wide.

"Yes, we've met once or twice."

Edward Covington leaned over to talk with Atherton, and within minutes both men were heading back to the table. "We are fortunate indeed," Edward boasted. "Mr. Atherton's friends were just leaving, and he's agreed to join us for dessert."

"I'm the fortunate one," Atherton gallantly replied, "to be in the company of three such lovely ladies." His gaze lingered appreciatively on each woman in turn.

Almost instantaneously a waiter appeared with a chair, and Atherton sat down between Edward and Harrietta.

"O'Connor, good to see you again. I've been hearing your name bandied about in political circles," Atherton said, then took a sip of the brandy Edward had poured for him. "Something about a congressional seat."

"There's always talk," Dev replied.

"True, true. But my sources seem well-informed."

He paused suggestively, but Devlin refused to take the bait. He wasn't sure he liked Roland Atherton and saw no reason to trust him. Besides, Dev hadn't decided himself where his future lay though the political arena did present an interesting forum for some of his ideas.

When Atherton saw he would get no further information, he turned to Mrs. Covington. "How have you been enjoying our fair city?"

"Philadelphia is simply lovely," Harrietta trilled. "The stores are so elegant and full of the most luxurious items. Why, I could spend a month on Chestnut Street alone. What about yourself? I understand you are quite involved in the business community here."

"Why, yes. I have recently come to quite a tidy sum of money, if you pardon my bringing up the subject, and have been exploring the best avenues for investing it."

Harrietta's eyes lit up. Roland Atherton had all the requirements Harrietta needed in a prospective suitor for her daughter: good looks, charm, and social standing. As Devlin anticipated, she wasted no time ensuring the man would be available again in case things did work out between Alice and himself.

"Then you must join us for lunch tomorrow. Edward has the most excellent contacts in the city."

"I would be most pleased to have you join me at my club, if you would like."

"That is most gracious of you, sir," Edward put in while his wife beamed.

"And how many of you may I count on?" Atherton asked, looking round the table.

"Just my parents, I'm afraid," Alice answered for them all. She made an apologetic moue. "I'm afraid the rest of us have other plans. We're visiting the Exhibition tomorrow. Have you been there yet?"

"Several times. You must save your energy for it. The Centennial's the best thing to happen to Philadelphia since the Continental Congress. We're quite proud."

"And so you should be, Mr. Atherton," Alice said

and sent him a sultry smile. "Everything in Philadelphia has been most enjoyable. The people of your city have been nothing but kind and gracious. Why, they've made us as welcome as neighbors at a church social."

"Just remember, this is a big city," Devlin felt compelled to warn. "There are some unsavory elements moving in of late looking to take advantage of out-of-town visitors. You shouldn't be too complacent about your safety."

"Whatever does he mean, Edward?" Harrietta asked, looking anxiously to her husband.

"I believe Devlin's referring to the problem the city has with young pickpockets, my dear. I read an article about them just this morning. Shameful, really. You'd think they'd have some pride in their city."

"Not only pickpockets, but a burglary ring, too. They seem to prey on only the best hotels and visitors in town for the Exhibit," Barrett added.

"Why didn't someone tell us?" Bess asked, looking around at the men questioningly.

"Because there really isn't anything to worry about, Miss Richmond," Roland Atherton commented with a reassuring smile. "Mr. O'Connor is exaggerating the problem. This is all a tempest in a teapot — the newspaper publishers are merely jumping on the issue to sell more papers. You shouldn't worry yourself with such vulgarities."

"But shouldn't we take some precautions?"

"It might be to your advantage to do so —" Dev began, but was cut short by Atherton.

"Nonsense, O'Connor. There's no need to upset the ladies unduly. We don't want to mar any of their excursions," Atherton said, then looked over at Devlin. "You would do well to let others handle this matter and keep your mind on your own affairs, O'Connor.

It's much safer that way."

Something in Atherton's tone set Devlin on edge. "Safer for whom?"

"Why, for all concerned, of course." Atherton's even tone was a distinct contrast to the veiled message in his narrowed gaze. Then he turned to Harrietta and added, "I don't think you need worry overmuch, Mrs. Covington. The few trifling incidents have occurred far from here and need be of no concern to you. Have you been to Independence Hall yet?

Devlin toyed absently with his silverware as the conversation shifted to other subjects. Roland Atherton troubled him. He hadn't liked the fact that the man knew more than was public knowledge about Dev's political plans. Nor did he like the implicit threat about minding his own business. The man had appeared suddenly and somewhat mysteriously on the Philadelphia business scene, and no one seemed to know much about him other than the fact that he had money. Atherton could bear closer scrutiny, Dev decided.

As dinner was ending Barrett received a message that his presence was needed back at the office. A recalcitrant client was finally ready to close a particularly lucrative deal, and Barrett's employer was willing to accommodate the eccentric millionaire's wishes by opening the office after hours. Devlin had no regrets about the younger man's departure, especially when Harrietta Covington suggested the family and their guests take a stroll outside to admire the decorations set out for the upcoming Fourth of July celebration.

Roland Atherton was pressed into service as Alice's escort leaving Bess no choice but to take Dev's arm.

"It's a shame Barrett had to leave," Dev said, merely to get her reaction.

"Yes, I'm sure his family's upset, though of course they did get to spend the entire day with him."

Dev smiled to himself. He could have received no better response — Bess could hardly be pining for the young man if she viewed his departure strictly from his family's perspective.

"Besides," she continued, shattering his complacency, "he'll be coming to the Centennial Exhibition tomorrow so I'll have ample time to be with him."

As they walked out of the hotel, Alice said, "Where shall we go?"

"Why don't we walk down to Independence Hall, as Mr. Atherton suggested over dinner?" Harrietta replied. "I understand it's only a few blocks from here."

"An excellent idea," Atherton put in. "The grounds are quite festive, and we can see the statue of President Washington. You won't be disappointed, I'm sure."

"I can't believe there are so many people out in the evening," Bess remarked as they walked east on Chestnut Street, trailing the two other couples. "I guess Anna Hobart . . . I mean, Anna Moore, was right. Kansas City is provincial."

"Not completely," Devlin offered, embarrassed now to recall his unwarranted assumptions about Bess and Wylie Moore. "Kansas City has a lot to offer in its own right. Don't forget Philadelphia is the center of our country's biggest celebration right now. We have far more visitors than usual."

They walked at a leisurely pace. Dev was aware of Bess's delicate touch on his arm and the elusive wildflower scent that filled the air whenever she was near. Every time she smiled at him his pulse accelerated. She seemed to be enjoying their stroll, looking avidly around her as they talked. Whatever animosity had briefly flared between them before dinner had passed.

A horse-drawn wagon clattered down the street, and Dev used Bess's slight start to draw her closer. She didn't object to the increased intimacy, looking up at him with sparkling eyes and flushed cheeks.

"Oh, look at that," she said, suddenly stopping to gaze across the street. "What a magnificent building!"

"It's the old Masonic Temple. Quite a sight, isn't it?"

They paused to admire the structure's elegant lines, rising to the heavens in Gothic spires. While Bess stared raptly at the beautiful building, Dev looked only at Bess. Her skin glowed pearly white in the rosy light of late evening. He longed to touch her, to slide his fingertips over her smooth cheek, to brush his thumb over her strawberry red lips before enticing them open with his own. Instead, he put his hand in his pocket, knowing that if he yielded to his impulses, he'd frighten her.

"We'd better catch up with the others," he said in the hope that he would gain control of his unruly thoughts.

"Yes, of course," she answered.

She sounded disappointed, but Dev didn't trust himself alone with her. He guided her down the sidewalk past the Public Ledger building and across Sixth Street to Independence Hall. The Covingtons and Roland Atherton were nowhere in sight.

"Washington's statue is in front of the main entrance," Devlin said as they made their way through the crowd that had collected at the site of the signing of the Declaration of Independence a century before.

"I still don't see the others. Do you think they went into Independence Square to see the stands?" Bess asked. "The celebration on the Fourth should be grand. Just look at all the bunting already on the buildings!"

"We can go look in the square if you like."

"Could we?" She looked up at him with stars in her eyes, having picked up the excitement of the enthusiastic crowds of visitors.

He smiled down at her. "I don't know why not."

He led her behind Independence Hall then across the street to a park-like square where the enormous observation stands were being constructed for the upcoming celebration. Flags and decorative streamers flapped in the evening breeze.

The sun had long since slipped below the horizon, and the square was filled with dark shadows. They walked slowly, ostensibly searching for the others though neither seemed too anxious to find them. Near one of the stands, Bess stumbled over a stone on the path. Dev caught her, his hands on her waist. He knew he should let her go, but somehow he couldn't.

She stood looking up at him, her lips slightly parted. Unable to resist, he pulled her close. A quick step back and they were hidden by the bushes. His arms slipped around to her back, lifting her gently as he lowered his lips.

He touched her lightly, fleetingly, his mouth barely grazing hers. Her sweet taste merely whetted his appetite for more. When he would have pulled back for fear of frightening her, she lifted her arms and laced her hands around his neck, holding him in place. She had to stand on tiptoe to reach his shoulders, leaning on him in a way that pressed her entire length against his. Heat enveloped him, and his blood raced. Did she even know what she was doing?

Bess thought she would die from the excitement coursing through her. She'd never been this close to a man before, never felt a man breathe nor known the rapid beating of his heart. She'd never dreamed of such a match for her body, a place for her breasts to nestle, a hand to nip her waist or flare around a hip, a strength where she was melting softness, a plane where she was snuggling curves. Till now.

His breath was warm against her cheek then marked a path to her lips. This time his mouth was more demanding against her own, lingering warmly, beckoning her to draw him closer, to remove even the tiniest space between them.

She closed her eyes and gave herself up to the sensations surrounding her: the soft susurration of the leaves in trees, the murmur of the crowds just beyond their hidden haven, the smell of sea and salt . . . and man, the firmness of his lips and the pliancy of her own. She felt herself becoming lightheaded and clung more tightly to him.

His tongue breached the opening of her lips, shocking her with pleasure. He tasted dark and mysterious, like the finest wine. An ache built inside her, settling in below her stomach, filling her with longing for more, though what more there could be, she didn't know and dared not imagine. She reached out tentatively with her own tongue and met his. It felt like velvet, both rough and soft all at the same time, making the very fine hairs on her arms stand up. Every touch was magnified, every sound muted as she lost herself in the exploration of this new and tantalizing world. She lost all sense of time, all sense of place as desire swept through her.

And then slowly but firmly, Dev eased back from the kiss, pulling away even when she would have deepened their embrace. His hands gentled her, stroking down her back from her shoulders to her waist. When only their lips touched, he lifted his head and pulled her to him. She could feel the thunderous beating of his heart matching the cadence of her own. Wonder mixed with giddiness and a sense of unbridled elation. If he let her go now, she would float away.

Dreamily she opened her eyes. Though she stood in the dark shadows with Dev, the light from a nearby lamp glinted in his eyes, making them glow like coals in a midnight fire. She read passion in them and desire, and a depth of hunger she couldn't begin to meet. Half frightened, she took a step back.

Dev moved his hands to her shoulders, cradling her gently. "It's all right," he said in a soothing voice. "Nothing more will happen."

She could see, even in the half light, that he was as surprised as she by their kiss. She felt the fine trembling in his arms and realized just how much strength of will it had taken for him to bring their embrace to an end. She felt a surge of feminine power, an inkling of what it could be like to love and be loved, to let passion rule her life. Elation and trepidation filled her—the need to know battling with an instinct that told her now was not the time, and this was definitely not the place.

"We should probably find the others," she said softly.

He looked down at her with his dark, burning eyes. "Yes, we should," he agreed in a whisper, but he didn't move. "Will you be all right?"

She nodded though she knew she would never be the same. She'd changed tonight in some deep and unfathomable way. She'd glimpsed the darker side of human nature—her own as well as Dev's—and taken the first step from being a child toward being a woman.

He held her for another moment, as if to convince

himself she was really all right, then dropped his arms and placed her hand in the crook of his elbow. They stepped back onto the well-lit path, leaving their secret behind. The crowds surged around them, oblivious to what had occurred just minutes before, and they let themselves be swept along through the square to Walnut Street.

As they stepped onto the sidewalk, they heard Alice call out. In seconds the Covingtons and Roland Atherton were upon them, and Alice was chattering away about the grandeur of the sights and the excitement of the evening. Mrs. Covington beamed at her daughter and then at Bess, well satisfied with the evening's outcome. If she only knew, Beth thought, and her insides quivered at the memory of all she'd experienced.

She glanced up and caught Dev's gaze. His memories were there, too, and she quickly looked away. But when he drew her closer and covered her hand with his, she didn't pull back. She smiled and felt another surge of excitement pour though her. Whatever magic had occurred in the dark of the square still sparkled inside her . . . and inside Dev.

Five

"I can't believe these crowds," Alice exclaimed the next day as she and Bess descended from the train at the Pennsylvania Railroad Depot by the main entrance to the Centennial grounds.

Nearby, at the horsecar terminal, a crush of cars was also unloading passengers. On some days attendance at the exhibition reached over 40,000, far fewer than the Centennial planners might have anticipated, but far more than Bess had ever seen all in one place. She found the crowd quite overwhelming, but not nearly as overwhelming as the strain of juggling her attention between Barrett and Devlin.

Not that Devlin was demanding her attention. Far from it. He seemed more than happy to indulge Alice's every whim—and Alice was in a whimsical mood today, blossoming under his interest. Why, sometimes they stood so close together you couldn't slip a piece of paper between them!

"Here, Bess, hold on to my arm," Barrett offered and stepped forward blocking her view of Devlin with Alice. "We'll catch up with the others in a second. The turnstiles won't be open for a few minutes yet, anyway." He held up his watch. It showed another five minutes till nine. "Let's go sit in the waiting room and look over today's program. Have you decided what you want to see first?"

"I thought we might go to the Main Building. I want to see Mr. Bell's new invention. It sounds so interesting, being able to talk to someone who is far away."

"That does sound interesting. Would you like me to get you a rolling chair? It's quite inexpensive, especially without an attendant. I would be more than happy to push you." Barrett looked at her with soulful eyes as they made their way into the waiting room.

Bess laughed at his earnest expression. "Thank you, but I don't think that will be necessary. I'm quite able to walk." Maybe his eastern lady friends needed the rolling chairs, but she was made of sterner stuff.

"Good. Then it will be my pleasure to escort you wherever you desire. The Bell exhibit, wasn't it?" His eyes darkened, and he clasped her hand in both of his as they took their seats. There was no way she could tactfully snatch it back, but she wished something would distract him.

No sooner had the thought entered her mind than Alice called from halfway across the room, "What happened to you two?"

Bess looked up and saw Devlin following Alice into the waiting area. His gaze was fixed on her hand still held snugly in Barrett's grasp. "Surely you're not tired already, Bess?" he asked.

"N-no, of course not," Bess said hastily. She stood up and used her motion as an excuse to extricate her hand from Barrett's hold.

"We were just waiting for the gates to open," Barrett put in as he also stood.

"Well, they're open now," Devlin said sharply. Bess glanced at him, but he wouldn't meet her eyes. "Shall we go in?"

His words were more of a command than a suggestion. What a quandary! Bess could hardly expect Alice to accept her brother as an escort with Devlin here, yet she wanted nothing more than to be with him herself, especially after last night. Did he find this pairing as painful as she did?

She wished she knew more about men, enough to know if his controlled anger was at her or at the circumstances, but what could they do? Good manners prohibited them from changing partners.

The four of them passed through the turnstiles after waiting in line, each handing in a fifty-cent note — the guards would accept nothing but the exact amount of admission — and headed for the western entrance of the Main Building.

"Oh, look, there's a fountain. Let's go take a closer look," Alice urged before they had gone more than a few feet.

"Why, Alice, it's not even the best one here," Barrett said scoffingly to his sister. "It'll just be a waste of time."

"It will not. I want to see it, but you don't have to come along. Dev will take me, won't you?" She flashed her most winning smile at Devlin, and a knot formed in Bess's stomach when he smiled back.

"It won't take more than a minute, Barrett, and we can see all the other buildings from there. Let's go," Bess said. She wasn't about to get separated from the other two.

"Well, if you really want to, Bess, I'm sure it must be worthwhile," Barrett replied, giving her another of his calf-eyed looks.

Alice glared at her brother for a full minute, clearly angry at his sudden about-face. She looked ready to continue their bickering at the slightest provocation when Devlin took her arm and headed off without comment.

This close to the main entrance the crowds were still thick, and Bess was grateful for Barrett's assistance in forging a path to the fountain.

"I can't believe it's already so warm," she said as she wiped her damp brow with a lace-edged handkerchief.

"It's the humidity that makes it uncomfortable," Barrett corrected with uncompromising conviction. "This summer has been one of the hottest in years, so I've been told. That's why we've come so early."

Though Barrett spoke as if the idea of coming to the exhibition when the gates opened had been his, Bess knew better. The suggestion had been Devlin's, and initially Barrett had opposed it. He preferred a more leisurely start to the day unless he had to be at the office.

Bess was grateful now that they had taken Devlin's advice. Here in the city she followed fashion's dictates to the full—from chemise and pantelettes to multiple petticoats over her corset, the whole covered by a form-fitting basque top trimmed with lace and a fully flounced skirt and overskirt draping her bustle. Already she could feel a tiny rivulet of perspiration run down her back, not that she would ever mention it.

Alice, too, seemed hot—or at least her face was flushed. Bess wasn't sure whether it was from the heat or excitement.

"This is the Bartholdi Fountain," Devlin said. "Along there—" he pointed to Belmont Avenue "—is the main thoroughfare. The Women's Pavilion is down on the right. I understand you'll be going there on Tuesday, Bess."

"I didn't realize anyone knew of my plans," Bess said.

104

He smiled at her, that indulgent smile that set her back up because it made her feel inadequate and defiant all at the same time.

"I believe Alice mentioned it on our way up here," he explained. "She said you had met Mrs. Babcock. Isn't that right?"

"Y-yes, it is. We happened to run into each other, and she mentioned I might find it interesting." Bess chewed on her lower lip, hoping he wouldn't make the connection between seeing her on Chestnut Street the previous day and her meeting with her aunt. She hadn't told anyone, not even Alice, that she had deliberately sought out Mrs. Babcock by going to her house.

"How fortunate you are," he said. "Mrs. Babcock is widely known in the city and is very highly regarded."

Bess breathed a sigh of relief. He wasn't going to give her away.

"Do you know Mrs. Babcock, too, Dev?" Alice asked, pulling his attention back to her.

"Certainly. Everyone who is concerned with the welfare of this city has had occasion to meet her. She works tirelessly and has a reputation for getting results."

Bess heard real respect in his tone. What would it take to make him think of her in that way, she wondered.

"Bess says all Mrs. Babcock likes to talk about are her projects," Alice said. "Sounds rather dull to me, don't you think? At least that's the impression Bess gave."

Devlin gave Bess an assessing look, shrugged his shoulders, and looked away. "Everyone has their own interests, I suppose."

His tone hurt. In all honesty, Bess *had* found that

105

Olivia tended to carry on a bit about her causes. Of course, the older woman had been trying to convince Bess to join in her work. But while Bess was eager to please her aunt, she still needed to find a direction of her own in life; until she did, she couldn't offer more than to meet at the Women's Pavilion on Tuesday. Was that so terrible?

"Are we going to just stand here all day?" Barrett asked somewhat querulously.

"Not *all* day," Alice countered. "Let's just walk around the fountain once while it's still cool enough outside. Then we can go explore the buildings."

She latched onto Devlin and pulled him along beside her, leaving Bess no choice but to follow with Barrett.

Together they all strolled around the fountain which stood in the center of the square separating Machinery Hall from the Main Building. Eight paths, like spokes of a wheel, converged on the fountain, and down each was a different view of the exhibition grounds.

Devlin pointed out the sights as they walked, his voice flowing over Bess in rich, smooth cadences interspersed by the cheerful splash of water from the fountain and the indistinguishable hum of noise from the crowd. The smell of popcorn wafted in the air from vendors located throughout the grounds. The sun shown brightly in a hazy, blue-white sky.

Rather than focus on any one thing, Bess let her mind wander. It didn't have to wander far—just back to last night and those moments in Independence Square. There it stopped, and the memories flowed, bright and sparkling like the diamond beads of water from the fountain. Bess felt her heartbeat quicken and took a deep breath. When she licked her suddenly dry lips, she remembered Dev's taste, the rasp of his tongue on hers, the strength of his arms around her.

She tried to keep her mind on Barrett's comments, to feel for him even a portion of the infatuation he seemed to feel for her, but to no avail. She walked in a daze, following his lead, swinging her reticule back and forth in an arc and watching the spray from the fountain, her mind on Devlin.

All her muscles tightened when she saw Alice move closer to Dev as the other couple passed them. Did she have to press against him so, Bess thought, unable to look away.

Devlin's gaze fell on her, his expression no more pleasant than her thoughts. She realized with a start that he *was* finding the day as difficult as she was. She knew he didn't approve of Barrett's forwardness even if he did tolerate Alice's, but there wasn't much Bess could do. The siblings could hardly be faulted for their behavior considering their mother encouraged them at every turn and their father was preoccupied with business rather than with keeping his children in line.

Everything was suddenly so complicated. The Covingtons had set their sights on Dev for Alice. Alice herself seemed eager for the match, and Barrett had eyes only for Bess. But while Bess found Barrett a pleasant enough companion, she did not reciprocate his feelings for her, and her feelings for Dev were confused and confusing. Last night he had shown her aspects of herself she'd never even dreamed existed. Her insides still throbbed when she remembered his kiss, his taste. Yet this morning he'd seemed so aloof, as if their kiss had had no effect on him—or so she'd thought until she'd realized he was trying to make the best of a difficult situation.

Bess saw no solution to their predicament, at least

107

not one that wouldn't end up hurting Alice and her family. And she couldn't do that, not after the way the Covingtons had stepped in to help her just when her life was collapsing. She turned the problem over and over in her mind, trying to figure a way out, wishing everything were different.

Then without warning she felt a sudden sharp pain in her wrist. She gave a small scream, more from surprise than from real pain. In a flash Devlin was by her side, his eyes checking her for injury. "What happened? Are you all right?"

She grasped her right wrist with her left hand, and Dev immediately reached for her arm. "Here, let me look at that," he demanded.

His touch was warm and gentle yet sent shivers racing down her back. He turned her wrist over. The skin along one side was abraded; tiny drops of blood oozed in bright red dots, but all Bess noticed was how small and fragile her hand felt in Dev's, how strong and comforting he felt. His pupils had darkened when he first touched her, and he looked at her now with concern and something deeper.

"I'm fine, really," she said, her voice huskier than usual. "Someone grabbed my purse. I didn't even see who it was."

"Come sit over here." Dev led her to a nearby bench. When he was convinced she was safe, he turned on Barrett. "She could have been hurt! After our conversation yesterday, I expected you to be more on your guard. You were supposed to be looking after her."

"I had no way of anticipating this," Barrett returned indignantly. "And if you care so much, why don't you try to catch the culprit?"

Barrett sat down next to Bess and took her hand in his, clearly staking his claim. Bess didn't want him

108

touching her, especially not there where her skin still tingled from Dev's warmth, but politeness kept her still; like it or not, Barrett was her escort today.

"Did you see where he went?" Dev asked Barrett.

"Over there. The boy slipped behind Judges' Hall."

"The boy? Are you telling me you saw the whole thing happen and didn't stop it?"

"What could I have done? It all happened too quickly. Besides, you know how low-bred those street urchins are. I didn't want to touch him." Barrett made no attempt to hide his disgust, and Bess saw Devlin's jaw clench as if he had to use all his considerable will to keep what he was thinking from coming out.

"Did you see what he looked like or where he went?" Dev demanded.

"I told you: he was a street urchin, unkempt and dirty. He looked to be about seven or so. Took off like a shot. That way."

Barrett pointed again toward Judges' Hall.

"Are you sure you're all right?" Dev asked Bess.

She nodded and murmured, "I'm fine."

Dev turned back to Barrett. "Watch over the ladies. I'll be right back."

Without waiting for a response, Dev took off after the boy. Bess thought Barrett would join in the search, but he merely stood and watched as Dev forged a path through the crowd. Just as she was about to suggest that Barrett help Dev give chase, Barrett saw a couple of friends walking down the path to the fountain. Within seconds Barrett and Alice had waved them down and were deep in animated conversation. The Crawfords were a prominent Philadelphia family known to the Covingtons through their banking connections. Bess had met them once and found them pretentious. She wasn't looking forward to spending the day in their company.

She sighed and looked down the path Devlin had taken. What could be taking so long? Determined to see for herself, she motioned her intentions to the Covingtons and followed after Devlin, breaking into a most unladylike run as soon as she was out of sight of the crowd.

As she cut between Judges' Hall and the railroad ticket office, she wondered if the boy knew he was heading directly for the police station. Apparently so, for Bess caught up with him and Devlin just a few feet farther down the path where the boy had obviously reversed his tracks. Devlin stood with his hands on the boy's shoulders, holding him in place.

The strap from Bess's small, beaded purse hung out the front of the boy's tattered shirt where he had hastily stuffed it as he ran.

"Devlin? Have you found something?" she asked.

"Bess! What are you doing here? I thought I told you to rest for a few minutes."

"I just wanted to see what was happening. After all, it is my purse that was taken."

"She your lady, mister? You shoulda said so right away. I never woulda bothered her if I'da known. Not after what you did for me."

Bess saw a sly, calculating look cross the boy's face, a look much too old for his tender years. "Do you know each other?" she asked, curious about their obvious connection. How they might have met, Bess couldn't imagine. Well-brought-up young ladies did not consort with the lower classes—this truth had been drummed into her often during her tenure at Miss Fine's—and neither did gentlemen, if it could at all be helped. That this boy clearly came from the lowest of the low was undeniable.

His clothes were torn and dirty, his feet and hands unspeakable. His hair was matted and of an indeterminate color—a dark brown now, but with a good washing, who knew? A smudge of dirt was smeared across one cheek, and the smell emanating from him made Bess want to hold her nose.

But she didn't. Despite all there was to repel her, something inside her responded to his pride, to the defiant way he stood up to Dev, to the tolerant way Dev let him hang on to that pride.

"Have you two met before?" she asked.

"Once," Dev admitted.

"Yeah. He bought me a drink. Over at the Main Building, it was. From Tuft's."

Bess watched the boy's eyes light up as he remembered the treat. They were green and bright, inquisitive and sharp, hinting at an intelligence she wouldn't have considered had she merely seen him in passing.

"Tuft's?" she asked.

"The Arctic Soda Water concession," the boy explained. "You never had one?"

"I'm sure I must have," she said. *But I doubt I enjoyed it half as much as you did,* she added to herself, realizing that his pleasures must be few and far between.

"Your mister is a fine man, lady. He bought me one for free. Didn't make me do his shoes or nothin'." The imp smiled cheerfully up at her and seemed to relax despite Devlin's hold on him.

Bess smiled back, unable to resist the boy's charm, then glanced up at Devlin. His face had a pinched quality to it, the skin around his mouth pulled tight, as if the whole scene pained him in some profound way. Here was treacherous ground, Bess realized, though she knew not why.

"We'd best be getting back to the others, don't you

111

think?" she murmured cautiously, unsure what should happen next. Would Devlin insist on calling the police or should they let the boy go? At the very least, shouldn't they tell his parents so they could discipline him? The child couldn't be allowed to prey upon unsuspecting people like herself. It wasn't right.

"First, I believe Danny has something of yours he wishes to return. Isn't that so?"

The boy studied Devlin's expression for less than an instant before correctly answering the question. "Uh, yes ma'am. I do. If I'd'a known you were his lady, I never would have bothered you. I hope you believe that."

Honor among thieves, Bess thought, understanding the boy's tangled apology. "You mean you would have taken someone else's instead?"

"Of course — never yours." He reached into his shirt and pulled out her reticule. One of the straps had been torn off, the other was frayed. Even the beadwork had ripped and an entire row was missing. "Here." He held the now sorry object out to her. "I apologize for the inconvenience."

"Thank you," she said, accepting it solemnly, in the spirit in which it had been tendered. Then she looked over at Devlin for a clue about the next step.

"The police station is just up that path." He tilted his head in the proper direction and looked sharply at the boy.

"I know. That's why I was heading back this way when we crashed." Danny grinned again. "I surely didn't want to get caught by them." He rolled his eyes meaningfully.

Devlin didn't answer for a moment, seemingly lost in thought. For once Bess sensed where his thoughts were taking him. Danny was a likable child, child being the operative word. What would happen to

112

him if the police got word of his behavior? She shuddered to think, and yet she couldn't quite see letting him go blameless. Where were his parents, anyhow? By now they surely should have come to find him. Her father would have been frantic if she had been missing for so long when she had been this age.

"The police aren't terribly sympathetic to your plight, are they?" Devlin said, more to himself than to his listeners. Again Bess was struck by the tension in him, the way the stark angles of his face were suddenly more prominent. For a moment she wanted to reach out to him, to give him comfort and reassurance. Then he lifted his head to look past her, his expression suddenly hard, shutting her out.

"Bess? What's taking so long? Are you all right?" Barrett Covington called out.

Bess looked over her shoulder and saw her escort barreling down the narrow path toward them. "Barrett, what are you doing here?" she asked. "Did something happen to Alice?"

"No, what makes you think so?" He stopped at her side, panting from exertion.

"Why were you running?"

He looked at her with surprise. "To see if you were all right. You've been gone quite a while. What with talking to the Crawfords, I lost track of the time. Then I realized how long you'd been gone."

"I'm sorry to have given you such a scare, but as you can see, Devlin has everything in hand. We'll be done here in a minute."

She turned her head to look at Devlin, and Barrett followed her gaze, narrowing his eyes when he caught sight of Danny.

"So you caught the little wretch, did you?" Barrett curled his lip in distaste. "Nasty-looking bastard, wouldn't you say? Doesn't seem right, subjecting poor

Bess to his presence."

He reached for Bess's hand, but she jerked out of his reach, unreasonably angry at his reaction. She knew he was trying to protect her sensibilities, but she wasn't looking for protection. If anything, she realized with dawning surprise, she was looking *to protect*.

And the object of her unfamiliar urge was none other than the scruffiest, most disreputable boy in the whole of Philadelphia — and maybe, if she searched her soul carefully enough, the somber, troubled man at his side.

"Now, Barrett, there's no need to get excited. Devlin has everything under control," she said, trying to smooth things over. "We're almost done here. We'll rejoin you in a moment." She hoped he would take the hint and leave, but to her chagrin, he chose this occasion to be obtuse and assert his gentlemanly upbringing.

"I wouldn't think of abandoning you, Bess, not for the world. Fortunately, the police are only a block away. The Exhibition has its own special force, you know. We can just hand this urchin over to them. They'll make sure he doesn't do this again."

Barrett gave Danny a fierce, disapproving glare and once again reached for Bess's hand. This time she wasn't fast enough to escape him. Her stomach tightened. Though she knew Barrett's suggestion was the right thing to do — indeed, she had been considering that exact course of action herself — she also knew she couldn't bring herself to do it. Danny was just a child. Surely there was some other way of dealing with this situation.

She glanced at Devlin, pleading silently for his help.

Dev felt Danny stiffen the minute Barrett started

114

to speak. The boy had an instinctive feel for the man's enmity—a class hatred which he'd no doubt seen first hand before, if even half of Dev's suspicions about the boy's life were true.

As Bess and Barrett traded conversation, Dev considered his options. None of them were pleasant. In a perverse way, his sympathies lay with the youngster. Some nights, in those vulnerable seconds before sleep claimed him, Dev would still remember snatches of his own early childhood—the smell of poverty, the ache of hunger, the desperate need to survive by any means at hand. He understood the limits and pressures of the boy's existence, the harsh realities of life on the street.

He didn't want Danny to disappear again the way he had the other day. This time he wanted to be sure he could help the boy. Yet with Barrett around that option might not be available, especially if Barrett insisted on calling the police.

To top it all off, Bess was sending him such mixed signals. What did she want? For a second he had the insane notion she wanted him to free the boy. Even crazier, she seemed to have taken to Danny, liking him despite the proscriptions with which she'd been raised.

"Well? Are we going to turn him in or not? What's holding things up now?" Barrett demanded.

Dev hesitated no longer. "Nothing," he replied coldly. "Lead the way, why don't you."

"I'd be happy to. I don't know what you were thinking of, subjecting Bess to this miscreant's presence for an instant longer than absolutely necessary. This is exactly the kind of thing we read about in the paper. Come along, Bess."

Barrett pushed down the path, heading to the back side of Judges' Hall, a handsome wooden building used by the judges awarding the prizes from the Centennial Commission, and toward the police station.

Dev bided his time, waiting until Barrett had passed him and gotten well ahead. Slowly, he loosened his hold on Danny, knowing that the boy would escape, though which fate was kinder—being turned over to the police or being returned to the streets—he couldn't judge. He only hoped he was making the right choice.

By some mischance Barrett happened to look over his shoulder just as Danny made his break for freedom.

"Hey, he's getting away!" Barrett shouted.

Dev turned at the sound of Barrett's voice and saw Bess step forward quickly, right into Barrett's path. In the next instant, both she and Barrett were on the ground. Dev could have sworn she smiled before beginning to push herself to her feet.

"Oh, my goodness," Bess exclaimed. "I'm so sorry, Barrett. I don't know how I could have been so clumsy. Are you all right?"

"Mm—I'm—mpfumphn," the man mumbled from beneath the tangle of Bess's skirt, its yards of fabric muffling his words.

Dev glanced around, making sure Danny was out of sight, then came to help Bess disentangle herself from Barrett.

"How could you be so careless?" Barrett ground out, directing his fury at Dev once he was back on his feet. "Just look at my trousers. They're a sight! And that—that heathen—he's getting away scot-free."

Dev barely spared Barrett a glance. The pompous boor was of no interest to him. What did Bess see in the vain popinjay? He turned his attention to her, a much more worthwhile pursuit.

Her face was alight with mischief and energy. She

116

rocked up on her toes like a bird poised for flight, ready for any and all adventures. Her lips curved sensuously, looking ready to break out into laughter at the slightest provocation.

"Are you all right, Bess? I'm afraid you're going to have an unpleasant memory of the Centennial Exhibition. Let me assure you most visits are not this enervating," Dev observed.

She met Dev's gaze with an impish smile. "I think I'm going to treasure my memories of the Centennial far more than you imagine. It's been a most thought-provoking experience."

His heart doubled its cadence. He longed to reach for her, to touch her skin with his own, to press his lips against hers again and again. Her taste flooded his mouth, clean and pure and utterly feminine; his fingertips recalled her touch, soft and sweet, innocent and eager. If they'd been alone, he would have had her in his embrace again, savoring her budding passion, teaching her of desire. As it was, he could merely look at her and imagine . . . and wonder what thoughts had turned her eyes so blue and brought the becoming flush to her cheeks.

"We'd better get back to the others. They must be wondering what happened to us," Barrett grumbled, breaking the spell that held Dev and Bess in thrall.

"By all means," Dev agreed quickly. His thoughts and feelings were getting out of hand. Being in a public place with Alice draped on his arm would give him the harsh dose of reality he needed to put his fantasies in abeyance.

"What will Danny do now? Do you think he'll tell his parents what happened?" Bess asked in a low voice as they joined the others.

"His parents?" Dev asked, astonished at her na-

117

iveté. "He has no parents, Bess. He lives on the streets. That's why he took your purse."

She knew nothing of the ugly side of life, of its dirt and despair, of its poverty and hopelessness — in short, of his own humble beginnings. The distance between them was more than East and West, city and country, if she only knew it. How would she feel if she found out?

"What do you mean, on the streets?" she asked, interrupting his thoughts. "He has no home? No one to care for him? But he's just a child!" Her eyes widened with comprehension even as her mind fought with denial. "You weren't going to turn him over to the police, were you? You knew exactly how he lived?"

"Yes, I knew, and no, I wasn't going to turn him over to the police."

"Then what would you have done?"

How she would laugh at him, if she only knew! He'd had some vague notion that he might do for Danny what Patrick O'Connor had done for him. For the scene this morning had been like a ghost from the past — his past.

He'd forgotten it all, or tried to, but if he closed his eyes, he could see every moment again: Patrick O'Connor holding him up by the collar, shouting at him for having stolen his wife's purse, ranting at him until his wife said, "But, Patrick, just look. Sure and he has no parents. No mother would let her son out of the house like that. For all we know, he has no home."

She had become his mother, that fairy-tale woman with the voice of an angel, just as Patrick had become his father. And he had put his past behind him, far behind him. Or so he had thought until Danny had rubbed the scars raw. He bled for Danny as once

118

he had bled for himself, but he couldn't trust Bess to understand.

"I hadn't decided what to do, and then he escaped," Dev lied, "taking the matter out of my hands."

"I see," said Bess, but she didn't sound convinced, and for the rest of the day he caught her studying him intently whenever she thought he wasn't looking.

Six

Bess waited anxiously by the front door of the hotel. Her great aunt had said she would pick her up at ten o'clock, and it was already a few minutes after. She hoped Olivia Babcock hadn't been persuaded to forego their meeting by her granddaughter. If Catherine Sinclair's attitude exemplified that of the rest of the family, Bess feared her aunt might not be able to withstand the pressure to avoid "the nobody from the West."

"Here's the Babcock carriage now, miss," the doorman called as an elaborate carriage turned the corner.

Relief surged through Bess. Olivia Babcock hadn't been swayed from seeing her after all. The doorman opened the carriage door with a little bow and assisted her inside.

"Bess, dear, I'm so glad to see you. I thought you might have changed your mind," the older woman said with a smile. She patted Bess's hand with her own small, gloved one. "After all, going to the Exhibit with an old woman can't be very exciting."

"Oh, I'm quite looking forward to it. I was afraid *you* wouldn't want to go with *me*." Bess allowed herself to voice her own fears in the face of Olivia's similar confession as she looked into the older woman's eyes.

"I never pass up the opportunity to forward the goals of the League, and when it also means I can spend time with Victoria's daughter . . ." She sighed, seemingly lost in the past. Then she turned to Bess and said, "Now, you must call me Aunt Olivia or Aunt Livvie, just as your mother did."

"Thank you. You really make me feel like family," Bess smiled.

"What do you mean? You *are* family." A frown creased the old woman's brow. "I hope you aren't taking Catherine's comments too seriously. I know she didn't make a good impression the other day, but I hope you can forgive her. She feels she must to protect me — even when there is no need. Once the rest of the family gets to know you, I'm sure everything will work out — blood is thicker than water, after all." She settled back into the soft upholstery of the seat.

While the words were comforting, Bess had few illusions that any of the other members of her mother's family would ever be welcoming.

"Well, Bess, have you visited the Women's Pavilion yet?" Livvie asked as the carriage neared Fairmount Park and skirted the Schuylkill River.

"No, but I'm certainly looking forward to it. You mentioned that your League meets there?"

"Our offices are in the city, actually, but we occasionally meet out at the Centennial grounds. To be honest, we all like the excuse of meeting at the Exhibition because we can combine our work with a wonderful luncheon and a nice day out."

"What exactly does the League do?"

"I think I may have mentioned it's full title is the Women's League for Children's Welfare. We try to help abandoned children. There are so many of them here in the city, you know, and no one to look after them. It's a tragedy, but so few people really care."

Just then their carriage slowed, and Livvie looked out the window. "Ah, here we are. I always have Donaldson drop me off at the Belmont Avenue entrance. It's the closest to the Women's Pavilion, and there's a nice young man stationed inside the grounds who runs the rolling chair concession. He takes care of me very well."

After telling her driver to return at four o'clock, Livvie insisted on paying both admissions. Once inside, she led the way to the chair concession and within minutes was ensconced in an ornate rolling chair, pushed by a young porter.

"Are you sure you wouldn't like to ride, too?" Livvie asked as they started down Belmont Avenue.

Bess shook her head. "I enjoy walking. Since I've been in Philadelphia, I haven't walked at all except yesterday when I visited here with my friend's family." *And Devlin,* she added silently, unwilling to say his name aloud though her heart gave a little flutter as she thought of him. "I probably need to walk off all the pounds I've put on eating the marvelous food Philadelphia has to offer."

"Your mother also had a good appetite. I remember when she would come to visit with my daughter Regina. They were of a similar age, you know. They were forever pestering Cook for something to eat."

Bess was glad Aunt Livvie had brought up the subject of her mother again. Now she could ask about her without being rude. "Could you tell me about my mother? You see, she died when I was very young, and my father . . . well, you know how men are. There are so many things I wish I knew about her."

Livvie apparently understood Bess's need clearly. "Stop over by that bench," her aunt instructed her porter. "My niece and I wish to talk. You may come back in half an hour or so, if you don't mind."

The porter agreed politely and strolled away, no doubt happy to have the time to himself.

"I'll be glad to tell you everything I can, child, but you realize I can only tell you about her when she was very young, before she left Philadelphia. After she married I only heard from her occasionally."

"Anything you could tell me would be most appreciated," Bess said as she sat on the bench facing her aunt. Though she tried to appear relaxed, her fingers were laced together so tightly her knuckles were white. As a child, Bess had feared there was something wrong with her mother since her father never talked about her. Later she had come to understand he had his own unresolved conflicts with which to deal. Nonetheless, her understanding wasn't sufficient to quell her hunger to know more, and now, at last, some small part of that hunger would be satisfied.

"Your mother and I were quite close, considering that I was her aunt. Maybe it was because I understood her so much better than her parents." Livvie shrugged her shoulders. "When she left, though, we lost contact, for the most part. I think she was afraid her father would cause trouble if he found out she was writing to me. I always felt my brother, rest his soul, was at fault when he raised such an uproar about your mother's marriage. I know your grandmother dearly wanted to see Victoria. She was her only child. I'll never forget the day I told her of your birth."

Livvie shook her head, and the light in her pale blue eyes dimmed. "She wasn't well, you know—your grandmother, that is. She died not long afterward, but I think it made her happy to know that Victoria, too, had a daughter." The older woman reached over and patted Bess's knee. "Her dying wish was to have seen you."

"Pride is such a wasteful emotion, Bess. Remember

123

that. Too often people are overly concerned with stature and social class. They fail to see what is truly important, and their lives are the poorer for it." She stared sightlessly at the crowd wandering past them, absorbed in her memories. "You know, I have pictures of the family at home, if you'd like to see them," she offered after a brief silence. "Some portraits and a few photographs as well."

"I'd love to," Bess said. "It's most generous of you to offer."

Tears welled in her eyes as Olivia recounted stories of her mother as a child and young woman. Though the bench she sat on was hard and the weather hot and humid, Bess sat enthralled, unaware of any discomfort. Before this, her vision of her mother and her grandparents had been nebulous at best. Now she knew something about them, and soon, when she saw the pictures, she would be able to put faces with the names.

When the time came to speak of Victoria's marriage to Bert Richmond, Olivia tried to explain how matters had stood twenty-odd years ago.

"Your grandfather put a good deal of credence in social position and economic standing. For those reasons alone he condemned the marriage. He wanted a different way of life for your mother, but she wanted your father. Victoria always had a mind of her own, and she was not afraid to voice it, either. No one could stop her once she'd made her decision. I'm only glad she was so happy in the short time she had." Olivia sighed and sat silently, remembering the past.

"Ah, here comes the porter," she said a few minutes later. "We'll have plenty of time to talk later. You are staying in Philadelphia a while longer, are you not?"

"We're scheduled to stay for three more weeks," Bess answered as they headed for a fair-sized blue building

124

farther along the avenue on their left.

"Good. That will give us plenty of time to get to know one another. I especially want you to visit the League's offices in the city. I'm certain you'll be as moved as I was when you learn the extent of these poor unfortunate children's plight."

"I would love to visit again," Bess said. "Any time that's convenient."

Though she didn't see how she could possibly contribute to the League during her short stay in Philadelphia, her aunt's impassioned speeches on its mission and Bess's own encounter with poor little Danny the previous day had affected her strongly. She couldn't simply ignore the problems around her. Perhaps in learning about the League's operations she would find something she could do for Danny and others like him.

As they entered the offices at the Women's Pavilion, a woman of some sixty years hurried up to greet them. "Livvie, dear, thank goodness you made it. We were getting quite worried."

Aunt Livvie looked up in surprise. "Whatever are you worrying about?"

"Surely you realize how late you are, my dear."

"I'm hardly that late, Matilde, but you must forgive me. I've brought my grandniece to visit. I'm afraid we got to talking and forgot the time."

"Grandniece? I don't believe I remember you mentioning her before," the woman named Matilde returned, looking Bess up and down.

By this time the other women in the group had caught up with Matilde and introductions were made. All were apprised of Bess's recent arrival from Kansas City.

"Do you all volunteer your time at the League?" Bess asked.

"Why, yes. Some of us have more time to spend than others, of course," Matilde said, "but we all try to put in as many hours as we can spare."

"There's such a need you know," Abigail Prescott added. She was a young matron, perhaps a decade or so older than Bess. "I couldn't believe the number of children who have absolutely no one to look after them."

"We try to find homes and provide food for those who allow it," put in Lucy Dowd, a timid-looking woman with a querulous voice. "I'm sorry to say many of them have adjusted far too well to the injustices of the street."

Bess thought of little Danny, his thin young face smudged with dirt and his shirt ragged and torn.

"Yesterday when we were here at the Exhibition, we saw a young boy who appeared to be wandering alone at will," Bess said, deciding not to mention the incident with her purse. "Is that the type of child you're interested in?"

"I should think it very likely," Livvie confirmed. "It's really a shame. There are far more children than there are families willing, or able, to care for them."

A discreet knock sounded at the door, and a young man appeared with a large tray. "Excuse me, ladies. Your luncheon is here." He smiled widely, bantering with the women in a friendly way born of long acquaintance. Quickly and efficiently he set out a tea pot, a large plate of dainty sandwiches, and another of small cakes on the sideboard. On a separate platter, a selection of fruit and small tarts was arranged in a pleasing pattern.

"All set now," he said, straightening the row of cups and saucers. "Ring if you need anything else."

When he left, the ladies began serving themselves, encouraging Bess to sample their various favorites.

"You see, dear—I told you the food would be excellent here," Aunt Livvie said.

Bess smilingly agreed. When everyone was served, they sat around the large center table and began discussing their plans for the children and the need for raising more funds.

"We've opened a couple of homes for the children," Abigail informed Bess, "but they can't provide the same loving care a family can. And the children are still too close to their old lives. Many of them just drift back onto the streets, lured there by their old friends."

"Or intimidated by them," murmured Lucy Dowd, looking half afraid.

"Intimidated? What do you mean?" Bess asked.

"We believe the children are being used by unscrupulous adults to commit crimes," Matilde declared.

"Crimes? You mean like snatching purses?" The words slipped out before Bess could think better of them.

"Snatching purses, picking pockets, stealing—you name it," Matilde amplified. "That's why we're trying to find out a better way to help the children, to get them away from the evils of the city to a safer place, with people who will love them and raise them as God-fearing, honest-toiling adults."

"And now we think we've found a solution," Livvie said. "We've talked to some visitors from New York City; they work with the aid societies there and came here to exchange ideas. Some of the children's groups to the north have successfully found homes for their children out of the cities."

"Well, I don't think that's going to work," Lucy Dowd put in.

"You never think anything new will work, Lucy," Abigail snapped.

"I do, too. I just don't think *this* will work. It's too

127

complicated. And I'm not the only one who says so."

"Maybe not, but I haven't seen you come up with a better idea."

"I have, too."

The two women glared at each other.

"Uh, where do they send the children?" Bess asked, hoping to deflect the two women from what seemed to be a long-standing difference of opinion.

"Out West," Matilde explained. "They hire a train car and take groups of children to small towns all over. Before they get there, they put an advertisement in the local paper announcing they'll have children available for good families. Why, they've placed thousands of children over the years."

"But how do they know the children are happy?" Bess worried out loud.

"They keep in touch with them to see how they're doing," Matilde said. "The families are told in advance that they have to treat the children right or they'll be taken away. After all, they're not bringing them slaves or servants."

"Besides," Abigail added, "they work with the local clergy or sheriff—someone who knows the townspeople and settlers in the area."

"That's all well and good," Lucy said, "but we don't know any clergy or sheriffs out West. I just don't see how we're going to manage this at all."

"That's why we're meeting here today, Lucy," Aunt Livvie reminded her. "To make the plans. And, I might add, we're especially lucky to have my niece with us. After all, she grew up out West, in Missouri. She can tell us what opportunities lie in her area."

The early afternoon passed quickly as the ladies bombarded Bess with questions about Kansas City and its environs. They also discussed opening yet another home for the city's children and made plans for raising the money needed to keep up their operations.

Shortly before tea time, the ladies ran out of energy, at least when it came to any more work for the League. They insisted on giving Bess a tour of the Women's Pavilion before partaking of their final refreshments.

Aunt Livvie, pleading exhaustion, begged off. Bess noticed that fatigue lines which hadn't been apparent earlier in the day now marked her features.

"Maybe we should just head back into the city," she suggested. "I can come back here another day."

"No, no, I wouldn't hear of it," Aunt Livvie exclaimed. "I'll just stay here and rest. You go with the others and look around. When you're done, we can have afternoon tea together."

Reluctantly Bess joined the group of ladies for a tour of the building. She didn't want to leave her aunt alone but saw no graceful way to refuse. As they walked, the ladies gave Bess a running commentary on each exhibit. Bess found it interesting that the women demonstrated such a clear measure of pride in the pavilion. All of them were quick to point out the accomplishments attained by their peers and more than ready to jump to the defense when any part was criticized. The more Bess saw the more she came to agree with them.

Before she had visited the Exhibition, Bess had never seen so many different items gathered together in one place. And to find such a large collection supplied solely by women—this was a concept which Bess had never even contemplated.

The group stopped in front of a steam engine where a woman was adjusting the control knobs. The woman was dressed in a workman-like skirt and blouse and appeared to be at ease with her responsibilities.

Matilde nodded toward the woman. "That's Emma

Allison, the stationary steam engineer. She maintains the engine which runs the looms, spinning frames and a Hoe cylinder printing press. You must get a copy of *The New Century of Woman*. It's the official voice of the Women's Pavilion — completely written, edited and printed by the women here."

Bess nodded. She had never realized the women of America were involved in so many varied occupations. Besides the woman who ran the engine, there was one whole section on inventions developed and patented by women, not to mention the purely artistic endeavors such as the paintings and sculptures found in the northern and southern wings.

Bess felt strongly reassured. So many women had contributed to the works exhibited in this building — surely all of them couldn't be misfits. Creativity, whether of an artistic or mechanical nature, was not a purely male domain. For the first time Bess was brought face to face with the limitless capabilities of her own sex, capabilities she'd never dreamed possible with her more conventional upbringing.

Her vague notion that in Philadelphia she might find a direction for her life was already bearing fruit. Even though she did not yet know her exact goal, at least she had learned not to narrow her scope, not to settle for less than she was fully capable of.

"Why don't we take a short rest and have tea, and then finish our tour," Matilde suggested after a while. "I know I'm feeling a bit peckish."

"That would be lovely," Bess agreed. "There's so much to see here, I am truly impressed. I can't wait to talk it all over with Aunt Olivia."

The others smiled at her approvingly as if she had passed some secret test. "Come along, then, dear," one said. "I'm sure Livvie is anxiously awaiting your return."

* * *

Olivia Babcock heard a familiar whistle outside the meeting room door, followed by a perfunctory knock. Before she could say "Come in," Devlin O'Connor pushed open the door and stuck in his head. "Am I interrupting anything?"

"Devlin, my dear boy, how good to see you," Livvie cried. "Come in, come in. The others are touring the exhibit and will be back soon."

"Again? I would think by now your ladies know everything there is to see and would be getting bored."

Livvie laughed. "That's true. But today we have new blood."

Her eyes twinkled merrily as she waited to see his reaction.

"Ah, a guest? Someone new to the cause?"

"I certainly hope so. There can never be too many people involved in our work."

He turned serious then, as she knew he would. He was one of the few men of her acquaintance who treated their "women's work" as worthy of respect. In fact, he was a major behind-the-scenes contributor to the League's efforts, though few people knew it either within the League or outside it.

"I saw a new child this week," he said.

"And?"

"And nothing." He began to pace. "The circumstances weren't . . . right." He shrugged. "The boy got away before I had a chance to speak with him. Two times, in fact."

She could see the hurt of failure in his expression. "If you've seen him twice, you'll probably see him again," she said soothingly. Dev took these things too much to heart. Since his wife's death, he'd become withdrawn and moody; only the League's activities

131

seemed to interest him any more. No one seemed to know how he spent the rest of his time, though she had her suspicions.

"I hope you're right," he conceded and dropped back into his chair. "So, tell me about your 'new blood'," he asked, deliberately changing the topic.

Olivia was happy to oblige him. She wasn't above a bit of meddling in the lives of her friends when the occasion called for it, and Devlin was past due for something good in his life.

"Well, you'll never believe this, but remember my niece Victoria?"

"The one who left home in disgrace?"

"She did no such thing," Olivia snapped, "and you know it."

"Sorry," he said with a teasing smile.

"Humph," Olivia snorted, biting down on her own smile. Dev could be a rascal when he wanted. "In any case, as I was saying, Victoria had a daughter and now she's come to visit."

Dev sat up, wariness and excitement lighting his features all at the same time. "Victoria's daughter? Where did she come from?"

"Kansas City! For all you know you met while you were out there."

"I thought she lived in some nothing little town in the middle of nowhere, to hear your daughter carry on about her, no offense intended."

"She did . . . does. But she went to school in Kansas City, and now she's here."

"I can't believe it! Are you telling me Bess Richmond is your grandniece?"

"You've met her? Already?" Olivia would have been disappointed that her surprise was spoiled except that she saw something in Dev's expression, an elusive spark she hadn't seen in a long time.

132

He laughed out loud. "Met her? I traveled halfway across the country with her—to her great dismay, I might add."

"Dismay? Whatever do you mean? Did you do something rash?" Olivia enjoyed playing dumb with her younger friends and relatives. It always got them to reveal much more than they intended if they thought of her as a poor little old lady.

"Now, Olivia, you know me better than that. I was the perfect gentleman. In fact, that might be the problem. I'm afraid the West has spoiled your grandniece. She seems to have developed a taste for the more bloodthirsty kinds of heroism."

"Why, Devlin, you're speaking scandalously. Bloodthirsty, indeed." Olivia narrowed her eyes as she took in his sudden energy, the fire in his eyes, the interest in his voice. "No wonder my niece turned up her nose. She isn't used to your wicked ways."

"Wicked? Come now, Olivia, surely you know me better than that."

"Do I?" She said the words more sharply than she'd intended and saw him close up. She'd long suspected there was more to Dev than met the eye, but whenever she ventured near the forbidden boundaries, he shut her out. And since Julia's death, he'd placed more boundaries around himself than ever before.

"In any case," she said, deliberately lightening her tone, "I suggest you put on your best behavior now, because Bess will be coming back here any minute. In fact," she added as if she had just thought of it, "if you play your cards right, I might invite you to stay for tea. Wouldn't that be nice? A free meal surrounded by all manner of ladies just thrilled to hang on your every word."

Dev laughed again, as she'd hoped he would, the momentary tension in him easing away. "Now how

133

could any male worth his salt resist an invitation like that?"

"Good, then it's settled," she said, pleased to see the animation return to his face.

"I hope my presence at tea wasn't too intrusive," Devlin said to Bess as he escorted her to the annex of the Women's Building at Olivia's request.

"N-no, of course not," she answered, embarrassed that he had noticed her startled expression when she had first seen him and learned he was staying to have tea with them.

"I'm glad. I had a most pleasant time, myself," he said.

"Did you?" she asked with a broad smile, then recovered. "I beg your pardon." She felt a blush rise and silently berated herself for being so flustered. "You seem to know all of the ladies quite well," she said, desperate to put their conversation on a different footing.

"I guess I do. Many are friends of my family. Their husbands do business with my father's firm. Some were friends of my late wife. She was very interested in the League and its work."

For a moment, Bess almost stopped in her tracks. No one had ever mentioned that Devlin had been married. "I'm sorry, I didn't realize that you'd lost your wife. Has it been long?"

"Two years, but one learns to go on."

"Still, it must be difficult."

"It was, at first. Julia and I had known each other since we were children, and she was a very important part of my life. For a while everything seemed very empty, but I've stayed in touch with the League and some of her friends, and that's helped. She introduced

134

me to Mrs. Babcock. Have you known her long?"

It was obvious from Devlin's change of subject that he didn't want to talk any more about his wife. She thought of her father and how he'd never quite gotten over her mother's death, and she went along with Dev's wishes. "I only met her in Philadelphia. We're related. Perhaps she mentioned it?"

"Oh, yes, she did. I believe she's very pleased to have you here visiting."

"Is she?" She smiled, unable to disguise her happiness. It was one thing for Aunt Olivia to tell her she enjoyed her company, and quite another to tell someone else when Bess wasn't around to overhear. "I'm pleased to visit her, too. She seems a wonderful lady."

"That she is," Dev replied, and again she heard fondness and respect for the older woman in his tone.

"Where are you taking me?" she asked, looking up at him with friendly interest.

His pupils grew large as their gazes met, making his eyes look black, and her heartbeat gave a sudden jump at the intensity of his expression.

"Uh, Mrs. Babcock wanted you to see the kindergarten," he said, his voice low and husky. They stopped walking and their gazes held.

Bess was sure Dev was recalling the night of their kiss just as she was. A lock of dark hair fell over his forehead as he looked down at her. She longed to reach up and smooth it back, to feel its silken texture on her fingertips. She remembered it well, thick and resilient even in the back where the hairs curled slightly at his nape.

A family walked by, the children in high spirits. One of the younger boys jostled Dev as he raced by, ignoring his mother's protestations. The woman apologized to Dev as she hurried past, bringing Bess back to an awareness of where she was.

"You were telling me about the kindergarten," she murmured, collecting herself.

"Oh, yes." He looked as distracted as she felt, but following her lead, he started walking again. "The children are all orphans, and the school is designed to show how well young children can be taught."

"Is the League involved in education, too?"

"Not directly. Their work is confined primarily to raising money to run the homes and feed and clothe the children. But you should really ask Mrs. Babcock if you're interested. She knows the details of how the League works."

"We spoke for quite a while earlier today. She told me of their plans for sending the children out of the city to better homes."

"What did you think?" He sounded wary.

"I'm really not in a position to say one way or the other. You don't seem very enthusiastic. Do you disapprove?"

"Let's just say I'm reserving judgment. I don't see the necessity of removing children from everything familiar and known."

"But what if they fall back into their bad ways?"

"Not all of them do, you know, or do you think them all so low-bred they can never overcome their pasts?"

Bess bristled at his tone. She'd only been making reference to the comments she'd heard at lunch. "Tell me, do you make it a habit to judge all your female companions so harshly, or is there something special about me?"

He looked away with a pained expression. It reminded her of the way he'd looked with Danny the previous day when the small boy had stolen her purse.

"I apologize," he said stiffly. "Why don't we go inside, and you can see for yourself how well the chil-

136

dren are doing."

He opened the door leading to the spectator gallery of the well-lit wooden building and motioned her in. Several other people were already seated on the benches behind a decorative barrier. Bess perched with Dev on an adjoining bench and looked down a floor to where the children sat at low tables arranged in the shape of a rectangle with an aisle up the middle. The teacher sat at one end of the rectangle instructing the students on their lesson.

The children, all well-scrubbed and neatly turned out, listened avidly while the spectators watched, whispering amongst themselves at the children's antics.

"It seems very nice," Bess murmured.

"Yes, doesn't it."

She gave him a sharp look, but he fixed his gaze on the scene below. She didn't know what to make of him. One minute he was friendly and gracious; the next, he was as rude as ever. Her initial dislike had modulated to a combination of respect and curiosity, wariness and interest—and, if she dared admit it, something else, something new and different that she'd never experienced before.

She ached for him when he wasn't there, yet felt tense and drawn when he was. He stirred her as she'd never been stirred before. He was a deep man, she'd discovered, not at all like her first impression of him. She'd thought him a copy of Wylie, but she'd been wrong. He didn't flaunt his business acumen or trade on his family's position. He didn't gravitate to the most important person in the room nor fawn on anyone who could do him a favor. She had yet to successfully categorize him; he fit none of her preconceived niches.

They watched the children for a while longer then

137

slipped out the side door.

"You are right, at least about those children," she said as they walked in the narrow area between the New Jersey State Building and the Women's Pavilion. "They are bright and winsome, whatever their backgrounds, and bound to do well. But . . ." She hesitated, unsure how he would react to her mention of Danny.

"Yes?"

She bit her lip, then decided she had nothing to lose. Besides, her curiosity overcame her inhibitions — or maybe it was more than curiosity, this burning need to know and understand. "What about children like that little boy the other day?"

He stopped in the shadows of the trees and turned to face her. "The one who grabbed your purse?"

She nodded.

"What about him?"

The tightness was back; she felt his tension stretch taut like a piano wire, ready to snap at the lightest touch.

"How will he make out here?" she asked. "Who will want him? Who can save him?"

"There is no 'who.' There is only me and you. If you don't take responsibility for the conditions around you, you can't expect anyone else to either. 'Charity begins at home'," he quoted, "and so does concern for your fellow man, or child as the case may be."

Mesmerized by his intensity, she swayed toward him, placing her hand on his arm for balance. His eyes were dark in the shade, the brown irises blending seamlessly with his pupils, drawing her in.

"I should have asked what can *we* do? Is there something? Do you know? Can we even find him?"

He gripped her shoulders, steadying her. For a moment, she thought he would pull her close, and shamefully reveled in the thought. His touch was electric, waking her entire body from its somnolent state, bringing to life every part of her from her skin clear down to the innermost recess of her secret self.

"That's the hell of it," he said. "I don't even know where he is. But if I ever see him again, you can be sure I'll do something about it. That I promise you."

"If I can help, you'll tell me, won't you?"

He seemed to suddenly look through her, into her, seeking to know her better than she knew herself, to find the elusive truth she herself sought.

"Why would you want to?" he asked, his tone almost belligerent.

"Because, Devlin," she whispered, too caught up in his spell to be angry, "I care about him, too. As much as you do. Maybe more."

This time he did pull her close. Hidden by the trees at the side of a little-used alleyway, he held her to him, his hands slipping past her shoulders to settle at her waist.

His mouth closed on hers, and her lips parted. His tongue slid into her hidden recesses, exploring and tasting, awakening her again to the magic she'd experienced only once before — and that, too, had been in his arms. Daringly, her tongue flirted with his. His lips were smooth as he lured her to him, his teeth sharp. Following his lead, she delicately explored his mouth, finding his taste as dark and male as before.

When her tongue withdrew, his followed, and he took command of the kiss again, teaching her the complex subtleties of this most romantic duel. His hands caressed her back, pressing her against him from shoulder to waist. She reached up and threaded her fingers through his hair, angling her head to allow him better access. A moan escaped from her throat, and she heard an answering groan from his.

"Oh, Bess, I—" But before he finished whatever he was going to say, their lips met again, hungry and eager.

One of his hands slipped around her waist to her front and slowly rose until his palm claimed her breast. She could feel his heat burn through the layers of fabric though she wore a corset and chemise under her prim basque top. His hand moved higher and two fingers slipped between the buttons of her top. She could feel his skin against her own, the roughness of his fingertips rasping against the soft fullness above her breast. No man had ever touched her thus, and her heart beat like a wild bird trapped in a cage.

Her nipples contracted sharply, and an answering ache formed low in her stomach. Her legs began to tremble until she wasn't sure she could stand on her own. Still his lips moved against hers and his fingers softly caressed her, skimming along the top of her corset but going no farther though she hungered for more of his touch. The kiss consumed her, like a fire that fed on itself, blazing ever brighter on its own energy.

"I can't breathe," she finally gasped, pulling away from him. She gulped in great breaths of air, panting as if she'd done some great exertion. His breaths were no less forced though he seemed to retain his strength, holding her up when she feared she might collapse, her bones no longer able to support her.

She looked up at him, wanting him to kiss her again and fearing that he would. This was a kiss like none other, with a passionate intensity she'd never experienced. She felt wild and reckless, and somewhat frightened of the storm churning inside her.

"We'd best get back inside," Dev said in a soft voice. He sensed she was like a wild animal caught in a hunter's sight, wanting to run but not knowing in what direction. At the base of her throat he could see her pulse beating madly. He tried to calm her with just the sound of his voice, knowing that his touch would be too much.

She looked at him, her eyes wide, showing her confusion, her lips swollen and glistening from their kiss. It was all he could do to keep from pulling her back into his embrace.

"Olivia will be getting anxious, wondering what's become of us," he explained.

She blushed then, and put a hand to her lips. He wanted to smile, but didn't. She was so young . . . or maybe it was her innocence, an innocence he had left far behind, if, indeed, he'd ever had it.

"I'm afraid I haven't behaved quite properly," she finally said, pulling herself together with obvious effort.

"On the contrary," he said, giving in to the smile, "you behaved most properly, I assure you."

He watched the color flood her cheeks and the animation return to her eyes at his provocation. She lifted her head to a haughty angle, but before saying anything, she regarded him quizzically.

"You're very good at that," she said quite calmly.

Surprised at her controlled response, he lifted an eyebrow in inquiry.

"Getting me angry as a distraction," she explained. "You've done it before to good effect, I believe."

He couldn't help himself—he started to laugh. "You've seen through me," he admitted.

"I don't see why that's so funny."

"It isn't." He took her arm and began walking toward the Women's Pavilion. He'd started this flirtation lightly, intending it to last no longer than the trip to Philadelphia, but somehow it had gotten out of hand. Bess never responded as he expected—and to be honest, neither did he. He'd thought he could turn his back on her once they arrived in the city. He'd been wrong. Now he had to make a choice, and so did she. It was only fair to put her on notice.

"You know," he confided, "if we aren't very careful, I might end up really liking you. And even worse, if you search your heart deeply, you might find you like me, too."

He could see her getting angry again, then thinking better of it.

"A true gentleman would apologize," she said instead.

"A true gentleman would not *have* to apologize," he corrected as he opened the door of the building and let them both inside. "Besides, why should I apologize when I wouldn't really mean it? Given the same circumstances, I'm afraid I would behave in exactly the same way, so consider yourself warned."

"Why, I never —," she started to say, but before she could finish he cut in with, "In any case, you'll have some time to decide what to do. I have to be out of the city for a few days."

He ushered her into Olivia Babcock's presence and wished her good day, then took off before she got her wits back. He'd given her enough to think about, one way or another. Now she needed some time so she could make her decision.

Devlin edged his way down the dark alley. At the sound of rolling pebbles, he halted and pressed himself against the side of the building, the bricks pressing into his back. He had the advantage of a cloudy night as he headed down Spruce Street near the docks. Crossing Front Street without the light of the moon and taking the steep drop down to Water Street suited his needs perfectly.

He didn't want anyone to know where he'd come from or that he knew his way around the better part of town.

Since returning to the heart of the city late in the afternoon, he couldn't shake the feeling that he was being followed. He'd not seen anyone unusual, but some sixth sense wouldn't allow him peace.

He glanced down the dark expanse behind him. A shutter creaked in the late night breeze, and a light flickered from a second story window, casting pale shadows on the opposite wall, but no one lurked behind him. Though the area seemed empty, he didn't feel alone. He'd do well to be careful. Very careful. This part of town had a violent feel to it, and a reputation to match.

As if to confirm his instincts, a door down the block flew open amid much shouting and cursing. Two men, fists flailing, tumbled down the steps leading from the establishment, bringing their brawl out into the middle of the street. The remaining patrons of the tavern followed them, pouring onto the sidewalks with raucous cries.

Dev folded himself into the shadows and watched.

"Kill 'im, Mick!" a voice shouted, and the cry was taken up by the others.

"He'll never get 'im. I've got my money on Bob."

"Yeah? How much?"

"A tenner."

"Too late, too late. Bob's got a knife. It ain't no fair fight now."

Dev sidled away, working his way down Water Street to the bar he wanted, carefully avoiding the myriad pitfalls lurking in the dark: wooden crates, stacks of lumber, basement doors sticking out at a slant into the sidewalk.

143

He'd come to the docks to meet a contact, someone who knew about the burglary ring using street urchins. The man was known to deal in stolen merchandise. Devlin's job was to locate him and offer his services, hopefully without arousing suspicion. It was the break Pinkerton's had been waiting for, the chance to infiltrate the organization with one of their own.

Dev pulled the bill of his coarse woolen cap lower to cover his face and eased himself down the stairs to the basement bar, ducking his head as he entered the low-cut door. Inside, it was dark and fetid, smelling of unwashed sailors and cheap beer.

The man Dev hunted was nowhere in sight though this tavern was his known hangout. It looked to be a long night. With one hand on the knife strapped to his belt, Dev made his way to the bar and ordered a drink. With any luck, Paddy O'Donnell would come by soon or send one of his flunkies to bring Dev to him.

Dev sat at a corner table, his back to the wall, and waited. The seconds stretched into minutes and the minutes into an hour and still not a soul entered the pub.

The texture of his cheap cotton shirt rubbed against Dev's skin, irritating him. He hadn't worn these clothes in over two months, not since the last time he'd been in this area. His stay had stretched into a month then. He'd make sure this didn't take as long.

For the first time in years he had something to go home to. Granted, it wasn't a tangible something, just a hint, a tantalizing whisper of possibility, and it had Bess Richmond's name on it. He thought of their last moments together. She hadn't been sure if she were coming or going—and all because of him.

He almost smiled, then berated himself for losing his concentration. Agents had lost their lives for such lapses. Before, he wouldn't have cared. Now, suddenly, it mattered. He didn't want to get careless when it counted.

Lately he'd found his taste for this job waning, the unrelenting demands on his time wearing, the constant danger draining. Had he been given a choice, he would have refused this assignment. Of course, the choice wasn't there, not when all the groundwork had been so carefully laid and he was this close to breaking the case. But things had definitely changed. He no longer had that unsettling disinterest in his future, the fatalistic acceptance of whatever fate held in store, be it life . . . or death.

The thought cheered him. He was like a bear coming out of hibernation after a long winter, ready to take up life again, eager for the joys of spring, of love, of new beginnings.

Lost in his thoughts, he didn't notice the newcomer to the pub until he was nearly past. A subtle tilt of the man's head indicated he wished Dev to follow. Dev surveyed the room as he slowly got to his feet, checking for signs of danger or threat. There was nothing specific other than the vague sense of menace familiar to all patrons of bars in this part of town. Anything could happen at any time, but nothing seemed deliberately planned at the moment.

Dev followed the man out the back, into a dark, private alleyway by the side of the building. The only light came from the windows of the tavern itself, filtered through glass so dirty it was nearly opaque. Dev kept his distance, stopping when the man in front of him stopped, waiting for him to make the next move.

Still, he was caught off guard when the man finally turned. Before he knew what was happening, Devlin felt the hot slice of a knife across his left arm. He ignored the pain as he pulled out his own knife, keep-

145

ing his eyes trained on his assailant. He didn't recognize the man but his intent was clear. He'd been sent to kill. Someone had breached Dev's cover.

The two men circled each other in the narrow alley. Neither wanted to make the first move. Devlin weighed the man's ability as they edged around each other. His arm was throbbing from the wound, and he held it pressed tightly to his side, keeping the man on his right, away from the injury. Devlin knew he would have little chance if he was charged on his bad side.

Just when Devlin made the decision to move in, a sound at the other end of the alley broke both men's concentration. It was all Dev needed. With a cry, he charged his assailant, knocking him flat to the ground. A couple of blows and the man was unconscious.

Dev made his escape before the other patrons of the bar got too curious and made their way to the alley. The only trace of his presence was a fine trail of drops which would have been bright red in the light of day. At night, they were too faint to see unless you knew where to look.

Seven

True to his word, Dev was gone from Bess's life. No one she talked with knew where he was or what he was doing. While she tried to keep her questions discreet, Alice had no such compunction. For the first time since this trip began Bess appreciated her friend's inquisitiveness though it, too, brought no results. Dev had disappeared without a trace.

Bess didn't know what to think, of him or herself. Her response to his touch had been so spontaneous, so unrestrained. Her lips tingled whenever she thought of him, and shivers would raise bumps on her skin as she remembered her wanton behavior. It was as if he held the key to the secret heart of her; he could unlock emotions even she was unaware existed.

Was she the reason he was gone so long? Perhaps he had found her response too forward. She wondered what his wife had been like . . . and how she compared, then put aside the thought as unworthy. She wished she knew more about men, but her father had been most reticent about discussing the intimate details of men and women. And her girlfriends were as ignorant as she, their speculations filled with giggles and rolled eyes but little real information. If only she had someone to confide in, someone who could give her motherly advice, but there was no one she dared ask.

She ached to see Dev, to know what he'd meant when he said he might end up really liking her. She was afraid she was already really liking him, probably too much considering she'd never felt the same heat or loss of control with Wylie — and she'd seriously thought of marrying him! But Dev was another story. Bess didn't know where she stood with him, and after her humiliation at Wylie's hands, she'd promised herself to be more careful. She had yet to decide if she would act flattered by Dev's attentions or furious at his boldness. All she knew was that she wanted him near.

As the Covington's expanded their social circle to include more and more of the well-to-do business community of Philadelphia, Bess was swept into a never ending round of social engagements. At first she went eagerly, thinking she might see Dev, or at least hear of him, since his family moved in these same circles. But her hopes were in vain. After a while the socializing became a drain.

Thoughts of Dev dominated her days, memories of his firm lips moving tantalizingly against her own, his hard, masculine body pressed to hers, his blazing eyes piercing her very soul. Her lips would tingle, and she'd blush at the oddest moments and lose her train of thought. It was a relief when Olivia sent word inviting her to visit the Women's League office in the city. At least now she'd have something to keep her from dwelling upon Dev all the time.

Filled with anticipation, Bess rode the few blocks to Broad Street the next morning. The driver let her off in front of a four-story brick building with signs set high on its walls proclaiming the tenants at each floor. Craning her head back so she could see up to the third, Bess made out the raised bronze letters of the League's name. As she headed for the front door, a soft whispering sound drew her attention. She stopped and cocked her head.

"Psst, lady. Come here a second," she heard coming from behind a wooden crate on the sidewalk.

When she realized it was the voice of a child, she cautiously approached the source of the sound, all her senses alert. She remembered all too well the dinner conversation about crime in the city. Though she had no wish to become another victim, there was something familiar about the voice that compelled her response.

"Who's there?" she demanded, stopping several feet from the edge of the crate.

A small head peeked around the slatted wood. "It's me. Danny Jenkins. Remember?"

Bess nodded, recognizing the young boy who had stolen her purse. "Do you need help?" she asked,

"Help?" he scoffed. "Me? Nah. I do just fine for myself. I just wanted to say hello since I reco'nized you from before."

He came around to the front of the crate though he kept his distance—like a half-tamed animal that had yet to learn how to trust. Bess noticed he wore the same clothes as the last time, though they were even more threadbare and torn. "What are you doing here?"

He looked warily over his shoulder. "I'm just looking around. Passing the time of day." He rocked back and forth on his heels. "Well, I guess I better get going now. Bye."

"Wait," Bess called out, but he was already halfway down the block. He stopped and looked back at her, his expression questioning. She ran toward him, heedless of propriety.

"I want to talk to you for just a minute. Please," she added breathlessly as he started to turn away.

He eyed her suspiciously. "Whatcha want?"

To help. See that building I was just going into? The Women's League meets there. They help children like you find homes. Why don't you come with me; they can help you, too."

"Why?"

"Why what?"

"Why will they help me?" he asked. "What do they want?"

He broke her heart. How could someone so young be so suspicious? What had his short life been like to make him like this?

"They just want to help. That's all," she said earnestly.

The boy gave her a pitying smile. "That's never all," he said and took off again.

Frustrated, Bess called out after him, "Please, Danny, wait," but this time he kept on going.

There had to be something she could do. The boy's plight fired a determination in Bess that sent her marching back to the building housing the League offices and up to the third floor.

Matilde Brown greeted her warmly when she knocked at the door. "It's so nice to see you again. How have you been?"

"Fine, thank you. Aunt Livvie suggested I come and see your offices. I hope I'm not in your way."

"Not at all. Let me just call your aunt."

Olivia Babcock soon appeared from a back room. She looked more fragile than when Bess had last seen her, but her embrace was as vigorous as ever.

"Bess, dear, how good to see you. I'm so happy you were able to come. What can I show you?"

"I'm interested in how you find the children the League helps. Do they come to you or do you go out and find them?"

Olivia regarded her thoughtfully, perhaps sensing

the change in her. "Come and sit," she said and gestured to a plush sofa. "I'll show you how we work."

She gathered some documents from a desk across the room then joined Bess.

"This is a picture of our first house," she said proudly. "Tabitha Grimes died and left it to us." She showed Bess a series of drawings as well as brochures describing the League's projects. "We use these when we solicit funds. They describe much of what we do."

Bess listened as the older woman began talking about the League's history. She had reason to be proud of what the League had accomplished, and at any other time Bess would have listened with interest, but now she wanted more specific information.

"But where do you get the children?" she asked again. She didn't want to appear rude, but just thinking of Danny and how she had failed him pushed her to probe more deeply.

"Different ways. The police know about us and frequently bring us young miscreants to care for. The local churches also help out. Sometimes the children just come in off the streets themselves. Word gets out. They know they can get a good meal, a warm bed. You seem to be troubled. Is it about the children?"

"I saw a boy today out on the street."

Olivia gave her an expectant look, encouraging her to tell more.

"I've seen him before," Bess confessed. "Today I tried to talk to him, but he didn't want to listen."

Olivia nodded her head. "It's terribly sad, I agree, but one of the things you quickly learn is that not all children can be helped. Some are too damaged by the streets to ever trust again."

"So what do you do?"

The older woman placed her hand over Bess's and squeezed gently. "We do the best we can and pray for the rest. Maybe your boy was on his way here when you saw him. Maybe he needs a little more time to make up his mind. You never can tell. Don't lose hope," she said, patting Bess's hand.

"I won't," Bess promised, but she knew she had to do more than just hope. "In the meantime, how can I help here?"

Olivia beamed at her. "Follow me," she said, and led Bess to a back office where she gave her over to Matilde with instructions on what needed to be accomplished that day. Matilde set her to work writing letters to convince potential donors to give to the League and thanking those who had already contributed. While they worked, they talked about the various children the League had helped.

"My biggest worry is that we lose so many of the children. The city is not the best place for them, not once they've lived on the streets," Matilde said, shaking her head sorrowfully.

"You mentioned sending the children West when we met at the Centennial Exhibition. What's happened to those plans?"

"Not much, I'm afraid," Matilde admitted. "We need to establish contacts with reputable people. We can't just send the children off to some unknown fate, you know."

"I have such contacts," Bess volunteered. "As I mentioned last time we met, my father is sheriff in a small town, and I have friends in Kansas City. We could put together a list of people who might help."

Matilde looked at her with dawning excitement. "Do you really think we can do it? It would take a lot of work, though. We'd need to set up a system—some way to get the children west and then to find them homes. And that wouldn't be the end of it, either. We'd have to be sure each child was well taken care of. Someone would need to be in charge out

152

there to keep an eye on everything."

"I know just the person to ask," Bess said, thinking immediately of Laura Christy, her former teacher. Laura's brother, Arthur, was influential in political circles, and the family was involved in many charitable causes. "I'll write to her immediately, and to my father, too."

"That would be wonderful. I can hardly wait to see what happens. This is so exciting. I've had this dream for a long time. Now you be sure to tell me if there's anything I can do, you hear?"

"Don't worry," Bess said with a laugh. "I'm sure there will be more than enough for all of us to do if this plan works."

Bess got out a clean piece of paper and gathered her thoughts. Then she started to write, explaining the children's plight in detail and the League's plans for helping them. When she was done, she ran to post the letters, as impatient as Matilde to get a response.

For the first time in her life she felt she had a direction outside of her own narrow interests. This work was important—meeting Danny had brought that home to her, making her aware of the plight of homeless children in a very personal way. And if she were very lucky, maybe she could help Danny, too. She hoped he would come back to the League offices, that his presence on the sidewalk outside meant he was looking for a different life. And when he came, she intended to have a different life available.

For the next two days Bess worked tirelessly. She was up early and at the League's offices before anyone else. She made lists, put together a new brochure to solicit funds for what she was coming to think of as "her" project, and helped out at the League office. At the same time, she kept an eye out for Danny, looking for him every chance she got—on the way to

153

the League offices in the morning, when she took the stroll Livvie and Matilde insisted upon each afternoon, and on her way back to the hotel at dusk. But there was no small, dark head to be seen.

She had just gotten back to her desk after another fruitless search when she heard the front door open. She ignored it, knowing that Aunt Livvie would greet the visitor and handle whoever had come to call. She heard the murmur of voices from the front parlor and noted that one of them was male, a most unusual occurrence but still not enough to draw her from her desk.

It wasn't until she heard that same male voice calling out for help that something struck her as familiar about it. But it was the urgency in the tone that sent her rushing toward her aunt's office, filled with foreboding.

"Aunt Livvie? Are you—Dev?" Her surprise over seeing Dev was quickly eclipsed when she saw he was leaning over Olivia, who lay prone on the settee.

"What happened to Aunt Livvie?" Bess asked with alarm. She dropped by her aunt's side and reached over to pick up her hand. It was flaccid and limp.

"Don't worry, Livvie. You're going to be fine," Dev was crooning reassuringly as if he hadn't heard Bess's questions.

He had propped the older woman's head up with a loose cushion and now placed the afghan over her.

Olivia tried to speak, but nothing recognizable came out. Fear and confusion showed in her eyes. A cold chill raced down Bess's spine, and she looked to Devlin for an explanation.

"I think it's apoplexy," he whispered. "Can you stay here with her while I send for the doctor?"

Bess tried to swallow past the sudden knot in her throat, but her mouth was too dry. Tears filled her eyes. Aunt Livvie was so spry and alert that Bess sometimes forgot just how old her relative was. How could she stand losing her when she'd only just found her?

Dev must have sensed her turmoil, and most likely shared it if the look in his eyes was anything to go by. His face appeared unusually pale, and Bess felt her own panic grow, but he laid a reassuring hand on her shoulder.

"Don't worry. I'll be as fast as I can," he promised.

When he left, Bess tried desperately to hide her terror and comfort her aunt. The minutes until Dev's return seemed endless. Bess looked up sharply when she heard his footsteps bounding up the stairs.

"How is she?" he asked as he came through the door.

"The same." Her voice quavered, and she forced a wan smile onto her face for Livvie's sake.

"The doctor will be here any minute," Dev told her. "How are you doing?"

Bess looked down at Livvie lying so still on the sofa, then helplessly back at Dev. He understood the unspoken message and knelt down beside her, taking her free hand in his.

"She'll be fine, Bess," he whispered. "She's a tough, strong lady, and she won't let this get her down. You'll see."

She wished she had half his confidence. Right now her fear was a bottomless pit, drawing her deeper and deeper. Only his hand holding hers kept her from falling over the edge and being consumed.

Livvie lay still beneath the afghan, her eyes closed, her hand trembling slightly in Bess's. Or maybe it was her own hand trembling. Bess couldn't tell.

A knock on the door was followed by the entrance of a portly, bald-headed man carrying a leather satchel.

"What are you doing here?" he growled at Dev as

he extricated Livvie's hand from Bess's and felt for her pulse. "I thought my instructions were clear."

"I'm fine," Dev responded just as firmly as he got to his feet. "See what you can do for Olivia."

"I plan to. But you go sit down. I won't have my good efforts go for naught because my patients are too stubborn to follow the simplest of instructions."

He glared at Dev, then gave his full attention to Olivia. "Well, now, Mrs. Babcock. What have you gone and done to yourself, hmm?" he asked in a surprisingly gentle voice. "If you'll excuse me, miss," he said to Bess as he helped her up then pulled over a chair. He eased his large bulk into it and added, "While I see to my new patient, why don't you take Mr. O'Connor to the kitchen and get some coffee? I'll call you when I need you."

Having dismissed them, he turned his full attention to Olivia. Bess gave him a worried look over her shoulder, unwilling to leave quite yet.

"Come on," Dev said right by her ear. "Let's go get that coffee ready. We're of no use here for the moment."

He put his arm around her shoulders and led her down a darkened hallway to the kitchen beyond. There he lighted the lamp and pulled out a chair and nodded toward it.

She collapsed onto the seat and watched absently while he stoked the fire in the old fashioned stove and set water to heat. All she could think of was Aunt Livvie lying so still in the front room. Then Devlin turned toward her, and she saw unfamiliar lines of strain on his face.

"Have you been unwell?" she asked, suddenly recalling the doctor's first words. The doctor had implied Dev was his patient, but at the time, Bess had been too overwrought to notice. Looking at Dev now, she remembered noticing his pallor and the fine sheen of perspiration on his forehead when she'd entered Olivia's office at his call. At the time she'd attributed it all to her aunt's condition. Now she realized there was more to it.

"It's nothing," he replied, but she sensed he was lying. He stood stiffly before her, one arm held tightly to his side. His jaw was clenched, the muscle in his cheek working. Bess suspected it was from pain as much as concern over her aunt.

"The doctor clearly thinks otherwise," she said.

"He just likes to worry. That's his job. How are you holding up? Can I get you something to eat?"

The change of subject was deliberate, and Bess was not in the mood to fight him. He appeared to know his way around this kitchen for he reached into a cabinet and pulled down a tin of cookies without having to search.

He placed the tin on the table then got a couple of small plates from another cabinet. She noticed he used only the one hand; his other arm remained awkwardly close to his body.

"Let me do this while you sit. It's obvious you've hurt your arm," she said, getting up to help him. She wanted to keep busy, and fussing over him would take her mind off what was happening in the other room.

"All right," he agreed readily. Too readily.

"How bad is it?" she ventured, noticing his wince as he sat.

He looked like he was preparing another lie, then he shrugged and said, "It's better now."

"But it was pretty bad?"

"Bad enough," he acknowledged.

She felt a welter of emotions: concern for his welfare, hurt that he had not informed her before, anger that he'd left so long without calling, surprise that he'd given her the truth now. It was too much for her

157

to sort out, especially coming on top of her anxiety for Livvie.

"Let me get you a drink," she said, turning from him and going to the stove where the water now boiled.

"I'm sorry," he said as if he sensed her turmoil and understood his part in it.

"It's all right," she said over her shoulder. But it wasn't. A wall had grown between them, a wall she didn't know how to scale. Too much had happened between them—and too little, as well. He was still a stranger to her even though he'd held her in his arms. She knew nothing of his past, of his hopes or his dreams. Part of it was her fault. She'd had ample time to learn about him on the train east, but she'd been too busy trying to avoid him, running away from the feelings that even then were burgeoning inside her.

Now she understood her mistake. They'd kept too much from one another and thus had no common ground. Wrapped in their own thoughts, they sat in silence on either side of the table and waited for the doctor to finish examining Livvie.

"We'd best get her home," Dr. Hiram said when he entered the kitchen. He poured himself a cup of coffee and stood by the stove to drink it. "She's resting quietly. I gave her a bit of laudanum. It won't cure her, but at least she'll get some rest."

"What's going to happen to her?" Bess asked.

Dr. Hiram gave a shrug. "It's hard to know in these cases. Sometimes a body recovers and goes on as if nothing ever happened. Other times . . ." His voice trailed off, his silence eloquent testimony to all that could go wrong. "She's a strong lady for her age. We can only hope for the best."

"When will we know for sure?" Bess pressed, her voice shaking.

158

"Be a few days yet. Right now she needs rest and familiar surroundings," the doctor replied.

It was not the answer Bess was looking for but probably all that could be expected at this time.

"I've had her carriage brought around," Dev said, rising. "Let me check if it's downstairs, and I'll take her home."

"Fine. I'll stop back at my office and meet you there."

Dev and the doctor left together, and Bess returned to her aunt's side. Asleep, Aunt Livvie looked almost the same as usual. Only the slight tugging at the side of her mouth revealed her condition. Bess sat in the chair the doctor had vacated and held Livvie's hand as she waited for Dev's return.

While Dev and the doctor moved Livvie to her carriage, Bess closed up the League offices. By the time she reached the street, Dev was sitting in the carriage with Livvie cradled tenderly on his lap.

"There's no room in here, I'm afraid," he said apologetically. "I've arranged for a cab for you. You can follow us to the house."

Bess nodded and climbed into the vehicle that stood in front of the carriage. It seemed to take forever for the small caravan to reach Rittenhouse Square. Once there, Bess was shunted aside as the rest of Livvie's family crowded around.

Half an hour later, Dev came into the front parlor where she was anxiously pacing, awaiting word on her aunt.

"How is she?" Bess asked the minute she saw him.

"As well as can be expected. There's not much more we can do. Dr. Hiram says the next few hours are critical. Once she's past this crisis, he'll be better able to evaluate her condition."

"Can I see her?"

"I'll take you up, if you like. But I'd better warn

159

you she's not alone. Her daughter's sitting with her now . . . and Catherine."

Bess bit her lip. How she wished she could be with her aunt, but that was not to be, at least not now. She wouldn't put it past Catherine to cause a scene if she appeared, and she doubted Catherine's mother would be any more welcoming. Olivia was the only one who recognized the familial bond, and she was in no position to assert her point of view. It would serve no purpose to upset the family.

"I guess I might as well go back to the hotel. Mrs. Covington will be wondering where I am."

"May I escort you?" he offered.

"Thank you. I'd appreciate it."

She had no desire to be alone with her fears for her aunt, not that Dev himself was immune. He looked tired and worn, though the vulnerability only added to his rakish good looks. He sent her an encouraging smile. "Don't worry, Bess. Olivia will be fine I just know it."

His confidence calmed her inside even though she knew he had no more basis for his statement than his instincts.

"I hope you're right," she whispered.

He ordered round Olivia's carriage and helped her into her wrap. His hands felt warm on her shoulders where they lingered a moment longer than strictly necessary. She leaned into his strength then pulled herself together as the butler announced the carriage was waiting.

The ride to the hotel passed quickly, leaving no time for conversation, not that Bess knew what to say.

"We need to talk," Dev said as they pulled up in front of the Continental Hotel. He placed his hand over hers.

She looked down at their entwined hands. She

wanted nothing more than to melt into his arms, to forget everything that had happened. She wished she could go back a week to when Aunt Livvie was well and Dev hadn't disappeared. Things had been complicated enough then; now they seemed overwhelming.

"This isn't a good time," she finally said, unsure of so much. She tried to free her hand from his.

"You're right," he said, allowing her to pull free. *"Now* isn't a good time, but soon. *Very soon."*

The words carried a conviction that made Bess's heart race. There was still a barrier between them, but maybe it wasn't as insurmountable as she feared. Time was what they needed — time together to share their dreams, to exchange the stories of their lives, to really get to know each other.

"Maybe tomorrow?" she suggested tentatively.

"I'd like that," he replied, his dark eyes warm on her, holding the promise of days to come.

Though Dev wanted nothing more than to be alone with Bess, he had little opportunity over the next couple of days. No matter where he looked there was a crisis waiting to be resolved — from dropping in on the Babcock family to see how Olivia was doing to meeting with his Pinkerton contact to conferring with his political allies.

At the same time, Bess was devoting herself to the Women's League, working long hours in their city office. Olivia's family had made it clear she was not welcome at the invalid's bedside, and Bess claimed being at the office made her feel close to her aunt. Dev couldn't fault her and took pains to pass messages between Bess and her aunt, knowing both women benefited from even a remote contact.

When Bess wasn't consumed by League business,

she had obligations to the Covingtons, who were still pursuing an avid social life and expected Bess to join them. Dev managed to get invited to some of the same affairs, but all too often Barrett was in attendance, and Dev could hardly get in a private word, let alone a dance, with her.

Memories of her innocent fervor haunted his dreams, and the scent of wildflowers evoked her presence when he was awake. She had thrown herself into the League's work with a dedication he could only admire and was turning out to be a far cry from the spoiled, willful society debutante he had first thought her. Dev was determined to make time for Bess, and he knew the perfect occasion: the torchlight parade on the eve of the Centennial. What better time to be by her side, sharing her wide-eyed wonder, her small-boned hand snuggled carefully in his own, her lovely lips smiling up at his face? Just thinking of it made his blood heat.

Fate, however, stepped in to thwart his plans. On the third of July, Dev was more alone than ever. The events of the day had surprised him, catching him so profoundly off guard that he had yet to recover. His political allies had turned on him, and in a way he would never have anticipated. At first he thought of staying home and avoiding the celebration entirely. Then his pride came to the fore.

He wouldn't let his erstwhile friends and current enemies shut him out so easily. While they might no longer support him for public office, he wouldn't let them dictate his actions. He set out on the crowded streets, wandering aimlessly, or so it seemed at first. Philadelphia was filled with people bent on inaugurating the nation's centennial birthday with a frenzy of celebration. Every hotel was full with out of town guests, and those who couldn't get a room encamped near the Exhibition grounds in Fairmount Park.

Flags and bunting adorned every building. Triumphal arches had even been set up on Chestnut Street.

Every hotel had at least one ball going on, or so it seemed to Dev as he made his way through the city. But as he walked, his path was no longer quite so aimless, for he found himself listening for mention of the Covington party, and soon his feet were taking him in their wake, following them from one ball to the next, always a step or two behind but slowly gaining on them — and Bess.

Everywhere he went he could feel the eyes of his former friends and colleagues. Some looked away when he returned their gaze; others smiled uncertainly. A few came up to him to say it made no difference — too few considering the number of friends he had thought he'd had in this town. Suddenly he needed to see Bess, to know if she, too, thought less of him or if she would brush aside society's prejudices as she had when offering young Danny her compassion.

Near the Centennial Exhibition grounds, Dev entered the ballroom of the newly built Globe Hotel, thinking he would at last catch up with Bess and the Covingtons. As he came up unnoticed behind two of his acquaintances, he overheard one say to the other, "Would you ever have imagined it?"

"Are you sure it's true?" the second one, James Gordon, asked.

"Of course I am. Roland Atherton told the nominating committee this afternoon, and I got it directly from Clarence Potts. He's on the committee, you know. Used to be one of O'Connor's greatest supporters. He was extremely disappointed, but what could he do?"

James Gordon shook his head. "I don't know, but it seems a shame. O'Connor never showed any signs of meager beginnings."

"Maybe not," his companion replied, "but it was merely a question of time. His true background would have come out at some point—the low-bred are different, after all. There's no disguising one's origins."

"You have a point there. Who knows what crisis might have provoked a lapse on his part."

"I'm just grateful that this entire fiasco occurred now rather than right before the election."

"That's certainly true," James replied. "I can't imagine what Devlin had in mind. If word had gotten out in the middle of the campaign that Patrick had picked him up off the streets, he would have lost the election for sure. At least now we have a fighting chance."

Gordon nodded his head. "That Roland Atherton will make an excellent candidate. I've no doubt about it. Why, one only has to listen to him speak for five minutes to know he's exactly the type of man we're looking for—one with the *right* background. Besides, O'Connor has always had a soft spot for the poor, though he disguises it often enough. Who knows what secret agenda he had in mind when he decided to run. Why, for all we know, he would have put *other* interests ahead of our own. He's one of *them,* after all, so his loyalty would have been misplaced."

The pair continued to talk about the election, but Dev had no stomach for more. James Gordon had been a schoolmate and known him well—well enough to have denied all that bunk about "breeding". Yet he'd quietly agreed when Dev's character was slandered. Like many others from the upper classes, James and his companion apparently believed that the poor deserved their fate and could not be redeemed. It didn't matter that Dev knew differently. Roland Atherton had worked quickly and lethally, striking where he'd known he would have the most

164

effect — Dev was persona non grata.

Dev made his way through the crowded ballroom, overhearing bits and snatches of other conversations, all of which confirmed how well Atherton had done his dirty work. There was no sign of Bess, and Dev decided that perhaps he should not meet her after all, at least not in public where his newly destroyed reputation might tarnish her. He left the ballroom from a side door.

As he crossed the wide veranda encircling the building, he saw the shrouded figure of a woman making her way out. She was dressed for the ball but had thrown a shawl over her head as if to hide her face. She stumbled as she stepped down onto the lawn that separated the hotel from Belmont Avenue and drew the shawl closer. Dev noticed her trembling hands even from the distance. He started toward her to see if she needed help and nearly collided with James Gordon.

"Dev!" the man said and had the grace to blush though he had not seen Dev behind him earlier. "What are — I mean, uh, I haven't seen you in a while. How are you?"

"Well enough, under the circumstances," Dev allowed, and James Gordon turned a deeper shade of red.

"Yes, well —" Gordon took in a lung full of air and glanced around, his expression both fearful and somewhat desperate, as if he was afraid of being seen with Dev and did not know quite how to go about leaving.

As Dev had no interest in prolonging the contact himself, he merely said, "If you'll excuse me," and hurried across the lawn, not waiting for the other man's response.

Outside, the woman who'd been fleeing the ball was gone. Dev looked around for her in the shadows, but his eyes had yet to adjust from the bright lights. Another carriage stopped in front of the hotel, and as he watched, Catherine Sinclair and her entourage descended from it. A couple of the young men in her party tottered as they walked, clearly in their cups from earlier balls they'd attended.

The Babcock carriage pulled away, and the attendant motioned to a hansom cab. The young woman in the shawl darted out from behind a bush and made for the cab. As she scurried past Catherine's group, head down, one of the inebriated young men bumped into her. Her shawl slipped off her head.

"Bess!" Dev exclaimed under his breath. Her face was tear-stained, and the bodice of her dress was torn at one shoulder. She held it in place with one hand while she clutched at the shawl with the other. Dev rushed to her side, pushing two of the men out of his way.

"My God, what happened?" he asked as he tried to shield her from view. When he put his arm around her, he could feel her whole body shaking. She shrank away from him, fear darkening her eyes.

"Who did this to you?" he demanded as fury surged inside him. If he could get his hands on the man who'd done this . . .

"Please, just let me go home," she pleaded and turned her head away, hiding her face.

"Was it Barrett?"

"Please," she implored, her voice breaking. "I just want to go."

Dev couldn't bear seeing her like this. He curbed his anger, knowing it would only upset her. "I'll get you home," he said in a gentler tone. He turned to check with the attendant just as Catherine Sinclair approached

"Well, well," she said, stopping to peer more

closely. "What have we here?"

"Nothing that need concern you," Dev said, stepping protectively in front of Bess.

"How can you say that?" Catherine countered, leaning around to see past him. "Isn't this my little *cousin* you're trying to hide so gallantly?"

"Catherine," Dev said warningly, but she only laughed.

"You're hardly in a position to threaten, Dev, even if only half of what I've heard today is true."

"I'm sure you've heard more than enough, some of which might actually contain a grain of truth. Nonetheless, as a close friend of your family, I'm asking that you not make a scene."

"Me? It would seem that the scene was already made—and by my fair *cousin*. You can't fault *me* for that. Besides, with the current scandal attached to your name, you'd do well not to lay claim to my family, other than my grandmother, that is. She's always had a soft spot for the lowly and downtrodden. She certainly took to little Bess, here, even threatened to change her will. Did you know that?"

"You'd hardly want for anything, Catherine, even if she were to change it."

"Maybe not—but don't you think your advice is a bit suspect? What if Patrick O'Connor were to change *his* will? Then what? You wouldn't be talking so glibly then." She turned to Bess, her face twisted in anger. "Is that what you're hoping for? To be like Dev here and have someone rich take you in?" she asked with a sneer in her voice. "Well, I've got news for you. I won't stand for it and neither will my mother. We'll fight you tooth and nail. Do you hear me?" She drew closer to Bess as she spoke and her voice rose, attracting the attention of the crowds passing along the street.

"I don't know what you're talking about," Bess said

in a bewildered voice. She clutched her shawl more tightly around her. Seeing the motion, Dev slipped off his jacket and placed it over her shoulders.

"I don't want any money," she continued. "I just want to go home."

"Good idea," Catherine replied. "All the way home—to Missouri—if you know what's good for you. Otherwise I'll tell my grandmother what happened here tonight."

"You don't know what happened," Dev objected, once again stepping between Catherine and Bess.

"Don't I?" she asked, malicious intent hardening her tone. "It seems clear enough. Her dress is ripped, and she's wearing a man's jacket. Yours. What do you think people will make of that? You can hardly deny that they're all too willing to think the worst, now can you? The low-bred lying with the under-bred. You make the perfect couple." The mocking laugh that escaped her lips was ugly.

Of its own volition Dev's hand came up as if to strike his viperish foe. A day's frustration and anguish raged through him, drawing bead on this shining example of the greed and coarseness of the so-called "high-bred" classes. It took all of Dev's control to refrain from bringing his hand down in the resounding slap she so richly deserved.

"If I were you'd I'd leave now," he got out from between clenched jaws, "or I won't be responsible for my actions."

Catherine stepped back, her face pale, as if even she realized she'd gone beyond the bounds of propriety. Not long ago she'd been assiduously courting his attention—back when he was considered a prime catch. If she was an example of what the higher classes were like, he'd made a lucky escape.

"You're right. It's time we made our appearance," she conceded, "but understand one thing. If *she* isn't out of Philadelphia within forty-eight hours, my grandmother will hear all about her wanton behavior tonight. And I don't think you'll be in any position to defend her, not after what everyone is saying about you. Is that clear?"

She turned on her heel and left without looking back. She didn't have to. Dev knew she would make good on her threat, especially now that a considerable fortune was apparently at stake. Dev suspected that Livvie wanted to return Victoria Hendrick's share of the family assets to its rightful place—to Victoria's daughter, Bess. Victoria's father had written his daughter out of his will when she'd gone off with Bert Richmond, but Dev knew Livvie had never felt comfortable receiving her brother's entire estate. She'd written to Bert Richmond offering him what should rightfully have come to his wife, but he'd wanted no part of it. Catherine had no such reluctance.

When Dev turned to look at Bess, he could see the devastating effect of Catherine's words. Her face was even paler than before, and her eyes looked huge and lost.

"Aunt Livvie will never want to see me again," she whispered.

"That's not true," Dev contradicted. "You know her better than that."

"Maybe if she was well," Bess agreed, "but right now she can't decide for herself. I doubt they'll give me a chance to explain my side."

"You can tell me, if you like."

She looked up at him, her eyes swimming in tears. "I—I can't. Please, I just want to go back to my hotel."

Dev saw the fear and desperation in her expression and yielded. He would find out what happened later, after he had her safely away from prying eyes and wagging tongues. He slipped the driver some change and helped Bess into the cab, then instructed the driver to go to the Continental Hotel. There they entered at a side entrance where Bess would be less likely to run into anyone. From the little she'd said en route, Dev concluded her escort had had too much to drink. The rest of her story was too incoherent to decipher.

Once they were in the front parlor of Bess's suite, Dev rang for some hot tea while Bess went and changed out of her tattered clothes. She came into the room a short while later dressed in a warm, fleecy robe that covered her from chin to toes. It's bright blue color should have been cheerful but served only to accentuate the pallor of her face and the bruised-looking circles under her eyes.

"Come sit. I've made you a cup of tea to warm your insides. It will make you feel better." He couldn't count how many times his mother had said those words to him growing up, and somehow she'd always been right. He hoped the home remedy would help Bess, too, and if the tea and sugar didn't help, perhaps the dollop of brandy he'd secretly added would.

"Here," he said and sat beside her on the small settee. He handed her the cup, then placed his hands around hers, warming them on the outside while the tea heated her palms. He could still feel her trembling and saw the occasional shiver shake her body. Gently he lifted the cup to her mouth and coaxed her to take a sip.

"Can you tell me what happened?" he asked a few minutes later when she seemed more calm.

Bess looked away from him and shook her head. "Not much. There was . . . a tussle, but I got away."

"You weren't hurt?"

"Not really. My dress was torn . . ." Her voice quavered and another shiver shook her.

170

"Finish up the tea. We can talk later." Dev could see she wasn't ready to think about her ordeal yet. Maybe in the morning.

"What am I going to do?" she asked when she finished the last of the tea. "Once Catherine talks, there's no telling what Aunt Livvie will think. And the Covingtons!"

"You mustn't worry about that now. They're your friends, and they'll think the same as I."

"But there's no telling what everyone else will think."

"You can't worry about that. The people who count will know you well enough to discern the truth."

She tipped her head back and looked at him. "Do you really think so?"

"I'm sure of it," he promised. He wished he could believe his own words. Two days ago, he would have said them in full faith. After the events of today he knew otherwise, but Bess was in no shape to hear the ugly truth.

"Actually, I'm feeling much better already," she said.

Mostly from the brandy, Dev thought, though he didn't say the words aloud. "Why don't you settle back and rest for a while. No matter what you say, you've had a very eventful night. And you'll want to be calm and collected when the Covingtons return."

Bess leaned back and closed her eyes. "You're right," she murmured sleepily. "I'll need all my wits about me when I see Alice in the morning."

Dev held her in the shelter of his arms, cradling her head in the hollow of his shoulder. She felt warm and soft and infinitely feminine. The room was quiet except for the gentle hissing of the gas lamp on the table nearby and the soft ticking of the clock on the mantel. Dev felt the tension slowly leave Bess's body

171

as she eased into sleep. He shifted position slightly, wanting to make her more comfortable, and her eyes fluttered open.

"You're not leaving, are you?"

Her voice was husky from sleep, and her expression was once again tense.

"Not yet," he said soothingly. "Just close your eyes and rest."

Reassured, she lay her head back on his chest and snuggled close. His arms closed around her again, cherishing her trust in him. There was nothing he wanted more than to stay here with her, but he knew he shouldn't linger. The Covingtons would be back around dawn when the parties petered out. By then, he'd best be gone.

But it wouldn't hurt to stay just a few more minutes, to gently run his fingers through her silken hair where it escaped from her elaborate coiffure, to feel the satin softness of her skin beneath his fingertips. He sighed and closed his eyes. Just another minute, and then he'd leave . . .

Eight

The heat was dark and enveloping, an all-encompassing warmth that surrounded her on every side. When she breathed, there was a weight pressing against her, but she felt no fear, only comfort and safety. She reached out her hands blindly, and the heat took form, warm and solid, strong and sheltering. She didn't question its source as she burrowed closer, wanting to lose herself, to escape the thoughts and nightmares that lurked just beneath her wakefulness, just beyond her dreams.

She nuzzled against the heat, feeling its textures, acknowledging its strength. It formed an impregnable barrier that shielded her from things she could not face. At least not yet.

She wanted to linger in the dark warmth, to revel in the security she felt there. When she breathed, the dark had a scent, enticing and alluring. She imagined wide open spaces, the freedom to fly and know she would be caught, the courage to dare and know she would not fail—not in his eyes.

The thought made her blink, and the dark disappeared, but the heat remained and took shape—a face lying close to hers, a lock of black-brown hair draping over the forehead. Eyelids edged by thick, dark lashes hiding eyes as black as midnight. A long narrow nose leading to a well-shaped mouth, the lower lip sensuously full even in sleep.

She lay sideways along the back of the settee, her body nestled against his, his arm thrown across her waist as he gathered her close, one bent knee resting on her legs. She would have felt trapped, except that this was Dev, Dev who had listened without judging, who had at every turn been helpful, who'd accepted her assertions of independence with equanimity, coming back to give her another chance when others might have spurned her for her clumsy rejections.

His tie had loosened as he slept and a shirt button had worked itself open. In the softly hissing light of the gas lamp on the table, she could see a tuft of tawny hair through the opening in his shirt. Her fingers itched to touch him. She reached out slowly, careful not to wake him, and slipped one finger inside his shirt. The hairs were springy, their texture so different from what she'd expected that she worked her hand in deeper so she could feel more.

One fingertip accidently brushed against his skin. It was warmer than a furnace, the source of his heat, and smooth as satin where no hair grew. The flesh beneath felt firm and muscled, a man's body, strong and powerful. She raised her head to gaze again at his face and found him watching her, his eyes gleaming with dark intent.

She gasped and tried to pull her errant hand back, but he clasped it with his own and pressed her palm to his chest. She could feel the thunderous beating of his heart and the way his chest moved as he breathed, deep laboring breaths that spoke of primal desire tautly held in check. A quickening of excitement laced with anticipation started low in her stomach and spread rapidly through her body.

The heat she'd felt before grew hotter and changed character. No longer dark and safe, it roared like a wildfire and beckoned like a burning flame, mesmerizing her. Her eyes widened as Dev shifted positions, tucking her under him so that she lay on her back while he loomed over her. Her hand now stayed on his chest of its own accord as he supported his weight with his arms, then lowered his head till his lips touched hers.

Her eyes drifted shut as a sudden languor overcame her. She wanted to lose herself in him, to give her femininity over to his care. When his tongue gently stroked her mouth, she opened hungrily, seeking to taste him as deeply as he tasted her, wanting to know everything there was about him. Feverishly she unfastened the remaining buttons of his shirt so her hands could have greater access. She then reached around his chest to run her hands up and down the valley of his spine, over muscle and sinew and slick, bare skin.

A low, guttural sound escaped from his throat as his entire body shuddered at her touch. He angled his head so he could take her mouth more deeply, drinking from her as if she were the source of all light and heat and life—as if he just couldn't get enough. His tongue swept her innermost recesses, probing in every corner, blending her taste with his until they were one. Like him, she wanted more, wanted the kiss to go on forever until she felt consumed by it. She responded eagerly, letting herself go, trusting her very essence to his protection as he guided her into new uncharted territory. Then slowly she felt him ease back, the pressure on her lips decreasing until he rested above her drawing in breaths as ragged as her own.

She opened her eyes with reluctance, leaving behind the passion-dazed world they'd created. The room was unchanged in every detail save one: *she* was no longer the same. Something profound had shifted focus inside her, opening her heart and her soul to new possibilities, to worlds she'd never dared imagine.

"We'd better stop while we can," he whispered as he stroked her hair back off her forehead. His fingers left ripples of awareness along her skin.

"No," she protested and reached around his neck to pull him down again.

He lowered his head at her tug and brought his lips to within a breath of hers. His tongue swept from one side to the other along her upper lip, then lingered on the return trip along the lower making her greedy for more. But when she would have opened her mouth in welcome, he again pulled away.

"You don't know what you're asking for, my sweet," he crooned, and she knew he was holding himself back only with the greatest of effort, for his arms were trembling as they supported his weight.

"But I want to know, Dev. I want you to show me."

His smile was bittersweet. "You say that now, but think what it would mean."

She shook her head, denying his objections. "I know exactly what it will mean—good memories to replace the bad, someone I can trust. Please, Dev." The last words were whispered as she raised her head, letting her tongue stroke his lips the way he'd done just minutes ago.

For a second she thought he would resist, but then, with a muffled groan, he took charge of the kiss, plunging them both back into a world of desire where passion ruled. With unsteady hands, he reached to the front of her robe, slowly undoing the buttons. As each one yielded, the sides of the robe inched apart, baring her to his gaze. She would have been embarrassed had she not seen the look of unadulterated admiration in his eyes.

"You're beautiful, so beautiful," he murmured and bent his head to nuzzle the newly bared flesh above her breasts. When she'd removed her dress to don the robe, she'd also taken off her voluminous petticoats, leaving only a thin, low-cut chemise over her corset. Now, as the two sides of her robe slipped away, they left her more naked than she'd ever been in a man's presence.

His lips felt hot against her skin, and as they worked their way down to the top of her corset, she felt the most indescribable sensations, not just where he touched her, but throughout her entire body. Her blood raced through her veins, and still she felt light-headed—more dizzy than she'd felt atop a steep bluff she'd once visited back home. Then, as now, she'd been filled with exhilaration, with the sense that the world was at her fingertips and all she had to do was reach out to grasp it.

But when she'd reached out before, there'd been nothing but air and dreams to fill her hands. This time there was Dev, solid and real, bigger and more masculine than her foolish girlhood dreams. A man who made her feel like a woman, ripe with secrets ready to unlock, filled with mysteries. A heady feeling of feminine power arose inside her as she tangled her fingers in his hair and held him to her breast.

His hand reached between them and pushed aside her chemise then tangled with the top fastening of her corset. She could feel the instant he released the spring clasp. Cool air rushed along her overheated skin, drying the sheen of perspiration that had formed. He moved again, and another clasp opened. When he reached into the opening, his fingertips were tantalizingly rough against her much smoother skin. She could feel her nipple pucker in anticipation of his touch the way it did when she was cold. Except she wasn't the least bit cold — just filled with wanting.

His finger grazed the tip of her breast, and a fierce yearning raced through her then settled deep in the heart of her most feminine part. The yearning ache consumed her, making her writhe beneath him. As if he understood her need, he worked one thigh between her legs and pressed it hard against her. At the same moment, he took her mouth. It was like drowning in a sea of passion, feeling the dark and the heat closing in on her, enveloping her entire being.

Never had she felt so much. Never had she been so aware of her body, of its pleasures and its almost-pains. She arched her back, pressing against him as she thrust her breast into his palm.

"Oh, God, Bess," he murmured. "Stop me now. Please!"

She heard the urgent plea in his voice. But she couldn't obey it. This was what they'd been made for. She'd never felt like this before, never looked at a man and saw the completion of herself the way she did with Dev. And in some primal, instinctive part of herself, she knew she would never feel like this about another. This was their moment, and she wanted to experience him in the most profound way she could.

"Don't stop," she pleaded. "Please."

Her words were his undoing, for his mouth found hers again, and his fingers quickly dispatched the remaining clasps of her corset. The restricting garment fell to the side to be replaced by the blanket of heat formed by Dev's body as his chest covered her. Her breasts swelled to meet him, responding to the delicate abrasion of his hair-roughened skin as he moved against her.

The pressure of his leg between hers grew, driving her deeper into passion's realm. She could feel the length of his arousal against her hip and for a moment felt panic. Bits and snatches of stories she'd heard made her stiffen in his embrace, stories of pain and lost virtue, of self-respect forever sacrificed to the demands of a moment. Fear fought with overwhelming desire, and she pushed him away with her hands at the same time that her lower body arched against him.

"Don't fret so, love," he murmured, sensing her wild confusion. "You're safe with me."

His words soothed even as their raw tone excited. He was as much a captive of desire as she, yet for her sake he was holding back. His hand stroked along her side, cupping her breast then sliding along her ribs to her waist. He shifted his weight more to the side, and his hand moved lower, touching her where he'd never touched before, at the indentation of her navel, the rounded curve of her stomach, the nest of curling hair where his leg was pressed against her.

Her pulse thundered in her ears, and a molten heat swept through her limbs to pool at her very center. When his hand moved lower, barely skimming the heart of her, she thought she would explode in a shower of heated sparks. She moaned, and he captured the sound with his mouth as he drove her higher. His fingers found the hidden treasure he sought, and as he rhythmically stroked her, the explosive waves she'd both feared and desired began to build in time with his movements.

She lost herself in the ebb and flow of sensation, in the pounding of her blood and the heated rapture of his touch. Her body became his, responding to his lightest caress, anticipating his every move, working

179

with him toward some unknown goal—unknown to her though she reached for it with every particle of her being, wanting, needing, longing for fulfillment.

And when it came, it was like the explosion of a volcano, lighting up the night sky in every direction, shattering the calm of everyday life and replacing it with a wondrous, heated conflagration. She was shaken to her very core by the forces pulsing through her and clung to Dev. He was both the source of her upheaval and her anchor in a world turned upside down.

His soft kisses gentled her, bringing her down from the pinnacle to the safety of his embrace. As she slid into sleep, some distant corner of her mind was aware that Dev was still aroused, that he'd given her the joy of consummation without taking it for himself. She stirred in protest, but he stilled her with a touch.

"Sleep, now, sweetheart," he whispered close to her ear. "Morning will bring another day. We'll talk then."

He held her close, and once again the heated dark enclosed her. She snuggled against him as he lay alongside her, his body a bulwark against the harsh events of the day. She lay her cheek against his chest and listened to the regular beat of his heart until it lulled her into a deep and dreamless sleep.

Her breathing became regular, and Dev knew she had fallen asleep. Her eyelashes lay like golden fans above her flushed cheeks, and her lips were still moist and swollen from his kisses. His pulse quickened as he watched her, and he ached to touch her again, to meld his mouth to hers and drink of her sweetness. His loins throbbed with unappeased desire, but he knew he would not take her, not tonight when she was so vulnerable. If he'd had more strength, he'd have avoided even touching her, but it would have taken a colder man than he to resist her tearful pleas and pull back from her loving embrace. At least he'd kept his wits about him and not taken full advantage of her.

Oh, she'd wanted him, he had no doubt of that. She'd responded with a sweetness and urgency he'd never known before, leaving him feeling full of confidence in his masculinity and her approval of it. Her wildflower scent permeated his skin in a heady mixture that filled his lungs with every breath and made him question his restraint. But how would she feel at morning's light? Would she look back on this interlude with loving pride or shame?

He feared the latter and wondered if her response was as much a reaction to the evening's nasty turn as to him as a man. Only time would tell, and he would give her that time if it killed him. Which it just might, he thought as he gingerly swung his legs off the settee and came to his feet.

He looked down on her sleeping form, her breasts luminescent in the filtered gaslight, their proud pink tips pouting at him as if begging for his caress. A tidal wave of desire surged through him, and he had to turn away, afraid he would succumb to the overwhelming need to once again hold her in his arms. Quickly he buttoned his shirt and tucked it back into his pants, hoping that bringing order to his appearance would quell the throbbing urgency between his legs.

He did up his collar and tie and donned his jacket. He turned back to the settee and caught sight of himself in the cheval mirror standing in the corner. The vision did little to calm him for he saw Bess's mark on his every feature—in the dark, heated wanting in his eyes, in the finger-combed disarray of his hair, in the deep red flush on his cheeks, and most of all in the sensual curve of his lips, lips as swollen as hers. He brushed his hair back with one hand and turned to look at the mantel clock. Nearly two in the morning. Not much time to get away before the Covingtons found him and felt he'd compromised Bess.

He went to the bedroom and pulled back the covers, then returned to the sitting room. Kneeling beside the settee, he eased his arms under Bess, and stood. She curled into him as he lifted her, her head finding its home on his shoulder, her lips against the bare skin of his neck. He could feel the soft warm puffs of air when she breathed, and the scent of wildflowers engulfed him.

He carried her to her bed and gently laid her down. He arranged her robe around her, fastening each button with fingers that trembled even more than when he'd opened them. Oh, how he longed to climb into the bed with her! To feel her close around him. Instead, he pulled the cover up to her chin and strode from the room, breathing hard.

He stood by the open window and looked down on the street. In the distance he heard musicians and singers still rejoicing noisily now that the Fourth had finally arrived. An occasional firearm discharged in celebration, joining the sound of steam whistles and bells. The jumble of bodies in the streets, the crowds at the balls, the air of festive merriment all seemed so remote. He wished he and Bess could have stayed cocooned here forever, just the two of them in a world of their own, far from the strife and petty jealousies of politics and family ties, the greed and ambition of friend and foe.

But that was not to be, he knew. The outside world would crash in on them soon, as soon as the Covingtons returned to the hotel. If they'd heard any of the rumors circulating about him, they would not be pleased to see him even if he had not spent this time alone with Bess. They were much too conscious of social standing and position to pursue their acquaintance now that his reputation was tarnished.

And Catherine would waste no time making her influence felt as well. Dev turned away from the window. It was time for him to leave. There was much he had to do—foremost of which was finding a way to stop Catherine. He'd have to handle the Covingtons later, for whether they liked it or not, he had no intention of disappearing from Bess's life.

He straightened out the cushions on the settee, resisting the urge to linger, and collected Bess's belongings, taking them into the bedroom. He didn't want to leave without a word and debated whether to write her a note or wake her, when her eyes fluttered open at his entrance.

He sat on the edge of the bed and took her hand in his.

"I have to go now, Bess," he said as his fingers drew an aimless pattern on her palm, relishing the feel of her smooth skin. "The Covingtons will be here soon. I'll call on you tomorrow as soon as I can. Go back to sleep and don't worry overmuch. Things will work out."

Unable to resist, he leaned over and dropped a kiss on her forehead. She smiled sleepily at him and tucked his hand under her cheek as her eyes closed again.

He waited until he knew she was asleep, then gently extricated his hand, and with one last look, let himself out of her room.

* * *

When Bess awoke, she was alone. The sky was just turning light, and she wasn't sure what had prompted her to open her eyes. Then she heard the knock at the door. Where was Dev? Had last night been a dream? She threw off the covers and found she had slept in her robe. She jumped from bed and ran into the sitting room. Everything was tidy, not a thing out of place. How strange! She put her hand to her mouth. Her lips felt tender.

She stopped in front of the cheval mirror in the corner and found her skin was pink and flushed. A closer examination showed it was slightly abraded. Last night had not been a dream. Dev had really been there, had really held her in his arms and kissed her mindless, the rasp of his evening beard leaving its mark.

The knock on the door sounded again, more demandingly.

"Bess, are you in there?" a frantic Alice called and immediately fell to banging on the door again.

"I'm coming, I'm coming," Bess called back and ran around the settee without looking at it, afraid it would make her blush—and then what would she tell Alice?

"Oh, thank goodness. You're here!" Alice exclaimed.

"What did you expect?"

"I didn't know. We were so sure you were with Barrett last night that no one thought anything of it when you both disappeared. Then later we saw Barrett alone, and he didn't know where you were. I can't tell you how frightened we were."

Bess clenched her jaw. The less said about Barrett the better. In fact, the less she said about last night altogether, the happier Alice would be. Anything Bess could say would end up hurting her dear friend one

184

way or another.

"I'm sorry to have frightened you," Bess said. "I should have tried to find you and tell you I came back here. I'm afraid the evening was just too . . ."

"Overwhelming," Alice supplied, nodding her head. "I know just what you mean. I had such a wonderful time I just didn't think how tired I was getting. You probably did the right thing. I'm afraid I'll just be exhausted all day today."

At that moment Mrs. Covington came bustling down the hall. "Alice, there you are, and Bess, too. Now, girls, this is no time for chattering. Today will be a big day. The parade has been rescheduled for early this morning because of the heat so you don't have much time to catch your beauty rest. And then we'll have to find our seats at Independence Square. Edward managed to secure tickets. Now don't dawdle, Alice."

"All right, Mama, I'll be along in a minute."

"See that you are. And let Bess rest. At least she had the good sense to come back at a reasonable time." Mrs. Covington continued on to her room, then stopped at her door and looked back at them. "I won't sleep a wink until I hear your door close and know you're in bed, Alice, so don't keep me waiting."

"Yes'm," her daughter dutifully replied, though she rolled her eyes at Bess. "I guess I'd better go or she won't let me see the parade. It feels like it's going to be even hotter today than yesterday, so be sure to dress in something light. I'll come see you before we go down. I can't wait to hear what happened and tell you everything I did, too."

Alice leaned into the doorway to give Bess a quick hug, then she ran down the hall to her own little suite, connected by an inner door to that of her parent's on one side and Bess's on the other.

185

"See you later," she trilled, her face alight with excitement. Then she entered the room and shut the door behind her.

Bess shut her door, too. She'd had a lucky escape. Alice had been so full of her own adventures, she hadn't stopped to think what might have caused Bess to come home early. Now Bess had to think of a story — and quickly. She knew that the moment Alice awoke, she would come back to Bess's room with her questions. But what could Bess say? She knew she was being a coward, but she wished she didn't have to face Alice so soon.

Inside the sitting room, Bess plopped onto the settee. She closed eyes and imagined she could still detect Dev's scent on the cushions, still feel his hands gripping her shoulders, still taste his lips as they nibbled hungrily on hers. She should be feeling ashamed and hiding in the closet. That's what a normal young lady would do, or so she'd been told often enough. Only she felt neither shame nor embarrassment; she felt exhilaration and anticipation as if she were poised on the brink of discovery.

And, oh, what she had started to discover! Every touch, every word, every feeling from last night rebounded in her mind, and in the center of it all was Dev. He was the one who'd brought her to such awareness, who'd taught her what pleasure two people could create together. She'd never imagined anything quite so wonderful — and all because of him. She wanted to shout her happiness to the world.

She sat daydreaming a while longer, lost in memories of a pleasure so strong she only believed it possible because she'd experienced it herself. But gradually other memories crowded in, memories less pleasant, memories more menacing. Memories of Catherine and the hatred in her eyes. Memories of

186

what had happened earlier. She had made two enemies last night, enemies she had never wanted, but
enemies nonetheless.

One way or another, she threatened them both.
Catherine because of some unknown—and un-
needed—inheritance, the other because of his ambition. All Bess had ever wanted was to know her
mother's family and have them recognize her existence, to learn about her background and heritage.
She neither wanted nor needed their wealth, no matter what her cousin or her well-meaning great aunt
thought. Yet now she was at odds with them,
through no fault of her own.

The man, too, had misunderstood her motives,
taking advantage of her good manners and closeness
to Alice to impose himself on her. But when she
hadn't responded as he'd wished, he'd become nasty,
frightening her. She'd barely made her escape, and
now she would have to face him again, thanks to her
connection with the Covingtons. Though her reputation would be tarnished if word got out, so would
his. In business circles that would leave him suspect,
perhaps not so much because of his actions, but for
being indiscreet enough to get caught.

Of course, if Catherine spread her venom about
Bess and Dev, both of Bess's enemies would come out
victorious. The irony of it all was that Catherine
wouldn't even realize that Bess and Dev had indeed
been intimate with each other, wonderfully, blissfully
intimate—but not until *after* Catherine had seen
them.

What a mess! Alice and her parents would assur-
edly be hurt, and Bess shuddered to think how Aunt
Livvie would react.

Bess spent the next couple of hours anxiously pacing her room, trying to discover a way out of the

morass she found herself in, to no avail. Her greatest fear was that what had happened would reflect badly on Dev, and that would be something she couldn't bear. Though he hadn't declared his feelings in words, Bess remembered the fevered look in his eyes, the intense emotions that engulfed them both. In her heart of hearts she felt they had communicated without words. And even if they hadn't observed the proprieties to the letter, Bess had no regrets.

She only wished Dev would return. She had the haziest memories of their parting, but she was sure he had said he would call on her as soon as possible. Where could he be? She needed him by her side when she faced the Covingtons; even more so when she had to deal with Catherine and her innuendos. Why didn't he come back?

She checked the clock on the mantel. The morning was getting on. Soon she would have to join the Covingtons for breakfast, and once they all left the hotel to see the parade, Dev would never be able to find them.

As she was making the fourteenth circuit of the parlor, having taken time out only to dress and complete her toilette, a knock sounded on the door. Hoping it was Dev, but fearing it might be Alice, Bess ran to the door, then hesitated. She had yet to decide what she was going to tell her inquisitive friend. Taking a deep breath, she said a heartfelt prayer that the right words would come and flung open the door.

To her surprise, neither Dev nor Alice stood there. Instead, she saw a bellman holding an envelope in his hand.

"Good morning, miss. This just came for you." He smiled and held out the letter.

For a moment, Bess was afraid to take it. She was expecting no missives. What could this mean? Had

Dev had second thoughts? Had he come to the conclusion that a real lady would never have acted as wantonly as she had and decided not to see her again?

Filled with trepidation, Bess took the note from the bellman and pulled a coin from her reticule lying on the table by the door. She closed the door and leaned back against it, her knees suddenly weak.

She eyed the spot where so recently she and Dev had lain entwined, and memories coursed over her. She lifted a trembling hand to her lips then made her way to a nearby chair. Now was not the time to relive what had happened last night. There would be plenty of time for regrets later, if need be.

She stared at the envelope in her hand. It felt stiff and foreign, filled with portent. She ran her fingers across its back, dreading the thought of what might be inside. Slowly she pulled the letter from its pocket and unfolded the paper.

She immediately recognized the familiar letterhead. The note had come from the League office, not from Dev at all. She breathed a sigh of relief. How silly to think that Dev would have left a note for her downstairs. He would never have been so open about what they had shared, nor drawn attention to the fact that he'd left at such an unseemly hour. Bess didn't know what could have gotten into her.

In her relief that the note wasn't from Dev, Bess didn't immediately grasp the meaning of the words written so elegantly on the page. Then the name *Danny* caught her eye, and she made herself concentrate.

What she had hoped for had finally happened. Danny had come to the League offices this morning looking for her. The watchman had notified Matilde who was in charge during Livvie's absence, and she'd rushed down to the office. The boy stubbornly insisted that he would talk with no one but Bess. Matilde wrote that she hated to spoil Bess's holiday, but could she come to the office immediately?

Before Bess finished reading the letter she knew she would do whatever she could for the small, determined young boy. She sat down and quickly wrote a note to Mrs. Covington giving a rather vague explanation involving the League and Aunt Livvie. She knew the woman would probably be furious with her—it was one thing to disappear while supposedly being looked after by her son and quite another to go off on her own and miss the day's activities. She only hoped that mentioning the esteemed Babcock name would have its usual calming effect.

Secretly Bess was also relieved to have an excuse not to face Alice and her mother at least for a while longer. With a little more time she would be able to think of a good excuse for last night, an excuse that wouldn't hurt Alice as much as the truth. After slipping the note under Mrs. Covington's door, Bess gathered her things and went down the elevator.

Nine

Bess found the streets unbelievably crowded and noisy when she left the hotel. In the distance she heard the thunderous roar of cannon being fired to herald the new day. Church bells rang in the holiday, and people were already lining up along the parade route. The troops that had gathered for the parade were scheduled to come right down Chestnut Street, past the front of the Continental Hotel on their way to Independence Square. As a result, the road had been cleared of all traffic, and Bess nearly despaired of finding a hansom cab. She hurried down Ninth Street toward Market, hoping she would find a conveyance there. If not, she would have to walk, making her way through the gathering throngs.

The day was already hot and humid, one of the worst since she'd arrived in the city, and Bess did not relish the idea of going on foot all the way to the League offices. To her immense relief, a family was just disembarking from a cab as she came up. The driver was happy to take her in the opposite direction, since most of his fares this morning had been only toward the center of town.

The ride took longer than usual, but within the half hour, Bess had arrived at the League offices.

Matilde was waiting for her at the top of the stairs, just outside the League's rooms.

"I'm sorry you were called away from the celebrations," Bess said as she deposited her parasol in the stand by the stairs.

"I'm just glad the watchman had the sense to fetch me. When I got here and took one look at those children, how could I refuse them?"

"Them?"

"Oh, yes, didn't I mention it? Your Danny was the spokesman, but he brought along some friends as well. I put them in the kitchen. They looked so thin and hungry."

Bess thanked the older woman as they headed into the office suite. The front room was empty, but from the kitchen came the sound of whispers.

"I have some correspondence I can work on in case you need me," Matilde said and went into the back office. "It's simply too hot for me to be outside, even for this parade."

Bess wasn't sure Matilde was being totally honest about the parade, but she was grateful for the other woman's presence. Matilde knew all the ins and outs of the League's operations and, in the absence of Livvie, was the one person whose help Bess could truly count on.

Bess tiptoed to the kitchen door, wanting to catch a glimpse of what was in store before the children saw her. She found Danny standing near the table and two other small children huddled together on a chair, munching on the remains of a sandwich Matilde must have made for them.

"Hello, Danny," Bess said in as calm a voice as she could muster. She didn't want him to think she was nervous or unsure.

"Ma'am," he said, turning his head to look at her.

Now you can get Heartfire Romances
right at home and save!

GET ❤ 4 FREE
HEARTFIRE NOVELS
A $17.00 VALUE!

Home Subscription Members can enjoy
Heartfire Romances and Save $$$$$
each month.

ENJOY ALL THE PASSION AND ROMANCE OF...

Heartfire

ROMANCES from ZEBRA

After you have read HEART-FIRE ROMANCES, we're sure you'll agree that HEARTFIRE sets new standards of excellence for historical romantic fiction. Each Zebra HEARTFIRE novel is the ultimate blend of intimate romance and grand adventure and each takes place in the kinds of historical settings you want most...the American Revolution, the Old West, Civil War and more.

SUBSCRIBERS $AVE, $AVE, $AVE!!!

As a HEARTFIRE Home Subscriber, you'll save with your HEARTFIRE Subscription. You'll receive 4 brand new Heartfire Romances to preview Free for 10 days each month. If you decide to keep them you'll pay only $3.50 each; a total of $14.00 and you'll save $3.00 each month off the cover price.

Plus, we'll send you these novels as soon as they are published each month. There is never any shipping, handling or other hidden charges; home delivery is always FREE! And there is no obligation to buy even a single book. You may return any of the books within 10 days for full credit and you can cancel your subscription at any time. No questions asked.

Zebra's HEARTFIRE ROMANCES Are The Ultimate
In Historical Romantic Fiction.
Start Enjoying Romance As You Have Never Enjoyed It Before...
With 4 FREE Books From HEARTFIRE

TO GET YOUR
4 FREE BOOKS
MAIL THE COUPON BELOW.

Heartfire Romance

FREE BOOK CERTIFICATE

GET 4 FREE BOOKS

Yes! I want to subscribe to Zebra's HEARTFIRE HOME SUBSCRIPTION SERVICE. Please send me my 4 FREE books. Then each month I'll receive the four newest Heartfire Romances as soon as they are published to preview Free for ten days. If I decide to keep them I'll pay the special discounted price of just $3.50 each; a total of $14.00. This is a savings of $3.00 off the regular publishers price. There are no shipping, handling or other hidden charges. There is no minimum number of books to buy and I may cancel this subscription at any time. In any case the 4 FREE Books are mine to keep regardless.

NAME

ADDRESS

CITY   STATE   ZIP

TELEPHONE

SIGNATURE   ZH0793

(If under 18 parent or guardian must sign)
Terms and prices subject to change.
Orders subject to acceptance.

GET 4 FREE BOOKS

HEARTFIRE HOME SUBSCRIPTION
SERVICE
120 BRIGHTON ROAD
P.O. BOX 5214
CLIFTON, NEW JERSEY 07015

He looked scared but was putting on a brave face. "Sorry about gettin' you out on a holiday and all. Miz Matilde said I should tell you that, though I don't know all that much about this holiday."

"Philadelphia's celebrating the 100th anniversary of the signing of the Declaration of Independence," Bess explained, latching onto the neutral topic with relief. It would give them both a chance to get comfortable with each other. "The city decided to put on a celebration worthy of such a milestone and asked all the countries in the world to participate. That's the reason for everything going on out at Fairmount Park with the exhibition as well as here in town."

Danny tilted his head toward the children on the chair. "I don't let them go out to the Park."

For the first time, Bess really looked at the two sitting so quietly together, their eyes looking large in their small, thin faces, their expressions too knowing and suspicious for such young girls. They looked to be no more than four or five years old, certainly no older than Danny himself, whom she thought was seven or so. Her heart contracted with pity and anger, the anger directed at a society that could let such young innocents slip through its fingers like this.

"Why don't you introduce us, Danny," she suggested.

"What? Oh, sure. That there's Rosie and the little one's Polly. They're Nola's sisters. Nola and I decided they were too young for the park so's we do their share of the work."

Their share of the work! Bess shuddered to think what he meant, but now was not the time to pursue it.

"I'm pleased to meet you," she said to the two girls as they scrambled to their feet and gave her clumsy little curtsies. She smiled at them, and they smiled back.

"Will you take care of us like Danny said?" Rosie asked, her blue eyes wide and pleading. There was a smudge of dirt on her left cheek, and her clothes looked as though she'd slept in them for the last month.

"Of course I'll take care of you," Bess told the girl though she really had no idea what she could do. She saw Danny visibly relax and knew she had at least said the right thing. "Why don't we have some cakes while you tell me about yourselves. Would you like that?"

Danny and the girls nodded. Bess was sure they didn't get this kind of treat often, and Rosie's next words confirmed it.

"Ummm, good—specially if you have cakes with lots of pink on 'em," Rosie said, then added with a serious expression on her face, "That's Polly's favorite kind."

Bess knew in an instant that pink icing was *Rosie's* favorite kind, but she smiled indulgently. "Then I hope we have some of *Polly's* favorite. Let me check and see."

It didn't take long for Bess to find a tin of little cakes, and though they didn't have pink icing, they did have yellow. Neither Rosie nor Polly seemed to mind the different color.

After they'd each eaten two cakes with evident delight, Danny haltingly began to tell Bess about their lives. "We live with Harley. He and his wife takes care of us most of the time."

"Yeah, and you and Nola, too, right, Danny?" Rosie piped up in between licking off the last bit of icing from her fingers. "Nola says we're a little family."

"Don't be daft, Rose. We're not a family. You need a mother and father for that, and a nice house. I

194

remember . . ." Danny's voice became wistful before he was interrupted.

"But we're almost a family," Rosie insisted.

Bess watched Danny shrug his shoulders. He sent Bess a look that said he wouldn't argue any further because he had to let the little one have her fantasy, not because he agreed with her.

"Neither you nor Nola have any parents?" Bess asked Danny.

"Nope."

"And not Jesse, Victor, Raymond, Samuel, Max, or Lester, either," Rosie added.

"Jesse, Victor, Max . . . Who are they?" Bess wasn't sure she was ready for the answer to that question.

"The other children that live with us — at Harley and Bertha's."

Almost ten children all told! Whatever could she do with *ten* homeless children? Lost in her thoughts, Bess felt a tug on her sleeve. She looked down and found Polly standing by her side. She shared her older sister's blue eyes, but where Rosie's hair was bright red, Polly's was a softer, paler shade.

"Are you going to be our mother now?" the little girl asked.

Her question went straight to Bess's heart, firing her determination.

"I don't know that I can," she replied. "But I promise you I'll find someone who will want to be your mother as much as you want one. Now you three just wait here for a few minutes while I go talk to Mrs. Brown. You can each have another cake while you wait."

Their eyes lit up as Danny opened the tin and let each girl pick out the cake she wanted. Bess slipped out of the kitchen and went to find Matilde, hoping the older woman would have some advice on what to do.

As she neared the rear office, she heard Matilde speaking.

"I really don't think she has any personal papers here, dear, though you're welcome to look. I'll just go into the kitchen and check on how Bess is doing."

"Bess? She's here?" Catherine's all too familiar voice sounded in response. "Whatever for? How dare she come snooping to my grandmother's office!"

"Snooping? But what are you talking about?" Matilde replied, sounding perplexed. "Are you sure everything's all right with your grandmother? Perhaps the strain . . ."

Her voice trailed off as Bess entered the room. Matilde glanced worriedly from Catherine to Bess. She lifted one brow, as if to ask, "Do you know what's going on?"

Bess shrugged. "Is there a problem?" she asked, not knowing quite how to handle the situation. The last thing she needed now was another confrontation with Catherine, but she couldn't very well hide.

Catherine looked up from her rummaging through the upper cabinet of Livvie's large secretary.

"What did you do with it?" she demanded, her jaw set at a determined angle, her eyes glowing with an unnatural light.

"With what?" Bess asked.

Catherine took a step forward. "You know very well what. Don't try to pretend with me."

Matilde edged toward the door. "I'd better go check on the children," she murmured, then hastened out of the room, clearly not wanting to witness any dispute.

Catherine ignored the woman's departure. "Well?" she said. "Are you going to tell me where it is or do I have to find it for myself?"

"I don't know what you're talking about."

"All right, let's say you don't, not that I believe it for a second. I'll find it by myself."

She turned back to the secretary and slammed the cupboard doors shut. Then she lowered the slant-front desk and began pulling out the little drawers behind it, checking their contents quickly before shoving them closed and going on to the next.

"Perhaps if you told me what you're looking for, I could help," Bess offered, wanting only to get the woman out of the League offices as quickly as possible. "What does Aunt Livvie need?"

"*Aunt Livvie!* She's *my* grandmother, and if you think I'm going to let you poison her mind against me, you're crazier than she is. Now where did you put that will? I don't have all day. The parade will be starting any moment."

"I've never seen her will, nor do I want to. I'm sure you're getting upset for no reason."

"No reason?" Catherine's cheeks flushed dark red with anger as she turned on Bess. "You would say that. You think you're so smart, but you're nothing but an upstart, ingratiating your way into my grandmother's life, pretending to care for her stupid charities. You may have fooled her, but you don't fool me. Now where is that will? Give it over or I'll make good on my promise last night. You think Devlin O'Connor can take another scandal? Well, you're wrong. His reputation is in shreds enough without you adding to it."

"What do you mean? What happened to Dev?"

"*Dev,* is it? Well, your precious Dev is no more Patrick O'Connor's son than I am. Turns out Mr. O'Connor picked him up off the streets because he couldn't have any children of his own. Now what do you think of *that?*"

197

Her eyes glittered maliciously, as if what she'd said would forever tarnish Dev. And in Catherine's eyes, it probably did.

"Why should I believe you?" Bess challenged.

"Don't, for all I care. But when I'm through with him, he won't even be received at the back doors of the fashionable houses in Philadelphia, let alone the front. People are all too willing to believe the worst of him now." Her expression took on a sly calculating look.

With her words, Bess's heart sank. She could never risk hurting Dev, or her Aunt Livvie for that matter, and with this feud brewing between her and Catherine, someone was bound to be hurt.

"What do you want?" she asked dully.

Catherine's tight-lipped smile was smug with victory. "I told you yesterday. I want you gone from here, the sooner the better. And I want my grandmother's new will."

"Whatever use will it be to you?" Bess asked.

"Don't you worry about that. Just give it to me." She opened a last drawer and peered inside, then frowned. "It isn't here, damnit."

Bess's eyes opened wide at the swear word. Catherine was truly desperate if she'd forgotten herself so far as to curse. Bess had no doubt now of the other's intent. If she could harm Bess in any way, including destroying Dev, she would do it. She was that desperate and out of control.

"I can't help you with the will, assuming there even is one," Bess said, taking the only course she now saw open to her, "but I was planning to go home soon in any case. Just leave Dev out of it."

Catherine's eyes glittered again. "How soon?"

"As soon as I can make arrangements. Will that do?"

"Yes, as long as it doesn't take too long." She picked up her reticule from the chair by the desk and swept her gaze once more around the room. "Oh, and if you do happen to find Grandmother Babcock's latest will, do let me know, won't you?"

Bess hung onto her composure by sheer strength of will as Catherine swept out the door. Never had she felt so threatened, not only for herself but for those she loved. She now realized that she truly loved Dev, loved him so much she would make any sacrifice to protect him. And thanks to Catherine, she would be making the greatest sacrifice of all—never seeing him again.

"Is everything all right? The children are getting restless." Matilde's question penetrated Bess's torpor, reminding her there was more to the world than just her loss, just her misfortune. "She's gone now, isn't she?" Matilde added.

"Catherine?"

Matilde nodded and peered cautiously into the room. "I thought I heard the outside door slam."

"Yes. She left."

Matilde came more fully into the room. "Did she get what she wanted, then?"

"In a manner of speaking," Bess murmured. Matilde's expression showed confusion, but Bess had no desire to explain. "We'd best figure out what to do with the children," she said before Matilde could question her further. "Did Danny tell you there are ten of them, all told?"

"Oh, my goodness. Ten?"

"Give or take one, that's what it sounded like to me."

"What shall we do with them all? I don't know if we can find places for so many on such short notice, especially with this centennial celebration. Almost everyone is busy with visiting family and friends. Why, we were even thinking of closing down the office for the whole week."

Bess felt as if the weight of the world was on her shoulders. She couldn't let these children down, not after the courage they had shown in coming here today, even if it wasn't the best day to have chosen. Somehow she had to find a solution, and quickly, because in a day or two she would be heading west, leaving the city of Philadelphia behind her.

And then it came to her—heading west, leaving the city behind—that was exactly what she and Matilde had dreamed of for children. This was their chance.

"I think I know what to do," she said with a feeling of mounting excitement. "I'll be heading back to Kansas City any day now. I want to take the children with me."

"Take them west? So soon?"

"Why not? We've been talking this idea over for long enough. The time has come to try it, don't you think?"

Matilde looked at her doubtfully. "It's not that I disagree, it's just . . ." Her voice trailed off and Matilde frowned thoughtfully. "It would certainly take a lot of work," she said slowly. "I mean, you can't just leave on the morning train or . . ."

Bess held her breath when Matilde paused again, afraid if she said so much as a word, Matilde would object to the idea. The older woman had to decide on her own that this was the right thing to do, otherwise she wouldn't give the plan her full support.

"You know, I think you're right," Matilde said. She smiled then, her excitement building as the idea took hold. "Yes, let's do it. It will take some really hard work over the next few days, but it's worthwhile. We

200

may not have an opportunity like this again, with a group of children needing homes and someone right here in Philadelphia to take them west, someone we know and trust."

"There's just one thing," Bess broached a bit hesitantly. She didn't want to dampen Matilde's new-found enthusiasm. "I can't wait more than a couple of days. I'm afraid I really must leave Philadelphia as soon as possible."

"Oh, no. Is something wrong with your family?"

"You could say that," Bess agreed though she knew she and Matilde ascribed different meanings to the words. Matilde no doubt thought there was a problem in Missouri with Bess's father while Bess was thinking of Catherine and the trouble she was causing. No matter. As long as Matilde helped her leave on time, the exact reason was inconsequential.

"Well, I am sorry to hear that, but in that case we'll simply have to work that much more quickly. Now, let me see. As I recall, I have some literature from the New York Children's Aid Society. They've been doing something like this for years. Let me see if I can't find it." She started looking through the large secretary, the same one that Catherine had searched so recently. "I know it's in here somewhere," she murmured more to herself than to Bess as she opened the various drawers and searched through the numerous shelves.

"I'll go talk to the children," Bess said. "I want to make sure this is what they want, too."

"Yes, of course. What a good idea! I must say I see now why Livvie is so pleased with you."

"She is?"

"Oh, my yes. She's so very proud of you. Says it's wonderful that someone in the family is interested in the work she's doing and will continue the family

201

tradition of caring for others less fortunate."

The words "someone in the family" echoed in Bess's mind. At least Aunt Livvie had welcomed her wholeheartedly, accepting her without question. Maybe that would help some even after Catherine told the older woman her little tale. For Bess knew that Catherine was unlikely to keep her word even if Bess left Philadelphia, especially where her grandmother was concerned. Catherine wanted Livvie to think ill of her great-niece in case the will story were true. Bess could only hope that once she disappeared the story would die down so quickly it wouldn't have a chance to harm Dev.

"Well, I'll do my best to live up to my aunt's good opinion," she declared.

"I have every faith in you," Matilde said. "If anyone can do this, I'm sure you can." She smiled at Bess, then turned back the secretary to resume her search for the elusive Aid Society pamphlet.

Bess wiped an errant tear from her eye as she headed back to the kitchen.

"Didja finish talking to Miz Brown?" Rosie asked as Bess entered the room. The girl's grinning face was smeared with icing, but to Bess that only made her more appealing. It was the first sign that despite her harsh existence, the child still could indulge in the natural pleasures of childhood.

"Yes, I did, and I think we've come up with a wonderful plan." She smiled at each girl in turn and then looked over at Danny. "Since you're the man here, let me ask you this. Do you and the rest of the children want to find families of your own?"

Danny looked over at the two girls who both nodded emphatically. He didn't speak for a moment, and then he, too, nodded. "Harley and Bertha's ain't safe no more, so we gotta find somewhere else. The boys and I talked it over this morning."

"What about Nola?"

Bess looked toward the two girls, but it was Danny who answered. "Nola wants to keep her and the girls together."

"I see. Did she say anything else?" Bess could tell from the way he refused to meet her eyes that he hadn't told her everything.

"She's not sure you'll be able to do that," he confessed. "That's why she wouldn't come today."

Bess wanted to tell him not to worry, that everything would work out just the way they wanted, but she couldn't lie to him.

"I'm afraid Nola may be right. I can't promise to keep everyone together, but I give you my word I'll try very hard to do so. Why don't you bring her here so we can meet. We'll figure out where to go from there."

Bess had already realized that Nola's was the deciding vote for this motley crew. She was the person to convince if this entire scheme was to succeed.

"We'll tell her we like it here, and then she'll come," Rosie said with a young child's innocent confidence.

"Maybe," Danny responded. He wasn't willing to make any promises; he'd already learned the harsh realities of life: that wishing for something with all your might didn't necessarily make it come true. Bess wanted to change that—for him and for the other children. She only hoped she was up to such a monumental task. Looking down at the trusting faces of the two girls, she knew she had to try.

"Do you think you can get her and some of the others to come here?"

Danny shrugged, but Bess could see that the girls' confidence was contagious. "If you watch Rosie and Polly, I can try and round 'em up."

Bess turned to the girls. "Will you stay here while Danny goes to get Nola and the boys?"

They both nodded, happy to stay anywhere there was a whole tin of little iced cakes.

After Danny had gone to find the other children, Bess and Matilde set to work cleaning up the girls.

"Why don't we bundle these two off for a nap," Matilde suggested when the two were finally thoroughly washed from top to toe. "Then we can rummage about in the donated clothes and see if we have anything suitable. We'll want them to have at least three changes of clothes if we can manage it."

"Clothing, food, lodging. There's so much they'll need. And where am I going to get the money for ten more train tickets?"

"Let's work on the clothes, first. I'll see what I can do about the tickets. I just might have an idea. As for food, I'm sure the League will supply you with enough money to get you to your destination. Now stop worrying, and let's get to work."

Bess stood at the train station unable to believe that she would be leaving for Kansas City within the hour. The past couple of days had passed in a blur of activity, and now she and the children Danny had gathered together for the trip—ten in all—stood on the platform waiting for the train to pull in. Just as Matilde had promised, everything had come together, everything except her own life.

She hadn't heard from Devlin since he'd walked out her door in the middle of the night with a promise to call. His silence caused her both relief and agony, relief because now she would not have to explain her decision to leave, agony because she'd hoped, in her most secret heart, that their intimacy had meant something special to him, that somehow they could have found a way to circumvent Catherine's threat.

Fortunately she had been so busy helping to organize today's trip that she had no time for self-pity or despair. The Covingtons had been dismayed at her request to return home so precipitously. At first Mrs. Covington had objected to her departure even when Bess had invoked the Babcock name, but eventually she'd agreed, realizing that now Alice would be able to hold court among the eligible Philadelphia males with no competition.

Alice had been harder to convince, especially without taking her fully into Bess's confidence. By the end, though, she'd been astute enough to understand that Bess was nursing a broken heart even if Bess refused to confess the details.

And Bess's heart was broken, even if the choice had been hers to make. She consoled herself with the thought that she'd achieved her original goals in coming to Philadelphia: she had met her mother's family and now understood better her father's pain. Equally important, she'd found that elusive purpose she'd been seeking, the way out of her conventional existence and into a life of meaning.

She had come here determined to replace her old dream with a new one. The children standing around her were a testimony to that new dream, unconventional though it was. She looked at them with growing affection, already recognizing them as individuals rather than as a means to a new end for herself. She had learned their names and personalities, and was able to see beyond the ill-fitting but clean clothes Matilde had managed to find for them to their intrinsic worth as human beings.

The two youngest girls remained cheerfully optimistic, much as they'd been at the League office.

They had accepted their new clothes with enthusiasm, thrilled at the attention being lavished upon them, uncaring if the fit was not perfect. Their older sister, Nola, had yet to be fully won over. She stood slightly apart from the group, quite aware of her lack of proper attire. She tugged at the bottom of her shirtwaist and pulled up the skirt beneath, as if she could make the mismatched clothes fit better. Bess's heart went out to her.

"The train should be here any minute," Bess said.

"I'll get the girls," Nola replied, then called to her younger sisters. When they ran up, she put an arm around each one's shoulders and pulled them half in front of her, as if she wanted to hide her shabby attire behind their brighter clothes.

"It shouldn't be long now," Bess said and scanned the area, trying to keep an eye on the boys as they tousled with one another across the wooden planks. They were certainly rambunctious.

"Shall I get the boys, too?" Nola asked. "They don't know much about keeping themselves clean and all, living on the streets the way we do. They don't mean no harm or nothin'."

Her little face looked pinched and serious. Too serious. Nola was such a good little mother — but she shouldn't have to be, not at ten years of age. She should have been enjoying her life — learning to play the piano, mastering the art of needlework, playing with dolls as Bess had done — instead of worrying about a motley crew of homeless waifs like herself.

"Don't be concerned about the boys," Bess hastened to reassure the girl. "When we get to Kansas my friends will have new clothes for everyone — clothes that fit properly. They'll look smart enough then." Bess gave the girl's shoulder a pat.

"We'll all look smart then, won't we, miss?" Rosie

asked, obviously pleased to use the new word she just learned.

"Yes, then we'll all look smart and very fashionable." Bess smiled at the younger girl, then noticed Nola ease the weight of her body from one foot to the other. The shoes they had found fit her no better than the dress. "Why don't you girls go and sit on the bench for a bit. You don't want the boys to mistake you for a post and run you down," Bess suggested.

Nola nodded gratefully as the small girls laughed. She shepherded them to a long bench near the baggage shed, picking up the three small bundles of clothes Matilde had given them.

The boys continued to run around, poking at each other and generally acting as boys everywhere did. Bess could already see the difference in their behavior. When Danny had first brought his friends to the League office, they'd been very quiet, almost secretive. He'd told her bits and pieces about the lives they'd led with the Jenkins couple, and none of it sounded good. But now it looked as though they were recovering, all except for Danny.

He stood off on his own, alone and withdrawn. He didn't even watch the other boys; his eyes were focused on something far in the distance. There was a look of wistfulness on his face that made her want to hug him in her arms and keep him safe. But she stayed where she was, afraid that such a display would hurt his dignity.

He was so independent. While he had no qualms about having others depend on him, he didn't like it when the roles were reversed. And depend on him the others did, even some of the older boys. He had been the one to seek her out on their behalf, the one who had informed her of their needs, from clothes to food. They turned to him with their problems and questions, but he turned to no one.

There was something about him that touched her more deeply than the others, some intangible link. She'd felt it that first day at the Centennial Exhibition, and the feeling had grown stronger with every meeting since. He had so much to offer despite his perilous childhood — loyalty and courage, responsibility and self-reliance. She'd seen signs of all these traits in him, and if nurtured, she knew he would grow into a responsible, courageous adult, a credit to society. But he needed a chance, and she was determined to find it for him. That he would be worthy of her efforts, she had no doubt.

Even Devlin had seen the boy's worth — she'd seen it on his face that day he'd caught Danny with her purse. Now that she knew Dev's background, she understood some of the pain she'd seen in him that day. Had Devlin been remembering his own childhood, the days before Patrick O'Connor had picked him up off the streets? He must have been.

And at that moment, Bess felt even more sure of her goals than before — for if Patrick O'Connor could have raised Dev to be the fine, upstanding gentleman she knew him to be, she could do no less for Danny. It would be her way of honoring the love she felt for Dev, the love that couldn't be, for Dev was already battling a misguided society's scorn, and she could not add to his troubles.

"The train's coming! The train's coming!" eleven-year-old Samuel shouted. He jumped up and down.

"Where?" eight-year-old Lester demanded.

"There! There!" Samuel screamed, pointing down the track.

Lester jostled against Sam, and both boys fell to the ground together, laughing and giggling as they rolled into Jesse.

208

"Hey," the oldest boy, Jesse, cried out. "Leave off, will you?" The youth stepped out of their way, a scowl on his face. "You'd better get your things before the train leaves the station without you," he snapped at the two boys who were still cavorting on the platform.

Bess called to Nola and her sisters, then helped the younger boys, Victor and Max, collect their things. She lined the children up, ready to board.

"I think that's everything," Danny told her, taking on the responsibility for checking after everyone.

"Thank you," she told him with a smile.

He smiled back, but then his gaze returned to the station and the city streets beyond. This was the only home he'd known, and though he had not been happy here, Bess could understand his fear in leaving it. She'd felt much the same way when she'd stood with her father in Carlinsville before coming east. And now she felt that way again, as her gaze took in everything around her, the crowds of waiting passengers, the billowing steam from the approaching engine, the streets of the city she'd grown to both love and hate.

What she was hoping for when she looked so ardently up and down the platform? Was she hoping to see a set of wide shoulder pushing their way toward her? Did she expect a pair of laughing brown eyes to smile down into hers from Devlin's handsome face?

She knew that was what she longed for, no matter how unrealistic the thought. Dev had called her sweetheart, though whether he'd said the words aloud or only in her dream, she did not know. What she did know was that losing him was much harder than losing Wylie, and the pain of it would be with her for a long time to come. Wylie had been a girlish infatuation, and a misplaced one at that. Dev, on the other hand, deserved the best, and she wished him well—so much so that she was leaving for his sake as much as for her own.

She only hoped he understood her actions, that he would get on with his life in the best way possible as she had resolved to. In the meantime, she had ten children depending on her, and a train pulling into the station. The unknown lay before them—a challenge and an opportunity—and she planned to make the most of it.

Laura Christy and her father had written back after her first letter, approving, at least in principle, of her ideas and asking for more details. Two days ago she'd sent them a telegram telling of her sudden change in plans. With any luck, they still approved; they really had little choice. Like it or not, she and the children were about to board the train.

Ten

When Bess stepped off the train in Carlinsville, she was relieved and happy to find Laura waiting for her on the platform. She needed to see a friendly face very badly. With an impatient hand, she pushed the loose tendrils of hair out of her face and hurried toward her friend.

"Aren't you a sight for sore eyes!" Laura exclaimed as she hugged Bess to her bosom and then held her at arm's length. "Though a rather bedraggled sight, if I may say so."

"I was hoping you wouldn't notice." Bess knew her dress had seen better days. The remnants of Polly's breakfast soiled the front, while the entire back was terribly wrinkled from sitting for hours. Even the bright blue color didn't look quite as intense as it had at the beginning of the day.

"Was it a long trip?"

"I can't tell you how long! I can't imagine what I thought this trip would be like when I started, but it certainly wasn't like anything I've ever experienced before."

"Well, you're here now, and that's the important thing. Where are the children?" Laura asked.

"They'll be here soon enough, I guarantee it," Bess said with a laugh.

It had taken the children no time to lose whatever reserve they might have felt around a complete stranger such as herself. She realized it was one of the ways they'd learned to survive on the streets, taking whatever kindness they could because they had no way of knowing what the next day might bring. Granted, the older ones were more resistant to the offering of love, having been burned before, but she could see the flickering of hope in their eyes that it would happen.

"Your letter didn't say how many children you were bringing," Laura said. "I can't wait to meet them."

"Ten all together. Three girls and seven boys."

"Ten? And you handled them all by yourself?"

"The older children helped with the younger ones, and everything worked out one way or another." Not that there hadn't been times when she'd prayed for another adult to talk with, to ask questions of, but she had muddled through. More than that, she'd learned a great deal, and one of those things was that she truly liked these children.

Bess took a deep breath. The air seemed so much cleaner here than in Philadelphia, or maybe she was just glad to be home.

"I must admit, though, that I'm glad to be here at last. I can't wait to find homes for the children. I think they'll do well once they're sure of their future. Have you found anyone interested in adopting?"

Laura shook her head.

Bess's heart dropped. She'd hoped Laura might have come up with at least some families who'd shown a little interest.

"Now don't be so impatient, Bess. We'll find homes

for them all. We have good people living here in Missouri, people who are more than willing to give a helping hand. It's just going to take some time. Quite a few people have donated to the cause—linens, towels, crockery—and we've gathered a fair amount of clothing, too. Let's just take things one step at a time and start by finding the children you've brought and setting off to the house."

"Oh, did you manage to find someplace for us all to stay?" Bess asked with relief. She'd been worried about where to find lodgings for such a large group. Carlinsville wasn't exactly Philadelphia, not by any stretch of the imagination, and there wasn't a house to let on every corner.

The old Rutherford House seems like an ideal place, don't you think?" the older woman said with a twinkle in her eye as if she knew the reaction she was going to get from her young friend.

"We're going to be staying at the Rutherford House?" Bess asked in astonishment.

Before Laura could reply, the children swarmed around them, chattering away about all they'd seen.

"Quiet, quiet, everyone," Bess said with a laugh. "I want to introduce you to Miss Christy. She'll be helping to care for you while we're waiting to find you new homes."

The girls dropped small curtsies while the boys bobbed their heads. "Pleased to make your acquaintance, ma'am," Danny said after the murmuring abated.

Danny was constantly doing things which surprised Bess. Not that having good manners was amazing, but he'd shown himself to possess a hidden reservoir of all the social niceties. Someone somewhere had certainly taught him well.

"And you, too, young man," Laura replied.

Bess introduced all the children to Laura in turn.

"It looks like we'll be one big happy family," Laura said, "but you'll have to help me with your names in case I get mixed up. Are you ready to head for home?"

"I'm ready for anything that doesn't move," Rosie said. "Our new home won't move, will it, Miss Christy?"

Poor Rosie had fared the worst on the trip out. The movement of the train car had produced a very queasy stomach, and for the better part of the trip, she'd spent her time in the lavatory.

"I ain't sitting by her," Jesse said defiantly. "I ain't gonna have her pukin' all over me."

Bess saw Rosie's face begin to scrunch up and knew she was about to cry. Jesse had been the one sore spot on the entire trip. He'd been uncooperative and sulky. Bess had hoped getting off the train might improve his disposition, but it didn't appear that it had. Nola placed her hands on her hips, ready to go head to head with him to protect her younger sister.

One thing they didn't need was for petty quarrels to break out. They'd have enough problems without fighting amongst themselves.

"Jesse, there's no need—" Bess's reprimand was interrupted by Danny's voice.

"Why don't you sit on my lap, Rosie, and I'll tell you about the time I had that tussle with old man Rogers bulldog."

Rosie immediately brightened and put her hand into Danny's. Nola smiled and ushered Polly over toward Danny, too.

Bess breathed a sigh of relief that trouble was averted again. She couldn't begin to count the number of times Danny had stepped in to end a fight or stop a spat between two of the children.

"Rosie, I'm afraid we'll have to take a wagon to the house, but after that you won't have to ride on anything for as long as you want," Laura promised, then looked over at Bess. "I've hired one large wagon. Do you think that will be enough?"

"Let's take a look and see. Children, grab all your bundles and follow Miss Christy."

There was a lot of good-natured teasing and chatter as the children inspected the wagon and decided where they would each sit. Only Jesse hung back, silent, his face closed and brooding. Bess hoped a new home would bring some laughter back into his life.

The stationmaster loaded Bess's trunk onto the wagon, and the children settled down around it, excited about the prospect of finally ending their trip. Bess took the reins, and Laura sat beside her, but before Bess could urge the horses forward there was a yelp from the back.

"Miss Bess, Victor's pulling my braids," little Polly called out.

"Was not. They're so long I sat on 'em by mistake."

Bess doubted Victor's plea of innocence. She'd quickly discovered that whenever someone had a trick pulled on them during the trip, it was almost a given fact that the five-year-old boy was behind it. How he'd learned to be so devilish in so few years was beyond Bess.

"Victor, you move over and sit by Samuel. He doesn't have braids for you to sit on."

"Oh, Miss Bess, does he have to?" Samuel protested.

"It will only be for a short time, Sam. Soon we'll be at the house." Bess's look encompassed all the children. "Now, are we all settled and ready to go?"

A chorus of "Yes, miss" filled the air.

Bess nodded, then gave the reins a slap. The horses started off with a snort, taking the main road to the outskirts of town where the Rutherford House stood. Bess remembered it well. It was a beautiful old house with lots and lots of room. There had to be at least eight bedrooms, and that didn't count the servants' quarters on the top floor. She'd been to tea there once when Miss Rutherford was celebrating her eightieth birthday. She'd admired the house so much Miss Rutherford had taken her and her father on a tour.

Her father. Where was he? Why hadn't he come to meet her train? Bess tried to think of a good reason and couldn't.

"What's happened to Papa?" she finally found the courage to ask Laura.

"Nothing that I know of," Laura replied though she didn't look at Bess.

"Then why didn't he meet the train? Do you know?"

Laura hesitated for a moment. "He thought it might be best if he waited to come out and see you this evening."

"But why? I don't understand." This just wasn't like him.

"I think he wants some time alone with you, and he knew he wouldn't get it at the station. Besides, he does have a job to do, you know."

"But—"

"Now don't sass your teacher," Laura said in a teasing tone. "Everything will work out given time. I told you, just take things as they come. There's no use borrowing trouble."

Bess could tell Laura was trying to ease some of her pain at her father's desertion. Or perhaps he really was busy. No matter—Laura was right about not borrowing trouble.

216

"I'm no longer one of your students, or have you forgotten that?" Bess returned with a small smile, trying to keep her response light.

"You'll always be one of my students. That's just the way teachers are," Laura said fondly, then added in a more serious voice, "I think your father's concerned about you coming home without the Covingtons. You know how fathers are — they're a lot like teachers. They never think their little ones have grown up."

"You're right, I suppose. Did he mention anything about my trip? Anything unusual?"

"Not that I'm aware of. He did mention a letter he'd gotten and seemed a little preoccupied. Do you know anything about that?"

Bess shook her head, a feeling of dread filling her. Maybe it was just her own sense of guilt, but she had the feeling her father had somehow found out about her visit to her mother's relatives. Could that be the reason he hadn't come to the train?

Bess chewed on her lower lip. She'd known when she decided to get in touch with her mother's family that there might be repercussions, but she'd planned on bringing up the subject herself when the time best suited. Now it was probably too late, and Bert felt betrayed, perhaps rightly so. He'd been there every time she'd needed him, and now she'd abused his trust. But how could she have talked to him about it when every time she mentioned her mother's name he closed up and got that sad look on his face?

"Whatever problems there are will work themselves out," Laura said, evidently understanding Bess's distress. "Your father loves you very much. Don't forget that. If you need to talk, I'll be here." Laura gave Bess's hand a final squeeze. "Maybe over a cup of tea later when we're all settled."

217

"Thank you. I'd like that."

It was still hard for Bess to think of her teacher as an equal, but it was clear that Laura had no such qualms. So absorbed was Bess in her own problems that it didn't occur to her until later to question how Laura knew so much about her father.

A short while later they reached the Rutherford mansion. The house had been built twenty years before the war, and at the time of its construction had been way out in the country, but Carlinsville had encroached on it since. The building had lost some of its grandeur with time but was still a fine old house, though too close to town for society's elite — they preferred the houses out by the lake — and too big and costly for most residents of Carlinsville. Now Laura's brother, Arthur, had arranged for them to use it, and Bess couldn't have been more pleased.

Putting aside her concerns about her father, she urged the children up the wide stairs to the porch and to the front door. The house was all she'd hoped it would be: large enough to house all the children, yet still retaining the qualities of a home rather than an institution. The children were as pleased as she was, and they scurried about the various floors, peeking into the closets and under the beds.

Laura and Bess let them choose their own rooms and then went through the donated clothes, trying to decide who would get what. Nola was in the most need, and Bess paid particular attention to the oldest girl's wardrobe. She could remember her own years at school as the one girl who was never dressed exactly right. The other children had made comments, and she remembered how she'd always felt left out. If she hadn't had her father there to tell her he loved her and thought she looked beautiful, she didn't know how she would have survived. Since Nola had neither a father nor a mother to do that for her, Bess was determined to find her the best clothes she could.

The older children soon ran outside to continue their explorations while the little ones were put down for naps. Bess used the relative quiet to unpack her things and see to dinner. Fortunately Arthur had arranged for more than just the house, providing them with a cook as well as a couple of local girls to help care for the children.

By the time dinner was ready, Bess had even managed to catch a moment or two for herself, sitting with her feet propped on an ottoman and sipping a cup of tea. Then, before she got too comfortable, the younger children rose from their naps and the older ones arrived back from their explorations.

When they all gathered in the dining room, it was a sight to behold. The large rectangular oak table was like nothing Bess had ever seen before. None of the dishes matched. Some of the glasses were large and some were small, and the flatware was of every conceivable pattern, but the children didn't seem to notice. The older boys chattered about what they'd seen in town, and the younger ones sat in wide-eyed wonder. For that matter, so did Bess. The town they were describing certainly didn't sound like the one she'd grown up in, and she knew they were embroidering their descriptions for the benefit of their listeners.

The children cheerfully cleaned off the table after the meal and trotted everything back to the kitchen where the older ones helped wash and dry the dishes.

"I took the liberty of bringing some lesson books with me," Laura said as she and Bess straightened up the dining room. "I thought the children might need some tutoring so they'll be ready for school in the fall."

"That's a wonderful idea. I'm not sure how much schooling any of them have had. Danny can read and so can Nola, but as for the others, I have no idea. I'm afraid I didn't think that far ahead when I decided that the children should come out here. Rather foolish now that I think about it. The League gave me some money to get things started, but it won't last long."

"Don't worry, dear. Arthur has set up a fund to help meet the expenses of the house."

"A fund?"

"To cover any expenditures we might have."

"How nice of your brother to think of the children. It's so very kind of him."

"Well, I'm not sure it's from kindness. His final words before I left the lake house were, 'Since it doesn't look like I can talk you out of this foolhardy undertaking, I've set up an account at the local bank for your use. Can't have the good name of Christy bandied about or tarnished with you starving to death or getting into who knows what kind of trouble.' As you can see, his motivation stems from his pride more than his generosity."

"I think it stems from his concern for you. Men always seem to bluster when they're trying to hide their real feelings."

"You may be right, but I tell you, Arthur was not happy about my leaving his house and venturing out on my own."

Bess could sense Laura's unease. The older woman was doing what she wanted, but not without a few reservations. Bess could understand that. She'd had plenty of time to mull over her own reservations since leaving Philadelphia. Having full responsibility for ten children could make anyone have a few indecisive moments.

220

"Surely he's happy you've found something worthwhile to fill your time?" Bess questioned.

"He thinks my time would be better spent looking after him and his house. Why is it men think they know what's best for us when the end result always benefits them?"

"They're raised that way, but I think things are changing. At the Centennial Exhibition there was one complete building just for women, and the displays inside were amazing. I certainly think men's ideas about women's abilities will change after they've seen what I have."

"I can't imagine Arthur changing his mind, no matter what," Laura said over her shoulder as she hurried off to the kitchen.

Bess had to agree to a certain extent. The older men would probably never change. Her father fit into that category. He still thought women needed to be protected from life, going straight from their father's house to their husband's. He would never get used to the idea that some women might want something else from life—especially if that woman was his daughter. It was the younger men who would learn to accept change, men like Dev.

The thought of Dev's name brought his face to life in her mind. She wondered where he was at this moment, what he was doing, whether he ever thought of her. Not an hour went by without her thinking of him. Tingles would race down her spine, and then a cloud of sadness would descend upon her. She would never again feel the strength of his arms around her, know the joy and passion of his kisses, revel in the tenderness of his gaze. How she missed him—how desperately she longed for him.

Though her life was now filled with purpose, it also harbored a secret pain—the pain of losing Dev, of lying alone in bed at night and longing for him to the depths of her soul. But it did no good to bemoan her fate. There was nothing she could do to change things now, not with Catherine promising to do her worst. Instead, Bess had to get on with her life as best she could.

Picking up the last of the table linens, Bess followed Laura into the kitchen. The children depended on her and she would not let them down. Love was for other people, not her.

Dev paced up and down in the front hall of Olivia Babcock's house, impatient with having to wait one second more. He'd stopped by the hotel the minute he'd gotten back from Pottsville only to find that Bess was no longer registered. When he'd tried to get in touch with Alice and her family, he found that they were out for the day and not expected back until late evening.

Where had Bess gone? His one hope was that she might have moved in with Livvie, though he was sure if Catherine had anything to say about it, that would never happen. But if Livvie had her way, who knew.

Fear knotted his stomach. God, how he hoped she was upstairs sitting by Livvie's side. Just when he thought he couldn't wait any longer, Evans came down the stairs and stopped at the lower landing.

"Miss Olivia will see you now, Mr. Devlin. If you'll follow me."

Dev wasted no time in following Evans up the stairs and into Livvie's upstairs parlor.

Evans opened the door and nodded for him to go ahead in. With quick steps, Dev crossed the threshold to find Livvie reclining on a daybed which had been made up in the corner of the large room. There was no one by her side.

"Dev, how nice of you to visit." Livvie's voice contained just the slightest slur, and if he hadn't known her as well as he did, he might not have even noticed it.

"I'm glad to see you looking so well."

"I wish I could say the same for you." Livvie's tongue had lost none of its sting because of her unfortunate condition.

"It's been a long three days. I had to go to Pottsville on business."

"And it's business I'm sure I want to know nothing about."

Dev nodded his head in agreement. Livvie knew he did work that led him into danger. She never directly questioned him about his assignments, but there was an unspoken understanding of what he did.

"So tell me what brings you here on a visit in the middle of the week," she said.

"I've just been to the hotel and discovered that Bess is no longer staying there. Has she come to be with you?"

"I wish she had, but I'm afraid Catherine wouldn't hear of it."

"Do you know where she might have gone?" Dev asked when Livvie didn't say any more.

"Who? Bess?"

"Yes, Bess."

"Didn't she leave you a note?"

He shook his head in answer. Dev had asked at the desk, but there had been nothing. Since he'd found out Bess was gone, he'd been in a quandary, alternately blaming himself for her disappearance and asking himself what could have happened. After their night together, he'd planned on coming back the next

223

afternoon. There was so much they had to decide, so many plans he'd hoped to make. But Pinkerton's had had other ideas, all because of the Molly Maguire trials. The detective agency had infiltrated the radical group hoping to discover who was responsible for various murders. Dev's testimony had been crucial in one of the trials, and he'd had to head north for Pottsville immediately.

He'd stopped back at the hotel, hoping to see Bess long enough to tell her he would be gone, but she was out—as were the Covingtons—so he'd had no choice but to leave her a note. And now she had disappeared without a word.

"I take it you care a great deal about where Bess might have gone?" Livvie asked.

"Yes, I do."

"Good."

Dev gave her a questioning look.

"I was hoping you might."

"Do you mean you planned—"

"Not exactly planned, but certainly hoped after I found out the two of you knew each other. It seemed like an ideal solution. You'd have someone, and I'd have my niece nearby. Then when she left in such a hurry . . ." Livvie's voice faded away.

"Where has she gone?"

"She's taken the children and gone home."

"Children? What children?"

"That little boy named Danny and some of his friends, I believe."

Dev didn't know what to think. How had Bess found Danny and convinced him that going out to Missouri would be best for him? Dev had wanted Danny off the street as much as she had—he just didn't think Missouri was the answer. Of course he wasn't asked his opinion nor was he even informed about the proposed trip.

"What made her leave so quickly?" he asked.

"I think it might have had something to do with the man who'd been looking after the children, but I don't know for sure. I never got to see Bess for myself, so I've had to rely on Matilde for all my information. But Matilde wouldn't tell me much. She's afraid I'll get too worked up. I'm sure she would tell you more if you want."

"Thank you. I'll see if I can find Matilde right away."

"Are you going to go after Bess?"

Dev looked at his friend. "I don't know. Things have changed a lot here since you've been taken ill. Right now, I just want to make sure Bess is safe. After that . . . well, I'm not sure she would even want to see me if she knew everything."

"There's nothing not to want, young man," Livvie said with some of her old spark. "Do you think I don't know what's going on? You're wrong. Don't ever think less of yourself because of an accident of birth. That's what the League is all about. It's what you make of yourself that counts, not where you come from."

"I wish more people thought like you, Livvie," Dev said with a sad smile.

"They will as soon as I'm up and around. Just you wait and see."

"I'll look forward to that."

He leaned over to give her a quick kiss, then left before Evans could come back and berate him for tiring Livvie out. Once he was outside, he headed for the League office, hoping to find Matilde. As soon as he made sure Bess really had returned to Kansas City, he would know what to do.

By the time he reached home that evening, Dev's

plans were made. When Patrick once again asked him to go west and handle some business, Dev surprised his father by readily agreeing. Philadelphia held no allure now that Bess was gone and his opportunity for public office had been squelched as it had. He just hoped Bess was ready for him. He definitely had some questions for her.

When dinner was over, Bess sat in the front parlor mending some of the clothes that had been donated for the children, while Laura sat opposite her teaching Nola how to darn socks. The young girl was an eager and willing pupil, too willing. Bess's heart cried out for the young girl so anxious to be a part of a family, so eager to please. And Nola was not alone. *So many children all wanting a family.* Bess just hoped she was up to the challenge. With Laura and her father's help, the task didn't seem quite as daunting. She only hoped her father still felt the same way. It was so unlike him not to meet her when she returned from a trip.

"I think I'll go to my house tomorrow and pick up some of my clothes, if that's all right with you, Laura."

The older woman looked up from her darning. "Sounds like a good idea."

"Would you mind if I stayed in town for dinner with my father?"

Laura didn't answer her question, but spoke to the young girl instead. "Nola, why don't you put the darning away until tomorrow and make sure your sisters and the younger boys are ready for bed."

"Sure thing, Miz Laura. And thanks for helping me learn to mend those socks. That'll be a real good talent to have when folks come to find them some young'uns, won't it?"

226

Laura nodded. "We'll come up and tuck you in a little later."

Bess could see the pleasure the words brought to the young girl. She just hoped she would be able to find families worthy of the children—families that met the children's needs as well as their own.

Laura's voice interrupted her thoughts. "You're worried, aren't you?"

"Worried?"

"I've known you a long time and can tell when you have something on your mind."

Maybe it would help to talk about the way she was feeling. "I'm worried about Papa."

"There's no need, you know. He'll be out to see you as soon as he can," Laura said in a reassuring voice.

"But he's never not met my train before."

"And you're not a little girl any more, remember. You've been off to see the world on your own."

Maybe Laura was right, and she was putting more worry into this than was necessary. Her father was probably very busy, and as soon as he found time he'd be out to see her. But she couldn't stop thinking about other possibilities, other reasons why he'd stayed away, and they all centered on her activities back in Philadelphia.

She and Laura were just getting ready to go upstairs and tuck the children in for the night when there was a knock at the door.

Bess walked to the door and pushed the lace curtains aside to see who was calling at such a late hour. A smile tipped the corners of her mouth when she saw her father standing on the other side.

Turning the lock, she pulled the door open and ran into his open arms. "Oh, Papa, I'm so glad to see you."

227

"Me, too, Bessie," he whispered back. "You're a sight for sore eyes."

Bess laughed. "Laura said the same thing. You two must be spending a lot of time together."

Bess glanced over at Laura and noticed the blush on her friend's cheeks as she escorted her father from the foyer. She looked back at her father and saw that he looked equally uncomfortable. To cover her own uneasiness, she began talking about her trip and the children. "To bad you've missed the children. They went to bed a short while ago, but you can meet them tomorrow."

"I'm looking forward to it. How many did you bring?"

Bess told him, and they talked about what they would need to do to get the program started. But Bess could feel an underlying reserve in her father. Maybe if they sat down and talked privately . . .

"Why don't we go to the kitchen and I'll fix some tea?" she suggested, looking only at her father.

"Sounds like a fine idea. Laura, you'll join us, of course," Bert said as if he were afraid to be alone with her.

"I'm not sure. Maybe it would be best—" Laura started to say, but Bert interrupted her.

"Nonsense. We want you to join us. Don't we, Bess?"

"Of course we do," Bess replied, looking from one to the other. Of course she didn't mind Laura joining them. Laura had become a good friend and, Bess was sure, a future confidant. She just didn't understand her father's reluctance to be alone with her. What had come over him? And over Laura, for that matter.

They walked to the kitchen, and Bess set about getting the cups and saucers while Laura stoked up the wood stove. While they waited for the kettle to boil, Bert and Laura told Bess about what had been happening in town.

Laura and her brother, Arthur, had come out to the Christy's summer home on the lake outside of Carlinsville right after Bess had headed to Philadelphia. When Bess had written to both Bert and Laura, they'd joined forces in making arrangements for the children who would be coming west.

"So tell me about what you did in Philadelphia," Bert said after the tea was poured and everyone had taken a sip.

"The usual things. Our hotel was wonderful and the elevator—well, you'd have to ride on one to believe it. It does the strangest things to your stomach. The Centennial Exhibition was really exciting. I've never seen so many people in one place at one time. And so many exhibits—"

"Bess, I'm sorry, but I can't tip-toe around about this," Bert interrupted. "You know I'm not good at these social things, so I'm just going to come right out and say it. Did you see your mother's people when you were in Philadelphia?"

Bess's earlier uneasiness came back in full force. What she'd most feared was actually happening. Somehow her father had found about her visit to Olivia, and now he felt alone and left out. She could see it on his face.

"Oh, Papa, please don't be hurt," Bess begged. "I had to find out what they were like. Since I was so young when Mama died and you never talk about her, I thought this might be the perfect time to find out about her. I wanted to tell you, to share everything that had happened, but I didn't want you hurt. I just didn't know what to do. Are you very angry?"

Bess could feel the tears gathering in her eyes and

blinked them away. She refused to cry; it would only muddle things.

Bert sighed and rubbed his face with one hand. "Maybe I didn't do right by you, not talking about your Ma and all."

"You were the best father anywhere. I couldn't have asked for more."

"But you wanted to meet your Philadelphia relatives."

"Yes, I did, because they're Mother's family."

She looked into his face and saw the pain and confusion there. Maybe she really had grown up at last. For the first time she saw her father as a real person, with wants and needs . . . and even fears of his own, fears that involved her.

She got off her chair and knelt beside him, putting her arms around his waist. "Don't you see? I love you Papa—this had nothing to do with you. I love you with all of my being; you've been everything to me. But I also knew there was a part of me that was created from my mother, and until I found out about her I felt as if that part of me was missing. I couldn't know myself. Can you understand that?"

"I suppose," he answered, but Bess sensed he didn't really believe it.

She laid her head against his chest, taking some small comfort from the sound of his heartbeat, steady and sure. She wished there was something she could say, some way of convincing him that he still had her loyalty and love.

"I know this is hard for you to hear," she finally said, "but every time I tried to talk to you about Mama you always changed the subject. You never seemed to want to talk about her, and I knew how much you hurt inside, so finally I just stopped asking."

230

The tears that had threatened now slid silently down her cheek, but with her face against his shirt, neither Bert nor Laura would see them. Bess took a deep breath, then added, "I'm sorry, Papa, but I just *had* to know about her."

"Talking about your ma was always hard for me," Bert said slowly, as if even those few words pained him.

"I know, and that's why I didn't press you, but you do understand why I did what I did?"

She could feel him nod though she still didn't look up, afraid of seeing the sadness in his eyes. His hands closed around her back, holding her to him, and they stayed together in silence, each trying to come to terms with the change in their relationship, each hoping to bridge the chasm that loomed between them.

After a few minutes, Bess pulled back and quickly ran her fingers across each cheek so no one would see the traces of her tears. She sent Laura an apologetic smile, embarrassed at having her witness the scene. Laura gave her a sympathetic look that said she understood.

"Laura mentioned you'd received a letter," Bess said as she regained her chair. "Is that how you found out about my visits?"

"Yes. It arrived day before yesterday. It was a real surprise."

Bess could imagine it was. Here she'd been writing him about visiting all the sights of Philadelphia, and suddenly he received a letter talking about the time spent with her mother's relatives, something she had carefully omitted from her accounts. What she couldn't understand was who had written him the letter. "Was it from Aunt Livvie?"

"Who?"

231

"Was the letter from Olivia Babcock, mother's aunt?" Bess couldn't imagine Aunt Livvie writing a letter to Bert and especially not with her frail health, but who else could it be?

"It was from someone named Catherine. Said she was some sort of cousin."

Just the sound of Catherine's name sent chills up and down Bess's spine. All the threats Catherine had flung at her after the ball came rushing back. She'd known she couldn't trust her so-called cousin, but she'd never imagined this! What else had Catherine said? Surely Bert's distancing wasn't entirely due to Bess's having met her aunt. There must have been something more in Catherine's letter.

Though she feared the worst, Bess knew she had to know more. Hesitantly she asked, "What exactly did she have to say?"

"Nothing important."

"Maybe you should let Bess read the letter," Laura put in. Up until this moment she hadn't spoken, but sat unobtrusively by Bert's side.

Bert turned and looked consideringly at Laura, as if he valued her opinion. Then he slowly reached into his coat pocket and pulled out an envelope. For a moment he held on to it as if he still had doubts about the wisdom of what he was doing. Then Laura gave him an encouraging nod, and he reached across the table and handed the envelope to Bess.

The heat of the stove warmed the room, but Bess felt a chill invade her body. With fingers made clumsy from nerves, she extracted the letter from the envelope and slowly unfolded the stiff sheets. Taking a deep breath she quickly scanned the contents of the letter and then more slowly began to reread it.

If you think I'm going to let your daughter come in

and steal my grandmother's fortune, you have another thing coming. I won't stand for it, and neither will my family. We always knew exactly the kind of man you were, and no ill-bred Westerner is going to make a fool out of me.

Don't think appealing to Devlin O'Connor will make a bit of difference because the word is out about him, and he's no better than you. Just because Patrick O'Connor picked him up off the streets and took him into his home doesn't change where he came from. Lowbred backgrounds will tell out.

Just make sure you tell your daughter that I mean what I say.

Bess looked up and into her father's eyes. She could see the pain radiating from them. In her peripheral vision she saw Laura put her hand over her father's and his hand turn to clasp hers. Laura obviously knew what the letter contained.

While Bess felt relief that Catherine hadn't spread any vicious rumors about Bess's appearance the night of the ball, she could feel her father's pain as if it were her own.

"Catherine always seems to know exactly where to put the knife, doesn't she?"

Bert looked at her questioningly.

"She knew what would hurt you the most and used it."

"What did she hope to gain?" Laura asked.

"Who knows? Catherine has her own *carte du jour.* What I do know is that Catherine doesn't like me being a part of the family, and she'll do whatever she has to force me out. Even playing on my father's guilt. What she didn't expect was for you to show me the letter. And 'I can tell you that no one but Catherine believes such lies."

233

"At the time, I'm afraid that wasn't quite as true."

"Aunt Livvie explained it all to me. At the time, no one in the family understood how much my mother loved you. Now they do, and none of them think the things Catherine has accused you of."

"You talked about all this with your aunt?" Laura asked when Bert kept silent.

"Yes. She said she never blamed Mama for leaving with the man she loved, she only wished my grandfather hadn't been as rigid and unbending. She said my grandmother wanted to see Mama and me but was afraid of grandfather."

Bert nodded. "Your grandfather never backed down once he made a decision. It made him a good businessman, but it broke your mother's heart." As if he realized he was saying more than he'd intended, he pulled his watch from his pocket and flipped open its case. "I didn't realize it was getting so late. Maybe I'd better head out and let you girls get some sleep."

"Will I see you tomorrow?" Bess asked, afraid to let too much time pass in case her father had second thoughts.

"Why don't you bring the children into town and we'll all have lunch together? We can talk about how to get the townsfolk acquainted with the children."

Bess smiled. "That would be fine."

She was still smiling as he headed out the door.

"We'd better close up and get to sleep as your father suggested," Laura said. "The children will be awake earlier than you think."

Bess agreed, and she and Laura quickly locked up the house, turned out all the lights, and checked on the children.

Once she was in bed, however, Bess found she couldn't fall asleep even though she was tired. The events of the day and her fears for tomorrow kept intruding on her thoughts. There was so much to do, so much to plan. For one thing, she wasn't convinced everything was patched up with her father; she still sensed a certain reserve in his manner. And what was happening between her father and Laura? It would be nice if they found an interest in each other. Her father had spent almost a lifetime grieving for his dead wife. It was past time for him to move on.

Bess couldn't help but wonder if she would be like her father — unable to commit to a new relationship for years because of her love for Dev. Even now she could recall every detail of the time they'd spent together, the way he'd looked, the things they'd said, the excitement and wonder of his touch. All she had to do was whisper his name and an aching longing would grow inside her, leaving an emptiness only Dev could fill. Would time make his image fade, turning her pain into bittersweet memories, or would her memories stay so achingly alive?

Her life stretched before her, a road less traveled by the females of her day and age. Was it her fate to travel it by herself, finding homes for other people's children instead of having children of her own? Would she watch all her friends get married while she slept alone — and dreamed of love, of passion — of Dev? That thought was too much to bear. She closed her eyes and prayed for the oblivion of sleep.

Eleven

Dev stood in the shade of an old elm tree near the sprawling mansion just outside Carlinsville and watched the small crowd gathered on the porch that wrapped around the first story. Several of Kansas City's most prominent families summered in this small town by the lake, but this afternoon he saw mostly the local folk. He took pains to stay out of sight, not sure of his welcome here in Bess's home town. She'd left Philadelphia without a word more than a week ago, disappearing as surely as he ever did, and perhaps that had been a message of sorts in and of itself. Surely if she'd wanted him in her life she would have deigned to answer his letter.

Dev waited until the crowd ambled into the house before approaching the front door. He hesitated, torn between wanting to see Bess again, to know if she had truly intended to cut him from her life so completely, and needing to hang on to the last remnants of his dreams. For he still dreamed of her at night, longing for the touch of her soft skin, the scent of wildflowers in her hair, the sound of her laughter floating on the summer breeze. Was it all lost to him forever?

"Why, Devlin O'Connor! It *is* you," came a voice

236

from inside, and Laura Christy came out the door. "How good to see you!"

She took his hand and tipped her cheek up for his kiss of greeting. "Are you coming in? How was your trip out? I understand Arthur is loaning you the cottage. Do you have everything you need?"

Dev smiled. "One question at a time, please. The trip was fine, the cottage as you call it, is more than comfortable, and I'd be glad to come in, if you're sure I wouldn't be in the way."

"We are rather busy at the moment, but one more won't make a difference. Did Arthur tell you our exciting news?"

Dev arched an eyebrow. "He told me about the children, if that's what you mean."

Laura laughed. "He isn't too enthusiastic, is he?" She laughed again. "No matter. He'll come around. Today is our first meeting with some of the local families. We're hoping to place the children in this area. That way we can keep an eye on them and make sure they are being cared for properly."

Dev frowned. "What do the children think of all this?"

"They all want homes, real homes, and that's what we want for them, too. You don't agree?"

"I can't say," he answered honestly. "I have no experience in placing children so far away from all that they're used to. I don't know how they'll take to it."

"I imagine different children will react differently. The important thing is to find the best place for each one, don't you think?"

"Yes, providing you know what the best place is."

She gave him a sharp glance, then looked over her shoulder. "Well, we're about to find out," she said. "This is our first chance to see what we can do. You're welcome to stay and see for yourself, but I'd better get back. Bess is waiting to begin."

"Go ahead. I'll just peek in from the back and see how it's going."

She nodded, sent him a quick smile, and headed back inside to the rear ballroom where everyone was waiting. Dev was amazed at the changes he could see in Laura. She was so much more animated and full of energy than he remembered from having known her in Philadelphia years before. Something was different in her life, and he had to wonder if it was the children or something else.

He followed her inside and down the hall but stood just outside the door until he heard Bess's voice. Then he dared peer into the room. The townsfolk were seated in rows in front of a small podium. Bess stood behind the podium, ready to address her audience.

"Ladies and gentlemen, I'd like to welcome you to Rutherford House and the Women's League for Children's Welfare special project. As most of you know, we are hoping to find caring and loving parents for several children who for one reason or another have lost their homes in Philadelphia. We plan to use Rutherford House as a temporary living quarters until we can find the children good homes—homes which we're sure you can provide."

She looked more self-possessed, more poised and confident than Dev had ever seen her despite the slight tremble in her voice. She was doing something she believed in, he realized, though he wondered if she knew how perilous her undertaking was. She was not dealing in amusing pets for the gentry here; she was determining the lives of children, setting on a course that could be full of reward or full of heartbreak, for herself as much as for her charges.

"Our purpose today is to answer your questions," Bess continued, "to tell you a bit about our procedures, and to introduce you to the children. We hope we can keep family groups together and ask that you not discuss specific plans with any child until you have first checked with one of the staff."

She went on to introduce herself and Laura, explain the procedures they hoped to follow, and tell how they would check on the children once they were placed. Then she opened the floor to questions.

"I have a question." A burly man stood from his chair in the front row and turned to face the rest of the audience. "These here children without families, how do we know they're not troublemakers? Who's gonna protect us from havin' young ruffians loose on our streets?"

A murmur passed through the crowd, and Dev could see that the man's words had provoked a spate of opinion both in favor of and against the children.

"These children are not ruffians," Bess denied in a strong voice. "It's no crime to have lost your mother or father. Most of you know that I lost my mother, as has Mary Robertson. Isn't that so, Mary? We weren't ruffians or troublemakers."

"That's right, Ty." Mary Robertson answered. "And we weren't the only ones, you know."

The burly man turned around to face her. "That's true enough, but these children are different. They were runnin' on the streets. Ain't that so, Miz Richmond?"

"Yes, they were, but that doesn't automatically make them troublemakers."

"Don't it? You mean to tell me they survived by doin' good deeds?"

"Perhaps not, Mr. Jackson," Bess conceded, "but they had little choice in the matter. I brought them here to give them a chance at a better life. I'm hoping the rest of you will help make that come true."

"And what if there are problems?" Ty Jackson insisted. "Then what?"

"Then I'll take care of them," a new voice from the back put in firmly.

Dev looked at the man who spoke. He was of medium height with green eyes and light brown hair just beginning to turn gray. There was something about him that seemed familiar, something in the shape of his eyes, the gestures he used, though Dev knew he'd never met the man before.

"Maybe so, sheriff," the burly man said, "but by then someone will have been hurt. I don't see why our town has to be used for this project. That's all I have to say."

He sat down amid scattered applause and a few catcalls aimed against the newcomers.

"Please, everyone," Bess pleaded from the front of the room, "these are children we are talking about. Can't you give them a chance? How much harm can they do? You haven't even seen them yet."

"Bess is right," Mary Robertson spoke out. "We're talking about youngsters here, youngsters that need homes. And I, for one, want to meet them and make them feel welcome."

The sheriff walked to the front of the room. "Mary's talking sense here. The children need to be made welcome. Any of you have problems, see me. Otherwise, I don't want any trouble. Is that clear?"

Ty Jackson stood again. "I don't mean no disrespect, sheriff, but you have to admit you're prejudiced on this, Bess being your daughter and all. Who's looking out for the town? That's what I want to know."

"I've been sheriff for a long time, Ty. Are you questioning my integrity? I said I'd take care of any trouble, and I will. If that's not good enough for you, you can find someone else to fill my job."

"Papa, what are you saying?" Dev heard Bess whisper, her face ashen. He wanted to go to her, to put his arms around her and tell her not to worry, every-thing would be all right. But he knew this was not the time to spring his presence on her. Besides, her father seemed more than capable of handling this crowd. Protests at his leaving his post were already being shouted from the assembled group, and Ty Jackson himself was saying, "Now, Bert, you know I didn't mean nothin' like that. I'm just worried, is all."

Bert Richmond nodded. "I'm worried, too, but like Bess says, we've got to give these young'uns a chance. So what do you say?"

Ty nodded his agreement though a frown still creased his brow.

"There are cakes and punch over on the sideboard," Bess said, taking charge again. "Please help your-selves, and we'll bring the children in to take refresh-ments with you."

She went out a side door with Laura, and in min-utes the two women were back with two lines of chil-dren. The older boys looked defiant, the younger ones curious. The girls hung together. Dev recog-nized Danny at once and had to quell the urge to pull the boy out of the line. He had wanted a better life for Danny, as Bess obviously did; he just wasn't sure that this was it.

Ty Jackson stood staring at the oldest boy, disap-proval written all over his face. The boy stared back, his expression sullen and challenging all at the same time. As if sensing the byplay, Bess brought the boy over to Ty and introduced them. Ty nodded once then turned his back and left the room. Bess spared a second to glare at his back before taking the boy to her father. Dev wondered how the sheriff would react to the obviously troubled boy, but his worries were needless. Bert Richmond had a natural ease with children, it seemed.

Several couples hovered around the girls, the wives

241

especially taken with the youngest, a sweet, red-haired cherub with a ready smile. The men, in contrast, seemed more interested in the older boys, no doubt seeing them as workers more than family members. Dev couldn't blame them, not after the economic hard times of the past few years. If they had to take in another mouth to feed, someone who could pull his own weight would be more useful than a completely dependent child.

Danny fell in the middle—too old to be a small cuddly child, too young to be relied on in the fields. He stood on his own, watching the others but making no attempt to get to know anyone. Then, as if he sensed he was being watched, the boy turned to face Dev. A sudden smile lit his face, and he ran across the room.

"Hey, mister, what are you doin' here? I thought you were in Philadelphia."

"I'm here on business. You're looking well. How is everything going?"

"Pretty good. That Miz Richmond sure is a nice lady. She got us new clothes and brought us here. Now she wants families for everyone. Do you think she can do it?"

The boy looked up at him with such a mixture of hope and doubt in his face that Dev didn't know what to say.

"I think she's going to try very hard," he finally managed. "What about you? What do you want?"

The lad looked wistfully toward Bess. "I'd like a family, too," he said, but Dev heard the underlying pain.

"What happened to your folks, Danny?" Dev couldn't resist asking.

The boy looked up at him with alarm. "Nothin'. Nothin' happened. I gotta go now." He ran off without looking back.

Dev started after him, forgetting his resolve to stay away from Bess until her guests had left. The boy ran straight for her, and Dev heard him say, "I don't wanna stay here any more, Miz Richmond."

"Hush, Danny," she said soothingly, bending over the boy. "You don't have to stay in here if you don't want to. Has something happened?"

Her blond hair gleamed brightly in the afternoon sunlight slanting in through the window, and Dev had to tuck his hand into his pocket to keep from reaching out to stroke its lustrous silkiness.

Danny just shrugged, refusing to say any more than he had to Dev. At that moment, Bess looked up and saw Dev. Her face went white.

"Dev?" she whispered.

"I'm sorry, I didn't mean to surprise you like this. This obviously isn't the right time. Maybe I should leave and—"

"Leave? But—"

"Is something wrong?" Laura asked from behind Dev.

"I'm afraid I came at a bad time," he replied.

Laura looked from him to Bess. "Why don't I take Danny back to his room? He looks like he could use a break. Bess, if you like, you can show Dev to the door."

Bess didn't know what she wanted. The last thing she'd expected was to see Dev again. What was he doing here? Why had he come? Her mind spun with possibilities. He looked tired, she noted, but just as compelling as ever. His sable hair was neatly combed, and his dark suit fit perfectly. But more than his appearance, the emotions playing in his dark eyes reached out to her. She saw everything she herself was feeling and more—the confusion, the hope, the fear, and most of all, the longing.

"Will you be all right?" she asked Danny.

The boy nodded his head and let Laura take his hand. Then Bess faced Dev again. It was as if they were alone; everyone else in the room faded away.

"Will you join me outside for a moment?" Dev asked.

"All right," she replied and led the way, talking as if her life depended on it. "We decided to use the ballroom for our meeting because it's so large. We weren't sure how many people would show up, especially on such short notice. As it turns out, we had quite a few." She knew she was chattering but there was so much she wanted to know—and was afraid to ask. Talking about the meeting seemed safe. "I hope Ty Jackson doesn't cause more problems. Were you there to hear him?"

"Yes, I was, and you handled him very well." The look he sent her was full of admiration.

"Actually, my father was the one they believed in, not me." She grimaced. "I guess it's no different here than anywhere else. If a man says it's okay, everyone believes him, but when a woman tries to do something, no one has much confidence in her."

They reached the front of the house. "Would you like to sit down?" she asked Dev.

He nodded and followed her out onto the porch and around to where a rattan settee and two matching armchairs were arranged on either side of a low table.

"Laura's brother sent these. He seems to think Laura is some sort of hothouse flower and will wither away if he doesn't see to her every comfort."

"You're wrong, you know," Dev said.

"About Arthur?"

"No, about yourself. I have every confidence in you. If anyone can make this work, you can."

She looked at him, her eyes captured by the dark intensity of his gaze. "But you still have doubts?" she asked with that part of her mind that could still remember their conversation, the part that wasn't admiring his finely sculpted mouth, the deep flush shadowing his cheekbones, the desire simmering in the black pools of his eyes.

"Not about you."

He stepped closer to her, so close that his face blurred as he leaned down. His scent surrounded her, taking her back to the last night they'd spent together. Her lips parted in the instant before his mouth touched hers. Without hesitation his tongue plunged into the opening, making her his again. His arms closed around her, lifting her until her hips were cradled against him and she had no doubt of his desire.

"Oh, God, Bess, how I've missed you!" His voice sounded hoarse, ragged with emotion. "I thought I'd lost you . . ."

His words trailed off, and then he was kissing her again, tiny, nibbling kisses that covered her cheeks, her eyelids, the line of her jaw until he found her lips again. This time she was the bold one, searching out his taste and textures, probing the most secret recesses of his mouth, reveling in the rough texture of his skin against her own.

"Why did you leave without a word?" he asked at last, when they had satisfied the first strong demands of their craving for each other. They sat side by side on the settee, her hand clasped in both of his, as if he couldn't bear not to touch her.

She turned her head away from him, unable to face the hurt she heard in his tone. "I was afraid," she admitted.

"Of me?"

"Of everything that was happening — you, me, Catherine. I didn't want to hurt you, Dev, and I was afraid Catherine would use me against you. And

245

then, when you disappeared without contacting me, I thought you, too, had decided it was best this way."

"Without contacting you? Are you saying you didn't get my letter?"

She looked up then. "What letter?"

"The letter I left with the hotel clerk. I stopped by the hotel later that morning, but the front desk said you were out. At first I thought you didn't want to see me, but when I heard the Covingtons were also out, I decided you must be with them. That's when I wrote to you. I had to go, Bess. There was some testimony I had to give for one of the Molly Maguire trials. I couldn't put Pinkerton's off even for a day."

"Pinkerton's? The detective agency?"

"Yes. I do some work for them now and again."

Bess's eyes widened. "That explains your injury and your disappearances?"

Dev nodded.

So much became clear to her now—how Dev had disappeared so completely, why he was so secretive about where he'd gone. Even more, she realized he was now trusting her with one of his most well-kept secrets. Even Aunt Livvie didn't seem to know exactly what Dev did when he was gone.

"Isn't it dangerous?" she asked, remembering how stiffly he'd held his injured arm, how pale he'd looked.

"Not usually."

"But sometimes," she insisted, amazed to think how she'd underestimated him when she'd first met him, dismissing him as a "city man" rather than trying to see past his facade to the real man beneath.

"Occasionally," he conceded. "But I try to avoid that now. I didn't use to care . . . but lately life has become more meaningful, more vital and important."

From the way he was looking at her, she knew she was the source of his change. He tugged on her hand, pulling her closer as he lowered his head. She leaned toward him, her eyes closing in anticipation of his touch, of his lips on hers.

Just then Laura came around the corner of the house. "Why, there you are, Bess. Could you come back in? People are starting to leave, and the children are getting restless."

Bess hastily leaned back and quickly stood, her eyes wide. She'd completely forgotten about the children! She could feel a blush creeping up her neck and onto her cheeks. "I'm so sorry," she exclaimed.

Laura gave her a wry, understanding look. "There's nothing to be sorry about. Come now, and no one will have noticed you've been gone. You come, too, Dev. Now that you're staying at the guest cottage, I think of you as part of the family."

After another hour the children were either asleep or in their rooms, and Bess was finally alone with Dev. Laura and Bert had retreated to the kitchen to share a pot of tea. By now, Bess had realized that a fragile but budding relationship was building between the two, fragile enough that she dared not impinge with her curious questions though the bud seemed ready to burst into flower if allowed its natural growth.

She took Dev into the second parlor, a room designed more for comfort than formality. Large cushions adorned the tufted leather sofa and chairs; flowered cloths covered the two end tables, one of which held a gas lamp while the smaller one held a tea set of mismatched pieces. Bess collapsed onto the sofa and grabbed one of the pillows, hugging it to her. Dev sat diagonally at the opposite end, half facing her, one knee almost touching hers.

"Laura mentioned you were staying at their guest cottage," Bess said, a pleasant tiredness creeping over her. She'd never dared to dream that Dev would be here with her, close enough to touch if she moved her leg a mere few inches, near enough that his scent filled the air, bold and masculine and infinitely enticing.

Dev chuckled. "That 'cottage,' is larger than some houses I've seen. Arthur was kind enough to suggest I stay there, and as quite a few of my business colleagues will be visiting the Carlinsville area for all or most of the summer, it seemed convenient. Especially since you were so nearby."

His eyes darkened as he looked at her, and Bess felt her heart skip a couple of beats.

"I'm glad you'll be here, too." She wanted to ask how long he planned to stay, but she felt suddenly shy.

"What are your plans for the children?" he asked, and the moment was lost.

"We hope to hold more meetings like today's, to introduce the children to the local families. I want the children happy, Dev."

"I know."

"But you still don't approve."

He looked away. "It's not that I don't approve, Bess. I'm just not convinced that taking the children so far from everything they've ever known will work out well. Some of them even have families still in Philadelphia."

"Families who turned their backs on them," Bess replied, her anger and anguish at the children's plight bleeding into her tone.

"Maybe. Or maybe they just did the best they could at the time."

Bess stood. "What does that mean?"

Dev shrugged and ran his hand over his face. "I don't know. Maybe there were circumstances at the time, circumstances that could change. How will the families be able to come back together if the children are no longer in the city? Only time will tell what's right and what's wrong. I certainly don't have all the answers; I just don't want to see the children hurt."

"And I do?"

Dev got up from the sofa and came to stand behind her. He wrapped his arms around her waist and rested his cheek against hers.

"I know you don't. I don't want to fight. You do what you think is best, and we'll see how it goes. I want you to succeed, Bess. I want only the best for the children. I hope you believe that."

She turned in his arms to face him. "I do believe you, Dev, and I think I am doing the right thing. You'll see—just give me a little time."

Dev gave her a chaste kiss on the forehead. "I think we both could use a little time. Come walk me to the door. It's getting late now, and I'd better be heading home."

Keeping one arm around her waist, he led her to the front of the house. As they approached the front entrance, Laura and Bert joined them, and both men took their leave.

"Did everything work out all right?" Laura asked as soon as the door closed. Her face was flushed and her eyes bright with happiness.

Bess didn't know the answer to that herself. Dev had given her his qualified approval, wishing her well despite his own doubts. She understood his concerns and respected his honesty, but she wasn't sure where that left her. What if something went wrong? How would they survive the strain of waiting to see what would happen?

"Everything's fine," she said, not wanting to destroy Laura's happy mood with her concerns. "I'm just tired. Today was a long day, and tomorrow will be even longer once we start classes for the children."

"Giving the children something to do other than

worry about their future will be a help to them," Laura said reassuringly. "And I'm sure you'll do just fine as a teacher. I remember how well you helped the other girls at Miss Fine's Academy. You know very well that Alice Covington would never have made it through without your help."

"How did you know about that?" Bess asked, surprised.

"We teachers have our ways," Laura said with a mysterious smile. "You just wait and see tomorrow. Your students will think they're being so clever, but you'll know everything that's going on. The only hard part is deciding whether to let on just how much you do know."

Bess laughed, as she was supposed to, and went to bed with a lighter heart. Laura seemed to have every confidence that she would do well by the children, and Bess chose to believe her friend rather than focus on her own doubts.

The week passed quickly, what with caring for the children and spending time with Dev. He dropped in almost every night, often staying for the evening meal. He took time out to be with the children as well. Of them all, Danny was especially fond of Dev. Bess would notice him hanging on Dev's every word, copying his way of walking and talking.

Sometimes the three of them would take a walk together, and Bess would show them the secret places in Carlinsville she'd loved as a child. On Friday evening, they took a picnic supper out to the lake where it was a bit cooler. Bess couldn't get enough of seeing Danny's delight as he watched the fish jump out of the water to snap up low-flying insects.

When she glanced at Dev, she saw he was just as enthralled, his gaze pinned on the youngster, his mouth curved in a smile. Then suddenly he turned to her. She could see his eyes darken as they focused on her lips. His hand came up to cup her cheek, and she couldn't resist turning her head to nuzzle his palm. His skin tasted salty and male when her tongue flicked out to moisten her lips.

"Bess," he murmured, and his hand glided back until his fingers entangled in her hair, sending hairpins flying.

Gently he brought her face close to his and kissed her. She felt his passion, a dark, pulsating force simmering just below the surface, and knew his desire. She closed her eyes and heard the gentle lap of the water against the shore, the little splashes made by the jumping fish, the receding patter of Danny's feet as he ran along the shoreline. The kiss deepened, and Bess lost track of everything else, of the scent of wildflowers and mossy banks, of the wet earth and dried grass; of the hard ground beneath her and the darkening sky above.

All she was aware of was Dev and the magic his mouth was creating. Rivulets of pleasure ran through her. Her hands came to rest on his shoulders, then curved around the back of his neck as her world spun in eddies of delight. His tongue plunged deeply and then withdrew, teasing her and arousing her at the same time.

A small moan escaped from her, and Dev gentled the kiss. Slowly the sounds came back, the insects' chirping, the breeze rustling through the trees, the sound of Danny's footsteps once again drawing closer.

"We need some time alone, Bess," Dev whispered. "Time just for the two of us."

She nodded, still too caught up in the rapture of the moment to speak.

"When?" he prodded.

Pulling herself together, she said, "Sunday? After the meeting?"

"I'll come get you."

"All right."

She stood on shaky legs and looked toward the lake. Danny was squatting by the water's edge throwing in pieces of grass and twigs and watching them float away. On the western horizon, the sky blazed forth in shades of orange and red while overhead it was already turning dark.

"Time to be going," she called to the boy.

He looked up, and a smile lit his features. "I'll be right there."

She wished she could keep him with her forever. This evening felt so right, and the child seemed so happy. In some ways, she dreaded the meeting on Sunday. What if someone should want to adopt Danny? Should she let him go? Was it fair to him to keep him when she couldn't provide him with a real home?

She wished she could adopt him herself, but knew that dream was unrealistic. It was hard enough for widowed mothers to keep their children; in fact, some of the children on the streets came from just such families, families where the father and breadwinner had died, leaving the family destitute.

She knew her father would never allow that to happen to her, but would he accept Danny and what adopting him would mean? Bess knew Bert still harbored the hope that his daughter would marry into the social elite of Kansas City. Though he had spoken out in favor of the children at the public meeting last week, she realized he still had serious reservations about her new vocation. How much worse would he view things if she actually tried to adopt a child on her own? A single woman with a child would be of no interest to the type of husband Bert wished for her.

She sighed and began to pack the remains of their picnic.

"Is everything all right?" Dev asked.

"I was just thinking about Danny."

"He's a fine boy."

"I hope he finds a wonderful home."

She bit down on her lip so he wouldn't see it trembling. She felt near tears all of a sudden, as if her dreams were close by but hovering just out of reach, hidden from her sight so that she didn't know which way to turn to grab for them. She was filled with inchoate longings, wanting things to which she could put no name but which were real just the same. How could she explain to Dev what she did not understand herself?

Dev helped her finish packing, then picked up the basket and called to Danny. Together, the three of them headed back to Rutherford House — almost like a real family, though Bess's mind shied away from the thought. Dev would be near for only a short time, and who knew when Danny might be plucked from her life?

Dev arrived early on Sunday, in time to see the last few couples leaving Rutherford House after the meeting. He recognized a few of the faces, including that of Mary Robertson, the woman who'd spoken out in defense of the children last week. She was looking wistfully over her shoulder as her husband led her away, her glance held by one of the younger boys, shy and quiet Max. The boy stared back then lifted one hand in a small wave. Mary waved back and smiled.

Dev wondered how long it would be before the child went home with her. She and her husband seemed to be a nice couple with no children of their own despite having been married for several years.

Bess had told him how much Mary wanted a child, and now it seemed she may have found one.

As Dev came up the stairs, Bess opened the door. "I saw you drive up," she said with a smile.

She was wearing a sprigged muslin dress with a lace inset in the bodice. The deep blue color matched her eyes, and the tiny pink flowers brought out the pink and white glow of her skin. She looked fresh and cool despite the steamy heat of the afternoon. Dev felt his breath catch in his throat.

"You look beautiful," he whispered.

"Thank you." A blush tinted her cheeks as she lowered her lashes. "You look nice, too."

He'd dressed specially for her, getting out his good suit and a clean white shirt with a wing collar. He'd shaved a second time as well, remembering how his day's growth of beard had scraped her tender skin that night in Philadelphia.

"Are you ready to go?" he asked.

She nodded. "Laura and the two girls from town are going to take the children for a treat. They won't need me this evening."

"Come along, then."

He held out his arm for her and breathed deeply as she placed her hand on it. Her unique scent filled the air around him, the sweet fragrance of wildflowers and woman, feminine and sensual.

He helped her into the buggy Arthur had lent him together with the cottage. The small vehicle was designed for two, with one narrow seat and an overhanging canopy. When he sat beside Bess, he could feel the warmth of her body all the way up his side. She looked up at him with shining eyes, her lips slightly apart. He would have kissed her right then except he noticed the slight movement of one of the sheer curtains in the front window and knew they had an audience.

"Wave goodbye," he whispered with a smile.

"What?"

"We're being watched." He tilted his head toward the house just as the curtain fell back into place.

Bess shook her head and laughed. "Those children! It was probably Victor. He's always up to something."

The laughter lit up her face, gladdening his heart. Despite the heavy summer heat, it was a beautiful day, made perfect by her presence at his side. Joining in her laughter, he flicked the reins once and set the horse in motion, heading for the lake and the Christy's cottage.

The cottage was really a fair-sized house on the grounds of the Christy's summer home. It was separated from the main house by a brick wall covered with a thick growth of climbing roses, all now in bloom in shades of pink and dark red. Their heavy perfume hung in the thick summer air, lending the place a sultry air despite the cooling breeze from the lake.

"Would you like to stroll by the lake?" Dev asked. "It's a bit early for supper yet, unless . . ."

"A stroll would be perfect," Bess replied. "I've never been to this part of the lake."

"You haven't? But I thought Laura was a close friend."

"She is now, but before that she was my teacher. I really had no occasion to visit her then." She laughed, the sound bright and cheerful in the shade of the trees bordering the path they took. "You know how it is. Teachers always seem like such mystical beings to their students. I don't know if I realized she had a house — or even needed one. Since I only saw her in class, I never thought she had another life."

As they came by a dip in the path, a family of ducks crossed in front of them, squawking loudly at having their rest disturbed.

"Aren't they darling?" Bess asked, looking up at him with a smile.

She looked so beautiful standing there, her hair like spun gold in the sun, her face alive with good humor and happiness. Dev reached out to touch her cheek, afraid for a moment that she was some fantasy, a wood sprite conjured out of his own need and desire. But she was very real, with her face lifted in anticipation of his kiss. And he wanted her as he had never wanted another woman. For a moment his mouth hovered over hers. Her breath mingled with his, and he savored her scent. Then, suddenly, he could wait no longer. Want and desire and fierce longing compelled him. With a sigh that reverberated deep in his chest, he lowered his lips to hers.

Twelve

He tasted sweetness and passion. Her mouth opened to him, inviting his entry, and her tongue slipped around his, warm and velvety, gently dueling. He brought her closer, his hands moving from her shoulders to her waist, savoring the tensile strength of her petite frame. Though she was small, she was everything he wanted, and he shut his eyes and lost himself in her bounty. The tiny sounds coming from her throat urged him closer, and he slanted his head to deepen the kiss.

Her hands came around his neck, her fingers burrowing into the hair above his nape. His scalp tingled at her touch, and his blood thickened, settling in his loins with throbbing intensity. He tried to raise his head, to escape the narrowing spiral of desire before it claimed him, but she wouldn't let him go. Her mouth played with his, her teeth gently biting his lower lip before her tongue smoothed over the spot, taking away the tiny pain and replacing it with a smoldering heat.

Dev plucked the hairpins from her head, and her hair fell in long flowing tresses of light yellow satin, tumbling past her shoulders to her waist. The wind spun it around them, trapping them both inside a silken web, and Dev filled his hands with it, exulting at her throaty laugh.

She reached between them and opened the button holding his jacket in place. When her hands slipped inside and ran over his chest, he felt his muscles quiver. She pushed at the jacket, easing it off his shoulders, and he let her go, one arm at a time, just long enough for the coat to drop to the ground behind him. The wind felt cool against his back, even through the fabric of his shirt, but inside the heat was building, a heat she stoked with every touch of her lips, every stroke of her hands.

She fumbled now with his shirt buttons, her pupils so large they seemed to obscure her irises, turning her eyes the darkest blue he'd ever seen. The fire was burning inside her, too, the flames reaching out to capture him. When her hands touched his bare skin, he thought he would come apart in a million tiny embers, each glowing with the force of his desire.

He reached for her breast, needing to touch her more intimately. It fit the palm of his hand, and when his fingertips brushed the soft skin exposed above her corset, she trembled in his arms. He could feel her heart beating madly and saw the matching pulse point in the hollow of her throat. He bent his head and planted a feather-soft kiss there, then knelt before her and opened her dress, working each tiny button free with hands that seemed too large, too slow. Eventually the dress fell away, leaving her arms and shoulders bare, tempting him beyond endurance.

"Do you know what we're doing?" he asked, surprised that his voice sounded so hoarse.

"Yes, oh, yes," she replied on a moan as his fingers eased beneath the top of her corset, seeking their elusive goal. She grabbed at his shoulders when one finger grazed a nipple. "Please," she murmured. "Don't stop."

Her voice sounded as ragged as his, and he felt a flush of masculine triumph that he could give her such pleasure. She bent her head over his, and once again her hair swirled around them, filling his world with the scent of her. The quiet cove where they'd been walking was isolated from the rest of the houses. The only sounds were those made by nature . . . and by the two of them.

Dev carefully reached beneath her chemise and started unclasping her corset. When he reached her waist his progress was stopped by the brace of petticoats she wore. His fingers fumbled with the various ties trying to undo them all while she leaned over his back and ran her fingers up and down his muscles. She bent farther over and a shiver ran down his spine as he felt her lips nipping at his skin. When her tongue licked from his shoulder to his neck, he gave up and tumbled her onto the grassy verge, making sure she came down on his coat.

She laughed, and he trapped her hands above her head, his laughter joining with hers. The laughter suddenly stopped as their gazes caught and held. She eased one hand from his grasp and reached up to him, pulling his face down to hers. The time for teasing was past; with one kiss they crossed the boundary from playfulness to serious intent. There would be no going back now.

Bess couldn't get enough of him, of his taste, so dark and male, of his scent, mysterious and musky, of his feel, hard where she was soft, taut where she was all yielding. His weight pressed her onto the grassy bank, molding her into a liquid pliancy she'd never felt before. The sun beat down on them both, and the wind ruffled the feathered edges of his hair. The earth beneath smelled warm and fecund and bursting with life—the way she herself felt.

She felt him reach for the last of her petticoats and

eased to her side to help him. Her clothes had become an encumbrance, separating her from what she wanted most — to feel his skin against hers, to know him as she'd known no other.

He helped her shed the last of her underclothes, then quickly removed his boots and pants until the only garment between them was his light wool drawers. In the instant before he covered her again, she could make out his male shape, the ridge of flesh she'd felt so fleetingly before. A thrill of excitement flashed through her, and her lips were already parted when he took them.

The sensation of skin smoothly brushing against skin sent shivers of anticipation rioting all over her body, and she writhed beneath him, wanting to increase the contact, to eke every moment of pleasure from his touch. His hands stroked her body from shoulder to thigh, and his legs entwined with hers. Then when she least expected it, his hand cupped her breast, his thumb and fingers gently massaging her sensitized skin. She felt as if a wire had pulled taut inside her, a wire that connected her budding nipple to the very heart of her feminine center.

When his mouth left hers to lick and suckle at her breast, her heart nearly stopped beating. She felt she was on the brink of a precipice, waiting to tumble into the gaping void below. She clutched at his shoulders, wanting to push him away and hold him in place, all at the same time. He kissed her tenderly — soft, whispering kisses that blazed a moist trail from one breast to the other.

This time she knew what to expect and her body arched in anticipation. He held back for a moment, tantalizing her, building the tension between them until she thought she would snap. Then, when she felt she couldn't bear to wait even another second, she felt his lips close over the aching bud. Liquid heat pooled inside her, threatening to overflow in a torrent. She'd never known such wanting, never felt such an urge to surrender and conquer, to give her all and take everything he had to offer.

When he raised his head, she almost didn't recognize him as the man she'd first seen across a ballroom. Gone were all traces of cool sophistication and disdain. He looked all male, his cheeks flushed and his lips swollen. His eyes were darker than she'd ever seen them and burning with the force of his emotions. Her body responded to his look with instincts as old as time. Her hips pressed against his, finding the source of his desire.

A groan escaped from Dev at the contact. He couldn't believe how responsive she was, how his every loving touch was magnified and returned, building the tension in him until the slightest breath made him feel he would explode. Never had he felt this way, so consumed by passion, so filled with desire and something more, something that made this act take on a significance beyond this place and time.

Her fingers ran down the valley of his spine, her delicate touch nearly becoming his undoing. At his waist, her hands paused, then worked their way beneath his drawers to cup his buttocks and urge him closer. His blood surged in his veins until he throbbed with more longing than he'd ever dreamed possible. Reaching between them, he let his hand slide down her creamy skin to the juncture of her thighs.

She stiffened, and he whispered in her ear, words of love, words of passion, words that made no sense to anyone but lovers. His hand slipped lower and found her ready, her flesh moist and swollen. Her eyes were dark and wild as he touched her.

"Please," she whispered.

He drew in a deep, shuddering breath as she

moved rhythmically against his hand. Carefully he rolled to the side and shucked his drawers, then, afraid he might frighten her, he slid back over her body, making a place for himself between her thighs. He touched her again, with the most intimate part of himself, and again her hips flexed. His breath caught as he fought for control, wanting to go gently, but she wouldn't let him. Her hands kneaded his hips, pulling him toward her.

She could feel him pressing against her. A tide of pleasure swelled inside her, rising higher and higher, yet not high enough. She needed more — more of Dev — more of this feeling. Her hands dug into his muscles in her desperation, urging him forward. For a moment, her body resisted him, and the pressure grew and swelled, like a wave nearing the shore. And then it broke, and he was inside her, filling her, taking away the aching void he'd created with the magic of his touch.

He lay still above her, his hands combing the stray hair from her face. She thought it was enough, this feeling of being full, this closeness she'd shared with no other nor even dreamed was possible. Then he lowered his mouth to hers, and as his tongue mated with hers, he began to move. The sensations were indescribable. The tide she'd thought was at its peak swelled higher, carrying her with it — and Dev, too. Higher and higher it took her, until with a shattering cry, she felt the world fall away, and she went spinning into a different place, a place where there were no limits, no boundaries — only her and Dev with nothing between them, a unity of body, a oneness of soul.

She opened her eyes and saw the sky above her and felt the warm earth below. It was like the first joining, the mating of heaven and earth, and she tried to hold on to the moment, to grab it with both hands and never let go for she knew she would never be happier nor more content. Her life had been made complete.

By the time Bess arrived home, she felt she was living a dream, a delicious, sensuous dream. Though she could barely remember what she'd eaten, the meal she'd shared with Dev had been a sensual delight. They'd sat side by side, feeding each other between long, languorous kisses, more intent on satisfying their hunger for each other than their hunger for food.

Every time Bess looked into Dev's eyes she saw her image and more — a depth of emotion she would never have thought possible, never imagined existing between two people. Where he touched her, her skin came alive, tingling with an excitement that quickly spread to even the farthest reaches of her body. When he kissed her, she was filled with rapture, her heart soaring like an eagle, lifting her spirit to the skies.

The more he gave, the more she wanted — and her growing desire was reflected in his every gesture, his every word. Lying in her bed that night, she blushed to remember all the intimate things they'd said, the tender ways they'd touched. The fine fabric of her night dress caressed her sensitized skin every time she moved, reminding her most vividly of Dev's touch, and she fell asleep to dream again and again of their time together.

In the morning, she awoke with a smile on her lips and a bounce to her step. Today would be a wonderful day! And all the days after, even better. When she came down the stairs, the children responded to her good mood with sunny smiles of their own, and even Laura made a comment about how living in Rutherford House seemed to agree with Bess.

Bess simply smiled, hugging her secret to her heart, not ready yet to share with the world her burgeoning love for Dev, her dreams of a bright future with him. She had just finished straightening up the dining room when a knock sounded at the front door. Her heart leaped at the sound. Dev had said he'd be over to see her early, and the thought that he might be there already sent tingles up and down her spine.

Eagerly she raced to the door, then stopped for a moment to make sure her hair was neat and her dress tidy. Satisfied that all was in order, she peered through the curtained window, wanting to catch a glimpse of him before he saw her. All her joy faded when she looked outside. Straightening her shoulders, she reached for the knob and pulled the door open, a false smile pinned to her face.

"Why, Anna, how nice of you to call and welcome me back to town."

"Oh, yes, of course," Anna Moore said with a small grimace that might have passed for a smile if Bess hadn't known her so well. "Actually, I've come about the children."

Wylie's wife walked into the foyer as if she owned it, surveying the house with a critically assessing gaze.

"The children?"

"Why, yes. Wylie and I have decided that this might just be the kind of charity I should be involved in."

"Involved in?" Bess felt like a parrot, repeating Anna's words, but she couldn't quite make sense of what she was hearing.

"I've talked with Lillian Bennett, and she agrees. As long as we're stuck here in the back of beyond, we might as well find some worthwhile project to work on. She suggested I come over and talk with you since we went to school together. Of course, I told her we weren't that close at Miss Fine's, but it's the contact, of course."

Bess ignored Anna's cut and said, "I take it you're staying out at the lake for the summer, then."

"Isn't everyone?" Anna returned with a smug smile.

She wasn't staying at the lake, as Anna well knew — only the most well-to-do could afford that. Apparently marriage to Wylie Moore hadn't smoothed away Anna's sharp edges.

"So what does that have to do with me?" Bess asked, deciding the quickest way to be rid of her caller was to let her have her say.

"A group of us thought your orphans would be the ideal summer project."

How like Anna to think of human beings as her own personal little project! Bess gritted her teeth, resisting the urge to tell Anna off. Like it or not, Anna and her friends could be a real help in finding homes for the children. For their sake, Bess would put up with just about anything — even Anna. Besides, she could afford to be generous now that she had a direction and purpose in her life — and Dev. What more could she want?

"I'm sure we can use all the help you can give, Anna."

"Yes, Dev said the same thing. He knows how important this type of work is." Anna paused suggestively, a sly and knowing expression on her face. When Bess didn't say anything, she added, "You may not know it, but his dear wife, Julia, was involved in any number of charitable organizations, and he doted on her. Of course, she also brought along her name. Why, the Whitlaw name would open doors that would normally have stayed firmly closed. And, as if all those qualities weren't enough, she was such a beauty, so tall and graceful."

Anna looked Bess over from head to toe as she said those last words, making it clear Bess qualified on none of those counts.

"She sounds like a true paragon," Bess stated.

"Oh, she was. Just before I started Miss Fine's, my father and I took a shopping trip to Philadelphia and stayed with Dev's father. Julia took pity on the poor motherless child I was and took me to all the best stores. With her startling violet eyes and dark hair, she made heads turn wherever she went. I felt like I was in the presence of royalty." Anna pressed her hand to her heart. "She was such a dear."

"I'm sure she was lovely," Bess said calmly, refusing to let Anna see her inner turmoil. Anna was deliberately trying to make her feel bad, but even though Bess knew that, the barbs struck home. Julia sounded like the perfect wife, and if Bess had held any doubts on that score, Anna's next words dispelled them.

"More than lovely—she was absolutely exquisite. Dev just adored her. He treated her as if she were the perfect summer rose. It was so romantic." Anna's eyes closed, and she sighed. Then as if suddenly remembering where she was, she opened her eyes and declared, "But I mustn't prattle on so, I'm sure you have your hands full cleaning up after and feeding this menagerie you've carted here from Philadelphia."

"Actually, we have help in from town."

"Of course, you'd have to, wouldn't you? *Miss Christy* isn't used to doing manual labor."

Bess ignored Anna's implication that such work was suitable for *her* but not for Laura. She was still agonizing over Anna's description of Dev's wife. Dev had spoken only briefly of her in Philadelphia, never providing this richness of detail. Bess could imagine how lovely Julia must have been, how striking the two of them were as a couple, with Dev so handsome and both of them dark-haired and tall.

From what Anna had said, it sounded like Dev and Julia had had a perfect marriage, each complementing the other. Was that why he'd been so reticent about discussing her? Did he still miss her too much? And what did that mean about his feelings for Bess?

Bess had no chance to worry the point, for just then Laura came through the front door with Nola, Rosie and Polly at her side.

"Anna, how nice of you to come and visit us," Laura said in greeting as she removed her hat.

"Oh, Miss Christy, you're looking wonderful. I heard you were out here organizing this project, and my friends and I think it's just the most wonderful thing."

"This is Bess's venture, not mine, but of course we all try and do our share. Don't we girls?"

Nola nodded shyly, as did Polly, but little Rosie didn't have the inhibitions her sisters did about speaking out in front of a stranger. "I help with the dishes, and I've only broken one glass. Isn't that right, Miz Bess?"

Bess smiled down at the small girl. The child's bright red hair shimmered in the morning light, and Bess couldn't resist giving a playful tug on one of her long braids. "That's right. Only one glass. We're very proud of her."

"Well, you'll have to be more careful if you want a good family to adopt you. People don't like their belongings mishandled."

Though what she said held some truth, Bess thought the rebuke a little too harsh. Why spoil the girl's enthusiasm? Laura must have sensed her growing anger because she quickly intervened.

"Rosie's so small and earnest, we must forgive her almost anything, mustn't we?"

267

"Of course, Miss Christy, if you say so," Anna acquiesced.

Laura smiled at Anna and then down at the children. "Girls, why don't you run out back and play while I talk with Bess and Mrs. Moore. We'll be in the front parlor if you need us. All right?"

The girls chorused their agreements, happy to be on their own. They ran off, chattering about what they would do with their unexpected free time.

"Come take a seat in the parlor, and we can talk more comfortably," Laura invited.

When Anna was seated with every ruffle and skirt placed in just the right position, Laura said, "Now, what can we do for you?"

Rather than allow Anna to sugar-coat her plans, Bess answered for her. "Before you came in, Anna said she thought the *orphans* might be a good *project* for her and her friends." Bess paused, allowing Laura to take in the full impact of Anna's statement. "And I was about to ask her if she thought any of the families out at the lake might care to adopt a child."

"What do you think, Anna?" Laura asked when Anna didn't speak.

"Adopt?" Anna replied in an appalled tone. "I'm sure no one has any plans to adopt. Why would we ever . . ." She stopped suddenly in midsentence. The realization of what she was saying and how it would be taken must have struck her, for she glared at Bess as though it were all her fault.

"You were saying, my dear?" Laura prompted.

"Actually, I'm not sure of anyone's plans. What we'd intended was to have the ladies meet once a week for a light luncheon to discuss the project and how we could be involved."

Bess didn't want to be small-minded, but this sounded more like an excuse for Anna and her friends to get together and have lunch than a true charitable venture. She was almost sure the children would come last, after the gossip of the day and who was in and out of town.

"I've gotten together a list of things that we need. I'm sure you and your friends could help with that, don't you think?" Laura prompted.

"I'm sure that's something we can handle." Anna looked in Bess's direction and gave her a very toothy smile then turned back to Laura. "Miss Christy, why don't you attend one of our meetings and give us talk about the orphans?"

"Bess is the one who does the speaking for the group. I prefer to do my work outside of the public eye. But I'm sure she'll be happy to come out any time you like, won't you, dear?" she said, with an encouraging smile at Bess.

Bess could think of any number of things she'd be happy to do, and speaking to Anna's group certainly wasn't one of them. Nonetheless, she didn't feel she had a choice, not where the welfare of the children was concerned.

"When are you having your first meeting?" Bess asked, summoning up a forced smile.

"Why don't I let you know? We haven't set a firm date. I'll send you a note. How will that be?"

"I'll look forward to hearing from you." It was clear to Bess that Anna was no more eager than she to have Bess come to her meeting. Anna still thought of Bess as the interloper, too poor and too low in social standing to mix with society's elite. With any luck, Anna would find some other cause to espouse and the whole issue would simply fade away.

"I really must be getting along," Anna said. "I have to make sure the cook has dinner ready exactly at six. Wylie likes to keep on his schedule even when we're away from the city. Father's so pleased with him. He's thinking about putting him on the company board."

Bess just smiled in response. She rarely thought of Wylie these days, and when she did, her thoughts were less than complimentary. What had she ever seen in the man, she'd wondered more than once since the night of the ball. He lacked all the qualities she found so appealing in Dev—honesty, caring, and concern for others. If she never saw Wylie again, it would be too soon.

Fortunately, Laura took over with her usual social aplomb. "Tell me more about this board appointment as I walk you to the door, and be sure to give Wylie and Gunther my regards. I hope to see them both soon."

Laura's voice faded as she and Anna walked out.

Bess took a deep breath. Well, she'd faced Anna and not come off any the worse for wear. After Catherine, Anna was a mere pussycat, her claws hardly worth commenting upon. Bess smiled to herself and started for the rear of the house so she could check on the three girls.

"Bess, are you still here?" Laura called from the foyer.

"Yes," Bess called back and retraced her steps. "Did you need me for something?"

Laura gave her a serious look. "I didn't want to say anything when Anna was here, but I'm afraid you'll have to go into town tonight."

"Go into town? Whatever for?"

"While the girls and I were at the mercantile, we heard there was trouble brewing."

The hairs on Bess's neck stood on end. "What sort of trouble?"

Laura twisted her hands nervously. "Some of the ladies were talking in the store when we arrived. As soon as they saw me, they stopped, but the proprietor told me the gist of the conversation after they left.

270

"He says there have been all kinds of malicious pranks in town—the kind that usually get blamed on children. He gave me a funny look when he said it."

"Did he give you any details?

"A few. There was a dog with some cans tied to his tail, some outhouses tipped over as well as a few pies and some fruit disappearing from windowsills."

"Did he come right out and blame our boys?"

"No. He merely said nothing like this had happened before they came, and that he found it curious that this all started since we've brought the new children into town."

"That's so unfair."

"They're having a town meeting about it tonight. You'll have to have some sort of rebuttal ready. We have to convince the townsfolk they're wrong about who's at fault."

"Tonight? Were they even going to ask us to come and defend ourselves? Or just run us out of town at daybreak?"

"I don't know. Even Arthur's incensed. I saw him in town and told him about it. He said he'll bring some of his friends to the meeting tonight to speak on our behalf, but I think one of us should be there, too."

"I thought he didn't want you working with the children."

"Arthur has certain ideas about how *I* should act and behave, but they have nothing to do with the children. He was very taken with them when we met in town last week. Even had a few sweets in his pockets for the girls today." Laura shook her head as if she couldn't believe the about-face her brother had made. "I can't say I'm not glad on a number of counts. Having Arthur on our side will be a big help—and his friends are all influential too."

"That will be a decided advantage, I'm sure, but I

just don't know what I can say to convince people that what's happening has nothing to do with us."

"Maybe Dev will have some ideas. He said he'd come out to fetch you around seven. Arthur was taking him to meet the Bennetts for lunch—quite an honor, I must say. The Bennetts are one of Kansas City's most influential families, you know. That's why Anna was so anxious to work with the children when Lillian Bennett made the suggestion. And Arthur doesn't take just anyone on his business lunches. He must have something important in mind if he's asked Dev along."

Bess felt a little more of her morning euphoria slip away. It was bad enough that her day had started with Anna. Worse by far was knowing she would not see Dev again until so late. The hours until seven stretched before her, each minute filled with a different worry. For when she finally would see Dev, it would be for a purpose she'd never imagined: defending the children from this outrageous attack.

She'd always thought of Westerners as an open and friendly people, welcoming strangers into their midst. And she'd always admired Carlinsville for being the heart of what the West stood for: a town where neighbor talked to neighbor, where independence and endeavor were prized, where the only limitations were those imposed by the land itself.

Now she was learning otherwise. Between Anna with her stuck-up ways and the townsfolk with their suspicious minds, many of Bess's illusions were being stripped away.

At six-forty-five, Bess stood on the porch steps waiting for Dev, feeling edgy and worried. If he'd come this morning first thing, before Anna had filled her with doubts about her ability to interest him after

Julia, before the troubles with the town and the children had distracted her beyond endurance, she might have fallen into his arms. Now, she wasn't sure how to behave in front of him.

Did he regret their actions yesterday now that he'd had time to think? Their lovemaking had been so spontaneous, a natural outgrowth of their time together. Out in the woods along the shore of the lake, the inhibitions and constraints of society had fallen away, leaving the natural world supreme. And Bess had succumbed to the beauty of the day, the glories of nature, the light in Dev's eyes.

His touch had been more important than the rules that governed her life, his pleasure more essential than her next breath. He'd been prey to the same storm of emotion, she would have sworn it. But that had been then, in another world and another time.

A swirl of dust told her Dev was finally arriving. She waited on the steps until his buggy came to a stop, then stepped forward. He jumped down from the seat, and before she could think another thought, he took her into his embrace.

"Bess," he murmured in the instant before his lips met hers.

For a moment, her worries fell away. She reveled in the feeling of coming home again, of having found her true place. When his tongue insinuated its way between her lips, she moaned and her entire body shook with tiny tremors.

"God, how I've missed you," he said, after a minute. She could feel his heart galloping in his chest, its rhythm in cadence with her own heartbeat.

"I've missed you, too," she confessed, her earlier awkwardness forgotten. This was Dev; her heart recognized him as her other half, no matter what concerns tormented her mind.

"Good." He flashed her a purely masculine grin

273

laced with a hint of triumph and a deeper satisfaction that echoed her own feelings. "Are you ready to go into town?"

She nodded. "I'm a little worried about it, though."

"Well, we'll know soon enough what's really going on. Let me help you up, and we'll be off."

The drive passed quickly. All too soon Bess stood outside the church where the meeting was to be held, Dev beside her. She was a bundle of nerves, unsure what she or anyone else could say to defuse the situation. It wouldn't be enough to claim her children weren't involved. Someone was pulling these pranks, but who could it be? The only other suspects were the town's own children. She didn't think the people at this meeting would be too pleased to hear that.

She was afraid to ask Dev what he thought, afraid to find that he agreed with the townspeople. He'd said often enough that bringing the children west might be a mistake, that they would be out of their element here, unsure how to behave, unable to really fit in. Though the subject had not come up lately, she was sure he hadn't changed his mind and worried how he might take this turn of events.

The clamor of voices stopped as soon as she and Dev stepped into the small sanctuary. Everyone turned in their seats to look at her, some with friendly smiles, others with ominous scowls. Dev gave her hand a squeeze.

"Everything will be fine," he whispered, reassuring her with just his touch. He might not agree with all she'd done, but he was making it clear that he was on her side at this moment.

She gave him a grateful look, and he held on to her hand a second longer, as if he realized his touch gave her strength. Before she could thank him, a voice called out, "Here she is now. Maybe she'll have some answers."

"What do you have to say, Miz Richmond?" another man called out.

"Yeah, this kind of thing's never happened here before. Not until you brought all those young ruffians here," the mercantile owner added.

Several people in the crowd began nodding their heads and muttering their agreement. Bess shrank back a step at the sight of such hostility, not knowing how to respond. Dev stepped in front of her, shielding her with his body.

"Please calm down," he said. "This is supposed to be a civilized discussion. Miss Richmond has come here of her own free will and deserves some respect."

"Mr. O'Connor is right," Arthur Christy joined in from up front by the pulpit. "She'll be glad to answer all your questions, just give her a moment to gather her thoughts. Isn't that right, Miss Richmond?"

"Of course," Bess answered as Dev escorted her to the front of the room. She was very conscious of the angry glares sent her way and was glad her voice sounded stronger than she felt.

Arthur Christy gave her an encouraging smile. As always, she was a bit taken aback by his looks, for he was much younger than Laura made him sound. When his sister talked about him, Bess always got the impression of a much older, much stuffier man. But to the contrary, he was several years younger than Laura and dashing in a stiff sort of way. Though Bess did not find him nearly as attractive as Dev, she could see he was capable of turning heads just the same.

As she turned to face the townspeople, Dev moved to one side of her while Arthur stood on the other.

"What do you want to know?" Bess asked when the crowd had quieted down.

"How do *you* explain everything that's going on?" a man called out from the back.

"Why don't you tell me exactly what *has* been going on?" Bess countered.

"Just what I said would happen," Ty Jackson said stepping forward. "I tried to warn you, but no one would listen."

"Tyler Jackson, you know that's not what's happened," a woman called out.

"The hell I don't. It was my privy that was knocked over. And a fine mess it made, too."

"Is that the only damage done?" Bess asked.

"I lost two pies from my windowsill yesterday afternoon," a small gray-haired woman said from the middle of the crowd. "And Mrs. Johnson had her laundry thrown to the ground and trampled."

"And don't forget my dog," added another gentleman. "He came running through the house with cans tied around his tail. Knocked the table over as he came through and the lamp just missed falling on the ground. Then he ran out the door, and we haven't seen 'im since."

"I told you there'd be trouble," Jackson reiterated.

"Mr. Jackson," Bess called out. "If you'll allow me, I'll give you my answer."

With ill grace, Tyler Jackson conceded.

"I can't tell you unequivocally that the boys at the Rutherford House didn't do this."

"See, I told you."

"But I also can't say they did, and neither can you. Has anyone caught even a glimpse of one of my children either before or after these incidents?"

The woman whose pies were stolen shook her head as did the man whose dog had disappeared.

"Even so," Jackson put in, "you have to admit it's mighty peculiar that nothing like this ever happened before them ruffians from the East came out here."

"Now, Mr. Jackson," Arthur spoke up. "I've heard that you've had problems with your outhouse on several other occasions. Isn't that right?"

For a moment, Jackson hemmed and hawed, and when he couldn't come up with an answer, he turned to the people sitting in the front pew, friends of Arthur's from the area near the lake.

"What would you know about it anyway?" he said, waving his hand in their direction. "You all don't live in town. All of you with your fancy houses down by the lake don't have to put up with what we do here. Of course you say not to worry; you can hire guards or go back to the city if things get too dangerous. We can't."

There was a general buzz of agreement, and Bess could see that Arthur didn't quite know how to respond, nor did she.

"Mr. Jackson," Dev spoke firmly. "I understand your concern. My name is Devlin O'Connor, and I'm a businessman from Philadelphia. I've worked with the Women's League for several years, and let me assure you that the League has had excellent success in caring for homeless children. If there are any problems here, you can be certain they'll be taken care of, but until we know for certain who's behind this mischief, I don't think it's wise to point too many fingers."

"Well, if it isn't your children, whose is it? 'Cause someone for sure is causing these problems. Are you saying it's our own boys?"

Indignant mutterings rose from the crowd, and Bess took a deep breath.

"Unlike you, I'm not making any accusations," Dev stated. "All we know for sure is that one or more persons have been causing problems, problems that are more inconvenient than truly dangerous, at least so far. There's been no evidence to link the League's children to these activities."

"Mr. O'Connor is right, not that I think it's any of

our own boys, either," Mary Robertson stated. "But we don't really know *who* is doing this. Maybe we should try and catch the culprits."

"Good idea," the man who'd lost his dog called out. "And I know just how to go about getting those good-for-nothin's."

At that moment there was a commotion at the back of the sanctuary. When Bess looked up, she saw her father striding down the middle aisle.

"I think you should leave catching these *good-for-nothin's* to the law," he said once he reached the front of the church. "We don't want anyone getting hurt."

"My thoughts exactly," Jackson said, sending a smug look toward Bess. "How you plannin' on stoppin' 'em, sheriff?"

"Not by going off half-cocked," the sheriff replied looking around as if daring someone to disagree. When no one commented, he continued, "I think it's time we all went back to our homes and settled down for the night. You can't do anything standing around here. And like I said before, I can handle whatever happens."

"So far you haven't done a thing. Why should we believe you're gonna change?"

"Now you listen to me, Ty Jackson, and you listen good. If you want to spend the night in your own bed rather than the jail's, you'll simmer down. If you'd'a come to me right away instead of getting everyone here so excited, maybe we'd'a caught the culprit by now."

"All right, I'll go. But you just make sure you catch him—and soon. An' if you want to know where to look, just ask your little girl up there. I bet she knows a heck of a lot more than she's tellin'."

"You tell 'im, Ty," one of Jackson's friends called out as a group of them walked out with him, slapping him on the back as they went.

The rest of the crowd slowly stood from their seats and gathered their belongings, preparing to leave. Bess watched them, wondering what, if anything, to-night's meeting had accomplished. This certainly had not been the reaction she'd expected when she brought the children west. How could everything have turned around so much?

Thirteen

Dev looked at the two men standing near Bess and was glad of their presence. Among the three of them, they had managed to keep the crowd from getting out of hand. His biggest concern was for Bess. This evening had been hard on her, and she looked somewhat shaken. Though the townspeople had been satisfied for the moment, Dev knew Bess still faced a crisis: she had to go home and ask the children if any of them were responsible for the pranks.

"Bessie? Mary wants to have a word with you," Bert said, as the discussions drew to a close and the remaining people began to leave. He pointed to the woman in the fourth pew.

"I might as well go talk to her now," Bess said. "Will that be all right?"

Both Dev and Bert gave their agreement, and she left them to find Mary.

"I'd better be heading back out to the lake," Arthur said as the crowd thinned out. "One of my friends gave me a ride in, and I see he's ready to go."

"I want to thank you for speaking out," Bert said to the man. "I know from what your sister said you didn't think this business with the children was too good an idea."

"I didn't think it was a good idea for Laura to be involved in this way," Arthur corrected. "The children are an entirely different matter. They deserve to have a chance. I hope you discover who's behind all this." He turned to Dev. "Keep in mind what you and I talked about. I think it could be a very interesting proposition."

"I will. And thanks for your help tonight. Things could have gotten ugly if Mr. Jackson had his way."

Arthur made his way out of the church with a last wave. Although he was a few years older than Dev, they'd discovered they had a lot of common interests this past week. With Arthur staying at his lake house and Dev in the nearby guest cottage, they had had plenty of opportunities to talk, and their conversations had been most intriguing.

Arthur was trying to persuade Dev to go into Kansas City and meet some of his business friends—that was why they had gone to the Bennett's today. There'd even been some talk about Dev joining the Board of Trade, but at the moment Dev found he didn't have the stomach for anything political. After the way Roland Atherton and his cronies had treated him, Dev wouldn't be ready for that particular arena for a while, if ever. Besides, he had something much more important on his mind—Bess and what was happening between them.

As Arthur walked away, Dev looked over at Bess and murmured to himself, "I just hope she's right."

"Who's right?" Bert asked, overhearing him.

"Bess," Dev said and nodded to where she was still deep in conversation with Mary Robertson. "I think she'll be heartbroken if it turns out her children are involved in these incidents."

"And you think they might be?"

Dev shrugged. "As I said before, I have no information, but it's not outside the realm of possibility. These are city children she's brought here, children from a different way of life. Carlinsville is nothing like what they're used to. One of them might be unhappy and wanting to go back or so used to stealing he can't stop any more. Don't forget, these youngsters have had a very rough time of it, right up to the moment Bess put them on the train. You can't expect them to become angels overnight."

"That's true enough, but the townsfolk got a right to an orderly life, too. That's what they pay me for, and I ain't looking for any extra disruptions. If Bess weren't my daughter, I'd probably be on the same side as the complainers myself. Though, since she is my daughter, I'm mighty glad to see you're backing her, even if you don't see eye to eye."

Dev gave him a questioning look.

"You're good for Bessie," Bert explained. "I can tell from the way she looks when she's with you that you're important to her. And you're a fine gentlemen, coming from a good family like you do. I may only be a sheriff in a small town, but I can see the importance of having the right family background. These children are going to have a hard time of it, I'd bet my bottom dollar."

Family background! Could it be that even here all that mattered were family connections? At Bert's first words, Dev had been pleased; Bess was important to him, too. But by his last words, Dev felt he was back in the same old bind—judged more by his family connections than by his own abilities. Did Bess share her father's ideas? A chill ran down his spine at the thought. He'd never told her the details of his problems in Philadelphia nor had he confessed his humble origins. He'd meant to, but the time had never been right, and from the night of the Centennial celebrations to the day she'd left on the train, he'd had little opportunity to tell her anything.

He looked over in her direction and saw her smile and bid farewell to the other woman, then hurry back toward him.

"I hope I haven't kept you waiting, but it looks like Mary and her husband might be interested in adopting one of the children."

"That's good news," Bert said, smiling down at his daughter.

"Yes, it certainly is. After what happened tonight I had my doubts about placing any of the children. Everyone seems so angry."

"Actually, it was only several people, but they were about to incite the rest. If nothing else happens this should all settle down," Dev said.

"You don't sound too sure. Do you think something else will happen?"

"Only time will tell. Right now, though, I think I'd better get you back to the house. If that's all right with you, sheriff?" Dev added, turning to the other man.

"Sounds fine. I'll be out tomorrow to see how things are going. I might ask some of the boys a question or two, too, just to see if they know anything."

They parted company on the lawn in front of the church where Bert mounted up and headed toward the jailhouse and Dev helped Bess into the carriage. She sat back and closed her eyes, not even opening them when the buggy began to move. She seemed too quiet, too controlled. He could see the muscle at the corner of her jaw clench.

This day had not gone according to plan, he thought ruefully, but then, none of his plans had worked out for a very long time. He flexed his muscles and stretched. Nothing had mattered for so long that he'd gotten into the habit of letting things slide, but that was about to change.

Bess had taught him that life was worth living again. He hadn't felt that way in a long time, not since Julia's untimely death. But now he felt that way again, and he couldn't wait to tell her. There was so much for them to discuss, so many plans to make.

If only she would look at him. But she sat with her eyes closed and her face turned away from his. He let her sit for a while longer, knowing the evening's events had been a blow to her. Then he decided the time had come to talk.

"Are you all right?" he asked.

"I think so. I'm just so angry. I tried not to let it show at the meeting, but now . . . How could anyone think our children would be behind this? You've only to look at them to know they couldn't do anything like this."

"Can you honestly look at Jesse and say that? I know I can't."

"But then you never believed this was a good idea from the beginning."

Dev should have known better than to say anything so blunt. Bess felt very protective of her brood, and when they were under attack, she would feel compelled to defend them, no matter what the truth might be.

"Now, Bess—" he began, trying to undo the damage.

"Don't try to deny it. I know it's true, but I'd hoped you had at least come to realize that the children are flourishing here. They've all done so well. Even Jesse's gotten over his initial hostility."

They drew up in front of the house, and Dev turned to Bess.

"I'll admit that you see more of the children than I do and probably would be a better judge—"

"Probably? What do you mean, probably?" Bess's voice rose with each question.

"Bess, please—" As he started to speak, Bess stood as if to jump down from the carriage. He grabbed her arm and pulled her back onto the seat. "Are you daft? You could fall and break your leg and then where would your children be?"

284

"Right back in Philadelphia—where you want them."

"Oh, you're so stubborn. I knew that the minute I ran into you in the hallway at the ball in Kansas City." When she would have risen from her seat again, Dev took hold of her other arm as well and tugged her into his embrace. "I knew you were trouble the first time I laid eyes on you."

When he said the word "trouble" she squirmed on his lap, her bottom pressing against his thighs. His heart raced. How she tormented him without even realizing it! Every time he looked at her his blood boiled.

"You were trouble from the start," he repeated, "but I couldn't get you out of my mind." He stared down into her eyes. "Your eyes, your lips." He rubbed his thumb over the surface of her lips and they parted. "How you taunted me."

"I did no such thing," Bess protested. "A well-brought-up lady never—"

The last of her sentence was swallowed as his mouth closed over hers, stopping all arguments.

He could feel her resistance but for once didn't heed its command. With all the upheavals in his life, there was one thing he was sure of and that was what he and Bess shared together when their bodies touched. It was a magic he had never known before and was sure he'd never find again.

He felt her hands pushing against his arms, and he eased the pressure of his lips from hers.

"Dev, let me go," Bess asked her voice low.

"I can't, Bess. You've entered my soul. Please don't ask to be freed."

Dev's words tore at her heart. Her eyes met his, and she melted against him, wanting everything he had to give. She'd known his touch and his love, how could she deny him anything? She loved him with all her soul and all her being.

His hand came up and cupped her breast, and she

sighed with pleasure. She wanted him near, nearer. After their night together, she had discovered desires only he could satisfy.

She felt Dev pulling away and mewed her disapproval.

"Listen," he said in her ear.

"Hello, down there, Miz Bess. Is that you?"

"Oh, no. It's Rosie," Bess whispered.

"What are you doing down there, Miz Bess?"

"You'd better say something," Dev urged.

"Hello, Rosie," she said in a strangled voice.

"Can we come down and see you? Nola and I are both awake."

Bess peered cautiously around the buggy's canopy. She could just make out the outline of Rosie's head in her upstairs bedroom window. As she watched, Rosie turned her head back toward the interior of the room, and they could hear her talking with Nola. "What did you say, Nola? Of course, Miz Bess wants to see us now. You want to see me, don't you?" Rosie called out the window.

"Rose Louise Somers, get your head back in here right this minute. Miz Bess don't need you spying on her," Nola's frantic voice called out, its high pitch carrying across the room and down into the yard.

"But—" The younger girl's head disappeared from view, taking along the rest of her sentence.

Suddenly Bess realized she was still sitting in Dev's lap. She was about to scramble off when she felt him shaking. She looked into his face and saw it filled with laughter. She pushed at his shoulders, but he couldn't stop.

"You have to admit, it's funny," he said, still chuckling. "I wonder what married people do?"

"Married folk don't sit in carriages and . . ."

"And what?" he teased.

"You must know what, since you seem to be so good at it."

"Am I?"

"Don't act so surprised. I'm sure you've been told that before."

"Never by you," he said, his voice soft and intense.

And then his lips touched hers again. For a moment, she allowed herself to fall back under the spell of his kiss, the sweet, sensual web he was spinning. Then she remembered the children.

When the kiss ended, she reluctantly slipped from his lap. "This is what it must be like having children — never knowing when they're going to pop up unexpectedly."

"I'd better get you inside before they set off an alarm, and everyone in the house comes out to have a look."

Bess agreed. She wouldn't want to explain this to Laura. "Will I see you tomorrow?" she asked.

"I have some business I need to discuss with Arthur Christy before he leaves for Kansas City, and several of the men out at the lake have expressed some interest in my father's investments. How about tomorrow evening?"

Bess hid her disappointment. She knew he had business to attend to — most likely he wouldn't even have come west if it hadn't been for his father's business interests. "In the evening, then."

He lowered her to the ground and gave her one more quick kiss, then jumped back into the buggy. It never failed to amaze her how agile he was, not at all like the other businessmen she'd met — men like Wylie and even Arthur Christy, more at home in the board room or ballroom than with physical action. She'd have expected Dev to be more like them, if she'd thought about it. But the reality was far different. She experienced it every time he held her in his arms, every time she closed her eyes and saw him as he'd been at the lake, his muscles well-formed and rippling with strength, his body supple and fluid in motion.

How did he do it, she wondered, not for the first time. What did he really do with his life when he wasn't handling his father's business affairs? He'd mentioned testifying for some trial or other, but that wasn't a job. He'd also talked about helping out Pinkerton's. But what, exactly, did that entail beyond his sudden disappearances and the potential for injury?

She watched him drive off and thought how little she knew of him — and also how much. She knew him to be honorable and proud, independent yet vulnerable, courageous in standing up for what he believed in yet compassionate enough to understand another's point of view. She knew he had once been married, and from all accounts, very happy. Could he be as happy again? Would it be with her?

The questions churned in her mind. Just yesterday she'd thought her life had found a new direction. In the space of a day, her most deeply held wishes had become uncertainties again. What if the children *were* involved in the pranks in town? What if Danny disappeared from her life? What if Dev had only come out west for business reasons? Would she be enough to hold him here?

The questions multiplied and grew, each feeding on the others, but the answers remained elusive, as elusive as Dev's image when he turned the corner and disappeared from sight.

By the end of the following week, Bess had successfully settled three of the children in area homes, two on farms and one in town. Mary Robertson and her husband Peter had taken shy, young Max, and Lester had gone to live on a nearby farm with a large family who had opened their arms and homes to one more. Samuel would be living just up the street from the Rutherford house with the family that ran the leather goods shop.

Bess and Laura had made arrangements to visit with the children weekly for the first few months. Though she missed them terribly, the important thing was that they were happy.

Her first home visit was to the Robertson's and Max. Bess really had no doubts that Mary and Peter would make excellent parents. They loved children, their only regret being that they had none of their own. In their first interview they'd told her adopting one of her children was God's answer to their prayers. At the Robertson's first meeting with Max, Bess knew she had a match.

When Bess rode into the front yard of the home, she saw Max in front of the barn together with Peter, standing over an upturned wagon wheel. Their two blond heads were bent close together as they studied the problem at hand. At the sound of her approaching buggy, they both looked up.

For a moment Max looked frightened, then he spotted Mary coming out of the house and ran to her side.

"How are all of you doing?" Bess asked as she tied her horse and carriage up to the hitching post. Her question encompassed the entire group, but she looked at Max.

"I can stay here, can't I? I don't have to go back to Philadelphia, do I?" Max asked in a quavering voice.

It was the most Bess had heard him say since she'd met him. He had been the quietest of all ten children, never arguing with the others or laughing along either.

"Of course not," Mary said, bending down and pulling him into her arms. He went willingly and snuggled against her breast. "Isn't that right, Bess? He can stay here forever and ever."

"Mary and Peter are your mother and father now, Max. Forever and ever."

Peter bent over and tousled his hair. "Come on, son. I thought you said you were going to help me weed in the garden this morning. Are you still interested?"

Max nodded his head and put his small hand into Peter's large one. "We'll be done before lunch, won't we?" he asked.

Peter smiled. "I should hope so."

Max looked back at Mary. "We'll be all washed and ready when you ring the bell."

"Do a good job on the weeds."

"We will, Ma," he called over his shoulder as he walked with a jaunty swagger out past the barn.

Bess could see the tears gathering in Mary's eyes. "That's the first time he's called me that."

"You mean Ma?"

Mary rose from her bent position and pulled a handkerchief from her pocket. "I never thought I'd hear that word."

"It would appear you're going to hear it a great deal from now on."

Mary gave Bess a happy, if slightly watery smile, and then invited her up to the house for a cup of coffee and some cake.

They'd been chatting for about fifteen minutes when Mary brought up the other children.

"Have you placed any of the rest yet?"

"You know about Samuel and Lester?"

"Yes. We were really pleased that the Barclays took in Samuel. It will be nice for their Jimmy to have a brother. I always wanted a sister to talk and share with. I think most children do."

"Does that mean you think Max should have a brother or sister?" Bess asked, eager to place as many children as possible.

Mary laughed. "Give me a chance to adjust to this one first, and then we'll see."

Bess could tell that Mary was already half convinced.

She might not be ready right now, but there was a good chance that if the League sent out another group from the city, one of them might just find a very good home here.

She was glad that Mary seemed so happy with her life. She and Bess had known each other since childhood. They'd lost contact once Bess had gone off to school and Mary had married, but now the two women resumed their friendship without skipping a beat.

"I heard Selma Thompkins might be interested in the girls."

Bess brightened at the thought. "That would be wonderful. Keeping them together has been on my mind a lot."

"I'm afraid she was only interested in the two younger ones," Mary confessed. "Said something about not wanting a child that already had too much burned into her, whatever that means."

Bess knew exactly what that meant. The woman wanted young, cute children, not someone as old as Nola. "I promised Nola I wouldn't separate them, and I'm not going back on that promise," Bess said, but she was worried. She'd known three children would be hard to place, but she'd kept her hopes up. So far, though, no one had expressed an interest in adopting an entire family.

"I'm sure you'll find someone who wants all three. You've only looked in Carlinsville so far. There are lots of other places to search," Mary encouraged her.

"I hope you're right. I think I've found a home for Raymond, too. There's a family out by Parkton who's interested. They've been staying out by the lake and dropped in just yesterday. I have to find out more about them before saying yes, but they seemed like good people."

"Sounds like everything's going well at that end. Now

291

let's talk about you. Tell me about this new beau of yours. He certainly is handsome."

Bess felt herself blushing. Just the thought of Dev sent her temperature rising. She'd missed him this last week—missed the closeness they had achieved, the sense of belonging which filled her each time they were together. Arthur Christy had changed his plans and Dev had been spending more and more time out at the lake.

"So it's that serious, is it?" Mary teased when she saw Bess's reaction.

"I care about him a great deal."

"Like you don't want to start a day unless you know you're going to see him?"

"How did you know?" Bess asked for that was exactly how she'd felt this week when she knew he wouldn't be coming into town.

"I felt the same way about Peter, and then I married him."

Mary's eyebrows rose in silent question, but Bess didn't know what to say. She and Dev hadn't really talked about the future, and she wouldn't let herself dream because she feared their dreams might be too different, especially if what Anna had said was true—that Bess was nothing like Dev's first wife, that he needed more than she had to give.

"I'm just not sure what we have," she admitted in a soft voice.

"Well, the whole town is talking. Your keeping company is one of their main topics of conversation."

"It is?" For some reason, Bess had supposed that what they did was their own business. Now she wondered exactly what the town was saying. "What have you heard?"

"Oh, nothing disreputable, of course. Just that you two have been seen all over town together and that Mr. O'Connor spends a great deal of time at the Rutherford

House. Between you and your father, the town's abuzz."

"My father?" Bess asked, unable to believe there were tales floating around about him, too.

"Well, you know—he and Miss Christy have begun keeping company."

While Bess knew that there was something between Laura and her father, she was surprised that anyone else did. "People are saying this?"

"Sure are. I've even heard the men tease your father about it. And he hasn't denied it, either, so they say— just ducks his head and blushes." Mary grinned.

"How long would you say they've been keeping company?"

"Ever since you went off to Philadelphia, I'd guess. Miss Christy and her brother came out here about that time. Now, there's a handsome man. Too bad he's so set in his ways. Why, I heard he pitched an absolute fit when Miss Christy rented your house for you. If he hears the rumors about your pa, I can't imagine what he'll do."

Neither could Bess. It seemed she and her father were the latest nine days' wonder. She only wished the talk about them would be so interesting that the townspeople would forget about the mischief that continued to plague the area.

Mary began filling her in on all the latest news from town, but Bess listened with only half an ear. Her mind wrestled with what to do about the latest rash of problems to beset the small town.

She had gathered all the children together the morning after the town meeting and questioned them about the pranks. Some of them had heard about the incidents, but not one of them had any idea who was doing the deeds. She had let the matter drop but had kept her eyes open.

Then just yesterday, at the mercantile, she'd heard something that had her very worried. She'd been told someone had broken the front windows out of the Smith house and then done the same to the house next door. These were no longer childish pranks, and Bess feared the consequences of these acts.

"We should find someone for him, don't you think?" Mary's words broke through Bess's thoughts. "He seems like a really good sort, especially the way he defended the children at the meeting."

Who, Bess almost asked and then remembered Mary had been talking about Arthur. "Oh, yes, he certainly stood up for the children. Speaking of which, have you heard anything about these latest incidents?"

"Just that the Smith's are pretty upset about their windows. They said it was done in the dead of night, and all they saw were two figures running away. This really is a puzzle, isn't it?"

"One that I hoped would straighten itself out before this. The culprits will have to be found so all this suspicion can end."

"Are you sure none of your children are involved?"

Bess couldn't believe it! If even Mary had her doubts, then how could she expect anyone else in town not to harbor suspicions?

"I don't have any proof, Mary, but we're very careful with the children, especially lately. What cause would any of them have to do this? You know yourself that half of them have homes already, good homes. This just doesn't make any sense."

"Maybe not, but if someone doesn't find out who's behind all of this soon, I don't know what's going to happen. Ty Jackson and his friends might take matters into their own hands, you know."

"I certainly hope not, but if they do I'm sure my father will be there to stop them from doing anything too foolish."

They chatted for a while longer, and then Bess said

goodbye, wanting to get back to the house and the children.

She had just pulled into the drive of the Rutherford House when she heard voices raised in anger. She ran into the house, then stopped as she recognized the speakers.

"I will not let you or Arthur interfere in my life," Laura said in a much louder tone than Bess had ever heard her use.

"We're not interfering," Bert nearly shouted in return, his voice as loud as Laura's. "We're worried about you. What if some of the boys here *are* involved? What if something happens to you?"

"I'm a grown woman, Bert. I can hold my own against a handful of children. If you tell Bess she has to send them back, I'll never speak to you again. Do you hear me?"

Bess didn't know what shocked her more—learning that her father wanted her to send the children back or hearing Laura defend her so vehemently. And then Bess got the biggest shock of all.

"Laura, honey," Bert said, his voice suddenly soft and beseeching. "I don't want to fight you. I want to protect you, you and Bess. I only want the best for you, surely you understand that?"

"The best is for the children to stay. Believe me. Just give us a little more time. I'm sure once you find the culprits, you'll see that this whole mess has nothing to do with us."

"I doubt that, Laura, but I'm willing to wait a while longer," Bert conceded.

Her father backing down? Bess could hardly credit her ears, but that was what had just happened. She heard the faint rustling of fabric and quietly peeked into the back parlor. Bert and Laura stood locked in an embrace, oblivious to anything that might be going on around them.

Bess quickly tiptoed away, her heart beating wildly. All her life she'd thought of Bert as her father, unaware that he was also a man with needs and wants of his own. The sight she'd just witnessed shook her to the core, not because she didn't wish for Bert's every happiness, but because she'd never thought of her father as a man — a man who could desire a woman and be desired by her. Yet the truth of her eyes was impossible to deny.

She stayed in the hall, leaning against the wall for support, feeling slightly shaky inside. She felt such a welter of emotions, ridiculous emotions for a woman already past twenty, but real enough just the same: feelings of jealousy and abandonment fought with relief and a certain giddiness. Of all the women in the world Bert might have chosen, he couldn't have done better than Laura. And there was something heartening in knowing that at last he had put the memories of her mother in their proper place: as memories to cherish rather than as limitations on his life and future happiness.

"Now tell me more about this rock," she heard Bert say a few minutes later.

"It came through the dining room window just after breakfast this morning," Laura replied.

"What rock is that?" Bess exclaimed, making her presence known without preamble. The last thing they needed was trouble here at Rutherford House.

"Oh, Bess, you're back." Laura blushed prettily and shot a quick glance at Bert.

Bess pretended ignorance. She would let Laura and Bert explain things when they were ready. There were more important things to discuss right now, things that could affect the safety of the remaining children.

"Yes. I had a nice long chat with Mary Robertson, and everything is going very well with her new family. Max is thrilled. He even called her Ma." Bess smiled at the memory of Mary's heartwarming happiness. "But

296

what's this I heard about a rock coming through the dining room window?"

Laura gave Bert a questioning look. "You'd better tell her," he said in a resigned tone.

Bess glared at him. "Of course she should tell me. I'm not a child any more. I don't need to be coddled."

Bert rolled his eyes. "Yes, ma'am," he said with a mock bow. "It seems the ladies in this house have gotten mighty independent all of a sudden. Maybe there's no room for an old man like myself."

"Papa, that's not true—"

"You're not old at all, Bert—"

Bess and Laura had spoken at the same time. They stopped together, then laughed.

"Come on, Papa," Bess said, looping her arm through his. "Sit on the sofa and let Laura tell me what happened this morning. Then you can tell us both what you think we should do. How's that?"

"I can tell you what I think right now," he said gruffly but let himself be led to the leather sofa.

When they were seated, Laura picked up a good-sized rock from the table and handed it to Bess.

"I heard a crash from the dining room when I was in here doing some mending this morning. When I ran out there, I saw the window was broken and this was on the dining room floor. Unfortunately, I didn't see any-body around. With those woods right at the back of the house, anybody could have found a hiding place. That's when I sent for Bert."

"Why would somebody do this? Are you sure it wasn't an accident? Maybe the boys were just playing around and someone tossed it through the window by mistake," Bess said.

"I don't think so. This was tied around it." Laura held out a creased piece of paper.

Bess smoothed it out. Crudely-formed, jagged letters

297

spelled out an unmistakable message: "Go hom were yoo bilong."

"Who do you think sent this?" she asked, feeling sick inside at the sight of the angry words.

"Looks like a child's handwriting," Laura opined.

"Not necessarily," Bert said. "Some folks out here don't read or write too good. They can spell their names if they have to, but not much else. Either of you recognize this handwriting?"

Bess and Laura both shook their heads, though Laura seemed more hesitant.

"If you think you know something, it's better to tell me, Laura," Bert said. "I'll keep it in confidence, but I can't do my job if I don't know what's going on."

Laura looked away, not facing either Bess or Bert. "It could be one of the older boys' writing. None of them write very well, but I've never seen them write this . . . angrily. I just don't know."

The letters indeed looked angry, each stroke dark and slashing across the page.

"Like Jesse?" Bert prodded.

"I don't know," Laura murmured.

"Well I do, and I just don't believe it was anyone here," Bess insisted. "Especially not Jesse. He's improved so much lately. There's got to be another answer."

Bert ran his hand over his face. "Maybe so. I just don't know yet and until I do I think you should get away from here for a while. You and the children. If someone's taken the trouble to come all the way out here, who knows where they'll stop."

Bess looked up at him. "You think someone might try to hurt us?"

"I can't tell. But I'll sleep better at night knowing you and the children are somewhere safe."

"But where can we go?"

Laura sighed. "I guess I can take Arthur up on his

offer, after all. We can use his house in Kansas City."

"Are you sure?"

Laura nodded and then smiled wickedly. "I don't think he intended to have a houseful of children, what with all his fancy belongings and art work, but it'll serve him right for interfering in the first place. I'll go and stay with him out at the lake. He's been hinting for me to do so ever since I moved in here. That should make him happy. You can handle the children can't you?"

"There's fewer than when I came out, so there shouldn't be a problem. Are you sure Arthur won't mind?"

"Don't worry about that. I'll handle Arthur."

With Bert encouraging her, Bess made plans to leave the next morning by train. When Dev arrived that night for dinner, Bess told him about their arrangements. She wasn't sure how he would react, whether he would be glad of this opportunity to be away from her, to let things die down between them, or whether he would feel the way she did: torn in two, knowing she had a responsibility to the children but aching for the toll it would take on her own life.

"Bert is right. This is no place for you and the children now. I've been putting off going to Kansas City for a while, but if you're going there too, I'll come along as your escort. How does that sound?"

Bess's last worries fell away. "That would be wonderful."

She tipped her face up and his lips claimed hers. Desire swept through her, igniting a deeper passion. Their kiss was long and complete, beginning in fierce ardor, then gentling to tender communion.

"I wish we had more time together," she whispered at last, her fingers still entwined in his thick, sable hair. Her lips felt swollen and tasted of him.

"Me, too. I just have so much to work out right now,

but soon I'll have more time. Can you just bear with me a while longer?"

She could bear with him forever, if only she had the courage to admit it. How would he react if she told him? Would he welcome her commitment to him or would he find it a burden? Before Anna's insidious remarks, Bess might have taken a chance. Now she wanted more time, time to show Dev how full his life could be with her, time to work her way into his life until he couldn't envision living without her.

She gave him her answer with her lips, plunging them both into that magic world they alone created. His arms closed around her as his mouth opened, and she forgot her immediate worries in the rapture of their embrace.

The train was still a couple miles down the track. Harley Jenkins watched it approach, a smile on his face. Just a few minutes more and he'd be done with his job. And this time, the boss would have nothing to complain about. How was he supposed to have known that Danny would take it into his head to run away? And why did the boss care, anyway? The kid was out of Philadelphia for good. It wasn't as if he could talk to anyone who cared about what'd happened.

Too bad Bertha had taken a liking to the squirt. Harley could have gotten rid of him right away, just like the boss had wanted. Instead he'd given the kid the use of his own last name, mostly to hide him from the boss, if the truth be known, and now he was paying for it! Not only was he supposed to get rid of the boy, he had to deal with that businessman, too.

Well, this should do it, Harley thought. They were all on that Kansas City train together. Luckily he'd overheard the talk in town and knew where to find them. With the sheriff always out at Rutherford House to see his daughter, Harley hadn't had a chance to grab Danny. But now he had a crack at them all.

The train chugged round the curve and ran along the edge of the cliff, right under the place where Harley sat waiting. He gave the signal, and one of the men he'd hired lit the fuse. Only a couple more seconds now, and Harley would be home free. The boss couldn't threaten him and Bertha no more, not if Harley did the job right—and this time, Harley had no intention of failing.

Fourteen

The explosion was followed in quick succession by several jolts and a loud grinding sound.

"Hang on," Dev cried. The train car began to tip as it charged off the rails, bucking and weaving as it went. Dev put his arm out in front of Bess, trying to hold her in the seat as the train finally came to a jarring stop. "You okay?"

She nodded, too out of breath to make any other response.

"Stay here and make sure the children are all right. I'm going to check outside."

He lingered only long enough to make sure Bess followed his orders, then made his way over the jumbled boxes, debris, and human forms littering the sharply angled floor. The explosion had been no accident, of that he was certain.

As he reached the near door, shots rang out. "Dev," Bess screamed.

He looked over his shoulder. "Stay down!" he commanded. "Everyone!"

He waited as the other passengers huddled against the floor, then reached into the side of his boot and came out with his knife. He sensed that Bess was watching him and spared her a quick glance. She was looking at him as if she'd never really seen him before, and maybe she hadn't. He felt savage and raw at this threat, consumed by a primal need to protect and defend what was his.

"I'll be back as soon as I can," he called to her. "Stay down."

She nodded and gathered Danny and the three girls into her arms, positioning them in the shelter of an overturned table. Jesse grabbed Victor and knelt down beside her, using his body to help shield the children.

A dozen more shots rang out from either side of the train car, and Dev turned his attention to what was happening outside. A conductor and another man joined him.

"Here, take this," the conductor said, and shoved a Colt into Dev's hand.

Dev weighed it assessingly, then checked to see that it was fully loaded. "Thanks," he said.

"Don't thank me yet. First we've got to get out of this."

The third man said, "Looks like there are at least four of them out there. Two on each side."

"What do you think they're after?" the conductor asked.

"Robbery?" Dev suggested.

The conductor shrugged. "Seems like a lot of effort for nothing. This here's just a local—no mail or anything. If they wanted to rob something, why not wait the extra hour for the mail train?"

"What's happening with the engine crew?" Dev asked.

The conductor looked out the window on the opposite side of the train car. "We're disconnected from them. The engine's on its side. Looks like it's all twisted up and burning. I don't see the crew."

"Can you make it into the other train car?"

The conductor turned around and shoved his way

into the passageway between the two cars. He tried to open the door to the next car. "It won't budge."

Dev and the third man added their weight to his, and it suddenly gave. Several men came up from the other side, guns in hand.

"We can't get out back there," one of them said. "That part of the car is perched over the cliff. The whole thing could fall any second. We've got to get everyone out."

A couple of shots came through a window, and one of the men shot back.

"I winged him," he crowed. "Let's go get the rest of those bastards."

He raced to the window and started climbing out before anyone could shout a word of warning. Then it was too late. The gunshot caught him in the middle of the chest and sent him flying onto the floor.

The two women in the half-empty train car screamed, and the conductor bent over the injured man and tried to staunch the bleeding with his hands. It didn't help. The blood pulsed rhythmically out between his fingers. The conductor cursed and shook his head. After a few seconds, he stood and wiped his hands on the back of his pants.

"He's gone. Now what?"

Dev flattened his body against the side wall of the train car and sidled to the nearest window. A shot nearly picked him off. He scrambled back to the passageway.

"There's one man beyond that rock." He pointed to the place a third of the way up the hill. "And a couple more, it looks like, by the trees to the left."

The train car creaked and trembled, the back end shifting slightly.

"We're falling," one of the men shouted. "Let's get out of here."

In a panic, he tried to storm through the passageway leading to the first car.

"Wait!" Dev cried out, but the train car shifted again and the man ignored him. He manage to clamber out the door and jump off the teetering train, only to be stopped by a well-aimed bullet.

"What the hell!" yelled the conductor. "Why'd they kill him? This is crazy! What in heaven's name do they want?"

"Whatever it is, we'd better get them before they get us—or this train falls into that ravine. There isn't much time," Dev said.

"What can we do?" one of the passengers asked, turning to Dev. The others looked to him as well, their eyes wide with fear. Most of them were farmers and businessmen on their way to Kansas City for the day. None of them had come prepared for battle.

"First, get everyone into the front car. It's more stable," he said, instinctively taking command. He pointed to one of the calmer men. "Can you stand guard on this car so no one gets in?"

The man nodded. Dev helped herd the other passengers forward, placing them as far to the front of the other car as possible.

"What's happening?" Bess asked as he passed, her expression worried.

"I'm not sure. There seems to be several men outside, but none of them have stated what they want." He didn't tell her about the two dead men.

"Hey! Come quick!" The man guarding the rear car yelled.

Dev turned on his heel and ran back down the passageway. "What's the matter?"

"Someone's working under this car. I saw him run over, then he ducked under."

"What's he doing?"

"I don't know. He was carrying something. That's all I know."

Dev cursed under his breath. He should have stayed

305

here himself. This man was too nervous to keep track of what was going on, endangering them all. "Think, man. What was he carrying? A rifle?"

"N-no. It was several sticks of some sort."

"Dynamite?"

The man's eyes widened until his irises were surrounded by white on all sides. "Oh, my God. We're doomed!"

"Hang on, mister." Dev gave the man a quick shake. "There are women and children in the other car. Your panic won't help anyone and might set them off. Now think. Where did he go under?"

The man stood shaking his head for a couple of seconds, overwhelmed by his fear. Dev gripped his shoulders tightly. "This is important," he whispered in a tense voice. "Think."

The man pointed with a shaking hand to the balance point of the train car as it lay half on its side, its back end hanging over a sheer drop of at least fifty feet.

"Damn. They're trying to kill us all! What the hell for?"

There was no answer to his last question, and the other man began to whimper.

Dev sent him to the front car. "Send back the conductor," he ordered.

When he again cautiously approached one of the windows, a shot rang out. There was no choice. He would have to try to get out on the cliff side and hope he wasn't spotted—and that his weight wouldn't be the straw that sent the train car over the edge.

The conductor ran up at that moment. "You need me back here?"

Dev nodded. "What's going on up there?"

The sound of sporadic gunfire split the air.

"I don't rightly understand this. They keep shooting, like they want us to stay in the train or something. So far, no one's tried to get in, but they sure aren't letting

306

us out, either. What's going on?"

"Damned if I know. I'm going to try to get out."

"How? The other two were shot dead."

"They went out on that side. I'm going to go out here."

The man paled. "Over the cliff?"

"There's no other choice. They're setting dynamite under this car. Looks like they aim to get us all killed one way or another. This may be our only chance. Will you help me?"

The conductor looked him up and down. "Doesn't look like I have any choice, does it? What should I do?"

He held a rifle in his hand and a gun like the one he'd given Dev was tucked into the waistband of his pants, within easy reach. Dev nodded at the weaponry. "Keep them distracted while I go out one of the windows on the back side."

The conductor nodded and worked his way to a window facing the attackers. A shot rang out, just missing him. The instant he shot back, Dev was out the other side.

The train car bobbled, and Dev didn't dare look down. He maneuvered himself to the rear end of the car. A motion in the corner of his eye caught his attention. Without a second thought, he turned and fired. The man screamed and fell forward, dropping his rifle as he rolled down the hill.

Another of the outlaws shouted, "Hurry, you fool," and fired in Dev's general direction, but the upturned edge of the train car shielded him. He worked his way lower, then peered under the train. A third man was lighting a match, ready to set the fuse afire.

"Stop," Dev yelled. The man looked up with a startled expression and reached for his gun. Dev fired in the instant before the outlaw did, catching him in the shoulder. The outlaw's bullet flew uselessly in the wrong direction as the man fell to the ground.

Dev wasn't sure if the man was unconscious or simply wounded. In either case, he had to get to him before he tried to reset that fuse. The train car was so precariously balanced that even the slightest explosion would take it down — and the car in front of it as well, the car with Bess. Dev would gladly die before he let that happen.

The conductor shot a few more times from his perch above Dev. His shots were answered from a couple of directions. There were at least two men still out there. Worse, Dev could now see a cloud of dark smoke drifting over from the front of the train. The fire in the engine was spreading, perhaps to the front car where Bess crouched with the children.

He had to take the risk. Jumping to the ground, he raced forward and slid under the car, barely escaping a volley of shots. The injured outlaw lay unconscious. Dev rolled him away from the dynamite and dug out the sticks. He worked his way to the front of the leaning train car and peered around the edge. A bullet whished past his ear, then ricocheted off a metallic portion of the car with a loud bang.

Working a match free from his vest pocket, Dev lit the long fuse on one stick of dynamite and tossed it in the direction of the closest gunfire. The resulting explosion sent a shock wave of dirt and dust in Dev's direction. The train car bobbled again, and Dev held his breath, unsure how much more the disabled car would take before sliding down the cliff side to oblivion.

As the car settled back in place, Dev could just make out the sound of retreating hoofbeats. He stayed in the shelter of the car as the conductor continued to fire, but when there was no response, the conductor stopped firing and called down. "Think they're gone?"

"Seems like it. Let's get everyone out of the train before it goes over," Dev called back.

"Okay. I'll meet you in the front car."

By the time Dev climbed back onto the train, he found Bess had organized the frightened children and adults so they could disembark in an orderly fashion. The rear car lurched, shaking the front car as well.

Bess gave him a worried look as he walked up the center aisle.

"Are you all right?" he asked.

"Yes. And you?"

He nodded. He'd survived with only a few scrapes, better than he'd expected, given the odds. "Let's get you out of here."

Dev got a couple of the men stationed just outside the train car. One after another, he and the conductor lowered the children and remaining adults into their arms. Bess soothed the people still in the train, keeping them from panicking. Every couple of minutes, they all froze in their spots as the train shuddered and the rear car slipped a little farther down the cliff.

"Hurry! There's no time for that!" Dev shouted as one of the passengers ran back to his seat to grab what appeared to be a heavy bag.

The man ignored Dev, struggling with his carrying case despite the ominous grinding noises coming from the rear of the train.

"Bess, get down. Now!" Dev shouted, furious with himself that he'd let her help instead of forcing her off with the children.

This time she heeded his words. "You come, too," she pleaded as he turned around to help the stubborn passenger.

"In a second." He grabbed the man's bag in one hand and shoved him forward with the other. "Go, damnit!"

The man stumbled forward. As soon as he jumped off, he turned around. "My bag," he cried.

The train gave a last ominous groan and the last car began its inexorable slide backward.

"Dev!" Bess screamed in terror. Why had he gone

309

back to help the man? Why hadn't he saved himself? Her horror knew no bounds. She flung herself at the train, reaching for its frame as if one frail woman could in fact halt its certain progress. The conductor grabbed her from behind and pulled her back.

At the last possible minute, she saw Dev push his way through the door and jump. He landed in the dust near her just as the two train cars slid out of sight.

"Dev!" Bess screamed over and over again.

He simply held her. "Hush, it's over now," he crooned in her ear, but panic still surged through her. She'd almost lost him, and in that instant she realized just how deeply she loved him. Her life would be meaningless without him. She held tightly onto him, needing the solid reality of him to dispel the nightmare images still haunting her mind.

"Where are the children?" she asked when she felt more in control.

"Jesse has them. They're just up the hill over there."

"Are you all right?"

He smiled at her, his face somewhat grimy and sweat-streaked from his ordeal, but she'd never seen him looking more handsome, more ruggedly masculine than he did at that moment.

"I'm fine now," he said, his voice suddenly husky, and she realized he was holding onto her just as tightly as she held him.

She looked into his eyes and asked, "Do you always carry a knife in your boot?"

He raised an eyebrow. "Afraid so. It comes in handy now and again."

An image of him sitting on the train on the way to Philadelphia came to her mind, the day the drunken man had tottered down the center aisle and threatened one of the passengers. At the time, she'd barely paid attention to Dev beyond noticing that he was asleep. Now, with the advantage of hindsight, she realized how wrong she'd been.

"You weren't asleep at all, were you?"

"When?" he asked, but she could tell by the gleam in his eye that he remembered the incident as well as she did.

"You know exactly when—that day on the train, on our way to Philadelphia."

"Oh, yes. That day."

"Why didn't you do anything? You must have had your knife in your hand the whole time." She remembered how he'd shifted in his seat, lifting his foot so it was within easy reach. At the time, his action had been mystifying; now she understood its significance.

"There was no need," Dev said. "The others were able to quell him without any trouble."

"And if they hadn't been?"

"Then I wouldn't have had a choice, would I? I would have done what I had to do, then as now."

She smiled up at him, knowing he didn't realize how honorable a man he was, how effectively simple his creed. It explained so much about him. Though he moved through a world that could sometimes be violent, he himself was not a violent man.

For a moment, she'd wondered—in those first seconds when he'd pulled his knife in readiness on the train. The Dev she had thought she knew had disappeared, replaced by a fierce-looking man with cold, dark eyes. The planes and angles of his face had seemed harsher, more finely drawn, and she had recognized in that instant the source of his lithe movements. The civilized facade had been stripped away by danger leaving the primal male inside bared to her scrutiny.

But now, with the danger past, he was once again the Dev she recognized, gentlemanly and civilized, but with a core of steel—a core she could rely on whenever danger threatened.

She stood on tiptoe and snaked her arm around his

neck, then pulled his head down to her level. Placing her lips on his, she gave him the tenderest, sweetest kiss she knew how.

"What was that for?" he asked when she pulled away.

"Just for being you." He gave her a puzzled look, but she simply smiled. "And maybe a little for saving our lives." She turned her head to look up the hill. "Jesse seems to have his hands full. We'd better go help him with the little ones."

"Let me check with the conductor first, then I'll join you. We'll need to signal the next train before it comes round the track and causes another accident."

Bess shivered. "What do think those men were trying to do? What did they hope to gain by derailing the train and then shooting us?"

Dev shrugged. "It seems they wanted to destroy the train with all of us on it. I just don't have any idea why. We'll check with the railroad office in Kansas City. Maybe they know something."

For a second, Bess had another glimpse of the determined, cold-eyed stranger she'd seen on the train. She knew then that Dev thought of this as unfinished business, and her heart contracted. What if the crazed gunman came after him? Maybe it would be better for Dev to let others investigate what had happened here today. But she knew he wouldn't do that. He had told her before that he believed in taking responsibility for the world around him. It was one of the reasons she'd fallen in love with him. So she held her tongue and went off to assist Jesse with the children, leaving Dev to help organize their rescue.

It was dark by the time Dev rode up the curved drive of the Rutherford House. He'd spent the rest of the day and most of the evening out at the site of the train wreck, assisting in the investigation and making sure not even the tiniest clue was overlooked. He'd sent Bess and the children home on one of the wagons the railroad had arranged to transport the passengers to their destination. Under the circumstances, neither Bess nor the children had wanted to go on to Kansas City.

Once the site investigation was over, Dev saw no need to linger. He wanted to see Bess, to hold her in his arms and know she was safe. He needed to assuage the anger that still raged inside him, and the only way to do that was to reassure himself that she was, indeed, unhurt. Simply stating the fact was not enough—he needed to see her, to touch her, to lose himself in her wonder.

Despite the lateness of the hour, lights blazed from the front hall, the yellow gleam spilling out onto the porch through the uncurtained windows on either side of the door. He dismounted from his borrowed horse, a sudden surge of energy at the thought that Bess was so close lightening his steps despite his fatigue and the aches of muscles sorely used.

He'd barely set foot on the lowest step when the front door swung open. Bess came flying out. He opened his arms, and she flung herself into them.

"I'm so glad you came," she said, hugging him hard around the waist, her head pressed against his chest. "I was afraid you'd just go straight home."

"No, I had to see you. Are you all right?"

She looked up then. "Yes, I'm fine. How about you? You look exhausted. Come in, first. I'll get you something to drink. Then we'll talk."

She put one arm around his waist and started up the porch stairs, urging him along. She smelled sweet and clean, her hair gathered in a loose plait that hung down the middle of her back.

"I didn't come here for a drink," he murmured, halting her in the front hall. "I came to tell you I love you and for this."

His mouth came down on hers hungrily, with no pretense of sophistication or tenderness, just unbridled need. He wanted to be gentle, but gentleness was beyond him. He'd nearly lost everything today, and now life pulsed within him, demanding affirmation in the most essential and primitive way known to man.

As if she sensed the desperation underlying his roughness, she responded fully, her mouth opening to his as her hips rotated to fit him. Her hands threaded through his hair, not to push him away, but to hold him ever closer. His hands raced up and down her back, measuring her supple strength as she arched into him. Through the fabric of her muslin dress, he could tell she wore no corset. Every muscle in his body tightened.

He captured the golden plait of hair running down her back, wrapped it around his hand, and tugged her head back so he could nibble at the tender skin of her throat. Her throaty groan nearly undid him. He could feel her pulse thrumming and reveled in her soft warmth. She was alive and safe and in his arms. There was nothing more he could want . . . and yet there was. He took her mouth again, deepening the kiss as if he could consume her, make her such a part of him that she would never go, never abandon him to his loneliness again.

When she first began to pull away from him, Dev tightened his hold, a low protest sounding in his chest. She eased back into his embrace, kissing him with an ardor that matched his own. Then once again she pulled back.

He opened his eyes, blinking against the too bright lights, feeling disoriented. She smiled up at him, a witch's smile, knowing and mysterious and filled with promises of seduction and fulfillment.

"Come with me, my love," she whispered and took his hand, guiding him up the stairs and down the hall, all the way to the last bedroom.

"Come," she said again and pulled him into the room, closing the door behind them both. "This will be our time. Everyone else is asleep.

A lone candle stood flickering on the night table by the bed. This was the guest room, Dev knew, and saw that the high, four-poster bed had been freshly prepared, the covers pulled back in welcome. The rest of the room was in shadows, but the dark was friendly, holding them in its quiet cocoon with only an occasional night sound breaking the silence.

He turned to face Bess, suddenly unsure. He didn't want to overwhelm her with his own needs, to take more than she was willing to offer. She took a step toward him, coming into the circle of soft light provided by the candle, and he saw his worries were needless. She wanted him as much as he wanted her. Her eyes devoured him, avidly searching his face then moving down his chest and lower. He almost thought he could feel her gaze, hot and blistering as it stole down his length, stopping at his very center, where his masculinity throbbed.

She smiled a secret, feminine smile, then slowly lifted her hands to the top button of her dress. Dev watched transfixed as she opened it and moved down to the next. One after the other, the buttons came undone and the sides of her dress fell back, revealing smooth, golden skin. Slowly, the dress slid to the floor. She stepped out of it, clad only in a thin chemise.

She raised her arms and reached behind her, pulling her hair up so she could release it from its thick plait. The motion pressed her breasts against the light cotton fabric, and Dev could make out the softly rounded contours of each full globe and the pale shadows of her nipples already puckering with desire. After removing the ribbon holding her braid, she combed her fingers through her hair, freeing it in all its glory. The candlelight shimmered in the blond tresses, making her look as if she, herself, were a flame, burning without being consumed.

And he was the moth, drawn inexorably to her beauty. Following her lead, he took off his jacket and started to unbutton his shirt.

"Let me," Bess murmured, halting his fingers in mid motion.

She ran her hands over the contours of his chest, then pulled his shirt out of his pants so she could reach beneath it and touch his skin. She felt heat and life pulsing beneath her fingertips. Quickly she unfastened the last of his buttons and pushed the shirt off his shoulders. Rising onto her toes she planted a trail of kisses across his chest, pausing to delicately lick one small male nipple.

Dev's hands clasped her shoulders, and he threw his head back. A low moan of need escaped from his throat, and Bess was filled with a heady sense of feminine exultation—she could do this to him, make him lose all sense of time and place until he thought only of her. How she enjoyed pleasuring him, discovering just where he wanted to be touched, how he wanted to be stroked.

Her hands slipped down past his waist until she touched him. A shudder ran through his body, but when she would have pulled away, he pressed against her. Her fingers curled around him, measuring his length, learning about this most intimate part—the part that had brought her such joy, taking her out of herself and into that special place where two became one.

She looked up into his face and saw it was flushed with desire, his eyes black, bottomless pools of longing. In a single motion, he reached for the hem of her chemise and pulled it over her head, leaving her all but naked in the flickering light of the candle. She tried to fold her arms over her chest, but he wouldn't let her.

"You're so beautiful," he whispered. "It's a crime to hide yourself."

He knelt before her and gently suckled one nipple, then moved to the other. She thought her knees would give way as waves of pleasure beat through her. His kisses moved lower and her legs began to shake. He eased her onto the edge of the bed, removing the last of her clothing and his. Then he knelt before her again. When he kissed her this time, her breath left her lungs. Her hands grabbed at his hair as he drove her past all limits. Her muscles tensed as her body reached for even greater heights. And then suddenly she was falling, freed from the restraints of daily life to float weightlessly in the air, her soul belonging to him as surely as her heart did.

Before the last convulsion had faded, leaving her all too earth-bound again, he was lying upon her, his weight pressing her into the voluminous feather bed. She felt surrounded by him, by his musky scent and dark, male taste, by the strength of his body and the intensity of his gaze, by the gentleness of his touch. His mouth took hers in a searing kiss, and in the next instant he was inside her.

She had thought she was sated, but now she knew a greater need—a need for all of him. He moved within her and her hips shifted in response, taking him deeper and deeper until he was a part of her. This time as she climbed the heights, he came with her, and they tumbled into ecstasy together, their mating a paean to life and love and survival.

They fell asleep still entwined with each other, and Bess awoke in the hour before dawn to find her head cushioned in the hollow of Dev's shoulder, his arms wrapped tightly around her. She tried to ease herself from his grasp, knowing her father would be upset if he found her in Dev's room come morning, but her movements woke him.

"Good morning," he whispered against her hair. He put his hand to her chin and tilted her head back so he could kiss her.

She kissed him back, then pushed on his chest so he would release her.

"I have to go," she murmured. "My father . . . he's here tonight, staying in the maid's room since Laura went out to the lake. I don't want . . ."

"I understand, my sweet love, but there's still time."

And there was. He claimed every inch of her body, marking her as his. She wanted it to go on and on forever, but all too soon dawn broke in the eastern sky and the first thin rays of sunlight made their way into the room. After a last lingering kiss, Bess drew on her chemise, picked up her clothes, and slipped down the hall to her own room.

Harley Jenkins was desperate. Ever since he'd blown up the train last week, the children at Rutherford House had been guarded more closely than ever. There was no way he could get to Danny. He'd hung around Carlinsville hoping to catch a glimpse of the boy, but to no avail.

Right now he was hungry and tired. He crawled out of his hideyhole and decided to prowl around for some food. He looked from side to side and though he didn't see anyone, he couldn't be too careful. He didn't want anyone paying too much attention to him. The boss was upset enough as it was. It wouldn't do to upset him more by failing to get this one right. The boss had made it clear this was Harley's last chance, and Harley knew the man could get real nasty when things didn't go his way—murderously so.

Harley was just about to turn the corner when he heard a noise. He stopped in his tracks and held his breath, ever conscious of being discovered. He pressed himself against the wall of the building just as he heard a man speak.

"I think someone is doing some imitating. These last few incidents seem different somehow, I'd bet my life on it. Something just doesn't feel right."

"I agree. The incidents have been meaner, more violent. Do you think they're related to that rock through the Rutherford House window?"

"Nothing's happened out at the house since then. Seems mighty peculiar, but I'm still having my men keep an eye on it."

Harley recognized the voices of the sheriff and Devlin O'Connor. Damn, he was in trouble now. O'Connor was just as dangerous as his boss if crossed. The boss had said so. And now O'Connor was suspicious about everything that moved. How was Harley going to make sure the boy didn't open his yap if he couldn't get to him? Harley cursed under his breath. There'd be no getting to him at the house, that was for sure. He'd have to wait for another opportunity like the train.

He should have been rid of O'Connor last week, but the dynamite he'd paid good money for had been less than expected. Whether it was too old or a bad grade he didn't know, but he'd expected the whole train to go up, not just the engine. You couldn't rely on good help anymore. O'Connor, his woman, and that wretch of a child would have been dead if Harley's scheme had gone according to plan. Instead, he'd watched from his hiding place in the bushes as his hired hands had botched everything.

"Where's Ben?" the sheriff asked.

"Over near the mercantile. We want to make sure everyone's got their eyes open. Frank's on the north end of town and Clyde's on the south."

Dammit, Harley thought, they had the town covered. It was bad enough that a place this small made anyone new stick out like a sore thumb, now people were actually standing guard. He'd almost been caught the other day when Jesse had been walking on the back side of the main street and stumbled upon the place Harley had been resting. Harley'd scrambled out of sight in the nick of time. He was lucky that all the other boys besides Jesse and Sam were out of town, adopted by families who fell for their beguiling ways.

That was what had gotten him in trouble in the first place. He'd kept Danny around because he'd recognized the boy's potential as a source of income and because Bertha had taken such a liking to him. All the little buggers were like that—full of charm and a kind of native cunning; that's why they'd done so well on the street. The kids had made him and Bertha a good living and didn't cause no trouble—until that bitch had come along, enticing Danny with promises of a new home. The kid had rounded up the others and taken off without so much as a by-your-leave.

He owed them all, the three of them—Danny, O'Connor and his woman—and he would make them pay soon. Then the boss would be off his back, and he and Bertha could get on with their lives. Harley stole back to the rear of the mercantile, knowing he wouldn't get anything to eat tonight, not with all of the sheriff's men out and around in the town. In a fit of pique, he pulled out a match and set fire to the stack of garbage by the back door, fanning the smoldering flames until they blazed brightly. Then he crawled into his hiding place to plan his revenge.

Fifteen

Bess sat on one side of the ballroom dreamily watching the dancers. She swayed in her seat, imagining Dev's arms around her. He would swirl her in circles until she was dizzy, then hold her tight so she wouldn't fall. She sighed and blinked, erasing the dream image to search the crowded room for Dev. He was still nowhere in sight, obviously taken up with the business deals that seemed to dominate his life lately. She would have been upset except for the banked excitement in his eyes when he told her to give him just a little more time. She was beginning to suspect there was a purpose to his dealings—a purpose that involved her and their life together—and if that was the case, she wanted to give him every opportunity to succeed.

After the events of the past week, she could no longer envision a life for herself that did not include Dev. Even Bert seemed taken with him despite Catherine's attempt to blacken his reputation in her letter. Bert's approval would make things easier, though Bess knew she had matured over the past few months to the point where she would do what was right even without Bert's full agreement.

Tonight she could hardly wait for Dev to finish his

321

business and rejoin her. She looked around the ballroom again, barely able to believe the changes Arthur had wrought here in Rutherford House. The room looked so elegant, a tribute to Arthur's connections and determination, for he had decided just last week, immediately after the train wreck, to celebrate Bess, Dev and the children's narrow escape. Moreover, he'd combined the celebration with a charity ball.

To that end, he'd refurbished and decorated the ballroom and planned on using the profits from the ball to buy the Rutherford House, making it the permanent home of the Women's League for Children's Welfare in Carlinsville. Bess was still overwhelmed by the generosity of Arthur and his friends. Everyone who was anyone was here tonight — people summering by the lake, people just in from Kansas City for the night, and people from the town of Carlinsville itself. Even her father had come, a most unusual occurrence, but one she immediately understood when she looked over at him.

Bert was standing by Laura's chair, running his finger inside his starched collar. He looked decidedly uncomfortable, but every time he looked down at Laura he smiled. Bess was still having a time trying to think of her father in his new role as suitor. She was happy for him, of course, and for Laura, too. They were an unlikely pair, but well-suited once you saw them together — her father somewhat gruff, with rough edges, but fiercely protective, and Laura with her impeccable manners and equally fierce loyalty to those she found deserving. They were a study in contrasts that complemented rather than detracted.

At the moment, her father was twitching, and Laura was sitting serenely listening to the music, a flowing waltz. Bess knew Bert had come expressly for Laura's benefit and admired his understanding of what was important to her. He'd even danced several times, much to

Bess's amazement. Now if Dev would get back, everything would be perfect.

"I think your father and Miss Christy make an absolutely wonderful couple," Alice Covington gushed in her ear as she took the seat next to Bess. Her friend had only been home for two days, but already knew all the latest gossip. She and her parents had come out to their lake home as soon as they'd returned from Philadelphia. The surprise had been who had come along for a visit — Roland Atherton.

Dev had not been pleased to see him. It was a good thing she hadn't told him what had happened in Philadelphia or he'd have more reason for his dislike. She had put that behind her, not only for her own sanity, but also because of Alice's attachment to the man, though, come to think of it, she hadn't seen them on the dance floor since the evening began.

"Are you enjoying yourself? You've certainly been the belle of the ball," Bess remarked.

"Yes, isn't this marvelous? Arthur was so kind to put this on. I was devastated when I'd heard what had happened to the train. You were so lucky. And I understand Dev was a real hero. Speaking of which, just how serious are you two? Mother and I were just as pleased as punch when we'd heard Dev had traveled out to Kansas City right after you. Of course, Barrett was devastated, but he'll soon get over it. He sends his best wishes. Were you surprised to see him? Dev, that is."

Alice hadn't changed one bit. She still didn't leave time for people to answer her long list of questions. So Bess picked the one she felt most like answering. And it certainly wasn't going to be the one about Dev or Barrett for that matter. "Arthur has been more than kind, not only has he organized and thrown this ball, but he's been a big supporter of the League's project."

"Mother couldn't say enough good things about him. She even managed to get Father to make a sizeable donation to the cause. And isn't he the most handsome man ever?" Alice asked, then frowned. "Why haven't I ever seen him before?"

It didn't take Bess long to realize Alice was talking about Arthur and not her own father. "You've seen him any number of times. He's been out at the lake every summer since we were thirteen."

"Maybe so, but he couldn't have been anything like he is now. He is a slightly bit stuffy, but in an endearing sort of way, don't you think?" Then without waiting for an answer, she added, "And I could probably cure him of that."

"I'll bet you could," Bess said with a laugh. Now that she thought about it, Alice and Arthur might just make an interesting couple. They had a lot of common interests and moved in the same social circles in the city. And if she had to make a guess, Mrs. Covington would find Arthur the perfect candidate for her daughter in every respect. Even better, Arthur seemed to return Alice's interest—they had already been on the dance floor together four times. The only sticking point Bess could see was Roland Atherton. What role did he play in all this? Though Bess wouldn't care if she never saw him again, she felt she had to ask for Alice's sake.

"What's happening with Mr. Atherton?"

"Oh, Roland. He has much more in common with my father than with me and not long after you left, he stopped calling on me altogether. Not that I minded. By that time I'd discovered I didn't really care for him at all. There's something kind of weasel-like about him, don't you think? Anyway, if it'd been up to me, I'd have left him in Philadelphia, but he seemed keen on coming. My father doesn't even think that much of him but couldn't discourage him from making the trip."

Bess was glad to hear of Alice's disaffection for Atherton. "I think Arthur's a much better choice."

"So do I, and he's so philanthropic. Look at all he's done for the children."

"He certainly has been a godsend to us. The League is very indebted to him."

"Speaking of the League, your aunt is so proud of you, you know. She visited us at the hotel before we left."

"How is she?" Bess asked eagerly.

"Quite well. Almost back to normal, thank goodness, and so pleased about what you're doing. She feels you're following in her footsteps. She also mentioned what a nice couple you and Devlin make and how happy she was that he followed you home."

"I'm so pleased Aunt Livvie is feeling better," Bess said, once again sidestepping Alice's curiosity about Dev, despite the blush she felt rising on her cheeks. "I've written to her, but I haven't gotten an answer."

"That's probably Catherine's doing. She has a reputation for being ruthless and not above subterfuge to get her way. She hasn't liked you from the beginning, so I wouldn't be surprised if she intercepted your mail. I know your aunt wants to hear from you—she said as much. Why not send a letter to the League offices? She's sure to get it there."

Sometimes Alice came up with the best ideas. "I'll do that tomorrow."

"Will your father mind? Your aunt seemed to think maybe you weren't writing because of the problems between him and her family."

"Oh, poor Aunt Livvie! That Catherine, I could just . . . !" Bess grimaced. "Well, to tell you the truth, Papa wasn't exactly thrilled that I wanted to meet Mama's family, but I think he understands that it has nothing to do with him. He just doesn't want me hurt by people like Catherine. And I guess he's right—that part hasn't been good, but meeting Aunt Livvie has really changed me. I guess you have to take the good with the bad, and just make the best of things."

"Well, speaking of the good, tell me all about Dev and what's been going on since you've come back. I don't want any more diversions and getting off the subject, you hear?"

Bess looked down at her hands. "Dev and I have been seeing each other," Bess answered somewhat shyly, knowing she had no choice this time.

"And?"

"And what?"

"And have you made any permanent plans? Plans that I should be aware of?"

Bess knew Alice was talking about marriage, but she didn't know how to answer. Of course she'd thought about it, but she just wasn't sure for any number of reasons, the biggest reason being Dev's silence on the subject. What could she say?

She was saved from having to answer by Arthur Christy. "Ladies, how are you enjoying the evening?" he asked, stopping in front of them. His eyes passed over Bess to focus on Alice. He looked very dashing tonight, and his smile widened as they rested on the dark-haired woman sitting by Bess's side.

"Everything is absolutely lovely, Mr. Christy," Alice answered and then blushed prettily.

"Please, call me Arthur," he directed, plainly mesmerized.

Alice smiled and coyly dipped her head. Bess could see that her friend had decided on her newest conquest.

"We really appreciate all you've done, Arthur," Bess said, deciding to break the silence that had become overly long in her estimation. "Much of what we have we couldn't have managed without you."

"My pleasure," he said, his gaze still fixed on Alice. "Might I have the pleasure of another dance?"

The small orchestra had just started another set, and

the floor was beginning to fill. Alice placed her hand in his and rose from her chair, her eyes locked on Arthur's. "I'll see you later?" she said absently to Bess.

"During dinner," Bess replied and watched her friend float into Arthur's arms and twirl onto the dance floor.

Bess began to feel like the ugly sister who came to the ball but never had a dance. Dev had left her over thirty minutes ago, and she hadn't seen him since. It would serve him right if she accepted the next invitation and left *him* sitting at the table alone. But in her heart she knew that wasn't true. She'd wait for him forever.

She was watching the last door on the right when it opened. Bess sat up, eager to see who would walk through, hoping it would be Dev. When she saw who it was, a shiver passed through her—Roland Atherton. Thank God Alice had seen the light and was no longer infatuated with the man. Bess averted her eyes from where he stood surveying the room and hastily slipped out of her chair, intending to vacate the ballroom lest he spot her.

She stepped into the nearby hall and stood just out of sight by the door. That way she could spot Dev the moment he returned to the ballroom. She suddenly needed to be with him with an almost desperate urgency.

"My dear Bess, you look lonely this evening. Could I convince you to dance with me?"

The closeness of the voice startled Bess, and she spun around to look up into Wylie's eyes. Why had she never noticed how closely set they were, how cold and calculating?

"I'm not in the mood to dance, thank you."

"Come now, Bess. Your escort has left you high and dry for the last half hour. Surely you'd rather be out on the floor," Wylie said, stepping closer.

"If dancing with you is the only alternative to standing here alone, I rather stay alone the rest of the evening. And I don't like being spied upon."

"I wasn't spying, only being observant."

"I'm sure Anna wouldn't call it merely observing. And quite frankly, after our last meeting, not only do I not want to dance with you, I don't wish to even talk with you."

Just when Wylie was about to reply, Anna came up and put her hand through his, drawing his attention. "Wylie, my father's been looking for you." She completely ignored Bess.

"Has he?" Wylie asked, his eyes avoiding those of his wife, but not looking at Bess either.

"Yes, darling. He says there's someone he wants you to meet. His name is Mr. Roland Atherton. He's from Philadelphia and traveled back with the Covingtons. He plans to do some business out here, and Father wants you to meet him."

It seemed Roland Atherton never missed an opportunity. Bess wasn't sure what she should do. She didn't think Anna would appreciate her sticking her nose into their business, but Bess also didn't trust Roland Atherton or his motives.

"Have you met Mr. Atherton?" Bess finally asked, wanting to find out exactly how entrenched Atherton might have gotten.

"Of course I have," Anna replied with the slightest touch of superiority in her voice. "And I find him the most fascinating man. We were all most impressed with him."

Wylie must have seen some of the unease in Bess's expression for he asked, "Don't you like him?"

"It's not a case of like or—"

"Wylie, I don't like to keep Father waiting," Anna said sharply. She obviously wasn't about to let Wylie solicit Bess's opinions.

Bess shrugged as she watched them walk away. At least she had tried to warn them, even if they had no inclination to heed her. Besides, she was grateful that Anna had appeared when she did. Bess had no desire to have anything to do with Wylie Moore.

Feeling thirsty, Bess made her way to the refreshment table. She'd just taken a sip of fruit juice when fate dealt her an unkind blow.

"Why, Bess, how good to see you again," said the one male voice that struck terror inside of her. "If I'd known you had so many influential friends, things might have been different back in Philadelphia."

Bess tried to swallow, her throat feeling dry as a desert despite the juice she'd just swallowed. She didn't say a word, but continued to watch the dancers.

"Aren't you even going to say hello to an old friend?"

"I have nothing to say to you. And if you don't get away from me and stay away, I'll tell the whole world what happened in Philadelphia."

"Now you wouldn't do that. Who'd believe you?"

"As you said, I have a lot of influential friends, both here and in Philadelphia. I suggest you take your wares and peddle them somewhere else."

"And if I don't?" he asked with silky menace.

She turned to face him, making no attempt to hide her contempt for him. "Do you really think people will want to do business with a man who abuses women?"

"An idle threat. Your reputation will be ruined as well if you say anything."

"But I'm still an innocent child—just ask anyone here, they all know me—an innocent child whose only sin was enjoying the sights in Philadelphia when she was beset upon by—"

"All right, I get your point."

"See that you remember, then, for I mean every word."

He turned on his heel and left, his face flushed with anger. Bess didn't bother to watch where he went. The ball had turned sour for her, between dealing with Wylie and matching wits with Atherton. She needed some time alone someplace safe where she wouldn't run the risk of being caught by either man again. She climbed the stairs, knowing just where to go — the special room set aside just for the ladies.

The room was nearly empty, and Bess sat down on a stool by the wide mirror, glad of a few minutes to sit unobserved. The door opened as she sat there, and Bess looked up to see Mrs. Covington enter.

"What are you doing hiding up here? Where's your handsome young man?" Alice's mother asked, echoing Bess's own thoughts over the past hour.

"Off busy with business, I expect," she answered, knowing Mrs. Covington, of all people, would understand that reply.

"These men, whatever will we do with them?" Mrs. Covington said and sat down in the chair as if she were happy to be off her feet.

"Put up with it?" Bess asked with a small smile.

"Quite right, my dear. We do that because we love them and have no choice but to be tolerant of their little foibles." The older woman returned Bess's smile, and Bess felt a sense of womanly camaraderie springing up between them.

"Is Mr. Covington off in some dark corner, too?"

"Unfortunately. He's been forced into showing that odious Roland Atherton around."

Bess raised her eyebrows in question and that was all that was needed to start Harriet Covington.

"Well, you might not be aware of this, but I never cared for the man. I mean, he might come off with a good show, but it's what's underneath that counts. The way he treated Alice in Philadelphia, and then had the nerve to ask us if we'd introduce him out here. Well, I've never seen such gall in my life! And I also heard he cast aspersions on your Dev, too. Something about some political thing Dev wanted and that Mr. Atherton made sure he didn't get."

Plainly Alice hadn't been as upset with Atherton's betrayal as her mother, but both of them wanted nothing more to do with the man. Bess could certainly understand that. She'd felt the same way even before hearing about his causing trouble with Dev.

Mrs. Covington finished primping and turned to Bess, her expression more serious than Bess had ever seen it. "I know you children think me frivolous, and maybe I am, but I also want what's best for my family. We women have to stick together. The men may think they know everything, but they aren't always aware of the subtle things. You know what I mean?"

Bess nodded, though she didn't really understand the point, only that Mrs. Covington was trying to convey something she thought was extremely important.

"Is there some subtle point you think the men are missing?" she prompted gently.

Mrs. Covington looked around before she spoke further. "Bess, you mustn't let friends get involved with him. I've heard some terrible rumors—about how he's destroyed people's lives with the lies he's spread."

"Atherton, you mean?"

Mrs. Covington nodded. There was no doubt she believed what she was saying. Bess didn't think it was just sour grapes over Atherton abandoning Alice back East, either. Whatever she had heard had truly put the older woman completely off the man. And if what she'd intimated about Dev were true, Atherton was even more of a menace than Bess had realized. She wondered why Dev had never mentioned it to her.

"I'll keep what you said in mind," she promised. "As you said, if we women work together, who knows what we can accomplish."

"Yes, but Bess," Mrs. Covington looked up at her with a worried frown. "Do be careful. That Atherton man is not to be trusted. I don't know to what lengths

331

he might go." She shivered visibly. "I just hope Alice is no longer interested in him."

"I don't think you have to worry there," Bess told her. "Alice seems well over him."

"Thank goodness for that." The older woman turned back to the mirror. "Now you listen to me, this room is no place for a young lady to hide. For all you know, your young man is anxiously awaiting you right now."

Bess smiled, knowing that Mrs. Covington was back to her old self. Taking one last look at the mirror, Bess started out the door. Behind her, Mrs. Covington was also finishing up.

Bess had just stepped out of the door when two arms closed around her and a voice whispered in her ear, "Can you ever forgive me?"

All thoughts of Roland Atherton vanished as Dev's touch sent tingles up and down her spine.

"It's about time you got here, young man," Mrs. Covington admonished as she came out of the ladies' room. "You're lucky Bess is still here. She's been inundated with young gentlemen asking for dances."

"Then it's a good thing I'm back. And I'm sure she's dying to get out on the dance floor, so if you'll excuse us, Mrs. Covington." Dev gave her his most charming smile.

"Get along with the both of you, now," Mrs. Covington said, shaking her head.

Dev whisked Bess down the hall to the ballroom and onto the dance floor. He held her closer than he should, but she didn't mind in the least. This was what she'd been aching for since they'd arrived.

"You look so beautiful," he whispered into her ear. "Your dress is lovely."

"This is the same dress I wore the first time we met." She'd wanted to wear something new, but had neither the time nor the money to get a new gown, especially as this one had only been worn once.

"And that's exactly when I fell under your spell."

"You had nothing but terrible things to say and, if I'm not mistaken, think, the first night we met."

"I soon learned I'd gotten the wrong impression, but I must confess I was so intrigued with you that I found myself attracted even when I thought you were dallying with Wylie Moore."

"Intrigued?" Bess was so absorbed in learning how long ago Dev had really noticed her, she didn't even bristle when he mentioned dallying with Wylie.

"Don't you remember I wouldn't let you go after we danced? I kept you dancing as long as I could then got you to sit and have refreshments with me. Even though I was under the impression that you were trifling with Wylie, I couldn't stay away."

"But I wasn't trifling with Wylie, as you put it."

"I know that. You're much too honorable a person, even if Anna isn't one of your favorite people."

They'd never talked about what had happened that night, and Bess decided the time had come to clear the air between them. "You're right. She isn't, but it would be better if I explained somewhere more private."

"You don't have to explain yourself to me, Bess. I trust you."

She smiled up at him. "Thank you, but it's for the best that you know exactly how things stand. I know you're close to her family, but . . ."

"That has nothing to do with us."

"Maybe not, but these things have a way of getting a life of their own, I've discovered. It's best that you know. Do you mind?"

"No. I know just where we can go to be alone."

He guided her through the maze of dancing couples and headed for one of the tall doors leading to the main part of the house. They slipped through the door and headed down the hallway to the rear parlor. Dev ushered her in and then closed the door behind them.

A gas light on one of the walls cast a pale light around the room. Bess sat on the leather settee, and Dev dropped down beside her. He took her hand in his and threaded his fingers between hers. She looked into his eyes and saw acceptance and encouragement.

"Take your time, Bess," he said, as if he sensed her embarrassment and uncertainty.

She looked down at their entwined hands and began to speak. "During my last year at school and then over the summer that followed, Wylie and I—well, he courted me, or so it seemed. All the girls at school envied me because Wylie was quite a catch. Maybe I read too much into his intentions, but I assumed that someday we would be married. I guess that was foolish of me, considering Wylie's father never approved, but Wylie acted as if that didn't matter. Then an announcement appeared in the paper that Wylie and Anna Hobart were to be married."

"And at the time you still thought you and Wylie . . ."

Bess nodded. "The ball was the first time I'd seen them since their wedding. By that time I'd convinced myself I was better off without Wylie. It wasn't until the incident in the hall that I *knew* I'd had a lucky escape."

"What happened?"

"Let's just say that his idea of what marriage was and mine were two different things. He thought he could have everything, but I let him know just what I thought."

"That son of a—I should have realized something like that had happened. And to think I prided myself on being such a good judge of character."

"From that moment on, I knew how lucky I was and . . ." Her voice trailed off.

"And Anna wasn't?"

Bess didn't answer. Even though she felt sorry for the girl, she couldn't like her and probably never would.

How could she tell Dev that when he was such good friends with Anna and her family?

"Anna isn't the easiest person to get along with, I know," Dev said, "but she hasn't had an easy life. She lost her mother when she was young, then she had a beau that left her for—" he suddenly stopped speaking and looked at her through narrowed eyes. "What a totally selfish bastard you must think I am. Everything I've described is your life, too." His voice was filled with self recrimination.

"Please Dev, don't feel badly. I don't. After all, I'm far luckier than Anna. I've got you."

Dev looked down into her eyes, and she saw his apology and something more. He bent his head, and his lips covered hers in the most tender kiss he'd ever given her. "You're a very special woman Elizabeth Richmond, very special."

Just as he finished speaking, the door opened and Danny stuck in his head.

Sorry, I thought everyone was in the ballroom," he said, drawing back out.

Dev looked at Bess, and she nodded her head. "Stay, Danny. We were only taking a rest, looking for some peace and quiet."

"Me, too," the boy said, coming in and standing beside them.

"Problems?" Bess asked.

For a moment he didn't speak, then in a quiet voice, Danny said, "I think I've found someone who wants to adopt me."

Whatever Bess had expected, it had not been those words. They pierced the softest core of her heart, leaving her bleeding. "You did?"

Danny nodded. "She seems like a nice lady. Maybe I could go with her right away?"

Bess felt her heart breaking. Somehow she'd thought she and Danny might find a way to be together, but now it sounded as if he preferred a new home. So far, everyone who wanted to adopt had come to her first. She always stressed that point whenever talking with prospective parents, knowing how easily the children could be hurt if things didn't work out. And whenever someone had seemed interested in Danny, she'd gently steered them away. Now, someone had gone around her, and it appeared Danny was all too willing to go. "Do you think you might want to live with her?"

"It'll be better than where I used to live. And she lives in Kansas City, so I can be far away." His face was pinched and he glanced worriedly at the door as he spoke.

"What do you mean far away?" Bess asked. Did he hate it here so much?

He backed away from her, looking even more worried than before. "I shouldn't have said that. That's not what I mean." He sounded very scared.

"Danny, what's wrong? You know you can trust us," Dev said, slipping to his knees in front of the boy.

"I promised not tell. He said he'd kill me if I did."

"He? Who threatened you Danny?"

"The man who killed my father," Danny said and then started crying. "I saw him. He didn't see me, but if he does . . . I thought when I came out here I'd be safe, but . . ."

"Oh, my God," Bess uttered and at the same time rose from the settee and gathered the small boy into her arms. This was the first time she'd seen him cry, ever. Bess looked at Dev, not knowing what to do. He shook his head indicating that they'd find out later what Danny meant. Right now the important thing was to get him calmed down.

A half hour later Danny had finally fallen asleep, but only after Bess and Dev had promised not to tell a soul of what he had told them. He couldn't identify the man who'd killed his father, but he did tell them the whole, harrowing tale. He'd never known the man's name, only what he looked like, but Danny's description would fit any number of people.

Bess and Dev weren't even sure the story was true. Danny had had such an unusual childhood, so full of disruptions and bad influences, it was impossible to tell what was real and what was a figment of his imagination, perhaps abetted in part by the stories other children had told in his hearing. All that was clear was that the boy truly believed his tale, becoming so hysterical in the telling that they'd promised not to mentioned what he'd said to anyone.

When he was finally asleep, Bess turned to Dev. "What do you think?"

"I don't know. The boy is so convinced, it's hard to disbelieve him, but his story won't stand up in a court of law."

"But you think it's true?"

"I think it's possible. Didn't you tell me he seemed more aware of the social graces than any of the other children?"

"Yes—do you think that may be because he grew up in a different environment? Oh, Dev, what can we do?"

"I'll make some inquiries, and then we'll see. In the meantime, we'd better work to reassure the boy. Something's obviously upset him."

He took her hand in his own larger one. She felt his strength and knew he would do anything possible to help Danny. The thought reassured her. As long as they were together, she could face anything, even something as heartbreaking as a little boy's nightmares—especially if they proved to be true.

Sixteen

The next morning Dev walked back from the telegraph office, pleased that he'd at least made a start on learning more about Danny. He'd sent a message to Pinkerton's and asked them to find out anything they could about the boy, though he didn't hold out much hope. He'd also decided to pursue his investigation of Atherton, an investigation he'd put aside upon leaving Philadelphia. Now that the man had shown up in Kansas, the issue was urgent again. One of Dev's Pinkerton colleagues had been looking into Atherton's background at Dev's behest. Now Dev decided he wanted the information sent to him here rather than held in Philadelphia.

Atherton was unscrupulous, as Dev had learned from bitter personal experience. Dev wouldn't put it past him to try some of the same tactics in Kansas City that he'd used in Philadelphia, if not against Dev, then maybe against someone else. When he had seen Atherton at the ball last night, he'd decided that his enemy needed to be stopped, and the first step was to learn everything he could about the man.

The second step was to defuse Atherton's possible

effect in his life. To that end, Dev had made plans to meet Arthur today and talk with him about everything that had happened in Philadelphia.

The two men met at the cafe for lunch. While they were waiting for their meals, and Dev was deciding best how to broach the subject of Atherton, Arthur began questioning Dev, instead.

"Have you known Miss Covington for some time?" Arthur asked as he fidgeted with his silverware.

"Only since my last visit. Her father had some business to conduct with mine."

"Do you know if she has—that is, does she have—is there anyone special in her life?"

"Not that I know of. Is there a reason for your asking?" Dev had never seen Arthur so rattled and unsure of himself and couldn't resist teasing him.

"No, just . . . well, actually I found Miss Covington extremely charming . . . and I just wondered."

Dev smiled inwardly. It looked like Arthur was quite smitten. For a man who was the epitome of the Kansas City businessman and rather conservative as well, he had a very bemused look on his face.

"I found her to be a very interesting girl," Dev said.

"She is a girl, isn't she? That might be more to the point," Arthur observed with a touch of disappointment in his voice.

Dev didn't quite know what to say. Alice was young—but *too* young? He certainly hadn't felt that way about Bess, and Arthur was only a year or two older than himself. "I've never thought age should play too large a part in such matters, not if you both care for each other. And there's no more than twelve years difference between you, is there?"

"Twelve years is a long time."

"Did she say so?"

Arthur looked aghast. "Of course not. I would never ask her such a thing."

"Why not?"

"What do you mean, why not? Why, it wouldn't be . . . seemly."

"What does seemly have to do with it? If you think there's something special happening between you, why not simply try to spend some time with her? If the twelve years bothers her, she can simply decline."

"Yes, and make me a laughingstock."

Dev narrowed his eyes. "It's none of my business, you know, but as a friend, let me give you the benefit of my own experience. What I or anyone else thinks is not the important issue here. Don't give others that much power over you. You'll only be the loser."

Arthur looked at him thoughtfully. "You may be right. I'll have to think about it."

"Good, and as long as you're thinking, I've something else to discuss with you, something highly confidential."

"I hope you know you can trust me," Arthur said.

"That's why I asked you to meet me. Do you mind?"

"Not at all. What is your problem?"

"Have you met Roland Atherton yet?"

"We had a chance for a little conversation last night."

"What did you think?"

"To be quite honest, and I hope I'm not stepping on any toes what with Miss Covington's father having introduced him and all, but I don't think he's the kind of man I want to do business with. Why do you ask? Is it something to do with your problem?"

"In a way." Dev was relieved to hear Arthur's opinion. It would make it easier for him to explain what had happened. "In the past, you and I have done some talking about the Board of Trade, and as you might recall, I've been reluctant despite your urgings."

"I didn't want to push you overmuch, but I thought

you have all the qualifications for the position. I still do."

"I appreciate that. My reluctance stemmed from what happened back in Philadelphia between Atherton and myself. I'd been stung and was leery of getting back into the melee, but now I'm not sure that was a wise decision. In Philadelphia I had my father's feelings and reputation to think about, but out here there are no such constraints. I wanted you warned just in case he tried to finagle a spot for himself out here."

"As I said, I haven't liked him from the first, even though he does have impeccable credentials."

"On the surface, you're right, but I'm not sure how far down that goes. I'm not so naive that I don't realize things can get nasty when you go onto politics. I just don't like Atherton's tactics."

"And what are they, if you don't mind my asking?"

"That he's willing to put innocent people up to ridicule, or worse, use their vulnerabilities to achieve his goals. My father adopted me off the streets in much the same way as Laura and Bess are doing with Danny and the children. Atherton planned on using my background to keep me out of the running. Because I didn't want my father hurt, I backed off, but now I have only myself to worry about, and he's not going to pull the same thing twice."

"Are you sure there's no one here who will be hurt?" Arthur asked.

"I hope not," he replied, thinking immediately of Bess, as no doubt Arthur was. "But I can't let that stop me—I would be living a lie, and I can't do that any more. I am what I am, and there's no hiding. That's what got me into trouble in the first place. If my origins had not been a secret all along, then revealing them would not have had the potential for scandal that they acquired in Atherton's hands."

"I see, and I admire your honesty. There are some who may hold your origins against you, even out here, Dev, but I think I speak for most of the business community when I say it would be a terrible waste for Kansas City to lose your obvious talents because of something over which you had no control."

Dev thanked him and hoped in his heart of hearts that Bess would share Arthur's enlightened perspective. After having heard Bert's opinions, Dev was unsure how Bess would feel. Could he risk losing her forever if she couldn't accept his background? He'd thought about keeping quiet, of letting Atherton win again, but he knew he couldn't let that happen. He'd have to hope Bess would understand. Besides, he couldn't live a lie his whole life, always fearing that his secret might some day see the light and destroy his life. It wouldn't be fair to him . . . or to Bess.

Her feelings toward Danny and the other children were a source of hope for Dev. He knew she loved Danny; he'd seen it every time she and the boy were together. He'd even recognized the secret yearning in her eyes and known how she ached to keep Danny by her side. But none of that had anything to do with how she'd react to what Atherton had to say.

"What are we going to do to stop Atherton?" Arthur asked, and Dev was instantly warmed by Arthur's willingness to go out on a limb by joining in his cause.

"I'm not sure yet. I've had a friend start a discreet investigation. I should have the details soon. Maybe then we can plan a counterattack."

"Well, the minute you hear anything, be sure to let me know," Arthur said. "This is my city, and I've worked hard for it. We're the heart of America, its very center, and I have big plans for Kansas City. I don't plan to sit by and let an outsider jeopardize everything by bringing in hate and divisiveness. Just let me know how I can help."

Dev was gratified by Arthur's faith in him. At least he'd made the right decision here. Arthur was a staunch ally and a formidable opponent. With Arthur firmly on his side, Dev knew he had a fighting chance, a chance he wouldn't pass up.

Bess stood in the kitchen and watched as Laura put away the lunch dishes. Now that the only children left in the house were the girls, Jesse, and Danny, the help from town only came in when needed, and she and Laura handled most of the household duties. In a few minutes they would be done and Laura would leave the room, and with her, a chance for Bess to ask the question that kept running around in her head.

The problem was she didn't know where to begin with such a delicate subject. In some ways it really wasn't any of her business, but she was worried nevertheless. She knew Laura and her father cared for each other, but she didn't want her father to be hurt, especially in the way he'd been hurt by her mother's family. The same bugaboo about social standing existed with Laura and Bess wasn't sure where Arthur stood on the issue. He might not want his sister, of whom he was so protective, marrying a small-town sheriff.

Laura reached up to place the last of the dishes in its cabinet. In a second, she would go on to something else, and the moment would be lost. Bess took a deep breath deciding she had no more time to lose. "Laura, can I ask you a question?"

"Of course, dear. What is it?"

"How serious are you and my father?" Bess blurted.

"Why? Is there a problem?" A stricken expression crossed Laura's face.

"No, of course not," Bess hastily tried to reassure her. "I just . . . that is . . ."

Laura still looked extremely upset. "I realize you and your father have a special kinship. I wouldn't want to do anything that would come between you. If you think that I'm not right for your father, or disapprove, then—"

"Oh, no, it's nothing like that," Bess hurriedly put in. "I think it's wonderful. I mean . . . you do love my father, don't you?"

"I do, with all my heart."

"And you're planning to make it—that is, are you going to . . ?" Bess didn't know quite how to phrase things. She'd never thought she'd be asking someone about their intentions toward her father.

"I hope your father and I will be married, that is, if you feel the same—"

"Oh, I do." A wave of relief washed over Bess. "You've made my father very happy. The happiest I've ever seen him, and I wouldn't want that to change. He's told me just how much you mean to him," she added softly, a bit embarrassed at revealing her father's confession, but knowing nothing less would restore Laura. "He never expected to find someone like you. It's changed his whole life."

"I'm glad, because he's made me the happiest I've ever been, too. Arthur has been surprisingly supportive. Of course, my brother's mind seems to be on other things lately. He couldn't stop asking about Alice Covington last night at the ball."

"She seems sweet on him, too. Does that disturb you?" Bess asked. "I know Alice is quite a bit younger than Arthur."

"I would be very selfish if I didn't wish him well. I couldn't very well tell him how to run his life when I want nothing more than for him to let me run mine."

"But how do you *feel* about it?"

"Of course, I worry. Alice is young and impetuous, but she may be ready to settle down. And Arthur has never been one to leap into something before checking it out very thoroughly. If he decides on Alice, it will be because he has good reason to suppose things will work out." A mischievous light entered her eyes. "In a way, Alice will be good for him. She'll certainly enliven his existence."

Bess smiled. Alice would certainly do that.

"Is it time to go to the church yet?" Nola called in from the hall.

"Oh, my goodness," Laura declared. "I've completely forgotten the weekly meeting of the Ladies Guild. Depend on the girls not to forget. They do enjoy it so. Of course, all the ladies make such a big fuss over them." She paused, and tears filled her eyes. "What will I do when we find them a home?"

She looked so forlorn, Bess didn't know how to respond. She knew that like herself with Danny, Laura had become very attached to the three little girls. "I don't know. It's hard, isn't it?"

"Oh, Bess, how unfeeling of me," Laura exclaimed. "I've seen it in your face when you look at Danny. We've both done the same thing, haven't we?"

"I know I shouldn't have gotten so attached, but I had hoped . . ."

"Don't we all. Do you know who wants to adopt him?"

Bess shook her head. "Danny can't remember her name. The whole thing seems a bit vague. I can't remember anyone showing a particular interest in him, but then I had my mind on other things. And no one's spoken up since then. What about you?"

"I didn't see anyone," Laura said. "Maybe it's all wishful thinking on his part."

"I don't know. He was so upset. He hasn't left the house since the night of the ball."

"Miss Laura, I'm all clean and dressed. Please hurry before I get dirty," Rosie called from the doorway. At the sound of her voice, the two women looked up at the little girl. She did look all clean and sparkling, her red hair neatly braided with ribbons tied to the ends.

"Will you be all right if we go?" Laura asked Bess in an undertone.

"I'll be fine. You take the girls and go to your meeting. Jesse should be home soon, and Danny promised he'd help me clean up one of the bedrooms on the third floor. We'll see you at supper."

Laura gathered the girls and set off for the church while Bess changed into her cleaning clothes and found Danny. They lugged several buckets of water up to the third floor along with a pack of old rags to use as cleaning cloths.

"Which room shall we start on?" Bess asked, putting down one of the buckets in the middle of the hall.

"How about this one? It has the best view of all. You can see almost to the lake except for the trees in the way. Can I have this room when we get it cleaned?"

Bess walked into the room. The view was lovely, she had to agree. Turning her head just the slightest bit, she could see the steeple of the church and the front yard and, as Danny had said, she could almost see the lake.

"The room is yours if you want it," Bess said softly, knowing that he probably would never sleep there.

Danny's bright eyes dimmed as he said, "I guess there's not much reason to change, not if I'm going to be going soon."

"Are you happy about being adopted?" Bess asked, keeping her voice bright.

"Have you ever been to Kansas City?" he asked, ignoring her question.

"I went to school there."

346

"Do they have lots of trees like here?" Danny wrung out a cloth as he talked and began cleaning one of the windows.

"In some parts of the city they do."

"I hope so. I really like the trees. I remember when I was little and we had this big tree outside our house. It was the biggest tree I ever saw. My father . . ?" Suddenly Danny threw down his rag and ran into Bess's arms, tears pouring down his face.

"It's all right, Danny. Dev and I won't let anything happen to you, I promise."

"Miss Bess, I don't want to leave you. I like living here. I like this room."

Bess thought her heart might break. "Danny, you don't have to leave if you don't want to."

"I do. Soon that man's going to come and get me. Why else would he be here? Harley must have told him where I went. Kansas City's big like Philadelphia. I can hide there."

"Darling, I don't want you going anywhere you don't want to. I know you're scared to stay here, but do you think Dev or the sheriff would let anything happen to any of us? To me or Miss Laura or the girls?"

"No, I don't guess," he said with a sniff.

"And they won't let anything happen to you, either. Don't think you have to be adopted to be safe. We'll keep you safe here."

Danny looked up at her with a glimmer of hope shining in his tear-laden eyes. Just then a knock sounded at the front door, and he stiffened in her arms.

"Don't worry. I'll see who it is," she whispered easing him onto his feet.

She left him at the top of the stairs and hurried down to see who was calling, hoping it was Dev. She could use his advice. Maybe Dev's contact had come up with something useful and they could figure out who was after Danny.

She flung open the door, and the smile on her face died.

"What are you doing here?" she demanded.

"Coming to see you. You are alone, are you not?"

Before she could slam the door, Roland Atherton shoved his way into the house. "Now, now, that's hardly the way to greet a guest. Where is that vaunted Western hospitality I've heard so much about?"

"You're not welcome here, Mr. Atherton. I must insist that you leave."

"Ah, such fire, such passion. Tell me, my sweet, does Devlin O'Connor appreciate what a gem you are?" He reached up and ran a finger down her cheek.

She flinched away, wishing for the first time in her life that she carried a gun in her skirt pocket.

"There's nothing for you here. Why don't you go before you get more trouble than you bargained for."

"I'm afraid, my dear, that that's not possible. You see, you have something that I want very badly. Now where is he?"

"What are you talking about?"

"Come, don't tell me he didn't mention me? I was so sure he would. That's why I had to come today, before you had a chance to spread the lies. So, where are you hiding him?"

As he spoke, Atherton advanced on her. Bess backed up until she was pressed against the wall, but Atherton didn't stop. He grabbed her jaw and slammed her head back, forcing her to look at him. Then he leaned over until his face was mere inches from hers, his breath blowing into her nose, its sour smell adding to the nausea she felt just from fear.

"I d-don't know what you're talking about," she stammered, her heart beating wildly.

At that moment, she heard Danny coming down the steps from the third floor. "Bess, where are you?" he called out.

"Ah, just the person I was looking for," Atherton said and roughly flung Bess aside. Her head banged against the wall, stunning her, but in that instant she knew Atherton was the man Danny feared.

"Bert, where are you?" Dev called as he entered the jail house.

"He's not here now. Can I help you?" a deputy asked.

"Where is he? Out at Rutherford House?"

"Well, no, not that I know of. I think he's just up-stairs," the other man drawled.

"How do I get there?"

"You can't just go barging in. That's his private quarters."

Dev looked around and spotted the stairs behind the half-open door in the back. "Never mind," he said to the deputy, taking the steps two at a time. There wasn't a minute to lose.

"Bert, you up here?"

He burst into the upstairs hall, the deputy hard on his heels.

"Sorry, Bert," the other man huffed as Bert came out from the kitchen. "He just wouldn't listen."

The deputy lunged, but Dev neatly sidestepped.

"It's all right, Leo. Dev's welcome. You go on back down." As soon as Leo was gone he turned to Dev and asked, "What's up?"

"I just got a telegram from Philadelphia. I think you'll want to see it."

"What is it?"

349

"Did Bess tell you about Danny?"

"You mean this crazy story about seeing the man who killed his parents?"

"I don't think it's so crazy any more." He laid the message on the table and pointed to the telegraph office clerk's neat script. "My friend Quinton couldn't find anything out about a Danny Jenkins, but listen to this. 'Nothing on Danny Jenkins. Found curious coincidence,'" Dev read. "'Roland Atherton has nephew, Daniel, same age, description. Parents of child killed. Nephew disappeared, no trace. Atherton in charge of estate. Money gone. Atherton, too.'"

"What do you think that means?"

"I'm not sure, but it sounds like our Danny may be Atherton's nephew."

"Do you think he followed the boy out here?"

"He might have, though Quinton also thinks Atherton is involved in a crime ring I was investigating in Philadelphia, maybe even as its ring leader. He thinks Atherton left because Pinkerton's was closing in on him. Quint will send us his information by mail. In the meantime, though, I don't want to take any chances with Danny."

"Let's find Atherton and see what he's up to, then we can ride out to Rutherford House and warn Bess."

"I'm right behind you."

Dev followed Bert down the stairs and out to the street. "Where shall we start?" Dev asked.

"The Covingtons are putting him up, as far as I know, but I understand he spends most of his days here in town. Let's check at the hotel and see if anyone's seen him."

The hotel was an old building, the same vintage as Rutherford House. When the lake had become more fashionable, the Grimes family had sold out, and the new owners had converted it into a hotel. To add an extra cachet to their establishment, they had imported a European chef, and now the best families dined there when in town.

Dev and Bert walked up the hotel's steps and straight through to the back where the dining room took up the entire area. A few people lingered over dessert or coffee, but Atherton wasn't one of them.

"Dev, how good to see you," Anna Moore called from a table near the center. "Do you have a moment to join me?"

She completely ignored the presence of the sheriff, Dev noticed. He wondered if Bert was aware of the slight. He glanced at him, but his expression was shuttered.

"Mrs. Moore, how are you?" the sheriff said, advancing to her table. "I wonder if I might trouble you with a question or two."

"Why certainly, sheriff. Is there some problem?"

She looked questioningly up at Dev. He gave her a reassuring smile.

"Nothing too serious," Bert told her. "We just wondered if you happened to take luncheon here today and noticed if Mr. Atherton was among the guests."

"Oh?"

"Yes," Dev said. "I've been trying to contact him and the sheriff volunteered to help me. Business, you know?" He knew he was stretching the truth, but he wanted Anna to give him the information quickly, not fence around with Bess's father. And if she had any inkling that Bess and her safety was at the heart of Bert's question, she might refuse to answer entirely.

"Well, as a matter of fact he was here. He even stopped at my table. You know, Dev," she said archly, "he and Wylie are putting together a business deal, too."

"Yes, I had heard," he said with a smile that hid his impatience. "Are the two of them together now?"

"No," Anna said with a pout. "Wylie had to go to

Kansas City today."

"Ah, and Mr. Atherton?" Dev had to put his hands in his pockets to keep from grabbing her by the shoulders and shaking the information out of her.

"I don't really know. All he did was ask me about Rutherford House—all about the children and how they were being accepted here in town, who they talked to, and where they went, that sort of thing."

"Did he say anything about going there?" Bert interrupted.

"Well, I don't know why he should. I told him today wasn't a good day to go out there, though, what with Laura here in town for the Ladies Guild meeting and Bess out there on her own. Why, Laura even brings those noisy little girls with her. That's why I'm here today. You know, sheriff, you really ought to talk to Bess about that. Those girls are so ill-mannered, why I just couldn't take another minute in the same room with them."

"What did Atherton do then?" Dev asked impatiently.

Anna shrugged. "He just said something about a ride in the country and off he went."

Bert sent Dev an alarmed look. "How long ago did he leave, ma'am, if you don't mind my asking?"

"Oh, not more than half an hour or so, I don't think. He could be anywhere by now."

Or he could be at Rutherford House, knowing Bess would be alone thanks to Anna's artless comments.

"Would you care to join me, Dev?" Anna asked. "I'm free for the rest of the day."

"Another time, Anna. Say hello to Wylie for me, won't you?"

With those words, he and Bert hurried out. "Are you thinking what I am?" Bert asked.

Dev nodded and as one they ran down the street toward their horses.

"Well, now, isn't this cozy?" Roland Atherton said as he brushed his hands clean on his trousers. He'd found a length of rope out in the shed and had tied Bess and Danny back to back, separately binding their legs together as well as their arms. They sat on the leather settee in the back parlor, propped sideways against its back.

"Comfortable?" he asked with false solicitude. "Well, it doesn't really matter. It won't be for long."

He gave a laugh then leaned close to Bess. "Of course, if you were to change your mind, I might be convinced to let you live a while longer. But you'd have to make it worth my while. What do you say?"

His hand came forward and touched her breast, and Bess jerked away as far as her restraints would allow.

"No?" he asked. "Too bad. You're a luscious young thing, and sweet, too. Not like my other women. They've all been around a time too often. It hardens them, if you get my drift. But you, you're soft as a feather and sweet as a peach."

He grabbed her by the hair and yanked back with vicious strength, turning her face up to his. When she moaned in pain, he closed his lips on hers. Without stopping to think, Bess bit down. Atherton pulled back with a yelp and fingered his bottom lip.

"Well, you might taste sweet as a peach, but you've got thorns as well. But that's fine, I like spirit in a woman. Makes it more fun when you finally break her."

He let go of her and walked to the window where he flipped the sheer curtain aside and checked the back yard. "Where the hell is that grifter? If he turns on me again, I'll kill him."

Bess felt Danny shudder and heard the boy

whimper.

"Shh-hh," she said as softly as she could. She knew from past experience that Atherton's violence fed off the fear of others. The best way to fend him off was to appear indifferent to his threats. Their only hope lay in stalling him until help came. Bess could only hope neither Jesse nor Laura arrived before one of her father's men—or even her father himself. The sheriff could take care of himself in this type of situation. The boy and Laura could not.

Atherton stayed at the window a minute longer, then threw down the curtain and stomped to the settee, looking down at them.

"Old Harley must be losing his touch. I'm going to check the front. Don't move, hear?" He strode out the door.

The minute he was gone, Bess tried to loosen her hands.

"Can you get free?" she whispered to Danny. There was no slack in their bindings, at least none that Bess could find as she tried to maneuver into a more comfortable position.

"I'm stuck," Danny whispered back. "I'm sorry, Miss Bess. This is all my fault."

She could feel him take one shaky breath and then another as he fought his tears.

"The only person at fault here is Atherton. This is all his doing, so don't take any of the blame. It's a waste of energy. What we've got to do now is figure a way out of this. Is there anything sharp in this room? Something we can use to cut the rope? A sharp piece of glass or pottery will do the trick. It doesn't have to be a knife."

"I have a small knife in my pocket," he said in an excited voice. "It's just a penknife, something Jesse gave me 'cause he was gonna throw it away."

"Can you reach it?" For the first time, Bess saw a

ray of hope. If they could get themselves untied, they might be able to escape, even if it were only deeper into the house, behind a closed and locked door. Anything was better than sitting here as captives, meekly awaiting their fate.

"I don't know. It's in my front pocket that's all squished. I can't get into it."

"All right, we'll have to move around a bit. Maybe I can help."

They struggled together, learning the limitations of their movements, trying not to fall off the settee or make any noise that would attract Roland Atherton's attention. Bess felt the skin on her wrists starting to rub raw, but ignored the pain. She worried even more about the child—his skin was so much softer than hers, but he, too, struggled gallantly against their bonds.

They twisted around, forcing their arms to bend in ways they weren't quite supposed to until Danny managed to squeeze his fingers into his pocket.

"I got it," he whispered exultantly, then groaned.

"What happened?"

"It slipped out of my hand."

"Where is it?"

"Somewhere behind me, I think, on the cushion."

They felt around as far as their arms could reach, then Bess felt the edge of something hard with one finger.

"I think I feel it. Slide toward me just a little . . . There."

"Do you got it?" Danny whispered.

"Yes."

"You better hide it. I hear 'im coming back."

Bess listened and heard the approaching footsteps. She closed her hand around the knife, deciding it would be safer in her grasp than hidden in her skirt where she might not be able to get to it if the opportunity arose.

"They're in here," she heard Atherton say as the door swung open.

"You wanna take 'em both?" an unfamiliar voice asked, his voice rising in surprise.

"I don't have much choice, do I?"

The two men entered the room, the second one unknown to Bess. His clothes were filthy and ragged, and he had a scraggly growth of beard. When he spoke, Bess saw he was missing a couple of front teeth and the remaining ones were yellowed and rotting.

"What ya want me to do?" the man whined.

"Help me get them away from this house."

"Why? Why not just kill 'em here?"

"Someone might have seen me come here. I don't want to be tainted by this. That's why you came west in the first place, wasn't it?" Atherton scowled at his cohort, and the man shrank away from him.

"I told you—I did my best. " 'Tweren't my fault it didn't work. I couldn't help it if that dynamite was bad. Otherwise, I would have had 'em on that train."

"Maybe so, but it didn't work, did it?" Atherton said, his voice full of contempt. "This time I'm here to make sure there are no mistakes. Now, how are we going to get them out of here?"

The scraggly man scratched at his thinning hair and walked closer to Bess and Danny. As he neared, Bess was overwhelmed by his stench.

"Harley," Danny murmured and shrank against Bess.

The man shook his head. "This is your doin', boy. You shoulda stayed with me and Bertha. Now you got me in trouble, too."

"Never mind that now," Atherton snapped. "Did you bring a wagon?"

"I couldn't find one."

"You what?" Atherton grabbed a stick up from the

hearth and started beating the man on his head and shoulders. "You stupid, incompetent, bumbling fool," he screamed with each blow.

Bess bit her lip to keep from crying out and hoped Danny had the good sense not to draw any attention to himself. Atherton's rage seemed murderous.

"I tried," Harley sputtered as he backed away, trying to protect himself from the worst of the beating. "Please, Mr. Atherton—I tried. Honest . . . Stop, please." He started to whimper as Atherton vented his rage. "The sheriff came down the street—I couldn't."

Atherton froze in place, the stick poised to strike. "What? What was that about the sheriff?"

"H-he was c-comin' down the st-street," Harley stammered, still cowering with his arms raised to ward off Atherton's blows.

Atherton dropped the stick and grabbed Harley by the shirt, lifting him off his heels. "Why? Where did he go?"

"I d-don't know why. H-he and that O'Connor man—they went to the hotel."

"Damn. There's no time left. No telling when they'll head out here." He shook Harley roughly. "Now you get out to the carriage barn in back and see what you can find. Hitch up your horse and drive up to the back door. You got that?"

"Ye-yesss," Harley managed to get out through his chattering teeth.

Atherton shoved Harley toward the door. Harley crumpled to the floor, then scrambled out on all fours, waiting until he was in the hall before getting to his feet. Atherton followed him out, and Bess could hear his footsteps heading for the front of the house.

"Quick, Danny," she whispered. "Help me get the knife open."

The two of them struggled until the blade was free. Unfortunately, the knife was small, its blade dulled from years of use. With a groan of frustration, Bess set to sawing at her bonds, knowing her progress would be slow given the thickness of the rope.

In minutes Atherton was back. Bess had barely sawed halfway through the rope binding her wrists. She quickly tucked the knife in her hands and slid her hands deeper between her and Danny.

"Okay, you two," Atherton barked. "On your feet."

He jerked them off the settee, but Bess couldn't find her balance. Atherton grabbed her under the arms and dragged her and Danny behind him. By the door, he dropped them on a small rug, then picked up the rug's edge and pulled them along the floor, down the hall, and into the kitchen. There, he dropped the rug and went to the back door.

"Where the hell is that damned bungler?" he mumbled angrily to himself.

Bess could see he was sweating freely and guessed it was as much from his excited state as from his exertion. His eyes had a wild look that sent chills racing over her skin. She'd seen hints of this mood already in Philadelphia but had never imagined he could lose control to this extent.

When he ran out the door, she breathed a sigh of relief. Her whole body was bruised and battered, and her wrists throbbed. She took a deep breath, afraid she would start shaking in another minute and be unable to stop.

"Are you okay?" she whispered to Danny.

"My arms hurt."

"Mine, too. Can you hold on just a little longer? I want to finish cutting through this rope."

"I'll try."

She maneuvered the knife back into position and started sawing, desperate to make headway before the small knife snapped in two. She was almost all the way through when the kitchen door flew open.

As Dev and Bert came thundering up the road to Rutherford House, a small figure came running out of the trees shouting for help.

Dev pulled up his mount, recognizing Jesse. "What's the matter?"

The youth was out of breath and tears were trailing down his cheeks. "Some man has Miss Bess and Danny," he blurted out breathlessly. "I saw him tie 'em up. I wanted to go in, but he has a gun. Please, you have to save 'em."

Dev realized Jesse must have run the mile from the house at top speed. Though he'd always been somewhat suspicious of the boy, there was no questioning the youngster's devotion to Bess now.

"All right. You stay here. The sheriff and I will handle this."

Jesse nodded and sank to the ground, gulping in air. "Be careful," he urged. "He's already killed someone out there in the woods. I found the body as I was coming home."

"Who was it? Do you know?" Bert asked.

"No one I reco'nized. Just some man with light hair and a mustache."

"Sounds like Royce, the deputy I had guarding this place. We'd better get going."

Dev spurred his horse to a gallop, and Bert followed suit. In minutes they were in sight of the house. They slowed down and pulled into the surrounding trees so they would not be seen. They approached the front of the house stealthily. Nothing seemed to move in any of the front windows, and they gained the porch without incident.

Bert eased the front door open and Dev plunged into the house, gun drawn. Everything was quiet. Bert joined him in the foyer, gun in hand.

"I don't hear nothin'." Bert whispered after standing quietly for a couple of seconds. "Why don't you check down here, and I'll head upstairs?"

Dev had just nodded when the crack of a whip split the air. Hoofbeats sounded from the back of the house. Dev and Bert ran through the house in time to see a wagon pull away, two men on the driver's seat and a rug-covered bundle in the back.

"It's Atherton," Dev shouted. "I'll get the horses. Watch where they go!"

inclination to heed her. Besides, she was grateful that
Anna had appeared when she did. Bess had no desire to

Seventeen

Dev ran faster than he'd ever run, cursing his lack
of foresight in hiding the horses rather than bringing
them to the house. He'd never imagined Atherton
would take off like this. Swearing under his breath, he
jumped onto his mount and grabbed the reins of
Bert's horse, releasing when he started past the
house and saw Bert running toward him.

Behind him, he heard Bert whistle for his mount
and the buckskin swerve in response. Without looking
back, Dev coaxed his bay into a ground-eating gallop,
following the cloud of dust raised by the wagon.

As he neared it, Atherton turned around, rifle in
hand, and fired a shot. Dev bent low over his horse's
neck. Though he held a gun in one hand, he was loath
to use it for fear of a stray bullet hitting Bess or Danny
in the back.

He had to assume they were alive—anything else
was unthinkable—so he held his fire. Atherton shot
again, and Dev heard the bullet whiz past. The man
was an excellent marksman, Dev recalled, but there
was nothing he could do about it other than hope the
jostling wagon continued to throw off his aim.

In the back of the wagon, the carpet shifted to the
side, and Dev made out Bess's blond head. She

moved, half sitting up as she grabbed the wagon's side. Relief that she was alive poured through Dev, but it was short-lived. She was still in grave danger. He wanted to shout at her to get down but didn't want to draw Atherton's attention to his cargo.

The road curved sharply at that point, and the careening wagon skidded. At the peak of the curve, a rider came bursting out of the woods, heading straight for the buckboard. In the same instant that Dev realized Bert had taken a shortcut through the trees, Atherton caught sight of the sheriff.

With the heightened awareness that comes in extreme situations, Dev felt as if time slowed. He could see Atherton raise his rifle in Bert's direction, saw Bess open her mouth to scream, then lunge toward Atherton, her arm upraised in attack. She struck Atherton on the shoulder, and he reared back, turning the rifle in her direction. Without stopping to think, Dev raised his gun and pulled the trigger, catching Atherton high in the chest. Atherton's rifle dropped to the ground, and he slumped against the buckboard seat.

Time suddenly sped up again as Bert pulled up parallel to the wagon and grabbed the reins, drawing the vehicle to a stop.

"Don't try anything," Dev ordered the driver, a disreputable-looking grifter.

"I didn' wanna do this," the reprobate whimpered, holding up his hands in surrender. "He made me. Said he'd kill me if'n I didn' do what he says."

"Shut up," snarled Atherton as he clutched his shoulder.

Blood oozed from two wounds, but Dev didn't bother to question the source of the second.

"Get down off the wagon," he ordered the two men, "and lie on the ground."

The scraggly one jumped from the driver's seat and threw himself onto the grassy verge by the side of the road, pleading for mercy the whole time. Atherton simply sat stonily in place.

"I said, get down," Dev repeated, enunciating each word. He could barely restrain himself from grabbing him and flinging him off the wagon.

"I'm hurt," Atherton said.

"Not as hurt as you will be if you don't get off that wagon."

Atherton stared at him, pure hatred shining out of his eyes, then obeyed. Dev was almost disappointed. He would have liked an excuse to beat the life out of the man for what he'd tried to do to Bess and Danny. When both men were lying facedown, Dev looked up at Bert. The sheriff was kneeling in the wagon bed, one arm around Bess as he bent over Danny.

"Are they all right?"

"Fine," Bert said, his voice suspiciously husky. He cleared his throat. "Here," he called and tossed a few lengths of rope in Dev's direction. "Use these to tie those bastards up."

It was a sign of how upset he was that he used such language in front of Bess and the boy. Dev couldn't blame him; he felt the same mixture of anger and relief, guilt and happiness. Unwilling to put aside his gun lest one of the men try to jump him, Dev held it in his hand as he first trussed up the whimpering man and then did the same to Atherton. At last he was free to do what he'd feared he might never get to do again.

He'd taken two steps toward the wagon when Bess launched herself into his arms. He caught her in midair, reveling in the warmth of her body, the sweet scent of hair, the delicate weight of her in his arms.

"Bess."

"Oh, Dev, I was so afraid for you." She wrapped her arms around him tightly and buried her head in his chest.

"*You* were afraid for *me!*"

"I don't know what I would have done if Atherton had shot you!" She trembled in his arms. "He's such an evil man. I'm glad I stabbed him."

"You stabbed him? With what?"

"Danny's pocket knife. That's how I got free. When I saw he was about to shoot again, I just hit him as hard as I could with that knife."

Dev couldn't believe how courageous — reckless — she had been. No wonder Atherton had two injuries on his shoulder.

"You won't have to worry about him any more. Bert and I will make sure he can't get near you again."

"I hope so. I don't think I can handle something like this again." She shuddered a second time, lifting her head long enough to cast a glance in the prone man's direction.

"Let's move over there where you don't have to see him."

"I don't know if that will help," she said though she let him lead her to the other side of the wagon. "All I have to do is close my eyes and I see him as clearly as if it were the third of July all over again."

"The third of July?" It took a moment for Dev to place the date. "Are you saying Atherton was the one who attacked you that night in Philadelphia?"

She nodded, then hung her head. Dev put his hand to her chin and gently lifted her face. "Why didn't you say anything then?"

A flush colored her cheeks. "I was so embarrassed by what had happened, and then Alice was so enamored of him I wasn't sure how she'd take it. Everything was so confused. I just felt the only thing I could do was go away — especially when Catherine came over to the League offices the next morning and threatened to use me to get at you."

"Catherine! That woman will get her comeuppance one of these days if I have to see to it myself."

"Don't let's talk about her. There'll be plenty of time later. Just hold me now."

Dev did that and more, lowering his mouth to hers in a kiss that celebrated life and love and washed away his fury and his fear. The kiss would have gone on forever if it hadn't been for Bert clearing his throat from just a few feet away.

"Uh, I hate to, uh, break this up, but I think we should take these two back to town and maybe stop at the doctor's office just so he can have a look at Danny and Bess. Don't you think?"

Bert stood with his back to them, the back of his neck bright scarlet.

"We'll be right there," Dev said, then turned to give Bess one last quick kiss.

The time had come to settle things between them. He'd almost lost her twice, once on the train and now with Atherton. He'd wanted to wait until he had everything tied down — a job here in the Kansas City area, a position among the city's elite to please Bert — before he asked her to commit her life to him. Now he knew that none of that mattered. All he wanted was Bess in his life forever.

But he couldn't ask her here, not with Atherton and his crony prone on the ground in the middle of nowhere, and Bert blushing fiery red with embarrassment, not with Bess disheveled and bruised from her ordeal and Danny still half-frightened of Atherton's threats. No, he needed her alone, and soon, and the best way to do that was to get back to town as quickly as possible.

Reluctantly tearing his mouth from Bess's, he put his arm around her and said, "We're ready now, Bert. Let's get going."

Bess cradled Danny by her side while Dev guided

the horse into town. They'd stopped briefly at Rutherford House to pick up the buggy while Bert had continued into town with Atherton and Harley tied up in the back of the buckboard. Dev had insisted that they leave immediately behind him so the doctor could examine Bess and Danny.

Though Bess wanted the doctor to check Danny, she knew she was fine. Still, Dev was so solicitous and concerned, she couldn't bring herself to tell him no. While her wrists did hurt, she knew the doctor would do no more than give her a salve that she had already planned to use. Danny, on the other hand, was small and had been through a great deal. She wanted to be sure he was all right.

They had just turned the corner, heading for the doctor's office, when a commotion at the jail house drew Bess's attention. She didn't take too much notice, more worried that the doctor might be out, until she saw Jesse in the middle of the crowd.

"Dev, quick. They've got Jesse by the scruff of his neck," she cried out. The boy was being pulled by Ty Jackson toward the jail house door with the youth resisting every step of the way.

"Hold on," Dev warned and turned the wagon toward the gathering crowd. "Stand back, we're coming through," he shouted as he maneuvered the wagon through the assemblage to where Jesse was standing.

"Are you all right?" Bess called out to the boy, when they were close enough for him to hear her over the grumblings of the crowd.

He nodded his head with bravado, but he looked terrified. As the wagon pulled to a stop, Bess told Danny to stay put and started to climb down from the buggy seat. Before she had one foot over the side, Dev reached up and swung her to the ground.

"What's going on here?" Dev demanded, turning to face Ty.

"We found the boy that's been causing all the trouble, that's what," the other man said, never taking his hand from Jesse's shirt collar.

"You can't mean Jesse!" Bess exclaimed in disbelief.

"Who else you see here, lady?" Jackson replied with a sneer. "Now he's gonna get what he deserves. You see, I was right all along. Them kids of yours were behind the trouble just like I said."

"They've never—" Bess started to say when the jail house door opened and Bert stepped out.

"What's all the commotion?" he asked, looking around the group standing by the door for an answer. Most of the men stepped back, all except Ty Jackson.

"We got the culprit who's been setting all them fires, Sheriff," he said proudly.

"Have you now?" Bert replied without too much interest, his attention on Bess. "You and Danny all right?" he asked.

Bess nodded and look over to see how Danny was faring. To her relief, she saw Laura easing the boy down from the buggy and into her arms. Bess felt like a weight had been lifted off her shoulders. She'd been torn between which boy to help. Now her full attention could be with Jesse.

"Well, Sheriff, what are you going to do?" Ty prompted.

"Do? First, I'm going to wait for you to let go of that child." Bert didn't continue until Ty had released Jesse with obvious reluctance. "Second, I've got a man in my jail right now that'll swear he committed most of them crimes."

A murmur rose from the crowd, but Ty's words cut them off.

"But not all. And I know who did the rest. I've seen this kid—" Ty jerked his head toward Jesse "—lurking around the mercantile for the past week. And I seen him before, too. Around places he shouldn't a'been."

367

"I *work* at the mercantile," Jesse said to Bert as tears collected in his eyes. "Honest, I do. And I been around those places because I thought I could help figure out who's doing all this stuff."

Bess walked to his side and placed her hand on his arm, knowing that if she enfolded him in her embrace as she wanted to he'd be too embarrassed.

"There's your explanation," she said to the crowd. "Jesse was only trying to find out who's been doing these things, same as the rest of us."

"Seems he's still the best suspect we have. I say we—"

"Wait a minute, Ty. There's something you should know," a new voice spoke out. "I can't let you blame the wrong person."

Orvis Barclay, the owner of the leather goods store, looked sad and resigned as he stepped forward.

"What are you talking about, Orvis?" Ty demanded.

"I'm saying I know who's behind the mischief in town—at least, the part Sheriff Richmond's prisoner hasn't confessed to."

"Who is it, Mr. Barclay?" one of the men called out.

"I'm afraid Jimmy's been doing it," Barclay answered, referring to his son. "Jimmy started it when we took in Sam. Seems he wasn't too happy about having Sam there and figured if he caused enough trouble, the children would all be sent back to Philadelphia."

"You can't tell me he let Mrs. Clarke's chickens out. I saw him myself at the mercantile right before it happened," Jackson said, unwilling to give up his claim that Jesse was also a suspect.

"Maybe Sheriff Richmond's man did that," Orvis said.

"He says not," Bert replied.

"How can you believe him?" Bess cried out, desperately afraid for Jesse. "After all that criminal's done, how can you trust him not to lie?"

Bert gave her an apologetic look. "So far, everything he's been sayin' has checked out."

Bess closed her eyes. Her muscles clenched, and she wanted to scream at the crowd that they were prejudiced fools, but that wouldn't help Jesse. She took a calming breath and opened her eyes. "Maybe so, but that still doesn't mean Jesse did it, or any of my other children."

Ty Jackson looked from Jesse to Orvis Barclay. "How come you never came forward before?" he asked suspiciously.

Orvis looked down. "I wanted to handle this quietly. I've already tanned Jimmy's hide. He won't do nothing like this again. I hoped everyone would just lose interest when the pranks stopped. I only spoke up today because I couldn't let an innocent boy be blamed."

"Well, Orvis, you'd better bring your boy by," Bert said into the silence. "The rest of you, head on home now. The show's over."

The crowd dispersed slowly, several people lingering to see if anything else of interest might happen. Dev walked to Bess's side.

"Laura's already taken Danny to the doctor. Why don't we meet her there? I still want him to take a look at you."

"I'm fine," Bess said, "especially now that Jesse's been cleared. But I'll go to the doctor—just for you. You coming, too, Jesse?"

Jesse hung his head and wouldn't meet her eye. "I'd rather not, if that's all right. I, uh, I have some things to do."

Bess sensed the boy was still troubled. "I'm sorry this happened," she said. "You must know I never suspected you or any of the others. It's just so unfair of the people here to be like this. But sometimes people

369

can be small-minded. I hope you put this behind you now."

He nodded but looked more unhappy than before. "I'll try," he said and walked slowly toward the mercantile.

Dev was watching the boy with a worried frown. "Maybe I'd better go talk to him. Would you mind going to the doctor alone? I'll be along as soon as I can."

Bess agreed, her own instincts also on alert. Something was certainly bothering Jesse, but maybe he would find it easier talking to a man.

She made her way to the doctor's office where both he and Laura fussed. She was greatly relieved to find that Danny was fine except for a few cuts and bruises similar to her own. Her main concern now was reassuring him that he was safe and Roland Atherton was out of his life forever.

"I'm so glad you're all right," Laura said once they were back at Rutherford House. "I don't know what Bert would do if anything happened to you. He looked ready to murder that Mr. Atherton when he brought him into town."

"I almost wish he did," Bess said with feeling. "He's destroyed so many lives, you wouldn't believe it. That Harley Jenkins couldn't talk fast enough when Dev and Papa got there. Seems he and his wife took care of homeless children for Atherton, organizing them to steal and such. Atherton grabbed the bulk of their take, blackmailing the Jenkins's into working for him. Sounds like Atherton had a whole ring of criminals under his thumb, one way or another."

"Did Atherton confess?"

Bess shook her head. "No, but Dev said he's going to telegraph Pinkerton's with the information Harley gave him, and they'll figure out soon enough exactly what Atherton's activities were."

"What about Danny?" Laura asked softly so the

child wouldn't overhear. He was sleeping upstairs, exhausted from the day's events.

Bess bit her lip. "It sounds like everything Danny said was true. Harley says he was told to take the boy and get rid of him. The only thing I can say in the Jenkins' favor is that they liked Danny enough to keep him. Danny was young enough that Harley could get away with telling him his last name was now Jenkins. I guess they hoped Atherton would forget about him. Then when I brought him out here, Atherton learned about it and flew into a rage. He threatened Harley unless he did something about it."

Laura's eyes opened wide. "My goodness. Is that why he pulled all those pranks in town?"

"I guess he thought the townspeople would get so upset they'd make sure the children were sent back to Philadelphia, and he'd have an easier time getting to Danny. When that failed, he went after the train. At least, that's what Papa and Dev think."

"How awful," Laura said. "Well, I'm glad none of his plans worked, not only because you're safe, but also for the children's sake. We've found almost all of them homes — good homes where they should be happy."

"We may have found homes for the boys, but I'm still worried about Nola and the girls. I wish I could find someone to take them all in."

"I think you may have," Laura said with an odd note to her voice.

"What do you mean?" Bess asked, amazed at such good news. "Who?"

Laura smiled a bit sheepishly. "I hope you won't mind this, but . . ." She bit her lip, looking vulnerable and more uncertain than Bess had ever seen her. "Well, there's no getting around this so I'll just say it straight out. Bert and I want them, Bess. We were going to wait until after our wedding to say anything, but I just can't see letting them go to anyone else."

371

"Why, Laura, that's wonderful!" Bess exclaimed, her heart filled with happiness for her friend and her father.

"You don't mind?"

"Mind? Why would I ever mind?"

"I don't know. I wouldn't want you to think Bert was deserting you or anything."

Bess laughed and gave Laura a hug. "Deserting me? Whatever do you mean? I'll be visiting you all so often, you'll think I live in your house. I can't believe how wonderful this is!"

Laura beamed back, clearly thrilled with Bess's ready acceptance of her and the girls in Bert's life. They were still talking excitedly when the bell rang.

Dev walked with Jesse. The boy barely looked at Bess as he mumbled something about turning in early and headed for his room.

"Is everything all right?" she asked once the boy was out of sight.

"More or less," Dev answered cryptically.

When he didn't say anything more, she said, "I have wonderful news. I've found homes for almost all the children now. You won't believe who's taking the three girls—Laura and my father. I couldn't be more pleased. This is working out better than I'd ever hoped."

Though he smiled at her words, Bess sensed his heart wasn't in it. Did he secretly disapprove of her success? A hollow feeling grew inside her. She'd known of his doubts about her project from the beginning but had chosen to ignore them. Now she feared their disagreement ran a lot deeper than she'd realized.

"What's wrong?" she asked, her voice tight in her throat.

Dev hated having to tell her what Jesse had confessed, especially now when she was so happy. After her ordeal today, she deserved to have time to relish her accomplishments, to enjoy the satisfaction of having set a goal and achieved it. Instead, he was about to bring her bad news. If she hadn't become so skilled at reading every nuance in his expression, he would have held off telling her until another day. As it was, he had no choice.

"I hate having to tell you this," he said and reached for her hand. She turned worried eyes to his face. "What is it?"

"Come sit beside me, and I'll tell you what Jesse told me."

She nodded, but when he sat on the settee, she did not sit by his side. Instead she perched on the very edge of the sofa like a prim and proper school girl, her hands folded in her lap.

"I know Jesse didn't do any of those pranks," she said before he could begin.

"I didn't say he did . . . but he does know who did do them."

"Someone other than Harley Jenkins or Jimmy Barclay?"

Dev nodded. "I know you're not going to like this, Bess, but you have to expect that any new project will meet with some bumps on the road to success."

"What does that mean?"

"It means you've done very well placing most of the children, and you have every right to feel proud."

She looked at him in surprise. "I thought you didn't approve of what I'm doing."

"I never said that."

"But you had doubts."

"Didn't you? You can't honestly tell me you never had a second thought about all this."

She looked down at her hands. "No, I can't. I just tried to keep my doubts in the background and concentrate on making the children happy."

"And for the most part, you've had every success. I

may not have said so, but I certainly think that."

He placed his one hand over her entwined ones, and she pulled hers apart so she could take his. She shifted on the settee so that she sat a little closer to him, and her shoulders were no longer so stiff or squared.

"I may not have given you a chance to," she admitted. "Especially in the beginning when I wasn't sure myself that things would work out."

"I've always had the highest confidence in you, Bess. And to be honest, you've convinced me that this plan will work — at least for some of the children."

"But not for all?"

He shook his head. "That's what Jesse and I were talking about. He didn't want to tell me at first — he was torn between his loyalty to you and his loyalty to his friend."

"Which friend?"

"Sam."

Bess looked up at him with a puzzled frown. "But I thought Orvis Barclay said Jimmy did the pranks because he didn't want Sam in his family. Why would Sam do anything?"

"Because he didn't want to be there any more than Jimmy wanted him. From what Jesse says, Sam never said anything and Orvis probably didn't realize how unhappy both boys were."

"Did Jesse tell you why Sam was so unhappy? I find it hard to believe the Barclays didn't treat him right, though maybe Jimmy was a problem. I feel so badly about that."

"Don't blame yourself, Bess. This has nothing to do with you or with the Barclays. It seems Sam's mother is still alive, though widowed. She asked a children's charity to look after him when she ran out of money. She planned to take him back once she found herself a respectable position. Then he ran away and everyone

374

lost touch. I guess he never realized what coming west would mean — that she might never find him again."

Tears filled Bess's eyes. "How awful for him. I wish he'd told us. Maybe we could have helped."

"We still can. I'll make arrangements for him to be taken back to Philadelphia and see if one of my colleagues can't find his mother."

"Oh, Dev, that's wonderful. Thank you." A smile worked its way through her tears. "Maybe you were right. This is so far to bring the children."

"I think it depends on the circumstances. You'll just have to check into the background of each child a little more closely next time."

"Next time?"

He smiled, glad of the surprise he had in his pocket. "Oh, that's right. I forgot to give you this, didn't I?" He reached into his inside jacket pocket and pulled out a telegram.

Bess took it. "It's from Aunt Livvie! Have you read it?"

"It was sent to the two of us. Take a look."

Dev watched her read, noting her surprise when she got to the part where Aunt Livvie said she'd changed her will and Bess would be getting what would have been her mother's inheritance. As he expected, when she read the next section her face brightened even more.

"Oh, Dev, did you see this? She says she's personally donating money to 'the Carlinsville branch of the Women's League for Children's Welfare'." She laughed. "I can't believe this. Catherine must be having a fit, and I can't say I'm unhappy. She deserves not to have everything go her way after all those tales she tried to spread about you and your father."

For a moment Dev didn't speak. "Those tales are true, Bess," he said in a slow even tone and then waited, his insides tied in knots.

"I know that, Dev," Bess said, still rereading the telegram. "It's just that she took such delight in telling them, as if that made a difference or something."

Something made her look up. Dev was staring at her as if he couldn't believe what he'd heard.

"You mean you knew all along that I was adopted?"

She saw his surprise. She could also see his doubt and confusion. "I've known since Catherine "confided" in me back in Philadelphia."

"And it didn't matter to you?"

Something in his tone made her look at him more closely. For the first time she realized he'd been afraid of how she'd react, how she'd feel about his not being an O'Connor by birth. How could she have missed it? That he showed her his vulnerability made her feel closer to him than before.

"Should it matter?" she asked, looking up into his eyes so she would know exactly what he was feeling.

"I'd hoped not, but there was something your father said once that made me think that you might see it as something to be ashamed of."

"Something my father said?" Bess repeated. "I'm sure you must have misunderstood. My father's known about your adoption almost as long as I have, Dev. Catherine made sure of it by sending a letter with all the details right after I left Philadelphia. As for me, how could I possibly love you less because of who you are and where you were born? When you first met me, did you think any the less of me because I was the sheriff's daughter?"

"You love me?" His expression filled with wonder.

"How could you ever doubt that?"

She placed her hand along the side of his beloved face. He turned his head and placed a kiss in the center of her palm, then took her hand in his. For a long moment he looked straight into her eyes as if he could see into her very soul. She could see that his eyes now held a light they hadn't a moment ago.

"Bess, will you marry me?"

Tears gathered in Bess's eyes, and she nodded, too filled with emotion to speak.

"And take Danny and me into your life forever?" he continued.

Dev knew her so well, knew everything she needed, everything she wanted. And now he was giving it all to her.

"I love you so much," she finally was able to say, pulling his face down to hers.

Their kiss was tender and warm, a kiss of promise and commitment, a kiss to last a life time. Slowly, he drew back and looked down into her eyes.

"Is that a yes?" He smiled at her.

Bess nodded, overcome with joy.

"Good, because you and I have to make some plans. First, we need to make arrangements for Danny's adoption. My contacts tell me he has no relatives left back East. That is something we want to do, isn't it?"

Bess smiled, thrilled at his use of the word we. "Of course we do," she replied.

Dev grinned. "Then there's the children Livvie has found and wants to send out. Can we handle that?"

"What children?"

"Finish reading and you'll see."

The last thing she wanted to do at this moment was read, but Dev's eyes were filled with promise and he held the now-crumpled telegram out to her.

The very next sentence told her what she needed to know—Livvie and the League had gathered together a new group of children to send west. In fact, Livvie wrote, she wouldn't mind coming west herself now that she was feeling better, just to check things out and see the two of them.

"Oh, Dev. This is wonderful. Only this time, we'll have to figure out a better way of deciding who comes west and who needs a home in Philadelphia. Then once the children are here, we'll have to organize a better way of finding them homes. Maybe we really should start a Carlinsville chapter of the League."

"There are certainly plenty of people who could help," Dev said. "Arthur introduced me to several, including Lillian Bennett."

Lillian Bennett was Anna's friend, and Bess had discounted her offer for help because of that. "Do you think she would want to get involved in something like this?" Bess asked skeptically.

"I don't see why not. She mentioned several times how impressed she was with your efforts."

Bess looked away. Perhaps she had judged the woman too hastily. "Well, she did ask me to join the Literary Society she heads. I believe several of the ladies out by the lake meet regularly to exchange books and do readings. I hadn't seriously thought of attending, but maybe now I should."

"Why not attend?" Dev asked.

Bess wasn't sure what to say. The main reason had been Anna, but Dev thought highly of the girl, even if Bess didn't, so she simply shrugged and said, "No particular reason."

But apparently Dev wasn't so easily fooled. "Surely you're not going to let a few supercilious barbs from an immature young woman like Anna stop you."

"Immature?"

"It's not an incurable disease," Dev said, an amused glint in his eye. "With any luck, Anna will outgrow her jealousy once she sees how everyone else accepts you."

Bess was not as generous-minded. She knew Anna would be most annoyed at having Bess invade her territory.

"I think you're being optimistic," she said, "but you may be right. It might be worth it to go just to see the expression on her face."

"Well, despite what you may think, Lillian Bennett herself has had only good things to say about what you're doing. Even Gunther Hobart mentioned it — and yes, Anna didn't like hearing what he said. Does that make you happy? I told you she's immature."

"I guess I'm immature, too, because I can't help feeling good about that."

"Maybe it's because you're still angry that she married Wylie."

"What!" Bess looked at him and caught the hint of laughter in his face. She laughed out loud. "Very clever, Dev. You're right, of course. I will try to be mature and generous and attend the next Literary Society meeting. Is that all right with you?"

"Only if it makes you happy. I just didn't want you to let someone else's foolish opinions rule your life — I think we've both suffered enough from that, don't you?"

She smiled at him. He was so wonderful and wise, and she loved him so much. They would build a wonderful life here together, maybe they would even buy Rutherford House for themselves — after all Aunt Livvie had sent them the donation to create a permanent home for the League's western operations. What more could she want? She had thought to leave behind her dreams of home and family when she started her new life. Now she was getting everything she ever wanted — a life with a purpose outside of herself, and husband and family as well.

Suddenly it came to her that she was making a lot of assumptions, foremost among them that Dev intended to stay in the west. It was time to have everything out in the open.

"Where would we be living?" she asked belatedly. "Back East?"

He looked a bit sheepish. "Actually, I've been working on trying to find a position here. That's why I've been so busy with Arthur and his business friends. Arthur has suggested that I serve as a Board of Trade representative. The Board wants to influence affairs at the national level, getting railroads and trade through Kansas City. The position might require my going back and forth between Washington and Kansas City on a regular basis. I could probably take in Philadelphia as well. What do you think?"

It was a tempting offer—traveling back and forth from Kansas City to the East would allow her to get children from the Women's League and bring them here. But was the Board of Trade job something Dev wanted for himself?

"What do you want? Will this kind of life make you happy? You're used to something much different."

"I was getting weary of my old life without even knowing it," Dev confessed. "After Julia died, I wanted to lose myself in the danger and excitement of working undercover. But once I met you, I knew that time in my life was over. There's nothing I want to do professionally in Philadelphia that I can't do here. This Board of Trade position is exciting—it's a chance to help build something strong and new. I think it will be every bit as challenging as anything I could do back East. And if we get back regularly so I can see my father and old friends, that will be perfect."

"I'm not Julia, you know," Bess reminded him, wanting to make sure he knew what he was getting into, especially after Anna's comments about what a wonderful wife Julia had been. "I don't know if I can be the perfect wife."

"Julia was a wonderful woman and I loved her very much, but she's gone now. She taught me a lot, about men and women, about how alike they are underneath the surface. I think if her health had been better, she would have wanted to do more, to make the world a different place, a better place, just like you are. I don't want you to be Julia. I want you to be Bess, the best Bess you can be. That's what will make me happy, not some foolish notion of what the perfect wife should be."

He took her into his embrace, and kissed her tenderly, deeply. "You're perfect already," he said. "Perfect for me."

She looked into his eyes and saw that what he said was true. No shadows lingered in their depths, only serenity and joy—and boundless love for her. Smiling, she whispered, "You're the one whose perfect." Then she kissed him, sealing the promise of their future together.